The Rule Breaker

STEPHANIE ALVES

Editing: Wonder and Wander Editing Co.

Cover designer: Claudia Bonet

ISBN: 978-1-917180-16-0

This book contains detailed sexual content and graphic language.

You can see the full list of content warnings on my website here: stephaniealvesauthor.com

Happy Reading!

Also by Stephanie Alves

Standalone

Love Me or Hate Me
Holly's Jolly Christmas
Strictly Business

Campus Games Series

Never Have I Ever (Book #1)
Spin The Bottle (Book #2)
Would You Rather (Book #3)
Truth Or Dare (Book #4)
The Final Game (Book 4.5)

Playlist

- **My Brother's Best Friend**
  Hannnah Trager
- **Into You**
  Ariana Grande
- **Single**
  The Neighbourhood
- **Let Me Love You**
  Ariana Grande
- **Boyfriend**
  Ariana Grande
- **Fuck Up The Friendship**
  Leah Kate
- **I Think He Knows**
  Taylor Swift
- **Pink + White**
  Frank Ocean
- **Come Thru**
  Summer Walker ft Usher
- **Nonsense**
  Sabrina Carpenter
- **They Don't Know About Us**
  One Direction
- **Touch It**
  Ariana Grande
- **Leave The Door Open**
  Bruno Mars

For those who prefer their men fictional, especially when they
have a hockey butt.

ONE

Ryan

I think my virginity is growing back.

I don't even know if that's possible, but honestly, at this point, I wouldn't be surprised.

I haven't hooked up with anyone in months. *Months*. I'm starting to wonder if I've forgotten how to talk to girls altogether.

Not that I haven't had opportunities. Because I have—plenty. But every time, something pulls me back. Hockey's basically taken over my brain. I can't stop thinking about how to improve my wrist shot or how to skate faster. Hell, I even dream about drills sometimes. It's sad, I know.

My life is one giant loop of eat, sleep, hockey, repeat. I can't even remember the last time I went to a party, or went out, or… well, did anything that didn't involve breaking my body in half on the ice.

The familiar smell of sweat and hockey gear fills the locker room as skates come off with a click. I yank mine off, place the guard on, and toss them into my locker.

As usual, Austin's phone is blasting some obnoxiously upbeat pop song as he bobs his head along, grinning, while half the guys groan in protest.

"Fuck, I'm dead," Logan exhales dramatically as he drops onto the bench, shooting a look at Nathan. "Hayes, you think you can convince your dad to cut us some slack tomorrow?"

Nathan scoffs, shaking his head as he peels off his jersey. "Yeah, that's not happening. My dad's a beast."

And he is. Coach Hayes is a goddamn legend, one of the best in the game. I respect the hell out of him, especially when he pushes us like that. We need it, especially after a practice like today.

"Heads up!" someone shouts.

I glance up just in time to catch a water bottle flying my way. Twisting off the cap, I take a long gulp, letting the cold water slice through the dryness in my throat. Around me, the guys are chirping each other, tossing jabs, but I can't shake the weight of practice. It's stuck to me like the sweat on my back.

"You sure you're not getting a contact high from your socks?" Logan laughs as he hurls his skates into his locker. "Pretty sure they could walk themselves to the laundry room."

Austin scoffs, flipping Logan off. "Who told the rook he could talk trash? Worry about making the starting lineup, buddy."

"Someone needs to tame your ego," Cole says, raising a brow, his voice dripping with the usual deadpan sarcasm. His tattoos, which cover pretty much every inch of his neck and arms, make him look like he just stepped out of a biker gang— if biker gangs wore hockey jerseys and chewed gum 24/7.

The rest of the guys erupt into laughter, but I've already zoned out. My eyes drop to the floor as I yank off my pads with a harsh breath. Practice was rough. Our game against Crestmont is tomorrow and I'm still making dumb mistakes.

My strides were too slow; I missed the puck a handful of times. I even somehow let the rookie knock me into the glass.

Fuck. I feel like I'm stuck on a broken record, repeating the same shit over and over. Skate faster, hit harder, play smarter. Always chasing the next win. And yet, somehow, it still feels like I'm not doing enough.

"We played like shit out there," I mutter, rubbing a hand over my face. The frustration spills out before I can stop it. "Maybe if you guys stopped bickering and actually pulled your weight, we'd play better."

The laughter dies, leaving only the faint buzz of Austin's playlist. A couple of guys glance at each other, awkward and unsure, before Austin—because *of course* it's Austin—breaks the tension.

"Relax. We'll get the win." He flashes that cocky grin that makes me want to either roll my eyes or punch him. Sometimes both.

I settle for the former. "Yeah? You do realize if you fail your classes, we're out a center forward, right?

He leans back, crossing his arms. "I'll pass… eventually," he says, his smirk way too confident for someone who's an F away from sitting on the bench for an entire season. "Don't worry. I've got it under control."

"Control?" I snort, zipping up my bag. "The only thing you've got control over is the playlist in here."

"Hey." Austin points a finger at me. "That's important, and you know it. Helps keep morale up and shit."

I bite back a laugh, shaking my head. Morale my fucking ass. His pre- and postgame rituals are so ridiculous they belong in a case study.

"Yeah, well, maybe start showing up to class," I fire back. "I'm not kidding, Austin. If you tank your grades, we're screwed."

His grin falters for a split second, just long enough for me to notice. But then he shrugs it off like it's no big deal. "Relax, Reed. I got this."

I shake my head, stuffing my gear in my bag. As much as I want to just let it go, I can't. Hockey's not just a game to me. It's my future. If one of us slips, it hurts the whole team. He should know that by now.

Grabbing my towel, I head for the showers without another word. I've got enough on my plate without adding Austin's bullshit to the mix.

The water hits my skin, hot and scalding, but it doesn't do much to clear my head. The game, the guys, the constant pressure surrounding me every single day… it's all closing in, and no amount of hot water is going to wash that away. I lean my forehead against the cold tile, letting out a long, slow breath.

I miss the way things used to be. Freshman year, hockey was fun. School was manageable. Back then, I could do it all— games, parties, school. Now it's like I'm on autopilot, stuck in some never-ending loop of practices, drills, and trying to stay ahead.

I finish up quickly, shutting off the water before wrapping my towel around my waist. When I step back into the locker room, Austin spots me, his grin widening. "Party tonight," he says, tossing a balled-up towel in my direction. "You in?"

I catch the towel and toss it back, shaking my head. "I've got stuff to do."

"Stuff like watching game footage?" Austin asks, arching a brow. "You can't be serious, man. It's Friday night. Loosen up a little. Maybe touch some grass or, I don't know… an actual human being."

"I'll think about it," I say, but the words feel hollow even as they leave my mouth. I know I won't go. I'll spend the night at my desk, buried in notes and clips from tonight's practice, trying to figure out what went wrong. That's what I do. That's who I am now.

"Ah, fuck," Nathan mutters, yanking off his jersey with a frustrated sigh.

"What's wrong?" I ask, glancing at him as he lingers by his locker.

He rubs his forehead, groaning. "Forgot my sister started school today. She's on her way to campus right now. I should go help her out, make sure she doesn't get lost or end up in some weird frat house."

Austin perks up immediately, his eyebrows practically launching off his face. "Another Hayes on campus? Damn, is she cute?"

Nathan spins on him so fast that Austin flinches. "Doesn't matter," Nathan growls. "She's off-limits," he warns, his eyes scanning the room. "If any of you fuckers even *think* about touching my baby sister, then you'll have me to deal with. I'm serious. Hands off. All of you."

I smirk, not fazed by his warning—monk routine and all that. I'm not hooking up with *any* girls, let alone Nathan's sister. He'd break my legs before I could even say hello. Besides, I've known Nathan since freshman year. He's become like a brother to me, and the last thing I'd ever do is cross that line.

"What if she thinks about touching me?" Austin asks with a shameless wink.

Nathan's eyes narrow, and I swear I can hear his jaw clench from across the room. "You want me to kick your ass in front of the whole team?"

Austin winces, holding up his hands in mock surrender. "Nah, I'm good. My ass is sore enough as it is."

"The hell?" Cole asks, leaning against his locker with a raised brow, gum still rolling between his teeth. "What the fuck have you been doing?"

Austin chuckles. "Some girl thought spanking me would be fun."

The room pauses for a beat with every head turning his way.

"And?" I ask, a little too intrigued to hide it. Sue me—it's been months since I've felt a girl's hand *anywhere* near my ass.

"Kinda was," he admits with a shrug. "But it hurt like a bitch the next morning."

The room breaks out into laughter and I breathe out a laugh, shaking my head. Jesus. Austin is out there getting spanked, and the closest thing I have to a date, is my right hand.

Hockey's my life, no doubt, but damn, I miss the other stuff. I miss sex. I miss kissing a pretty girl. Hell, I even miss watching these idiots get hammered.

"You seriously not coming out tonight?" Austin asks, elbowing me. "I need a wingman."

I scoff, shaking my head. "Yeah, you're good, man. You don't need one."

Austin could walk into a room, flash that cocky grin, and walk out with half the room's phone numbers before finishing his first drink.

"Come on," he groans, dragging the word out. "One night, Cap. We win tomorrow regardless. You're wound tighter than a drum. I'm seriously worried for you."

I laugh despite myself, but damn if he isn't right. My shoulders are practically locked in a permanent knot from all the tension I carry. I've buried myself in schoolwork and hockey for so long that I've forgotten how to have fun.

And fuck, do I miss it.

I let out a long breath. Maybe, just for tonight, I could let all the responsibility shit slide. "Fuck it," I mutter under my breath with a shake of my head. "I'm in."

Austin lights up like a damn kid at Christmas, throwing a playful punch at my shoulder. "Finally! Let's get you outta that dry spell."

I narrow my eyes at him. "What the hell is that supposed to mean?"

He lets out a scoff, tapping me on my back. "Please. You think I can't tell when someone's so backed up they're walking around like a damn statue?" He gives me a once-over, tilting his head. "Your right arm's looking a little too swole, man. Dead giveaway."

I shake my head, giving him a shove. "You're a fucking idiot."

He laughs, undeterred, swinging his bag over his head. "You'll thank me later, Cap. Trust me, the team'll play better with you a little less… wound up."

I snort, grabbing my bag. "I'm not thanking you for this."

Austin winks, already halfway out the door. "You will."

I roll my eyes, but a laugh escapes me anyway.

Guess I'll find out tonight.

TWO

Isabella

My arms are going to fall off.

How I thought bringing every single thing I own with me was a good idea, I'll never know.

I suck in a sharp breath, hoisting my suitcase up the last ten steps of this never-ending staircase from hell, groaning like a dying animal when I finally reach the top.

Holy fuck.

And to think this is only half of my stuff. I'm lucky Dad's bringing the rest up, because if I had to do this again, I'd be calling it quits on higher education. Not being dramatic, either. I'm pretty sure my lungs have reached full capacity.

Dragging my suitcase down the packed dorm hallway, I scan the numbers for 208, dodging stacks of cardboard boxes and the occasional human speed-walking with their parents trailing behind like lost puppies.

I can feel my curls frizzing up from the sweat on my scalp. If I had known move-in day was going to be a full-body workout, I wouldn't have wasted a hair wash this morning. That was premium shampoo, too. Devastating.

Room 206. Room 207.

208.

Finally.

I stop at the door, sucking in a deep breath before pushing it open.

Inside, my eyes land on, who I'm guessing is my roommate, balancing on her tiptoes, one hand pressing the last corner of a band poster onto her wall while the other clutches a can of soda.

Priorities.

My eyes drift over her long blonde hair and the short black playsuit that makes her legs look endless. She hums along to soft pop rock playing from her phone, taking a sip of her drink. Her gaze flicks down to me, her brows lifting before her lips curve into a grin.

"Hey, you must be my new roommate." She pauses, her brows tugging together. "Unless you want to switch rooms." She shakes her head before I can respond. "In that case, not fucking doing it. I don't care if your roommate has sleep apnea and needs a machine, I'm not—"

"No, I'm your roommate," I confirm with a laugh.

She relaxes, flashing me a smile as she hops down from her bed, and holy shit, her legs don't just look endless—they are. I'm not short by any means at 5'6", but this girl has to be at least 5'10".

"Isabella, right?" she asks, cocking her head.

I nod, dropping both of my suitcases on the ground. "Yeah, that's me."

"I'm Aurora." She pauses for a second, her head tilting to my bags. "Need help?"

I set them down with a small sigh of relief, my shoulders aching. "Honestly? Yes. I think I brought my entire house with me."

Aurora lets out a laugh, her shoulders shaking slightly. "Don't worry, same here." She gestures toward her side of the room. "My side looks like a disaster zone."

She's not wrong. Her clothes are everywhere. A pair of sneakers thrown on the floor. A coffee mug half-filled with something that doesn't look like coffee. But she seems cool, so I don't mind.

"I'm good with it," I reply with a chuckle. "Besides, this is just my clothes. All of my other stuff is at my brother's place off campus."

Her brows shoot up. "Your brother lives off-campus?"

"Yeah," I say, tossing my smaller suitcase onto the bed and unzipping it. "He lives with his teammates."

Aurora's eyes widen. "Hockey player?"

I pause, narrowing my eyes. "Yeah… how'd you guess?"

She shrugs. "My boyfriend's a hockey player. I just assumed." Then, with a smirk, she adds, "Hockey players are hot, and you look like you'd have a hot brother."

I choke out a laugh. "Uh… thanks?"

She winks. "You're welcome." She unzips a packing cube and starts stacking my neatly folded clothes onto the bed. Kinda digging that she's helping me out, given that we've only just met. "Is this your first time away from home?"

I shake my head. "I'm not really far from home. My dad's the coach, so we live close."

Her brows shoot up. "Wait, your dad coaches the hockey team?"

"Yep."

"Damn." She grins. "So, you've basically been surrounded by hockey players your entire life. That explains why you're immune to their charms."

I snort. "I wouldn't say immune. Just… conditioned."

She laughs, plopping onto my bed. "Well, I'm from California, so this is definitely far from home for me."

"Wow," I say, my brows shooting up. "That's far."

She stretches her legs out, tilting her head. "Yeah, well… Colton U has the best art program in the country, and, you know," she pauses, flashing me a wink. "I wanted to be very, *very* far away from my parents."

I breathe out a laugh. "Not close to them?"

She waves a dismissive hand. "They suffocate me, and I just needed space to breathe." She shakes her head. "Plus, they're not exactly thrilled about the whole art thing." She rolls her eyes. "Starving artist and all that."

Folding up my skirts, she glances up at me. "What's your major?" Her eyes narrow with suspicion. "Please, for the love of God, don't tell me it's something boring like business."

I let out a laugh, scrunching my nose. "Well… kinda," I admit, shrugging as I fold a sweater. "I'm majoring in sports management. It's necessary if I actually want to work with a team someday."

Her brows shoot up, and she lets out a low whistle. "Okay, I'll let that slide because that's actually really fucking cool. We need more women in sports."

I let out a laugh, nodding because… yeah, we really do.

She reaches into my suitcase and pulls out a purple mug wrapped in a t-shirt, her brows tugging together. "This a special mug or something?"

I breathe out a laugh. "Just one I made. I like doing pottery sometimes," I explain. "It calms me down and gives me something to do other than scrolling on my phone."

Her eyes widen as she inspects the mug. "This is really good." She tilts it in her hands, studying the design. "I mean, some of the details could be better, but I can help you with that," she says, flashing me a grin. "I might even commission one from you."

I grab the mug from her and place it on my nightstand. "First one's on the house."

Aurora grins and scoops up a handful of clothes from her pile, tossing them onto her bed. "I was kinda worried my roommate would be a total drag. I'm so glad you're not."

I let out a laugh. "Is that supposed to be a compliment?"

She nods, blowing me a kiss. "Closest thing to one you'll probably get."

I shake my head, a smile tugging at my lips as I dig through one of my bags. I pull out a framed photo of Jacob and me, and just like that, my smile fades. My stomach twists as I stare down at it, memories clawing their way back in.

I trail my fingers over the edge of the frame.

"Who's that?" Aurora asks, her gaze flicking over with curiosity. "Boyfriend?"

I lift my head, sighing as I slip the photo into my drawer and shut it a little too fast.

"Ex-boyfriend," I correct, the word feeling foreign on my tongue. "We broke up before summer. He went to Harvard, I came here." I shrug, forcing indifference. "He didn't want to try long distance."

Aurora's expression softens, but instead of pity, she gives me a knowing look. "Oof." She lets out a harsh breath and flops onto my bed. "Yeah, long distance sucks. My boyfriend goes to Westbrook. He's a sophomore, so we've been apart for a while. It really does suck sometimes."

I nod, my gaze drifting to the window. "I know. I know we did the right thing, but… he ended it so fast. Like flipping a switch. These feelings don't just disappear overnight. At least not for me."

Aurora watches me for a moment, leaning back on her hands. She smirks, her eyes glistening. "What you need is a rebound," she adds. "You need someone to fuck you so hard you forget about your ex altogether."

I huff out a laugh, shaking my head. "Yeah, don't think that's happening."

"Why not?" She tilts her head, studying me. "Are you a virgin?"

"No."

She hums, giving me a once-over. "Are you one of those people who need an emotional connection before sleeping with someone?"

I hesitate, my brows pulling together. "Maybe?" I shrug, shaking my head. "I don't know. Jacob is the only guy I've ever been with."

Aurora's eyes widen. "*Ever*?"

I scrunch my nose. "Is that bad?"

She doesn't reply, her brows tugging as she presses her lips together.

Growing up with an overprotective hockey-playing brother meant most guys didn't even try to get close to me. Jacob was the only one, and even he didn't stick around. The second we graduated, he packed up for Harvard and left me behind like a forgotten souvenir. He moved on so fast, I have to wonder… did he love me? Did *I* even love him?

"God." I drop onto my bed, rubbing a hand over my face. "I don't even know who I am without him." My gaze flickers to my closed drawer, where our picture is now hidden away.

Aurora slides closer, bumping her shoulder against mine. "It's not a bad thing," she says, tilting her head. "Just… unexpected. I mean, you're hot."

I snort, glancing at her. "That was a real compliment."

She sighs dramatically. "You looked pathetic. It felt necessary."

A laugh escapes me, but a groan follows it a second later. "We broke up months ago. I don't know why I'm acting like some tragic, lovesick loser today."

Aurora shakes her head, a chuckle leaving her lips. "You're not a loser. You're just long overdue for a little fun." She springs off my bed, planting her hands on her hips. "Which is why we need to pick an outfit."

I lift my head, already suspicious. "For what?"

"There's a party tonight." Her eyes gleam. "Welcome week rager. Filthy frat house, warm beer, drinking games…" She waggles her brows. "Am I selling you on it yet?"

I huff out a laugh, shaking my head. "Not even a little."

Aurora rolls her eyes. "C'mon. It'll be fun."

I flop back against my pillow. "I think I'd rather be in bed with snacks and a movie than stepping in questionable bodily fluids at a frat house."

She gasps, clutching her chest. "That is slander. This one only smells like stale beer and bad decisions."

I arch a brow. "Oh, well, in that case. Totally convinced," I reply, with a dry look.

"You're coming." She jabs a finger at me. "I refuse to let my hot new roommate rot away in bed on the first weekend of college."

I groan but can't fight the smile tugging at my lips. "Fine. But if some guy in a wife-beater breathes too close to me, I'm out."

Aurora's eyes light up. "Hell yes!" She jumps off my bed, already rifling through my clothes. "Okay, let's find something slutty but approachable."

I snort. "What does that even mean?"

She waggles her brows and flings a tiny black lace top at me. "It means this."

THREE

Ryan

"**A**bsolutely fucking not."

Austin's bloodshot eyes lock onto mine as I lean against the wall, holding what would've been his tenth drink of the night.

"Come on, man," he slurs, swiping for the cup. "Just one more."

I yank the cup back, watching as he nearly topples over. *Jesus.* "I told you to get your shit together. We have a game tomorrow. You really think showing up half-dead is the move?"

He scoffs, stumbling backward and nearly taking out two girls passing behind him. "I'm not drunk."

To prove his point, he attempts to walk in a straight line, only to bulldoze straight into a side table, sending a vase crashing to the floor.

"Fuck," he mutters, staring at the shattered pieces. "Where the hell did that come from?"

I drag a hand down my face. I love the guy, but fuck, he's a walking liability.

Nathan lets out a long sigh, then steps in and hooks an arm under Austin's. He groans as Nathan tries to haul him upright. "Jesus, you weigh a ton," Nathan grits out.

Austin gasps dramatically. "Rude. I'm bulking."

Nathan rolls his eyes and, with one final grunt, heaves Austin onto the couch. Austin flops back against the cushions like a rag doll, until he spots the girl sitting beside him.

His head jerks up, a lazy grin spreading across his face. In one fluid motion, he throws an arm around her shoulder. "Hey," he drawls. "What's your name, gorgeous?"

The girl barely glances at him before scooting as far away as the couch allows.

Nathan snorts. "Yeah, real smooth."

Logan, standing nearby with his arms crossed, watches Austin sway in place. "Hate to break it to you, but you can barely stand on your own."

Austin grins, slumping further into the couch. "That's why I'm sitting, genius."

Nathan grabs a water bottle off the table and chucks it at Austin's face. It bounces off his forehead into his lap. "Sober up. We need you tomorrow."

Austin blinks up at him with a lazy, wrecked grin. "You do?" he sighs dramatically, throwing his head back like this is the most touching declaration of his life.

Nathan scowls, shaking his head. "He acts like he's my fucking kid."

Logan elbows him, smirking. "Aw. How cute. Guess we know who the daddy of the group is." But his amusement fades the second he glances at Austin, who's now deadweight against the couch, head tilted back, mouth wide open, snoring.

He lets out a groan. "Dammit. He was supposed to be my wingman."

Nathan raises a brow. "You need a wingman?"

Logan shrugs, taking a sip of his drink. "Don't need one. But it helps." He tilts his head, eyeing Nathan. "You up for it?"

Nathan scoffs. "Watching you crash and burn? Absolutely."

Logan huffs. "You really have no confidence in me?"

Nathan lifts his brows. "In a rookie who still hasn't grown up? Yeah, not a chance."

Logan smirks, poking his cheek with the tip of his tongue. "Don't worry. My dick's fully grown."

Before I can drown out that horrifying sentence, his attention swings to me. He runs a hand through his messy blond hair. "What about you?"

Nathan snorts. "Ryan can barely talk to a girl, and you want him as your wingman?"

I can't even argue with the guy. I've been here for half an hour, and the only thing I've accomplished is grabbing a beer… okay, two. But besides that? I've just been standing here, listening to these idiots.

Logan, of course, isn't giving up that easily, his eyes locking on me. "You don't even have to do much. Just stand there, look friendly, and if a girl brings up, like, astrology or some shit, nod and smile."

I bite back a laugh, shaking my head. Normally, I wouldn't mind helping a buddy out, but since Logan's the rookie, he's got to earn his stripes. Giving him shit is part of the deal.

He exhales sharply, running a hand through his hair. "Fine. I'm better off on my own anyway." His lips curl into a smirk. "Bet I can get a girl to come upstairs with me in two minutes."

Nathan lets out a dry laugh. "Yeah, that's not happening."

Logan cocks his head. "You sure?"

Nathan's expression doesn't budge. "Positive."

Without hesitation, Logan downs the rest of his drink, the gulp loud over the party noise. He wipes his mouth with the back of his hand. "Watch and fucking learn."

He straightens, rolls his shoulders like he's warming up for a game, then strolls toward a pair of girls huddled near the staircase, deep in conversation.

Nathan shakes his head. "This is gonna be good."

I fold my arms across my chest, my amusement growing as I track Logan's movements. The girls give him a once-over, their skepticism practically radiating off them. I almost feel bad for the guy.

But then, one of them laughs. Then the other. His grin stretches wider, and before I can even process it, he drapes an arm around both their waists. Just like that, he's leading them up the stairs.

At the last second, he glances over his shoulder, locks eyes with us, and winks.

I blink. "You've got to be kidding me."

Nathan's mouth falls open. He looks from me to the staircase and back again, like he's waiting for his vision to correct itself. "He didn't—" He blinks a few times. "*Two* girls? Two fucking girls?"

I run a hand down my face. "And I can't even get one."

Nathan's gaze flicks to me, his brows drawing together. "Then why are you still talking to me? Relax and have some fun. We both know you desperately need it."

I scoff, shaking my head. "Pot, meet kettle."

He ignores me, clapping a hand on my shoulder. "I'm serious. You don't have to carry the whole team on your back 24/7. You might be captain, but that doesn't mean it's all on you." His lips curl into a smirk. "Have a drink. Find a girl. Take her home." He tilts his head. "Matter of fact, find a bedroom upstairs. I'm not trying to hear any moaning through the walls tonight."

I roll my eyes. "Fuck you. I do not moan."

Nathan grins. "No, but the girl will."

I'm about to shove him when a sharp shout cuts through the music. My head snaps toward the far end of the room, where Cole has some guy pinned against the wall, fists clenched. "Fuck my life," I mutter, already pushing off the couch.

Nathan's arm shoots out, pressing a hand against my chest before I can take another step. "I got it."

My jaw tightens, but I let him handle it, watching as he grabs Cole's arm and yanks him back. This isn't new. Cole's got a temper. Loves to fight. He's a right-wing for a reason.

Across the room, Tommy, the frat leader, sneers, beer sloshing over the rim of his cup. "Fucking told you hockey pricks," he says, jabbing a finger in Cole's direction. "If one of you started shit, you wouldn't be welcome here anymore. Get the fuck out."

Cole's jaw flexes, his hands balling into fists. "Fuck you." He shoves Tommy back a step. "I'm not going anywhere."

Tommy blinks, lifting a brow. "Yeah? I'm sure your coach would love to hear about his underage players getting wasted at some random frat party."

Nathan tightens his grip on Cole's arm, but it doesn't stop him from leaning in. "And I'm sure the school would love to hear about all the underage drinking going on in this house." His smirk widens. "This shit goes both ways, *Tommy*."

Tommy's jaw ticks. A second passes. Then another.

Finally, he exhales sharply, flicking his gaze to Nathan. "Get him out before you're all kicked out."

Nathan tugs at Cole's arm. "Come on, man. It's not fucking worth it."

Cole stays rigid, muscles tight like he's still debating whether to throw a punch. But after a tense beat, he exhales sharply through his nose and lets Nathan pull him toward the exit.

I drag a hand down my face and blow out a breath. I knew I shouldn't have come out tonight. If I'd just stayed in, I wouldn't be dealing with this shit, I wouldn't be freaking out about tomorrow and—

"Hey, Ryan."

The sound of my name cuts through my thoughts. I turn, finding two girls beside me, both flashing bright smiles.

"Hey," I say, forcing one of my own.

The brunette steps closer, her eyes twinkling. "Good luck in the game tomorrow."

Christ. I wish someone—*anyone*—would talk to me about something other than hockey for once in my life. It's all I ever think about. I came here to *stop* thinking about it.

"Thanks," I manage, forcing a half-smile.

Her friend, the one with light orange hair, places a hand on my arm, tilting her head. "You must be so nervous."

I shrug, trying to play it cool. "Nah, I'm fine. Just trying to relax a little—"

"You look so hot in your hockey gear," the brunette interrupts, tugging her glossy lip between her teeth, eyeing me like I'm her next meal.

I let out a low chuckle, shaking my head. I've heard that one about eighty times freshman year. Nice to know it still works for some girls. Not on me, though. Not tonight. Right now, all I want is to get the hell out of here and take a hot shower.

"Thanks," I mutter, already scanning the room for an exit. My gaze lands on Austin, who's laughing with a girl curled up next to him, looking like he's having the time of his life.

"Want us to help you release some tension?" The brunette's voice drops, a playful lilt in her tone.

I glance down at them both, her friend grinning at the question, and *god*, this is every guy's dream.

I push away from them, offering a tight smile. "I've got a massage gun at home, but thanks."

Their expressions shift, dropping at the rejection. I feel the awkwardness hang in the air before I turn away, squeezing through the crowd toward the exit.

I don't know why I thought coming out tonight would help clear my head. It hasn't. I'm not the same guy I was in freshman year. I can't just forget about hockey and party away like it's—

My rambling thoughts are interrupted when I get hit by someone and my skin chills as the liquid from their cup soaks into my shirt.

"Oh my god," a female voice gasps. "I'm so sorry."

Fuck. I grunt and glance down at my drenched t-shirt, feeling it stick to my skin. "It's fine," I mumble, wiping it off with my hand.

When I turn around, I'm met with the sight of a girl, her hands clutched to her mouth in shock, but it doesn't hide her big brown eyes widened in panic.

Fuck, her eyes are pretty.

She quickly drops her hands, shaking her head. "I really am sorry. I didn't mean to bump into you." she says, her brown wavy curls bouncing as she looks up at me. Her skin is flushed with embarrassment—or maybe it's just from the alcohol. Either way, it makes her even more stunning.

I clear my throat. "It really is fine," I assure her, raking a hand through my hair.

Her eyes widen, her lips parting slightly. "Are you sure?"

"Yeah." I shoot her a smile. "Not the first time it's happened."

Her pink lips curve into a shy smile as her fingers fiddling with the rim of her now-empty cup. "I didn't mean to push you," she says, letting out a breath. "I told my roommate you were kinda cute, and she thought I should come talk to you, so she gave me a nudge, and…"

I can't help but grin, a smirk tugging at my lips. "You think I'm cute?" I tease, leaning in slightly.

She groans, tipping her head back, her eyes fluttering shut. "I'm just dying of embarrassment tonight. Bye, I'm off to go kill myself."

I chuckle, taking a step forward and grabbing her elbow before she can slip away. "No, don't leave. It was cute."

She pauses, glancing back over her shoulder, her chocolate brown eyes locking onto mine. "You think?"

God, she's gorgeous. It's been so long since I've felt that electric buzz at the sight of a pretty girl. Her eyes, her lips, her hair—fuck, I want to run my fingers through it.

I nod, my smile widening as I gently pull her a little closer. "What's your name?"

Her throat bobs as she swallows. "Isabella."

I can't help the grin that spreads across my face. "Ryan," I introduce myself, holding her gaze. "You want another drink? Since yours kinda drenched my t-shirt."

Her eyes flick down, lingering on my chest a bit too long. *Is she checking me out?* Her lips curl into a sheepish smile. "I really am sorry."

"Stop apologizing," I say, lifting my shoulder into a shrug. "It's fine. Got me talking to you, didn't it?"

She blushes, and I feel my pulse quicken at the sight of it.

"So, you want that drink?"

She nods, her expression softening. "Sure."

I pour her a drink from the punch bowl, hand it to her, and take a sip of my own, unable to look away from her. "I haven't seen you around before. Are you a freshman?"

She hums, nodding. "Just moved into my dorm earlier today."

A groan leaves my lips. "I hated the dorms."

She laughs, a light sound that's cute as fuck. "It's not that bad. At least I've already made a friend."

"The roommate who nudged you into me?"

Her lips tug into a smile, and she shakes her head. "Aurora was doing me a favor, honestly. I would've never come and talked to you."

"Oof," I clutch my chest dramatically. "My ego's wounded."

"No. No," she laughs again, soft and light. "I wanted to, I just…" She chews on her lip, her eyes flicking away like she's searching for the right words. "I'm bad at this stuff, I guess."

I nod slowly, my gaze slipping down her body—those legs in that denim skirt, smooth and perfect, and that tight black lacy top that makes it hard to focus. *Fuck, she's a sight.* My fingers brush across my lips, trying to hide the smile that creeps up.

"You're doing pretty good."

She rolls her eyes. "What an endorsement."

I let out a laugh, feeling that easy confidence spark inside me again. *Fuck, I like this girl.* She's funny, gorgeous, and the best part? She's not blabbering on about hockey like everyone else in my life.

"You're better than you think, trust me. You just need to loosen up." I tip my head toward the beer pong table. "Ever played beer pong before?"

She shrugs, her pink glossy lips tipping up into a smirk. "Not really."

I raise an eyebrow. "Wanna give it a shot?"

She smirks, her eyes narrowing in a way that makes my body hum with heat. *Fuck, I missed this feeling.* "Depends. What do I get if I win?"

"Whatever you want."

Her smirk deepens as she leans in, her finger tracing the rim of her cup. "And what do you get if you win?"

Christ. *Dangerous fucking question.* I shrug, already picturing her panties on my bedroom floor. "Your number."

She laughs, her eyes lighting up. I'm not being coy here. I want her, and she wants me. If I have to play a silly game to get her, then so fucking be it.

"You're on."

We head toward the beer pong table, waiting for the group to finish their round. Finally, it's our turn, and we go to opposite ends. She places her hands on the table, giving me a teasing look. I can already picture her on her knees, her eyes burning with that same heat.

"Three cups?" she asks, raising an eyebrow. "Really?"

I smirk, grabbing a ping pong ball. "Hey, the fewer cups, the quicker the victory."

She smirks back, her eyes gleaming with mischief. "Yeah, sure. Or I could just win this in one shot."

I chuckle as she picks up the ball and tosses it. It misses, bouncing off the side of the cup before falling to the floor.

"Nice try," I tease, flicking the ball in my hand.

Her eyes narrow, but there's a playful smile tugging at her lips. "One shot doesn't mean I can't still win this."

I smile back, feeling more like my old self than I've felt in a long time. I pick up a ping pong ball, aiming carefully at her cup, and launch it, swirling around the rim before landing inside.

"One down," I say with a cocky smirk of my own.

She shakes her head, reaching for the cup, then takes a quick drink.

"My turn." Grabbing a ball, she tosses it with a quick flick of her wrist, and it lands right in my cup.

I raise an eyebrow, impressed. "Okay, alright. You've got good aim." I pick up the cup, take a swig, then grab the ball again, sinking another one in.

She takes a sip from her cup, her eyes never leaving mine before she grabs the ball and throws it again.

I raise an eyebrow when it lands in my cup. *Damn*. I take a quick sip of my cup and grab the ball, rolling it in my hands as I flash her a grin. "Ready to call it?"

She tilts her head, and arches a brow. "Not a chance."

My shoulders shake with a chuckle, and I blow on the ball, rolling it in my hand a few more times, before I take the shot. I watch it sink it into the last cup with a satisfying thud. *Fuck yeah*.

I strut toward her, a grin plastered across my face. "I win."

She scans me from head to toe, her eyebrow arched. "You win," she repeats, and fuck, I can't look away from her.

Her smile's got me hooked, and for a second, I forget where I am. My chest tightens, and my mind goes blank. Her lips, the way they curve—fuck me, I want to kiss her right here. Right fucking now.

She leans back against the table, hands gripping the edge as she gives me a look that damn near stops my heart. "So…" she draws out, her tongue swiping across her lips. "You want my number now?"

I swallow hard, caught off guard for a second, my thoughts spinning like crazy. The music, the party, even the damn beer pong cups—all of it fades away. All I see is her.

I glance at her lips again, heat crawling up my neck. Fuck it. I'm going for it.

I take a step closer, lowering my voice as I place my hand on her hip, resting it there. "Actually, I want something else."

Her gaze sharpens, a spark of challenge lighting up her eyes. "Yeah? What's that?"

I lick my lips, closing the distance between us, and—

"Izzy."

The name slices through the air, and Isabella instantly turns her head. I follow her gaze, watching Nathan push his way through the crowd, his eyes locked on her. She straightens, pulling back slightly, her eyes darting up to meet his.

"I didn't know you'd be here," Nathan says, his eyes flicking to me for just a beat, confusion passing over his features.

"My roommate kinda dragged me here," she replies with a sigh.

He nods. "Well, I'm glad to see you." Nathan slings an arm around her shoulders, and I can't help the way my muscles tense. My eyes flicker between the two of them. How the hell does he know her?

Izzy groans, visibly annoyed, and shoots him a glare. "Can you not stand so close to me? You're going to scare away every guy from talking to me."

Nathan scoffs, completely unbothered. "Good. I don't want some sleaze getting his hands on my baby sister."

Sister. The word hits me like a punch to the gut.

Nathan's little sister.

She rolls those pretty brown eyes of hers. "Nathan, I'm not a baby."

He shrugs. "You are to me. What were you doing hanging with my teammate, anyway?" He gestures toward me with a nod of his head.

My skin pricks. Fuck. He told all of us to stay away from his sister. Warned us off.

And here I was, two seconds away from kissing her. *God*, did I want to kiss her. My eyes slide to Isabella, a whole foot shorter than Nathan, the same hesitant, burning expression in her eyes.

"We were just… playing beer pong," I tell him with a shrug, shoving my hands in my pockets.

Nathan grunts, his eyes skeptical as he glances down at his sister. "You drink now?" he asks his sister.

She rolls her eyes, pushing him off her. "Do you really expect me to believe you don't drink?"

Nathan places his hand on his chest with a smug grin. "I'm a saint." I let out a loud scoff, which earns me an instant scowl from him. "Shouldn't you be heading off?"

The daggers in his eyes are sharp enough to cut my balls off, and that's just from a scoff. I can't even imagine what he'd do if he knew the dirty thoughts I had about his sister just two minutes ago.

"Yeah, I'm, uh… gonna go grab a drink," I mutter, gesturing behind me. I turn and walk away before Nathan realizes I wanted to do a little more than just play beer pong with Isabella.

I groan, rubbing a hand down my face.

Should've just been the rook's wingman.

FOUR

Isabella

Disappointment settles in my chest as Ryan disappears into the crowd.

I should've known it was too good to be true. Something always bites me in the ass when everything's going well. It's like the universe loves to remind me that I can't have nice things.

I haven't even *looked* at a guy since Jacob dumped me, let alone talked to one the way I talked to Ryan. But with him, it was easy. We joked, flirted, smiled, and for the first time in a while, I felt like *me* again.

Then my brother walked in.

Before that? Ryan was just Ryan. Fun, flirty, hot Ryan. But now? Now, he's Nathan's teammate. His best friend. His very hot, totally off-limits friend.

I shake my head, grabbing a cup from the ping-pong table and tossing back whatever beer's in it. It's warm and gross, but I don't really care right now.

"I don't know what's up with him," Nathan's voice breaks through my thoughts. I glance up to see him shaking his head. "He's been so off lately."

Off? Ryan was anything but off two minutes ago.

"What were you doing with Ryan, anyway?" Nathan raises an eyebrow, his eyes narrowing as he looks me over. "Didn't even know you two knew each other."

My eyes widen slightly. He can't know what really happened. Not when I'm still trying to figure out what *exactly* happened between us. So, I shrug and press my lips together. "I don't. We just met, and played a game of beer pong."

Nathan shoots me a dry look. "Izzy," he warns. "He's my teammate. Don't even think about it."

I hate that he can see right through me. It's like he has some radar that can detect when I'm up to something. I just want to be able to live my life without my big brother crowding me, judging, and controlling every single decision I make.

"Quit the protective big brother crap. Nothing happened." I roll my eyes and take a long gulp from my cup, hoping the alcohol will dull the sudden tension in my chest. "We were just talking."

Nathan shakes his head, but the tension in his shoulders eases. "Good. Cause he's not good enough for you."

I arch a brow, crossing my arms. "Isn't he your best friend?"

"Yeah, I love the guy," Nathan admits with a shrug, "but I also *know* him. I don't want him—or any other of my teammates for that matter—anywhere near you."

I let out a frustrated sigh. "You have nothing to worry about, because nothing was happening between us."

He groans, running a hand through his hair, clearly not buying it. "C'mon, you're hanging with me."

I raise an eyebrow. "I don't need you following me around. I'm not a kid, Nathan."

He shrugs, flashing me an arrogant grin. "Doesn't matter. I've been looking out for you since forever. You'll always be a kid to me."

I roll my eyes. He's two years older than me, not a decade. But, apparently, Nathan's always going to act like I'm still twelve.

I glance around, looking for Aurora. No sign of her. Where the hell did she go?

"Fine," I finally give in, shooting him a look. "Only because I can't find Aurora."

Nathan gestures for me to follow him with a tilt of his chin. I push off the ping-pong table and trail behind him through the crowded party.

People stop him left and right. Slaps on the back, handshakes, and a few girls trying to get his attention, running their hands over his arms or tossing him flirtatious glances.

I press my lips together, trying to stop the bile from rising in my throat. I could do without watching girls practically drool over him. I'd much rather hold onto the image of my overprotective, somewhat-innocent big brother... though I know that's a little unrealistic.

Nathan stops to talk to everyone who approaches, effortlessly flashing that trademark grin of his. It's a little surprising how well-known my brother is around campus. Especially since he tends to keep to himself.

"Hayes!"

My brother stops when a guy on the couch yells his name, giving him a lazy grin, drunk out of his mind.

"Where the hell have you been, man? I missed you."

My brother shakes his head. "Someone get this idiot some chamomile tea or something to cut the alcohol."

I come to a stop when I glance up and see Ryan, again, snickering as he takes a sip of his drink, his dark eyes shifting toward me.

The guy on the couch runs a hand through his light brown hair and whistles low, his smirk spreading. "Who's the hottie?"

Ryan jabs his elbow into the guy's stomach, making him grunt out an 'oof.' "That's Nathan's sister, dumbass," he grumbles.

The guy's face drops, eyes wide with surprise. "Oh, shit. Sorry."

Nathan narrows his eyes. "You'll be sorry when I kick your ass."

He chuckles, shaking his head, then extends a hand with a grin. "Nice to meet you, Baby Hayes. I'm Austin."

"Hi," I reply, shaking his hand and laughing softly. "Isabella."

I glance back at Ryan, still watching me, his gaze lingering as he sizes me up. *God, that look.* It sends a jolt through me, reminding me of how close we were just minutes ago, his body pressing into mine, the faint scent of his cologne still in the air, his lips a breath away.

Nathan nudges me with his shoulder. "I'm gonna grab a drink. You sure you'll be okay with these idiots?"

I snicker. "Yeah, I'll be fine."

Nathan walks off, leaving me with his teammates—one completely hammered, and the other… the one I almost kissed.

Austin leans forward, a mischievous glint in his eye as he shoots me a wink. "Don't worry. I don't mind a little ass-kicking."

Ryan's gaze snaps to him, his face hardening. "You're an idiot," he mutters. "Weren't you just talking to a girl?"

Austin shrugs. "She had a boyfriend."

Ryan scoffs, shaking his head in disbelief before his gaze shifts to me. His eyes soften as he arches a brow, his lips twitching into a smirk. "Wanna get away from this weirdo?" he asks.

I let out a soft laugh and follow him as he takes a seat on the steps, the sound of his sneakers scraping against the wood. "He's kind of funny," I tease, turning slightly to glance at Ryan.

Ryan shakes his head, a hint of amusement in his eyes as his lips curl into a playful smile. "Deranged, more like."

My eyes flicker to the side of his face, watching as he runs a hand through his messy hair. "So, you're a hockey player?"

He lets out a sigh, like my question's annoyed him, but the moment fades when he glances at me, his lips twitching into a smirk. "And you're Coach's daughter and Nathan's sister." He shakes his head, a small scoff escaping him. "Dangerous combination."

I laugh when he takes a sip of his drink. "You're scared of my brother?"

Ryan chuckles, his eyes locking onto mine again, and the space between us seems to vanish when his knee nudges mine. "I'm not scared of anyone. I just respect him, is all," he admits, his smile softening as he swallows, his gaze lingering on every inch of my face. "Besides, it would've probably been a mistake."

Yikes. His words hit me like a punch to the gut, but I force out a laugh, trying to brush it off. "You're probably right." I shoot him a smile. "I don't date hockey players, anyway."

"Really?" he asks. "Why not?"

I tilt my head, my eyes drifting over his face as I reply, my lips curving into a smirk. "I've been around them my whole life. Too many missing teeth and broken noses."

His laugh is quick, but it's followed by a smirk. "Well, I have all my teeth." He flashes a grin that seems to stretch just a little too long, and I catch myself staring at the way his lips curl. The ones I almost kissed.

I swallow, forcing myself to look up, but his eyes catch mine, steady and warm. My pulse quickens. I lean in a little, just enough for him to notice the way the air shifts between us. I catch the faint scent of his cologne, mingled with the hint of alcohol on his shirt, and it's a heady mix that makes it hard to focus.

"I see that," I murmur, my voice lower now as I inch closer. The scent of his cologne wraps around me, making it harder to think. "But you're still off limits."

His grin widens, and I can see the challenge in his eyes. "Well, that's good," he says with a smirk. "Because I don't date. Period."

My brows shoot up in surprise. "Ever?"

He shrugs, taking another sip of his drink. "I like being single."

I can't help but roll my eyes. "I'm sure. You flash that cocky smile, and every girl just drops their panties for you."

His grin widens, but his eyes flash with something challenging as he leans in, closing the space between us. "You're not immune, Isabella. Trust me, I know."

My chest churns, my heart skipping a beat, and for a second, I really wish he didn't care about my brother and just kissed me already. "If I remember correctly," I murmur, "you wanted my number."

He nods slowly, the corner of his mouth twitching slightly. "I did."

I pause, his words circling in my mind. Pressing my lips together, I lean forward, daring him—daring myself. "Do you still want it?"

The muscle in his jaw tightens, his eyes darkening as he seems to weigh the consequences. "Probably wouldn't be a good idea."

"Right." I nod, knowing he's right, even if it's the last thing I wanted to hear.

He keeps his eyes locked on mine, unwavering. "Nathan and your dad…" He blows out a breath, running a hand through his hair.

"Yeah, I know." I nod again, but my mind keeps circling back to the way his eyes had drifted to my lips just seconds ago. "I just keep thinking… if Nathan hadn't walked in…"

The tension between us grows as his gaze drops from my eyes to my lips. "Good thing he did."

"Yeah," I murmur, my voice betraying me. I don't believe a single word that leaves my lips.

His eyes snap back to mine, a smirk creeping across his face. "Cause you don't date hockey players."

"And you don't date. Period."

Ryan's smirk widens, his eyes glinting with amusement as he lets out a low chuckle, leaning back slightly. "Exactly."

A part of me wants to keep pushing him, but I know Ryan respects my brother too much to ever cross that line with me, even if it's what we both want.

"But we can still be friends, right?"

An amused smirk tugs at his lips. "You wanna be my friend?"

I pause, thinking it over. Can I really be just friends with Ryan when earlier tonight, I wanted nothing more than for him to have my clothes on his bedroom floor and his name slipping from my lips?

I haven't been friends with a guy since… ever.

But seeing as I now attend Colton U, and I'll probably run into my brother and his teammates often, it would be a lot easier if we just agreed to never cross that line.

"Yeah," I say, offering a smile, my shoulders lifting in a shrug. "Why not?"

Ryan's eyes linger on me, his gaze scanning my face as if he's searching for something, before he finally nods, the corner of his mouth lifting into a smirk. "Sure. Friends."

"There you are." I turn my head, seeing Aurora heading toward me, letting out a relieved sigh. "I've been looking for you all this—" She cuts herself off, her gaze flicking between me and Ryan. A smile slowly spreads across her face, growing wider with each passing second. "Shit, sorry. Was I interrupting something?"

"Not at all," Ryan replies with a laugh. "Just keeping her company." He grips the railing and lifts himself up. As he turns to walk away, he flashes me a smirk. "See you around, Isabella."

He walks away, hands tucked in his pockets, before disappearing into the crowd.

I glance up at Aurora, whose grin only makes me roll my eyes. "Thanks for pushing me into him, by the way," I tell her, lifting myself off the steps.

She chuckles. "You're being sarcastic, but you should be thanking me," she teases, wrapping her arm around mine. "If it wasn't for me, you wouldn't have talked to him."

I purse my lips. That's true, but then again, if I hadn't talked to him, I wouldn't have almost kissed him. And this weird tension between us wouldn't be hanging in the air.

An amused smirk tugs at her lips. "So, what happened? Did you kiss him? Give him your number? Hand stuff?"

I choke out a laugh, shaking my head. "Hate to burst your bubble, but none of the sort is ever going to happen."

"What?" Her brows furrow. "Why not? You seemed like you were having a good time."

We were. Until my brother showed up, and suddenly everything got complicated.

I shrug, trying to brush it off. "We're just friends."

FIVE

Ryan

"**N**ailed it!"

I skid to a stop as Austin lands a shitty ass spin, lifting his stick in the air as he lets out heavy breaths. Guess he's pretending to be a figure skater today.

Seeing as we lost the game last week—no fucking surprise there—he'd be better off focusing on drills, not spins.

Logan skates circles around him, arching a brow. "Is this hockey practice or a circus, because you look like a clown, my guy."

Nathan chuckles. "I've seen more coordination from a toddler with a sugar high."

Austin lets out a scoff, crossing his arms, his stick lodged under his armpit. "This shit's harder than it looks. You'll all be jealous when I'm famous."

Cole shakes his head, his mouth moving as he chews gum. "Famous for taking out half the team with your wild turns?" he replies. "You scared the rookie away."

"I'm not scared," Logan replies with a roll of his eyes. "Just didn't want to lose a tooth. I'm still young. I've got a lot going for me."

Nathan scoffs. "I'm sure. Like being a fuckboy for once."

Logan clicks his tongue, giving him a grin. "I prefer the term, part time lover."

Coach's sharp whistle cuts through the rink. "Alright. Rhodes, stop spinning and get your ass to those cones. Ellis, take that fucking gum out of your mouth. Rest of you, stop fucking around and get to warm ups. Now."

Austin lets out a low groan as he turns around and skates around the cones, doing some tricks, because he just can't help himself.

"Stop fucking around before coach rips you a new one."

He glances over his shoulder, shooting me a wink. "You know you're secretly jealous of my moves."

I let out a snicker, tapping his back. "It's good to have dreams, buddy."

I hear a laugh in the distance—a sweet, light sound I instantly recognize. My gaze snaps up, drawn to the entrance where Isabella is smiling up at her dad, his arms wrapped around her.

Haven't seen her since the party, and goddamn, she looks good. Too fucking good to be at an ice rink with a bunch of sweaty hockey players. What the hell is she doing here?

My eyes drift to her lips as she talks to her dad. I'm so caught up in watching them that, before I know it, my foot catches, and I stumble—crashing into Cole. "Woah, watch it!" Cole grunts as I land half on him, my knee jamming into his back.

"Fuck, sorry," I mutter, pushing myself up. I hold out my hand to help him to his feet.

He just stares back at me, shaking his head, his dark eyes hardened. "The hell was that?"

"I… slipped." I glance up again, and Isabella's still there, laughing with Coach. Her dimples make her smile even more infectious, and I can't help but look for just a second longer.

"Damn, Coach," Austin whistles from behind me, skating to a stop. "I thought you were some hard ass, not a teddy bear. Where's my hug?"

Coach turns, narrowing his eyes at Austin. "Still a hard ass. Get your ass in gear, or I'll have you running laps until your legs give out."

"Fuck that," Austin groans, rolling his eyes as he turns back to his drills. "Reed. You coming?"

"No, I'm… gonna do some stretches," I mutter, my eyes drifting back to Isabella.

Austin shrugs. "Suit yourself."

I watch Isabella for a little longer, the noise of the guys behind me fading as I focus on her talking with Coach.

Before I even realize what I'm doing, I'm gliding across the ice toward her.

Coach's expression hardens when he spots me. "Reed. What are you doing out here? I thought I told you to warm up."

Kinda wanna talk to your daughter instead.

"Just getting some water, Coach," I reply.

He grunts, glancing down at his daughter. "First order of business, keep an eye on that one." He points at me before spinning on his heels and walking away.

I turn my head and lock eyes with Isabella. She smiles the second I do, and I can't help but grin as I raise an eyebrow. "You're here to keep me in line?"

She scoffs, shaking her head. "That's my dad's job."

I pull off my helmet, grab a water bottle, and squirt some into my mouth. "Ah. Came to stalk me, then?"

She chuckles. "You wish."

My lips twitch. *Yeah, I do.* "So, what *are* you doing here?" I cock my head, my gaze drifting over her jeans and cropped flowery top, lingering a second too long on the curve of her cleavage before I drag it back up.

She lets out a sigh. "My dad thought it'd be a good idea for me to work under him for a while."

My brows shoot up, intrigued. "Yeah?"

She nods, a small smile tugging at her lips. "I want to work in sports. Maybe as a manager or an analyst." She lets out a breathy laugh, half-exhale, half-chuckle. "I know people think it's a stupid, unrealistic idea, but—"

My eyes widen, genuinely impressed. "Hell no, that's cool as fuck. You sure you want to spend your life dealing with a bunch of idiots, though?"

She chuckles, tucking a curl behind her ear. "If I can handle my dad and my brother, I can handle anything."

"Not so sure about that," I tut, shaking my head. "Especially when it comes to Cole. Your dad has a fucking field day with him."

She laughs, her eyes glimmering. "He doesn't have any trouble with you?"

I press a hand to my chest in mock offense. "I'm a saint."

"Right. Sure you are." She smirks, glancing at my jersey. "Reed," she murmurs quietly as her gaze catches the name. "Wait… *Reed?*" Her eyes widen. *Ah, fuck.* "Ryan Reed? As in Connor Reed, the hockey legend?"

Shit. Really hoped she wouldn't put that together. I've got enough people losing their minds and drooling over my brother—don't need her doing it too.

I sigh, dragging a hand through my hair and shooting her a sheepish look. "Would you believe me if I said it's just a coincidence?"

She squints, confusion flickering across her pretty face. Fuck. Stop looking at her like that. Off limits, Ryan. *Off fucking limits*. "Do you want it to be a coincidence?"

I shrug, shaking my head. "I don't know," I admit, letting out a groan. "I love my brother, I'm proud of everything he's done, but I feel like he's all anyone sees when they look at me."

She studies me for a moment, those big brown eyes softening before she shakes her head. "I don't think that."

I arch a brow. "No?"

"For one, he's taller," she says with a grin.

I scoff. "Thanks for that."

"And hotter, obviously."

I narrow my eyes. "Well, that's just not true."

"And *way* better at picking up girls."

I smile, loving how she's teasing me, turning the awkward as fuck situation into something lighter, though part of me wants to remind her that I had her lips an inch from mine not long ago, her body arching into mine, practically begging me to kiss her.

Fuck it, why not.

I reach out, twirling a brown curl around my gloved finger, my voice dropping a hint as I lean in, the scent of fresh strawberries filling my nose.

"Not how I remember it, Curls."

She stumbles back, her breath hitching in a way that makes my pulse race. God, I want to hear that sound again… and again.

"Well, then we'll need to cure your bad memory." She smirks, her voice hotter than hell, sending a shiver straight down my spine.

I let out a laugh, feeling my chest jump. I haven't had this much fun with a girl in… fuck. Ever.

I like how she can tease me and still flash me a smile that makes me want to thread my fingers through her curls and bring her lips to mine.

And that's when it hits me like a bucket of ice-cold water.

I can't fucking do that.

Her brother. *My best friend*.

Her dad. *My coach*.

Christ. There are so many rules when it comes to her, so many 'do not enter' signs flashing in my face, blaring red alarms, and yet here I am, a fucking dumbass ignoring them left, right, and center.

I pull away from her, my smile faltering the second I see that same damn look in her eyes.

"I'll, uh… see you." I shift awkwardly, trying—and failing—to ignore the sudden tension between us.

"Yeah." She presses her lips together, a soft chuckle slipping out that makes my brain short-circuit. Goddamn, I love that sound. "See you."

Like a complete moron, I give her a two-finger salute.

And then immediately want to disappear off the face of the Earth.

Did I just… salute her?

Someone fucking shoot me.

I spin on my skates, shaking my head as I shove my helmet back on, but it doesn't do shit to clear my head. Her scent is still clinging to me, and I can still picture those pretty lips parting when I leaned in close and twirled her hair around my finger.

Jesus. I need to get laid. Bad.

Austin's already waiting for me on the ice, eyebrows raised, amusement dripping from his smirk.

"Fucking dangerous, Cap."

Shit. My skin prickles, but I force a lazy shrug. "No idea what you're talking about."

Austin lets out a low laugh, shaking his head. "Come on. You're not that dumb. Pick literally *anyone* else. Hell, if you're that hard up, I'll kiss you."

Before I can react, he lunges, hands grabbing my helmet like he's actually about to do it.

I shove him away, laughing. "Get the fuck off me, you idiot."

He chuckles. "I'm serious, though. Nathan will beat you into next week if you even think about touching his sister."

Yeah. No shit.

I shrug again, keeping my face neutral. "You're dreaming. Nothing's going on."

But then, like a dumbass, I glance back at her.

Just one last look.

Nathan's got an arm wrapped around her, messing up her hair. She glares at him, shoving him off before fixing those brown curls, and I can't help but smile.

Austin lets out a laugh, and I snap my gaze back to him. His grin has only gotten bigger, like he already knows exactly how this is gonna end.

"I tried to warn you."

SIX

Isabella

I'm gonna die.

Okay, maybe not *die*, but Aurora is definitely going to dislocate my shoulder if she keeps yanking me around like a ragdoll.

"Come on," she wraps her arm around mine, tugging me along, "you need sunlight before you start hissing at it."

I squint against the obnoxious brightness, raising a hand to shield my face. "I appreciate the concern, but I'm good."

"Just looking out for you," Aurora says, throwing me a pointed look. "When's the last time you left our dorm for something other than class or hockey practice?"

I open my mouth to respond, but then I pause.

She smirks. "Exactly. You've been holed up in there for days."

I sigh, already regretting letting her pull me out of the dorm. "Aurora, I really need—"

She stops so suddenly I nearly crash into her. Placing her hands on her hips, she arches a brow. "You're coming with me to get some fresh air, coffee, and stop thinking about hockey for five minutes, before your brain turns into ice shavings."

I exhale, defeated. "Fine. One coffee. Then I really need to study."

Aurora grins, looping her arm through mine. "Good girl."

I scoff. "Do I look like a dog to you?"

She sniffs dramatically, then shoots me a grin. "You kinda smell like one."

I laugh, shoving her lightly as we cross campus, and okay— maybe this isn't the worst idea. The fresh air actually feels *nice*, warm sunlight spilling across my skin, the scent of coffee floating through the air.

It's been way too long since I've done anything but drown myself in school and hockey. Ever since the party last week, my routine has been nothing but classes, practice, and hiding in my dorm with my favorite sweatpants. The only time I see Aurora is when she's half-asleep with a face mask on, watching horror movies in total darkness like a psychopath.

The second we step inside the café, Aurora takes a deep inhale. "God, I love this place," she sighs, dreamily. "It's the only thing keeping me from committing crimes."

"You barely function *with* caffeine," I tease, heading for the counter.

"Rude." She flips her sunglasses onto her head, flicking her blonde hair over her shoulder. "What's the move? Stick to my usual or risk my taste buds and finally try a matcha?"

My face screws up. "Just get your usual. You're not that adventurous."

She gasps, scandalized. "Excuse me, I once did five tequila shots and rode a mechanical bull."

"And *cried* after."

She rolls her eyes. "That's not the point, Isabella. *God*, why did I tell you that?"

I let out a chuckle as I order a caramel latte, and hand over my card. Aurora, however—adamant on wanting to prove me wrong—orders a matcha, takes one sip, and instantly grimaces like she just licked the bottom of a lawnmower.

"This tastes like grass."

"Expensive grass," I correct, chuckling into my caramel latte.

She hums, smacking her lips. "With a sprinkle of regret."

Since I'm a good friend, I won't tell her '*I told you so*', but... I told her so.

We grab a small table by the window, warm sunlight spilling across our drinks, and Aurora is already scrolling on her phone before I even sit down.

"Party tonight," she announces, tapping out a quick text before looking up at me. "We're going."

I've only known Aurora for less than two weeks, but one thing is abundantly clear—this girl does not take no for an answer.

"Aurora." I shake my head. "If I ever want to work with a pro-team and not end up running them into the ground, I actually have to pass this class."

She eyes me over her cup, lips pursed. "Do you actually need to study, or are you just trying to avoid a certain someone?"

My fingers tighten around my cup. "I have no idea what you're talking about."

Aurora lets out a knowing chuckle, arching a brow. "Oh, please. You can't fool me. I saw you two talking at the party, and now you have to see each other every day at practice... You sure nothing happened?"

"Positive," I say, lifting my coffee to my lips. "Just a few quick conversations."

"About?" she pries, stirring her drink as she dumps in three sugar packets.

I press my lips together. Since my dad is always around, we never really... talk. Usually, he just skates past me, compliments my outfit, flashes me a wink or that smile of his that turns my knees to jelly, and then disappears into the locker room.

"Stuff," I reply, sipping my drink to avoid having to say any more.

Aurora smirks, snapping the lid back onto her drink. "I don't know anyone who avoids a guy this hard unless they hooked up with him... or committed a felony in his presence."

I shoot her a flat look. "First of all, *what?* And second of all, I already told you, nothing happened."

She hums, leaning in, her eyes twinkling. "But you *wanted* something to happen."

I open my mouth to argue, but before I can, Aurora suddenly chokes on her drink. She coughs, eyes going wide as she presses a hand to her chest. Then, a slow, wicked grin spreads across her face.

"Oh, this just keeps getting better."

I frown. "What?"

She doesn't answer; just tilts her head toward the counter.

I follow her gaze, and my stomach sinks like a rock.

Because standing there, looking unfairly good in a hoodie and joggers, is Ryan. His dark hair is tousled, sticking up in places like he just rolled out of bed, and he's grinning at something. Not just any grin—full-bodied, dimple-popping laughter, the kind that makes his shoulders shake and his head tilt back slightly.

And standing right next to him? My brother, Nathan.

Of course.

Aurora leans in with a smirk. "I know this is awkward for you, but I'm loving this right now."

I exhale through my nose, shooting her a dry look. "I'm transferring schools."

"You're being ridiculous," she scoffs with a shake of her head.

"I'm serious. I'll pack my bags right now."

Before I can make my escape, Nathan spots me. He lifts his hand, shooting me a smile before nudging Ryan and making his way over.

Ryan's gaze falls on me. Our eyes lock for a few seconds before he follows my brother.

I retract my earlier statement. I *am* going to die.

Nathan doesn't hesitate, flopping into the seat beside me. He throws an arm over the back of my chair. Ryan sits beside him.

"What are you doing here?" my brother asks, arching a brow.

Aurora answers before I can. "Trying to drag your sister out of our dorm for once."

Nathan snorts. "Is that why you look like that?" he asks, arching a brow, his gaze flicking to my hair.

My cheeks heat as I flip him off. "I hate you."

My brother laughs. "Yeah, right. Tell me that the next time you need a favor. Speaking of which," he says, shifting in his seat, "you still have a ton of crap at my place. Taking up all my space and shit."

I let out a groan, squeezing my eyes shut. "I completely forgot about that. Dad said he'd handle it."

Nathan snorts, jerking his thumb toward Ryan. "And yet she claims she's not a baby." He shakes his head, ruffling my hair. "You're such a Princess."

Why he continues to act like I'm a dog, I'll never know. I shoot Nathan a glare, swatting his hand away, and attempt to fix my hair.

I try desperately not to make eye contact with Ryan. One of the reasons I enjoy talking to him is because he doesn't treat me like I'm just Nathan's little sister. But after this? I wouldn't be surprised if he starts seeing me that way too.

"I'll deal with it later, don't worry," I mutter.

My brother scoffs, unconvinced. "It's *a lot* of stuff. Boxes and boxes of makeup and whatever other crap you hoard. No way you can move it alone."

I glance at Aurora, batting my eyelashes. "You'll help me, right?"

She sips her matcha, her expression blank. "I didn't sign up for manual labor."

I let out a chuckle and shake my head. Can't fault her for being honest.

Nathan leans back in his chair, his eyes flicking to me with an eyebrow raised. "Well, you need to figure something out. Can't have my room drowning in boxes." He pushes himself up, tossing his jacket over his shoulder with a shrug and arches a brow my way. "Brushing your hair isn't illegal, you know."

Ryan chuckles as my brother heads to the door, rubbing a hand over his mouth.

I narrow my eyes. "It's not funny."

Ryan presses his lips together, a smirk tugging at the corners as he stands. "No, of course not," he says, leaning in closer. His breath hits my cheek and I suck in a breath, feeling the air escape my lungs. "But if you ever need help with anything… I'll be your guy." He pulls back, his lips twitching into a smirk and I feel a shiver race down my spine.

Before I can even come up with a response, Nathan calls out from the door, already on his way out. "Come on, man. We're gonna be late."

Ryan straightens, his posture shifting, and glances at Aurora before tipping his head her way. "Aurora." His eyes slide back to me, and that damn smile of his stretches wider. "Later, Curls."

I blink, trying to shake off the tension in the air, but it lingers, thick and undeniable. My heart pounds in my chest, and I have no idea why it's affecting me this much.

Aurora chuckles from beside me, her voice dripping with amusement. "*Nothing happened*, she says."

I discreetly kick her under the table.

Her grin just widens.

SEVEN

Ryan

"**F**uck, I'm starving."

Before I can even kick off my shoes or close the door, Austin bursts through, practically launching himself at the fridge. I hear the familiar squeak of it opening, followed by a frustrated grunt.

"Either grab something or shut the door, man," Nathan calls out, rolling his eyes as he drops his gym bag onto the floor with a thud. "You're letting all the cold air out."

Austin groans, his voice muffled as he digs around inside. "Why the hell don't we have any real food?"

I give him a deadpan look as I peel off my jacket. "Because you eat everything the second it enters the house," I reply, raising an eyebrow. "Seriously, you're like a human vacuum cleaner."

Austin slams the fridge door with his foot, holding a pack of shredded cheese. He rips it open, not bothering with a plate, and dumps half of it straight into his mouth.

Nathan scrunches up his face in disgust. "Come on, that's just gross."

Austin tilts his head, chewing away. "You're just mad you didn't think of it first."

Nathan flops onto one of the stools at the counter with an exaggerated sigh. "I can confidently say I've never been jealous of someone eating cheese straight from the bag." He watches, wincing, as Austin grabs another handful. "Ever heard of a *real* meal? Protein?"

Austin lifts the cheese bag, waving it around. "Dairy's got protein, dumbass."

I snicker under my breath, leaning against the doorframe. "No wonder Cole didn't want to move in with us."

We'd asked Cole if he wanted to move in here with us, but he shot it down fast. Said he liked living in his dorm. Which, fine, whatever—but I have a sneaking suspicion he just enjoys being alone. Or maybe he just flat-out hates us. Can't say I blame him either.

Austin licks cheese off his thumb, his face scrunching up in thought. "Living here would do him some good."

Nathan snorts. "Pretty sure you alone scared him off."

I let out a laugh, shaking my head, but my attention shifts when my phone buzzes in my pocket. I pull it out, my eyes narrowing as I scroll through a sea of missed texts from a handful of girls—Sophia, Tara, Lana. Endless names light up my screen.

Then I spot the newest message, from Cassie, some girl I met at the bar last night—thanks to the guys dragging me out of my room.

Cassie:

What do you say we grab that drink later tonight?

I exhale a frustrated breath, rubbing my hand down my face. Cassie's cool, I guess. Last night, she made it pretty clear she'd be down for a quick hook-up. It'd be easy. *So fucking easy*. I could just send a quick 'yes,' and she'd be in my bed by the end of the night. No strings, no complications.

But of course, my stupid brain doesn't go down the easy route. Instead, it travels right back to the one girl who's off-limits.

Isabella is cool as hell, funny, smart, with a smile that makes me forget everything around me. And not to mention, she's absolutely drop-dead gorgeous. Those brown curls, those deep brown eyes that have me completely hooked.

But fuck, I don't want a relationship. I've never had one. Never wanted one.

And Isabella is not the type of girl you can just hook up with and pretend nothing happened afterward.

Besides, I couldn't do that to Nathan. He's one of the best guys I know.

And I know, without a doubt, if I had a sister, I wouldn't want any of these idiots dating her.

Another text from Cassie pops up on my screen, her address blinking at me. I let out a groan, running a hand over my face.

Just fucking do it.

Just… get her out of your system. Move the fuck on with someone else.

"What's wrong?" Austin asks, his voice muffled as he shovels more cheese into his mouth.

"Please, for the love of God, chew before you speak," Nathan replies, shaking his head.

Austin ignores him, still staring at me, intrigued. "Who you texting?"

I shove my phone into my pocket, wishing the damn thing would just stop buzzing. "No one."

Austin's brows shoot up, a wide grin spreading across his face. "Uh oh. He's hiding something."

I shoot him a glare, my jaw tightening. "Can you stay out of my business, please?"

But of course, Austin doesn't listen. He jumps off the counter, that grin still plastered on his face. "Come on, who is it?" he presses, his eyes bright with curiosity. I stay silent, but he keeps pushing. His grin falters, then grows again as he puts it together. "Wait… Is it—"

"No," I snap, my voice firm. The last thing I need is Austin dragging this out. He hasn't let it go since he saw me talking to Isabella at the rink. I thought he'd drop it, but of course, he hasn't.

His mouth doesn't know when to shut up.

Nathan looks at me, brow furrowed. "Who's he talking about?"

"No one," I snap, rubbing my temples. "Can you just let it go, Jesus." I exhale, running a hand through my hair, trying to shake off the tension building up inside me. "It's like I'm talking to a bunch of ten-year-olds."

Nathan chuckles, but then his face scrunches up as he groans, squeezing his eyes shut. "Speaking of ten-year-olds… I need a favor."

I snort. "Listen, I love you, but I'm not babysitting your cousin or some shit."

"No babysitting required," he says with an eye roll. "I just need help carrying my sister's stuff to her dorm. My mom called me out for not helping her, and I got an earful."

Austin snickers from the kitchen. "Aw, you a mamma's boy, Hayes?"

Nathan flips him off, but his eyes stay locked on me. "Will you help me out?"

I raise an eyebrow. "Now?"

He shakes his head. "No, not right now. I'm gonna grab a shower. But maybe around five? If you're free to help then?"

I should probably say no. I should probably avoid her. If I don't see her, I won't think about how my hands felt on her hips, or how her lips were an inch from mine.

But then again… I kinda wanna see those brown curls and that smile again.

And I did tell her I'd be her guy if she ever needed help with anything. I'd be an asshole to go back on my word and let her down.

"Yeah," I say, shrugging. "Sure."

Austin's smirk widens. "Oooh, you're helping baby Hayes? I might tag along."

"Get fucked," Nathan mutters, shoving him in the chest.

Austin laughs it off, rubbing at his chest. "Fine, fine. I'll stay here. Got some studying to do, or whatever." He sighs dramatically. "Take pictures for me, Ryan," he adds with a wink.

As I said… his mouth never knows when to shut up.

Nathan, however, doesn't seem amused. He throws me a glare, clearly not thrilled at the idea of Austin joking about me and his sister.

"Chill," I mutter, shaking my head. "Austin was just kidding."

Nathan grunts. "Better be."

He keeps glaring, and Austin just keeps grinning.

"Trust me," I say, forcing a chuckle. "I have no interest in your sister, alright?" *You dirty little liar.* "Besides," I shrug, hoping he buys the bullshit spilling out of my mouth. "I've got a date tonight."

Nathan's brows shoot up in surprise. "You do?"

Austin echoes, voice dripping with skepticism. "You do?"

"Yeah," I lie. "Some girl I met last night at the bar."

There's a beat of silence before Austin whistles loudly, then whoops, smacking me on the arm. "Bout fucking time."

Nathan shakes his head, chuckling under his breath. "Don't worry. I'll make sure we're done by then so you won't be late to your date. Lord knows you need it."

I hate them all.

Before I can fire back, the sound of pounding footsteps echoes from downstairs, and Logan comes barreling in, shirtless and only in boxers. "Who's got a date?"

Oh, for the love of God.

"Jesus. Put some fucking clothes on," Nathan mutters, narrowing his eyes at him.

Logan just smirks, wagging his eyebrows. "Turning you on, am I?" he teases.

Nathan rolls his eyes, crossing his arms over his chest. "You're an idiot, Gray."

Logan laughs, tossing him a wink. "Keep talking dirty to me, and I might just take that as an invitation." His eyes flick to Austin. "Now tell me who the hell has a date."

Austin lazily gestures toward me, his smirk widening.

Logan's eyes snap back to me, and his mouth practically drops open. "Reed's got a date? Fuck yeah! About time he got rid of his dry spell."

"That's what I'm saying," Austin agrees.

I roll my eyes, throwing my hands up. "Jesus Christ. I'm surrounded by children." I grunt, rubbing a hand down my face. "I'm out of here." I grab my gym bag, sling it over my shoulder, and head upstairs.

The second I close my bedroom door behind me, I strip off my clothes and toss them onto the floor. I make a beeline for the shower, turning the water to full blast. The hot spray hits me, and I close my eyes, letting it ripple over my skin as I inhale deeply.

Thoughts of Isabella start flooding my mind. I barely got a chance to talk to her at the café last week, since her brother was there, which pretty much put a damper on anything real happening, but I really like talking to her. I can't even remember the last time I enjoyed talking to a girl like I do her. Usually, all girls want to talk about is either hockey, my brother, or—let's be real—an invitation into their bed.

But with Isabella? It feels different. No hidden agendas. She's not interested in dating hockey players, and I'm not looking for a relationship, so we're basically on the same page. There's no pressure, just two people talking and actually getting to know each other.

Except… she's off-limits.

I let out a frustrated groan, splashing water onto my face, trying to wash away the tension in my head.

What the fuck am I doing?

I need to stop thinking about Isabella. This whole thing is probably just a side effect of not getting laid for way too long. Maybe my brain's just making up some weird obsession to fill the void.

Yeah, that's what it is. Just a weird delusion.

I run a hand through my wet hair and turn off the shower, the bathroom quickly fogging up with steam. Grabbing a towel, I wrap it around my waist and step onto the cold tile. Reaching for the massage gun on the counter, I start working it into the tight muscles in my neck, trying to ease the knots from practice.

I glance at my phone on the bed. With a sigh, I walk over, grab it, and scroll to Cassie's text with her address.

A breath escapes me. This is exactly what I need—a quick distraction. Someone to help me get Isabella out of my head.

Me:

Sounds great. 8 okay?

I hit send, before I can talk myself out of it.

Her reply is a thumbs up.

I drop the phone back on the bed, but before I can even get dressed, it buzzes again. Glancing at it, I expect another message from Cassie.

Instead, it's an incoming call from my Dad.

I stare at it for a second, debating. The last time we talked was… hell, I don't even know. A few weeks ago? Maybe longer. It's not like we have a schedule. He calls when he remembers, and I answer when I feel like it.

My thumb hovers over the screen before I sigh and swipe to accept.

"Hi, dad."

"Ryan." His voice is crisp, clipped. The same as always. "How's school?"

I shift on the edge of my bed, bracing my elbow on my knee. "It's fine."

"Your grades?"

"They're alright."

A short pause passes, and I picture him nodding silently, checking his watch. "Good." He pauses again for a second. "I caught your last game."

I rub a hand over my face. "Yeah?" I say, already bracing for whatever's coming.

"You let three shots in."

My jaw tightens, and I exhale through my nose. "I know."

"It wasn't your best performance."

"I know that too," I mutter, the irritation bubbling up, but I swallow it down.

He sighs, drumming his fingers against his desk. His version of a disappointed sigh. I've been hearing that sound for as long as I can remember.

"You were out of position on that second goal."

I frown, mentally replaying the game. "I was screened."

"You should've read the play faster."

My grip tightens on the phone. "I'll do better next time," I force out, my tone tight.

"Connor never—"

He stops short. But I already know where that sentence was headed.

I squeeze my eyes shut for a second, breathing in slow to keep my cool. "I'm *not* Connor."

Silence.

It stretches on so long I wonder if he hung up. But then his voice breaks through. "No," he says, almost like he's stating a fact. "I suppose you're not."

The words land like a punch, even though I saw it coming. It's not even cruel, not outright. It's just matter-of-fact, like a truth neither of us can change.

Like he doesn't even mean it as an insult.

And somehow, that makes it worse.

I shift, rubbing a hand over my jaw, my fingers scraping over stubble I haven't bothered to shave off in a few days. "How's Mom?"

"She's fine," he says, voice tight, clipped, giving me the bare minimum, like he can't be bothered to share anything more. No elaboration, no detail.

I glance at the clock on my nightstand. "Is she home?"

"I think so."

I think so.

I swallow down the bitter laugh that wants to escape. They live in the same house. Married for twenty-five years. And he doesn't even know if she's home.

I lean back against my bed, staring up at the ceiling. I really shouldn't be surprised. Their relationship's been like this for as long as I can remember. When I was a kid, it was nonstop fighting—yelling in the kitchen, doors slamming. Then one day, it just… stopped. No more yelling. No more arguing.

They didn't get better. They just got quieter.

I'm still not sure which one is worse.

There's some rustling on the other end of the line, and then a muffled voice. A few seconds later, Mom's on the line. "Hi, Sweetie."

I shift again, adjusting the phone against my ear. "Hey, Mom."

"How are you?"

I hesitate for a second too long, my fingers drumming lightly on the side of my bed. "I'm good."

"You eating enough?"

I can't help but smile at how much she worries. "Yeah, Mom. I'm good."

"Not just ramen and protein shakes?"

I huff out a laugh, rolling my eyes. "I eat actual food, I promise."

I can hear her hum in the background, unconvinced. "You're too much like your father sometimes."

The smile slips. My jaw tightens, and I look out my window.

"How's hockey?" she asks, shifting the conversation.

"It's good," I reply.

"I saw that highlight of you last week. That breakaway goal was incredible."

A slow exhale escapes me, the tension in my chest loosening just a little. It shouldn't matter, but it does. No one really comes to my games—hell, I can count on one hand the number of people who've shown up to support me in the stands. I wonder sometimes if anyone even notices. My dad watches, sure, but he's never one to say anything positive. It's always what went wrong. I swear, I could score a hat trick and he'd still find a way to tell me I should've had another assist.

"Thanks, Mom."

"We miss you, darling," she says, letting out a soft breath. "You have to come and visit sometime."

We. The word lingers in my head and I swallow, my throat tightening. "Yeah... Will do."

"I should let you go," she says. "Call me soon, okay? I love you."

"Love you too."

The call ends, and I lower the phone to my lap, staring at the black screen for a moment.

I flop back onto my mattress, staring up at the ceiling, letting out a long breath. Hearing about all the shit my brother's doing is like getting punched in the gut every damn time. He's ten steps ahead of me. By my age, he was already drafted. And here I am, just trying to figure out what the hell I'm doing.

I wanted to go to college. Thought maybe it'd be my way of doing my own thing. A chance to have my own identity before I get thrown into the league and have people compare me to him at every damn turn.

But what's the point in trying so hard when it feels like I'm always playing catch-up?

I close my eyes for a second, trying to shut out the noise in my head.

But it's still there—it's always there.

I run a hand through my hair, gripping the strands as I let out a frustrated breath. Same shit every time he calls. Nothing new. Nothing I don't expect. But, for some reason, I still wish things were different. Some part of me still wants to be enough on my own, without always being the guy who's compared to his brother.

Before I can spiral any further, a knock on the door snaps me out of my thoughts.

"Let's go," Nathan's voice cuts through. "Austin helped me pack the car."

I close my eyes for a second, wishing for a few more minutes of peace. But I know it's pointless. The longer I stay in here, the more I'll just stew on everything that's been eating at me. With a sigh, I sit up, pushing my brother and all the bullshit that comes with him to the back of my mind.

I grab my clothes and tug them on quickly, glancing in the mirror before I reach for the door handle and pull it open.

Time to go see Isabella.

And act like I'm not picturing her naked… while her brother's right next to me.

Yeah, this should be interesting.

EIGHT

Isabella

I thought taking ceramics as an elective would be cool and kinda fun. After all, I've been making random clay stuff every summer since I was fifteen—bowls, mugs, whatever I could shape with my hands. Sure, some of it had holes, leaked, or cracked, but it was fun.

Turns out, though, taking an actual pottery class is a whole different ball game. The sculpture I made today? Definitely… abstract. Maybe post-modern, if you squint hard enough and pretend you don't know what it's supposed to be.

By the time I get to my dorm, I'm itching to rip off my clay-covered jeans and hit the showers. Then maybe I'll curl up in bed, eat some junk food, and binge-watch a cheesy TV show.

I twist the door handle, pushing it open, and find Aurora lying on her bed, with her phone to her ear. Probably talking to her boyfriend again—they're always on the phone.

My mind drifts to Jacob, and for a second, I wonder if this would've been my life every night if we'd tried long distance. Would I be lying here, wondering where he was when I hung up, or who he was with, or what he was doing? The thought sinks like a rock in my chest, and I shake it off as I kick my shoes off. Maybe Jacob was right to break things off.

"Hey," Aurora mouths, flashing a quick smile before her eyes drift down to my jeans—now destroyed with clay. She chuckles. "Nice look."

I roll my eyes and head for the mini fridge, grabbing a Coke, and cracking it open before taking a long, refreshing sip.

"No one, just my roommate," Aurora says to her boyfriend as she lays back on her bed, twirling a strand of her hair.

I peel off my jacket and catch a glimpse of my clay-covered t-shirt and jeans in the mirror. Ugh. These stains are never coming out.

"Izzy, open the fucking door."

My brows furrow at the sound of my brother's voice, before heading toward the door and swinging it open.

My brother stands there, drenched in sweat, his face beet red and a vein bulging from his forehead like he's about to pop. "Holy shit," he grunts, dropping two massive cardboard boxes onto the floor with a heavy thud, wiping his forehead with the back of his hand. "How much shit do you need?"

I can't help but laugh and shake my head. "Didn't you tell me you weren't gonna bring this stuff up for me?"

Ryan steps into view just behind him, lugging two more boxes. He drops them with a groan, glancing up at me with wide eyes. "These boxes are fucking heavy. What the hell do you have in here? Rocks?"

I snicker, eyeing the two of them. "You'd think with all that hockey practice, your muscles would actually be useful." Nathan and Ryan shoot me simultaneous glares, and I can't help but chuckle. "Just kidding. Thanks for hauling all this up for me."

Nathan rolls his eyes dramatically. "I wasn't gonna help, but then Mom guilted me into it." He gives an exaggerated sigh.

"Something about looking after my baby sister, and being a good brother… blah, blah, blah."

I roll my eyes. "Love you too."

"Yeah, whatever. You owe me," he says, then gestures to the boxes. "Where do you want these?"

"Just leave them by my bed," I tell him, glancing at the mess I'll deal with later. "I'll sort it out when I get a chance."

He nods, lifting one of the boxes before squeezing past me, and I step out into the hallway to give him room. As I do, I almost stumble straight into Ryan. His hands catch me just in time, before I can crash into him.

"Shit. Sorry," I mumble, taking a step back.

"Don't sweat it," Ryan chuckles, his eyes flicking down to me with a teasing smile. "Not the first time you've bumped into me." His gaze trails down my clothes, brow quirking as he takes in the sight.

"I just came back from pottery class," I explain, motioning to my jeans, which are covered in what looks like a toddler's abstract art project. "Hence the disaster."

Ryan blinks, his eyes widening in surprise. "You do pottery? That's so frickin' cool. I can't even draw stick figures."

I laugh, tucking a curl behind my ear. "Debatable. Honestly, it's stressing me out way more than I expected, which totally defeats the point of doing it in the first place."

He shrugs, running a hand through his hair, and for some reason, I feel my stomach do this weird flip. *God*, why is that so hot? "Still cool." His lips twitch into a grin, and his eyes sweep over me again. "I'm kinda picturing you behind the pottery wheel now… your hands all covered in clay…"

I snort, shaking my head. "It's not as pretty as it sounds."

He clicks his tongue and tilts his head. "Somehow, I don't believe you."

I feel that nervous-flutter thing again, right in my chest. I clear my throat, trying to change the subject before I make a bigger fool of myself. "Are you nervous about the game on Friday?"

A sigh leaves his lips before he smirks, shaking his head. "Nah, we got this." He gives me a cocky grin. "Your dad busts my balls on the ice to make sure I don't slip up."

My face scrunches up. "Yeah, I really don't wanna hear about my dad and your balls," I joke, trying to hide my smirk.

Ryan laughs, tipping his head back, and I feel a shiver run down my spine. He has such a nice laugh.

He chuckles, pursing his lips. "You coming to the celebration party?"

I let out a scoff, arching a brow. "You're that confident you'll win?"

He shrugs, that smug smirk playing at the corners of his lips. It makes my knees feel a little weaker. "Confidence is attractive. Or so I've heard."

My lips twitch, my stomach flipping. "Are you flirting with me?"

Ryan studies me for a few seconds, long enough that I start to memorize every detail of his gaze. Then he tuts, shaking his head, as he steps closer. His cologne fills the space between us, and it's like everything around me fades. "*Baby*, if I was flirting, you'd know. You wouldn't even have to ask."

I suck in a sharp breath at the nickname and his gaze drops to my lips, his grin widening. Yeah, he's definitely flirting. And I'm definitely enjoying it.

"Ryan!"

The sound of my brother's voice snaps me back to reality. Ryan takes a step back, facing Nathan as he nods toward the hallway. "Bring the rest of the boxes."

"Better go help your brother." Ryan glances at me before lifting one of the boxes, the corner of his mouth tugging up into a teasing smirk. "All these purple throw pillows won't unpack themselves."

I roll my eyes. "I like purple. Sue me."

He chuckles, his eyes locked on mine. "Didn't say it was a bad thing. It's kinda cute."

My cheeks warm before I can stop them.

He carries the box inside and drops it beside my bed just as Nathan reappears at the door. His brows furrow when he sees me standing there, and flicks me on the forehead. "You look like shit," he says bluntly. "Go take a shower."

Heat rushes to my face as I rub my forehead, glancing at Ryan—who's failing miserably at suppressing his grin.

Nathan pats Ryan on the back. "Come on, man. You're gonna be late for your date."

My stomach drops at the same time Ryan's eyes flick to mine, a hint of something similar to guilt in his eyes.

I swallow. "You have a date?"

Ryan rubs the back of his neck. "Uh… yeah. Met this girl at the bar last night, and… yeah."

"Oh." I nod, forcing a smile that feels more like biting down on broken glass. "That sounds… great. Have fun."

Ryan nods, flashing me a small, half-hearted smile before following Nathan out of the room. I just stand there, blinking like an idiot.

I close the door, maneuver around the boxes, and flop onto the bed, burying my face in my hands with a long, agonized groan.

Aurora's voice drifts in from across the room. "What's with the dramatics?"

I groan again, dragging my hands down my face, scowling at her. "Why are brothers such assholes?"

Aurora laughs, tucking one leg under her as she settles beside me on the bed. "Probably a genetic defect. What happened?"

I hesitate for a second, then blow out a breath. "I think I like his friend."

Aurora's eyes practically sparkle, and her grin widens. "I knew it. And why is that a problem?" She cocks her head. "He's a good choice. Tall, hot." She nods, humming. "I approve."

I chuckle, swinging my legs off the bed to sit up. "As much as I appreciate your approval, my brother won't feel the same."

She shrugs, rolling her eyes. "Who cares? You're not a kid."

"I wish it were that simple," I mutter, shaking my head. "He still sees me as someone he needs to protect. And besides, I don't date hockey players. And Ryan doesn't date at all."

Aurora waves me off. "The last thing you need right now is a relationship. You've been in one since you were—what, ten?"

"Seventeen," I correct, rolling my eyes.

"Same thing." She leans in with a smirk. "You need to let go and have some fun. Whether it's with Ryan or someone else, you need a good rebound to make you forget about your ex." She shoots me a wink. "Hop on and enjoy the ride."

I laugh, grabbing a fluffy pillow and chucking it at her. She's half-joking. But also… she's right.

NINE

Ryan

All I wanted to do tonight was sprawl on the couch, put on an action movie, and pass out before midnight. Hell, I'd have settled for a rom-com. A sitcom. A damn infomercial. Anything that didn't involve standing in a room full of drunk, half-naked idiots.

But my roommates had other plans.

I forgot how much I hate parties.

I hadn't been to one in so long that I almost missed it. The noise. The chaos. The thrill of being shitfaced and waking up on some random bathroom floor.

Almost.

Because right now, being stone-cold sober, I wonder how the hell I ever thought this was fun.

Especially considering I'm currently wrapped in an actual fucking curtain. Full-length, hideous pattern, scratchy fabric that looks like it belongs on my grandma's couch.

This is all Austin's fault, of course. His genius idea was to make the celebratory party an 'anything but clothes' party, so naturally, no one held back. Including him—standing across the room in a concoction of saran wrap and tin foil covering only the most strategic places.

A loud rip snaps my attention across the room.

"Fuck." *Tear.* "Ah!" *Tear.* "Shiiiit."

I take a slow sip of my beer, watching Logan wrestle with the duct tape around his chest.

"Jesus," I shake my head. "That cannot be comfortable."

Logan groans, yanking at the edges of the duct tape strapped across his chest. "Austin called dibs on the saran wrap. I had to improvise."

"Yeah, well, at least it's better than my outfit," Nathan mutters, stepping into the room. I glance over—and immediately lose it.

My drink is gone, spit straight out of my mouth, my nose, probably every pore in my damn face.

Because Nathan is standing there, stone-faced, in nothing but a string of bananas covering his junk and a coconut bra.

I cough, wheezing. "Bro."

Nathan exhales, adjusting his banana thong. "Yeah. I know. Austin's a fucking idiot."

"Nah, you look amazing," Austin says with a grin.

"Hands down, best outfit here," I tease, grinning when he flips me off.

"What the fuck are you wearing?"

We turn at the sound of Cole's voice as he finally arrives, dressed like a sane person—jeans and a t-shirt. No surprise there. Kind of pissed I didn't think to ditch the dress code, too. This curtain is starting to itch.

Austin groans. "Aw, come on, bro. It's an anything but clothes party. That's so fucking boring."

Cole scoffs. "Coming from the guy wrapped like a sandwich."

Austin grins. "I'll take that as a compliment."

"It wasn't one," Cole deadpans.

I shake my head, handing him a drink. "Glad you're here. These idiots are giving me a headache."

He shakes his head, lets out a quiet huff—the closest thing to laughter we'll probably ever get from him. "When don't they?"

"Please don't lump me in with those two," Nathan sighs, running a hand through his hair. "I'm a victim in all of this."

I let out a chuckle, unable to stop laughing every time I look at Nathan.

"Hey." We turn as a brunette slides up next to Cole, her eyes shining as she looks up at him. "Cole, right?" she purrs, resting a hand on his chest.

He nods. Silent.

Her smile stretches as she rises onto her tiptoes to whisper something in his ear. He arches a brow, listening. Then, without a word, he takes her hand and leads her upstairs.

I shake my head.

Un-fucking-believable.

"Don't you dare go anywhere near my bedroom!" Austin yells after him, scowling. Cole doesn't so much as glance back.

"Fuck," Austin groans, rubbing a hand down his face. "He's gonna fuck on my bed, isn't he? Damn it, I *just* changed my sheets this morning."

Logan scoffs, popping a chip in his mouth. "You change them every fucking day, if the number of girls sneaking out of your room is anything to go by."

Austin chuckles, nudging him. "You're one to talk. I saw a girl sneak out of your room last week." His eyes narrow. "She ate my cereal, by the way."

Logan raises a brow, unimpressed. "Oh, the travesty."

"Dude, it was Cap'n Crunch. The limited edition," Austin blurts. "It's my favorite one!"

"You'll live," Logan teases with a wink.

I shake my head, glancing around the party, my eyes scanning the crowd for a glimpse of curly brown hair. I haven't seen her since that day in her dorm, but I did invite her to the party, and I wonder if she's going to come.

I shake my head, reaching for another drink, and stop cold.

My eyes lock on Isabella chatting with her friend, tilting her head back as she lets out a laugh, which makes my lips tip up into a smirk as my eyes graze over her body.

Even in a *garbage bag*, she looks hot as fuck.

She glances to her side, and her laugh fades the second our eyes meet, her lips twisting into a slow, knowing smile. She leans toward her friend, murmuring something. Aurora flicks her gaze to me, then back to Isabella with a grin, like she approves.

Of what? Couldn't say. Don't give a fuck.

Because Isabella starts walking toward me.

My grip tightens around my drink as her smile widens the closer she gets.

"Nice curtains."

I huff out a chuckle, glancing down at the stupid-ass fabric still wrapped around me. "Nice trash bag."

She sighs, smoothing a hand over the cheap plastic, cinched at the waist with a strip of duct tape. "So creative, I know." A smirk tugs at her lips. "Didn't know it was an ABC party until about two hours ago."

I chuckle with a shake of my head. "If anyone could make trash look good, it'd be you, Curls."

She clicks her tongue, shaking her head. "No curls today."

Her hair—which is usually curly and wavy and lives in my fucking dreams, apparently—hangs sleek and straight, brushing against her waist. "I can see that." My fingers reach out before I even think, rubbing a strand between them. Smooth. Silky. Different. My lips curl into a smirk. "Kinda miss them."

The space between us shrinks. I catch the faint scent of vanilla and something else just as sweet. We're so fucking close that her brother would kill me if he saw us together right now.

What the hell am I doing?

I straighten, tension locking my shoulders just as a voice cuts in.

"Hey, Ryan."

I glance down at the girl smiling up at me, her friend standing beside her.

I have no idea who they are. Still, I offer a polite smile. "Hi."

"Congrats on the game." She places a hand on my arm, fingers trailing just enough to make her intentions clear. Her friend watches, sipping her drink.

My gaze shifts—straight to Isabella.

She hasn't moved. Hasn't looked away. Just stands there, watching, taking a slow sip of her drink. If she has any thoughts about what's happening, she doesn't show it.

I glance back at the girls, shooting them a smile. "Thanks." My mom drilled manners into me. There's no need to be an asshole just because I'm not interested.

But right now, I *really* need them to leave.

Because the one girl I *do* have an interest in is standing here, watching another girl press up on me.

I step back, gently peeling the girl's hand off my arm. "Enjoy the party." Before she can respond, I turn to Isabella, grabbing her hand instead, and pull her toward the back of the house, somewhere quieter, somewhere no one can get in the way. And she lets me.

Once we're there, I blow out a breath, dragging a hand over my face. "Sorry about that."

Isabella just laughs, her big brown eyes glinting. "It's fine," she says, her lips twitching into a smirk. "You're clearly very loved."

I shake my head, scoffing. "Yeah, well… it's just because we won the game."

She laughs, shaking her head. "I don't believe that for a second. I think girls are like that around you no matter what."

I press my lips together, exhaling through my nose. She's not wrong.

I've always been popular, I guess. Even as a kid, I knew girls found me attractive. I had game. Still do.

She chuckles when I don't answer, knowing she's right. "Congrats on the game, by the way."

My lips twitch into a smirk, and I drag my thumb over my bottom lip. "Did you watch it?"

She lets out a soft laugh that makes me want to hear it again. *And again*. "Of course I was watching. My dad's the coach, and my brother's the goalie." She lifts a shoulder in a lazy shrug. "Kinda had to."

I hum, shifting closer without even realizing it. Close enough to catch the faint scent of whatever shampoo she uses. Close enough that I probably should step back.

But I don't.

"And maybe you were watching for me?" I tease, my voice dipping lower, testing the waters.

Because I *like* having her eyes on me.

She smirks, keeping her eyes locked on mine. "You wish," she breathes, lightly shoving at my chest.

I let out a low laugh. "You can admit you watched the game for me. It's not a crime."

No, but it is a crime against bro code.

I'm playing a dangerous fucking game. Because I *know* I shouldn't be here, in the corner, alone with her. Talking. Smiling. Touching. *Flirting.* And yet, here I am.

Can't help it.

She tugs her plump bottom lip between her teeth, and I swear to God, I almost lose my mind. "I might have *maybe* glanced at you for a quick second during the game," she says, rolling her eyes in a way that shouldn't be sexy but absolutely is.

Makes me want to grab her and kiss her right-the-fuck-now.
Step the fuck away, Ryan.

"I like hearing that," I admit, my voice a little quieter. Because I do. I like knowing she was out there, in the crowd, looking at me. Watching me play.

No one ever really does. Not like it matters. It's just a college game, not the fucking Stanley Cup or anything.

She inhales softly, swirling the liquid in her cup before bringing it to her lips for a slow sip. "So… How was your date?"

Ice cold fucking water.

That's what those words feel like. Dumped right over my head.

I don't want to think about another girl.

And I definitely don't want Isabella thinking about her, either.

"Great," I lie.

Isabella's brows shoot up, her drink hovering just below her lips. "Yeah? Do tell. Did you kiss her?" She tilts her head, pressing her lips together.

I scoff, shaking my head. She's trying to play it cool, but I see right through her. She's jealous. Or pissed. Maybe both. And I like it more than I should.

"Don't try and act coy," I say, tilting my head slightly. "Ask me outright, Isabella."

Her forced smile falters just a little before she masks it with a sip of her drink. "Did you hook up with her?"

My smirk widens. I like teasing her, talking to her like this, even if I shouldn't. "I didn't even go."

Her brows knit together. "What?"

I shrug, leaning back against the wall, letting my fingers graze the rim of my cup. "I didn't go on the date," I admit.

Ask me, I silently beg her. *Ask me why.*

"Why?"

My jaw clenches, a muscle ticking. "Kinda can't stop thinking about someone else."

Her lips part slightly, but she recovers quickly, arching a brow. "Oh yeah? Blondie and her friend back there?" she teases, tilting her head toward the party behind us.

I let out a low laugh. "Definitely not." My gaze drifts over her face, the curve of her lips, the way the dim lighting catches the gold specks in her eyes. "Kinda think this girl doesn't like me or something," I joke, letting out a dramatic sigh. "It's a tragedy."

"No?" She tuts, shaking her head. "Might be your overinflated ego." A smirk tugs at her lips as she lifts her drink. "Well, I'm sure there are plenty of girls willing to take your sorrows away. You won the game, after all. There must be thousands of girls willing to hook up with you tonight."

"Thousands?" I arch a brow, stepping just a little closer.

"You know what I mean," she says, waving her hand dismissively, but there's a challenge in her eyes.

I nod, taking a step closer, though every instinct in my body screams at me to take a step back. And then another. And another. But I can't help it. Not with her standing so close, her silky hair falling around her face, the scent of her shampoo filling the space between us.

"Yeah, I know what you mean." My gaze drops to hers, and for a second, I lose myself in those big brown eyes. They're pulling me in like gravity. Her words, though, feel so fucking arbitrary. If she knew just how often I think of those curls of hers, of her lips, of the way she fits into every thought I have, she wouldn't have even asked me that question.

"If I were interested in hooking up with anyone else, I wouldn't be here talking to you, would I?"

The silence stretches between us, and I'm very fucking aware of her breath, shallow and hesitant. The only sound is the trash bag crinkling with every breath she takes.

Her eyes flicker up to mine, a challenge in them. "Too bad nothing can ever happen between us."

Why is that again?

Right.

Brother. Dad… *Rules*.

There are a million barriers between us, but in this moment, it's just me and her, standing close enough to feel the heat radiating off her skin. No one else around to stop us. And all I can think about is the dirty thoughts running through my head—starting with those lips, and ending with ripping off that garbage bag off her body.

I hum, brushing my thumb along her soft cheek before cupping it, feeling her warmth seeping into my palm. "You're right." I stifle a groan when her lips part, and a soft noise leaves her lips. Fuck, I want to kiss her. Want to swallow those noises.

But I drop my hand and take a step back before I do something we'll both regret. Though, I'm not sure if I'd regret it all that much.

I shoot her a smirk. "But it's still fun to tease you."

She scoffs, shaking her head. "You're such an asshole."

I laugh, the tension between us easing as if nothing happened. "And you were two seconds away from telling me how you want to rip off my old lady curtains."

Her brow arches, her lips curling into a playful smile. "Definitely not."

I chuckle. "Uh-huh, keep telling yourself that."

I like Isabella. A lot. But I know better than to act on it. We both do. Hooking up with her would be a mistake. There are just too many lines I can't cross.

And besides, I agreed when I met her, I'd be her friend.

And that's all I can be.

TEN

Isabella

I should be used to this by now.

The sea of guys in my class doesn't faze me anymore, but I still feel the pressure. Being the only woman in a room full of sports management majors is like wearing a neon sign that says *Out of Place*, even though I know my stuff. I can name more hockey teams than half these guys can name cities. Last season's stats? I could rattle those off in my sleep.

My mom always thought I'd be a figure skater. After all, I spent more time on the ice than most kids did on their bikes. But instead of gliding gracefully, I spent most of my time knocking my brother over at every chance. Of course, that only lasted until he got bigger than me, and then I spent way more time picking myself up off the ice than I care to admit.

Dad's been a coach for as long as I can remember. He spent my whole childhood teaching us both. Playing hockey was never my thing, but the strategy? The plays? That's what always interested me. I loved figuring out how everything fit together, how the right pass at the right moment could change the entire game.

Being the only girl in this class isn't always easy, but I'm not backing down or cowering away. This is my dream, and I'm not going to let anyone make me feel like I don't belong.

So, when I catch the guy in the back corner of the room staring at me, I don't flinch. I've gotten used to it by now. But his gaze lingers longer than usual, and I can't help but wonder what his deal is.

When the professor finally dismisses us, I grab my things, mentally preparing to get out of here. But just as I start to stand, I feel someone approach.

"Hey." I turn to find the same guy from before, grinning at me. "I'm Luke. You new here? Haven't seen you around before."

I pause for a moment, glancing up at him. "Yeah, just started this semester."

He nods, his eyes scanning me thoughtfully. I do the same. He's tall, maybe a little over six feet, with broad shoulders and dark hair that's a little messy, like he's just run his hands through it, with a slight stubble grazing against his jaw.

"I'm not going to lie, you kind of caught my eye," he says, his gaze lingering a little longer than necessary, making a small flutter of warmth spread across my chest.

I can't help but laugh at that. "Guess being the only girl in a room full of guys kind of does that to you."

"Not complaining," he replies, leaning in slightly, his grin widening, the playful glint in his eyes making something warm settle in my stomach. "I like it. Makes things… interesting."

I roll my eyes but can't fight the smile tugging at my lips. "You don't get enough of that from the rest of your classmates?"

"Eh," he shrugs, the movement causing his muscles to shift under his fitted shirt. "They're not exactly my type." His grin deepens. "You, though? I think I could get used to that."

I laugh again, shaking my head. "Is that supposed to be a pick-up line?"

"I mean, it's working, isn't it?" he teases.

My lips twitch. "Maybe a little."

I like how effortlessly he's flirting with me, like it's second nature to him. It's kind of refreshing, actually.

But then, the thought of Ryan pops into my mind. I shouldn't be thinking about Ryan. He's not an option. He never was.

Aurora was right. I need to have some fun. Figure out who I am outside of all the baggage of my ex. I need a distraction— someone like Luke.

I glance back at him, letting my eyes drift over his broad shoulders and sharp jawline again. He's definitely attractive, no doubt about it. His smile's a little cocky, but there's a warmth to it that makes me want to get to know him. "Guess you'll have to try harder if you want to impress me."

Luke chuckles, stepping closer, but before he can say anything else, another guy walks up, slinging his backpack over his shoulder. He glances between me and Luke. "You coming?" he asks Luke.

Luke waves his friend off, his eyes still on me. "Yeah. I'll be right there."

His friend arches a brow, glancing at me once more. "You do know that's Isabella Hayes, right? As in Nathan's sister?"

I watch a flicker of recognition pass over Luke's face. His eyes widen, and for a second, his confident grin falters. "Shit," he mutters, taking a step back. "I uh… I gotta go."

I watch him walk away, the playful tension between us evaporating as quickly as it appeared. I let out a frustrated sigh, shoving my stuff into my bag. Great. Just what I needed.

Another guy who can't see me for me, only as Nathan Hayes's little sister.

I sling my bag over my shoulder and head up the stairs.

Walking down the hallway, I spot Nathan up ahead, his broad frame standing out in the crowd of students. He catches my eye and gives a subtle nod of his chin. "Hey, Izz. You just come out of class?"

I nod as Nathan steps in line with me, walking beside me.

"You okay?" he asks, furrowing his brows.

I open my mouth to respond, but I can't help but notice the way people glance at him.

It's like I'm invisible next to him.

I thought coming to Colton U and working beside my dad would be the best thing for my career. And, if I'm being honest, kind of fun too. But it feels like I'm just an extension of Nathan, a shadow instead of a person. Everyone sees me as his sister, and that's it. They don't look beyond that.

"Yeah," I reply with a sigh. "I'm good."

"How's everything going with classes? Any of those guys giving you trouble?"

"Not yet, but I keep to myself."

Nathan raises a brow, his expression softening. "You shouldn't have to. You've got every right to be there."

I shake my head, the smile lingering. As much as I resent the fact that every guy on campus is too scared to even get close to me because of Nathan, I can't help but feel grateful for him. I may not always like it, but having a brother like him—I wouldn't trade it for anything. He might be a pain in the ass, but he's never once made me feel anything less than supported.

"Thanks, but I can handle myself."

Nathan pulls me into a side hug, wrapping his arm around my shoulders. "Just looking out for you, Izz. The guys and I are going to the bar later. You wanna come?"

I flutter my lashes up at him. "Really?" I gasp, covering my mouth dramatically. "You're finally letting me out of my tower?"

He scoffs, the corner of his lips twitching into a grin. "Christ, you're such a drama queen. You wanna come or not? My invitation only lasts so long."

I roll my eyes. "How generous of you. Are you going to babysit me all night, or will you actually let me have some fun?"

He shrugs. "Depends what kind of fun. I'm not sitting around while you mack on some guy, but you can have a drink. I won't tell Dad."

I scoff, shaking my head. Nathan was never the kind of brother to snitch, and I wasn't either. We had an unspoken pact when it came to stuff like this.

"Fine," I relent, dropping my shoulders. "I'll come."

"Cool." He shoots me a smile. "Gotta get to class. See you later."

I watch him disappear into a lecture hall before pulling out my phone. If I'm going to survive a night at the bar with my brother's friends, I need backup.

Me:

Wanna come to the bar tonight?

Aurora:

???

Me:

I didn't think it was a hard question.

Aurora:

> Who is this? Because it can't be Isabella Hayes.
> She'd rather do homework than go to a bar.

Me:

> Funny. I guess I'll just go alone then.

Aurora:

> Oh, hell no. You'd be a disaster on your own.

I scoff out a laugh.

Me:

> Wow. Thanks for the vote of confidence.

Aurora:

> You know I'm right. You'd sit in the corner, sip your
> apple juice like a sad little Victorian child and then
> leave at 10 p.m. saying you have an early morning.

Me:

> First of all, I drank cranberry juice. Second,
> I make no promises about the 10 p.m. part.

Aurora:

> That's why I'm coming. We're getting you that rebound.

I hesitate, my fingers hovering over the keyboard. *A rebound.* The words make my stomach twist, but I push the feeling down. She's right. I need to move on, have fun, figure out who I am outside of my brother's shadow and the guy who's off limits.

Me:

Fine. But no setting me up with weird guys.

Aurora:

Define weird.

Me:

If he refers to women as 'females,' I'm out.

Aurora:

Fair. See you at 8. Wear something short and hot.

Me:

No.

Aurora:

Yes.

I don't bother replying. She's already won.

Shoving my phone into my bag, I blow out a breath. Maybe this will be a disaster. Maybe it won't. Either way, I'm done sitting in the corner.

Time to see what happens.

ELEVEN

Ryan

In one ear and straight out the other.

That's what Austin's conversation is doing right now because while he's rambling about—hell, I don't even know anymore—I'm too busy watching the door.

Ever since Nathan mentioned his sister was coming tonight, my mind's been running circles around the thought of seeing her again.

Haven't seen her since that party at my place. Since that night we got a little too close, a little too reckless. And fuck, I must have a death wish because all I can think about is doing it again. Talking to her is fun, flirting is even more fun, and playing with fire when I know I should be ten feet away from her at all times? A dangerous kind of fun.

I take a slow sip of my beer, barely tasting it as the door swings open, hoping it's Isabella.

I want to talk to her. Flirt with her. Make her laugh. Wanna kiss her.

Fuck. No. Bad idea.

Friends. Just fucking friends.

I take another sip of beer, forcing myself to focus on the cold bitterness sliding down my throat. It doesn't help. She's the first girl in months I've even been remotely interested in, and of course, she's the one I can't have.

Off-limits. Forbidden.

Nathan would break my jaw if I even thought about touching his little sister. Coach, too.

Kinda hot when you think about it.

Also fucking dangerous.

Austin's laugh snaps me out of my thoughts, and I blink back at him, realizing he's watching me with an arched brow.

"Reed, what the hell are you looking at?"

Shit. I shake my head, playing it off. "Huh?"

"You've been zoned the hell out," he says, smirking. "Thinking about your next hook-up?"

I almost scoff, but I just shake my head. "Yeah, something like that."

Austin chuckles. "What happened to that girl from the other night? Date went well, I assume?" He wags his brows.

Right. The date I never went on. Because, apparently, I'm an idiot who'd rather fixate on the one girl I can't have and risk my friendship—and my spot on the hockey team—than go out with any other girl.

"Didn't work out," I say, hoping he lets it drop.

"Why not?" Logan chimes in, brows knitting together. "Weird fetish?"

My forehead creases. "What?"

"Feet? Daddy kink?"

"What? No, you idiot." I laugh, shaking my head. "Just wasn't feeling it."

Austin snorts. "You overthink shit too much. She was into you."

"Wasn't into her," I reply with a shrug.

Logan scoffs. "That's the lamest excuse I've ever heard. You need to get back out there, man. Shake off the cobwebs."

Before I can respond, the door swings open.

Of course, my head snaps toward it, and just like that, every thought except *her* vanishes.

Wild curls that look way too soft not to touch. Big brown eyes that look like they belong in an animated movie.

Isabella walks in, laughing at something her roommate says, cheeks flushed from the cold. Fuck, she looks good. Too good.

And then she sees me.

Her step falters for half a second, but then her lips curl into a slow, pretty as fuck smile.

Wanna kiss it.

Fuck, Ryan. For the last time. Just fucking frien—ah, fuck it.

There's no point in denying it anymore. Nathan can't hear my thoughts.

I want to kiss the hell out of her. Want to slide my hands around her waist, pull her flush against me, tuck one of those curls behind her ear, and kiss the ever-loving crap out of her.

What would she do if I did it? If I just—

"What the fuck are you doing here?"

The words snap through the air, sharp enough to cut, and my head jerks toward the voice.

Cole.

His entire body is rigid, jaw locked, eyes locked on Isabella's roommate. His fists are clenched, chest rising and falling a little too fast.

I blink. *The fuck?*

His whole body is humming with tension, hands clenched at his sides.

Her roommate doesn't even flinch. Doesn't react at all, actually. Just lifts a brow, plants a hand on her hip, and tilts her head. "Didn't realize you owned this bar."

Cole's nostrils flare. "You know what I mean, Viper. What the fuck are you doing in Colton?"

She lets out a slow breath. "Getting a degree. Can you say the same?"

Cole's fingers twitch. His whole body coiled as he grinds his teeth together. "Why *here*?"

She shrugs. "Because I want to. My decision has nothing to do with you."

Cole's glare darkens, his voice sharp enough to cut. "You don't fucking belong here." He steps in closer, shoulders squared. "Why don't you run back to your boyfriend and get the fuck out of here?"

Her eyes narrow, lips pressing into a thin line. "Bite me."

Cole's jaw clenches, his gaze intense as his lips curl. "You're not my type."

"Tragic," she mutters, rolling her eyes before grabbing Isabella's arm. "Come on. I need a drink—and to get away from this asshole."

"Feeling's fucking mutual, Viper," Cole throws back.

They head toward the bar, and every single person at our table turns to Cole.

He ignores it. Just downs the rest of his beer in one long pull, like it might drown out whatever the hell that was. His jaw is locked so tight I half expect his teeth to crack.

Nathan leans back against the booth, arms crossed. "What the hell was that about?"

Cole drags a hand through his hair, exhaling sharply. "Nothing."

Nathan snorts. "Didn't seem like nothing."

Cole's glare snaps to him. "You wanna piss me off today?"

Nathan lifts his hands in surrender, but his brow furrows. "Just asking. She seemed nice enough when I met her the other day."

Cole lets out a low, humorless laugh. "Yeah, well, you don't fucking know her." His eyes flick toward the bar before he shoves himself up from the booth. "I'm hitting the can. Need a fucking minute."

He stalks off, shoulders tense as he heads to the bathroom.

Austin waits a beat before leaning in, lowering his voice. "Psst. What do you think that was about?"

I shake my head. "No clue."

My gaze shifts back to the bar just in time to see Isabella's friend walking toward the bathroom.

Kinda interested in what the hell will happen when those two cross paths.

But not as interested as the girl sitting at the bar, alone, twirling a straw in her drink, her curls bouncing as she laughs at something the bartender says.

The girl I *really* want to be paying attention to.

I swallow down the rest of my drink and slide out of the booth. "Gonna get another. Anyone want anything?"

Nathan shakes his head. "Nah. I need a clear head for tomorrow."

"Another vodka on the rocks, and I'll owe you my life," Austin says, blowing me a kiss.

Logan lifts his half-full beer. "I'm good."

I nod and head toward the bar. The closer I get, the harder it is to fight back the grin stretching across my face.

Isabella's sitting there, still twirling her straw, lips slightly pursed, deep in thought.

I slide onto the stool beside her. "Beer and a vodka on the rocks," I tell the bartender, slapping a twenty on the counter.

Then I nudge her shoulder, just enough to get her attention. "Glad you came out tonight."

She glances at me, amusement flickering in her big brown eyes. "My brother invited me. Though I'm starting to doubt whether it was a good idea or not."

I frown. "Why's that?"

She exhales, her gaze dipping to her drink. "Because whenever we're in a room together, he sucks up all the air, and I feel like I can't breathe. People only ever see me as his sister, like I'm an extension of him, not my own person."

Her words hit a little too close to home. My brows shoot up. "Yeah… I know what you mean."

She scoffs softly, shaking her head. "I don't think you do. Guys are too scared to even come near me."

I tilt my head at her, fighting a smirk. "I don't know. I'd say we're pretty close right now, and I'm not scared."

She lets out a cute little laugh, the kind that sounds like warm honey and arches a brow at me. "You bolted the second you found out I was his sister."

I groan, running a hand through my hair. "Alright, that's fair. But Nathan is my best friend. It's a respect thing. There are rules when it comes to the bro code."

She nods, swirling her drink. "I know. I just wish other guys didn't care about who my brother was," she admits with a sigh. "Getting a rebound is harder than I thought."

My body stiffens. My eyes widen. *The fuck?*

Hers do too, and she slaps a hand over her mouth. "I can't believe I just admitted that."

I let out a low chuckle, though my brain is stuck on one word. Rebound? She wants a fucking *rebound?*

"No, it's fine. Not a big deal."

She narrows her eyes at me. "Then why'd your eyes nearly pop out of your skull?"

I shrug, shaking my head. "Just a little surprising. I mean…"

My gaze drifts down her body before I can stop myself. The tight white T-shirt clings to her chest, a leather jacket draped over her shoulders. And that skirt—the skimpiest, hottest black skirt I've ever fucking seen—has my mouth going dry.

I swallow, leaning in slightly. "You *have* to know how hot you are."

Her lips twitch like she's fighting a smirk. "Did you just check me out?"

I let out a laugh, running a hand through my hair. "Sure fucking did. Impossible not to, Curls."

She arches a brow. "Thought we were friends."

Right. Yeah. *Friends.*

"We are," I say with a shrug, even though every bone in my body wants to disagree. Because I like her, like being friends with her, but I also want to do some very non-friendly things to her. "Which is why—as a friend—I'm calling bullshit."

Her brows pull together. "Bullshit?"

"On your whole rebound situation." I lean against the bar, watching her. "No way in hell you can't find someone who wants to sleep with you."

She clicks her tongue, shaking her head, those curls bouncing around her face. "I think you have more faith in me than I do."

I scoff, arching a brow. "There's at least ten guys in this bar who would love to strip that skirt off you." *Me included*. "And you wouldn't even have to open your mouth to make that happen."

She scoffs. "I mean, I'm sure I'd have to open my mouth at some point," she quips, eyes twinkling.

Fuck.

My lips curl into a smirk. "Did you just make a sex joke?"

She hums, feigning innocence. "Might have." She leans in, the smell of her sweet perfume hitting me square in the chest, making it even harder to keep my distance. "Did it turn you on?"

Thinking about her pretty pink, glossy lips wrapped around my cock? Hell. Fucking. Yes.

I swallow hard and shake my head, losing every inch of control I have. "Don't look at me like that unless you want to be pinned up against the wall," I warn her.

She smirks, not backing down, and leans in just a little closer. "Maybe that's exactly what I want."

I'm fucked. Her words, the look in her eyes... it's all too much. I rub my hand over my face and take a step back, rational thinking making a rare reappearance. Nathan. My best friend. His sister. Fuck. I shake my head, forcing a chuckle. "I shouldn't have said that. I'm not the guy for the job," I mutter, hoping she hears the strain in my voice.

She sighs, taking a sip of her drink, her tongue darting out to catch a drop of alcohol that spills past her lips.

And suddenly, all I can think about is tasting it for her. Leaning forward, cupping her face, running my tongue over those plump lips and finding out if she tastes as sweet as she smells.

She glances at me, and my hazy, heavy-lidded eyes snap open.

"You got any friends you think I'd be into?"

Something flares in my chest, my temper rising. I scoff, unable to keep the bitterness out of my voice. Is she really asking me to pimp her out to my friends? "Yeah, that's not happening."

Her brow arches, daring me. "Why not?"

The muscles in my jaw tighten, ready to fucking pop. "I kinda like them. I don't want to have to knock them out every time I think about them touching you."

She laughs, her shoulders shaking with the sound, and damn, it only makes me want to kiss her even more. "Alright. Not your friends." She eyes the crowd, her gaze flitting to the guy across the bar. "How about that guy? Think I'm his type?"

I don't know how anyone could look at her and not want her. Not want to know every curve, every inch of her body. But I turn my head anyway, my eyes sliding over to the booth where the guy she's talking about sits, drinking a beer and shoveling peanuts in his mouth as he talks to some girl.

"I think he's preoccupied." *And not fucking good enough for you.*

I can't stop the irritation that tightens my chest. The thought of her going home with someone else tonight, some random guy, getting hot and sweaty with him, makes me want to punch something. Hell, preferably myself for being too much of a fucking idiot to step up and give her the rebound she wants. I should be the one doing this for her.

But I made a promise to my friend. To her brother. And I keep my damn promises. I'm a big boy. I can handle being told I'm not allowed to have something.

I think.

She sighs, her shoulders deflating like she's given up. "Then what about him?" She points at a guy playing darts, laughing with his buddies, his eyes glazed over.

I shake my head. "Yeah, no. He's drunk."

She raises her drink, a mischievous glint in her eye. "I'm getting there, too."

I give her a dry look. "You really want to go home with a drunk stranger drooling all over you, unable to even get it up from the alcohol?"

She screws up her face in distaste. "I guess you're right."

"I know I'm right." My gaze locks with hers. "I don't know why you're looking for a rebound, but I know you don't want some quick fuck who you won't even remember the next day."

She doesn't say anything, but the way she bites her bottom lip lets me know I hit the mark.

"You want someone who'll kiss you like he's desperate for it," I lean closer. "You want someone who'll worship your body, make you the center of their attention. Make you scream their name. Take you to a different fucking dimension."

Her breath hitches, and those pink lips part in surprise. My eyes drop to them like a moth to a flame, drawn to them without the ability to look away. *Fuck.*

"I'm gonna head home."

We break apart at the speed of lightning when I hear Nathan's voice behind me as he approaches the bar.

I quickly sit back on the stool, grabbing my beer and taking a sip, avoiding Isabella's eyes as Nathan slaps me on the back.

"I'm tired of those dickheads, and I need to be up early for one-on-one training with my dad." He groans, shaking his head. "You good here?" he asks his sister.

She rolls her eyes slightly. "I told you; you don't need to babysit me. I'll be fine."

Nathan nods, his eyes flicking to me. "Keep an eye on her for me, will you?" He presses his lips together in a smile.

I swallow the huge rock lodged in my throat as I nod, and he turns around, pushing open the door.

I'm such an asshole.

Nathan trusts me enough to look after his sister, and here I am fantasizing about all the different positions I could put her in.

I can't fuck up his trust. No matter how much I want to. And *god*, do I want to.

I glance at Isabella, and the same look in my eyes is mirrored in hers. She sighs, shifting her body to face the bar. "I need a drink."

Yeah, me fucking too.

TWELVE

Isabella

Isn't alcohol supposed to loosen you up?

Because I feel like it's doing the exact opposite.

Three shots and a glittery pink drink with cotton candy later, and I'm tenser than I was when my brother approached Ryan and me. It was a good thing, really, because the way the conversation was headed would have only ended in destruction.

"You're thinking too hard." Aurora taps my forehead with a perfectly manicured finger, flashing me a grin. "Your brother isn't here anymore. You can have some fun." She glances around the crowded bar. "Where's that hot friend of his you like?"

I let out a sigh, shaking my head. "Not happening," I tell her.

I saw the look in Ryan's eyes when Nathan clapped him on the back and asked him to keep an eye on me. My brother doesn't hand out his trust easily, so for him to say that? To trust Ryan with me? I know exactly how much that means.

Aurora blows a raspberry, unimpressed. "His loss. You look sexy as fuck. You could bag any guy in here."

"I second that."

I snap my head toward the deep voice, catching sight of a guy sliding closer to me on the dance floor. He's tall, broad-shouldered, and grinning as his gaze drags down my body, shaking his head slightly before locking eyes with me again.

"You're the hottest girl in here by far."

I let out a laugh, tilting my head. "You must not have seen many girls."

He grins, stepping closer. "No, I have, and they don't even come close to you." He lifts his chin toward the dance floor behind me. "I've been watching you and your friend all night. Dancing. Grinding. Fuck, it's hot." His eyes darken, voice dropping. "I kinda want to recreate it."

He places his hands on my hips, tugging me closer, and I let him. He doesn't care about my brother—or doesn't know Nathan's my brother—and he's hot. A blond, which isn't exactly my type, but still attractive enough to hold my attention.

"Can you dance?" I ask, arching a brow.

He chuckles. "Oh, darling. I can do anything you want me to."

The music shifts, something faster, sexier, pulsing through the speakers. Mystery guy—whose name I still don't know— starts moving, guiding my hips with his hands, pressing his body against mine.

I should be enjoying this. I wanted this, didn't I? A rebound. Someone new. Someone to kiss, maybe more. Someone to help me forget Jacob—and Ryan.

But then my mind goes somewhere else.

I imagine those hands traveling lower. Or higher. Somewhere that takes this from PG-13 to R-rated.

And instead of heat, I feel cold.

It hits me all at once—the reality of what I'm doing. What this could lead to. The idea of going home with him, undressing, letting him touch me, expose me. I don't even know his name.

A bucket of ice-cold water crashes over me.

I stop moving.

He frowns. "What's wrong?"

I take a step back, my vision blurry as the alcohol in my system does its job. "I'm sorry. I thought I was ready, but—"

I offer him an apologetic look as I take another step. And another. And—

Slam into someone.

Hands grip my hips, and before I can react, I'm spun around. A gasp slips past my lips as I throw my hands up for balance, my palms landing flat against a solid chest.

My eyes widen as I look up at the familiar brown eyes, and gorgeous lips I almost kissed at the welcome week party.

"Ryan?" I ask, my eyes narrowing as the room spins, hoping this isn't just a mirage. "What are you doing?"

His jaw clenches, his grip tightening. "I don't fucking know," he admits, voice rough. "I saw you out here dancing with—and I—" His jaw locks again, his nostrils flaring.

I suddenly become aware of my hands on his chest, the heat of his skin burning through his thin t-shirt. I shift them slightly, feeling every hard muscle beneath my fingers.

Ryan exhales sharply, a low groan slipping from his lips—so quiet I almost wonder if I imagined it.

His tongue flicks out, wetting his lips. "You going home with him?" he asks.

"Who?"

His eyes flick over my shoulder. "The guy you were just dancing with." His hands flex on my hips, one last squeeze before they drop away.

I lower my hands and take a step back, shaking my head. "No, I'm not."

His brows furrow. "What about your rebound?" His eyes darken, jaw going taut. "Don't tell me he did something creepy." His voice drops, dangerously low. "Tell me he fucking didn't before I assume the worst and cut his hand and dick off."

A laugh bursts out of me before I can stop it. "As much as I appreciate you mutilating a guy for me, he did nothing wrong," I assure him.

Ryan exhales, shoulders dropping in relief. "Thank fuck. I almost committed murder."

I hum, swaying slightly as I blink up at him, the alcohol making everything feel a bit slower. "I know. It was kinda hot."

His brows lift, a slow, teasing smirk pulling at his mouth. "Good to know a criminal record turns you on."

I shrug, my lips quirking. "What can I say. I like my men like I like my coffee. Strong, hot, and guaranteed to keep me up all night."

That earns me a small chuckle. But his smile settles as his eyes lock on mine. "So, what happened?" he asks. "Why didn't you go home with him?"

I tilt my head, narrowing my eyes as I press a finger to his chest, pushing him an inch. "Are you jealous?" I tease, wagging my brows.

He scoffs, grabbing my wrist and lowers my hand, but doesn't let go, my skin breaking out in shivers when he rubs his thumb over my skin. "Not answering that."

I let out a laugh, but my balance wobbles, forcing me to grip his forearm for stability.

"Jesus. Yeah, I'm glad you're not going home with anyone. You're wasted."

My eyes find his and I let out a harsh sigh. "I just… don't think I'm the kind of girl who sleeps with strangers," I admit.

His lips twitch, his eyes on mine, but he doesn't say anything.

"Hey, Cap!"

We both turn as Austin and Logan stumble toward us, grins wide, drinks obviously long gone.

"We're heading home. You coming?" Austin slurs, barely staying on his feet.

"No," Ryan says, his gaze flicking back to me, softening just a little. "I'm staying."

Austin winks knowingly. "Ahhh. I hear ya."

Ryan groans, rubbing a hand down his face. "Get him the fuck to bed."

Logan scrunches his nose. "Y'know, I love the guy, but he's not my type."

Austin gasps, clutching his chest dramatically. "I'm a fucking catch, thank you very much."

Ryan pinches the bridge of his nose. "Christ. I'm dealing with children. Just go home."

They both saunter off and Ryan lets out a rough sigh, shaking his head. "Sorry about them. They need a fucking leash."

I chuckle. "I work with you guys practically every day," I remind him, lifting a shoulder in a shrug. "I'm used to them."

Ryan scoffs. "Beats me, cause I'm not." His lips twitch, but as our eyes lock, something shifts in his expression. "Back to what you said before we were interrupted by a couple of drunk idiots." He tilts his head. "You're not doing the rebound thing anymore, then?"

I kinda wish he'd forgotten about it because the alcohol is making me way too honest.

"I don't know," I admit with a sigh. "I wanted to move on from my ex, since he was the only guy I've ever been with, but—"

His head jerks back slightly. "What?"

"I wanted to move on fr—"

He shakes his head, cutting me off. "No, that wasn't the part I was shocked by."

A sheepish smile creeps onto my face. "I know it's the complete opposite of what *you're* used to, but…" I shrug. "I told you; guys are too scared to approach me, and Jacob was no different."

Ryan scoffs, pressing a hand to his chest. "Hate his name already. I'm an Edward guy, but continue."

I let out a laugh, shaking my head. "My brother made it clear no one was allowed to touch me—protective big brother and all that crap." I roll my eyes. "And guys listened. They stayed away… until Jacob. But, of course, he didn't want my brother to know, so we kept it on the down low."

I exhale, shutting my eyes for a second. "And after he dumped me, I couldn't shake him, even though he never wanted anyone to know about us. I just…" I trail off, feeling that familiar ache.

Ryan stays quiet, watching me, his brows furrowed.

I exhale a laugh, shaking my head. "Aurora told me I needed to find myself and I agreed. I thought sleeping with someone else would help me move on." My voice drops, my fingers absently toying with the hem of my dress. "I was hoping it would be *better* with someone else."

"Uh oh," Ryan teases, cocking his head. "My man Jacob have problems in the bedroom?"

I let out a short laugh. "No, it wasn't that. It was… good." I pause, frowning slightly. "But I just… I don't know. We did everything in secret. Bathrooms at parties, closets, his car. It was always rushed so no one would see us together." I shake my head. "I guess I thought maybe it would be better if we didn't have to rush, you know?"

Ryan nods, a hint of understanding in his eyes. "Definitely better when you don't have to rush."

I let out a breath, swaying a little, and I notice Ryan's hands twitch like he's ready to catch me if I tip over. "I thought things would be different when we got to college. That we'd finally have some time to ourselves. But then he dumped me before summer even hit."

Ryan's face hardens, his jaw tightening. "What'd he say?"

"Long-distance is too hard," I say, rolling my eyes. "Which, okay, I get it. He wasn't wrong, but I just… I don't know. I felt like—"

"Like you didn't matter to him," Ryan finishes, his voice quiet but sharp.

My breath catches, and I glance up at him, a little surprised by how easily he reads me.

I exhale sharply. "Yeah. I was so hurt by the breakup, but he seemed fine, like I was nothing." I tilt my head, the alcohol making everything a little hazy. "Hence the whole 'can't sleep with someone unless I know them' thing. I've only ever been with one guy, and he kept me a secret." My shoulders slump. "You probably thing I'm an idiot."

Ryan's brows pinch together. "I think you're gorgeous."

My cheeks flush, but I laugh anyway, shaking my head. "I bet you can walk into a room, glance at a girl, and boom, decide she's going home with you."

Ryan chuckles, dragging a hand through his hair. "Is that what you think of me?"

"Come on." I give him a dry look. "We're friends, right? No need to lie to me. I know how guys your age are. You fuck anything that moves and don't even bother learning their names."

Ryan tuts, shaking his head. "Damn, Curls, you're so fucking wrong."

"Really?" I arch a brow. "How so?"

He tilts his head, flashing me a teasing smirk. "Seeing as I haven't been with anyone in over five months, I'd hardly say I 'fuck anything that moves'."

My eyes widen so much they might actually fall out of my skull. "*Five Months*?"

Ryan shoots me a glare. "Say it louder, will you? I don't think people in Connecticut heard you."

I let out a laugh, covering my mouth. "I'm sorry, I just…" I trail off, still staring at him, trying to process what he just said.

"Yeah, I know." He sighs dramatically, rubbing a hand over his jaw. "My balls hurt all the time."

I snicker, heat crawling up my neck as my alcohol-fueled brain conjures up a very vivid image of Ryan—frustrated as hell, sitting alone in his room, his hand wrapped around his hard—

Nope. Nope. *Abort mission.*

I shake my head quickly, trying to rid myself of the visual. "Is there a reason why you're… out of commission?"

Ryan scoffs. "No logical reason. Just… my fucked-up head," he replies with a shrug. "All I can fucking think about is hockey, school, and my future. Girls are on the backburner for now, at least they were until…" His eyes catch mine, and he stops himself, lips pressing into a thin line.

Until what?

Until me?

The flutter in my stomach doesn't help the ache growing between my legs. *God*, I need that rebound. "Then maybe we should scratch each other's itches."

He snorts, shaking his head like I've lost my mind. "Funny."

"I'm not joking," I say, my frown deepening. "I want a rebound, but the idea of sleeping with a random guy freaks me out. You want someone to get you out of that dry spell." I lift my shoulders. "Seems like a win-win to me."

Ryan stares at me, mouth open, eyes locked onto mine. Then, slowly, he lets out a low laugh, shaking his head. "Holy fuck, you're drunker than I thought."

"I'm not drunk," I insist, though my words come out slurred. He raises a brow, giving me a dry look. I sigh, rolling my eyes. "Alright, maybe I'm a little drunk, but I mean it."

Ryan exhales sharply, running a hand through his hair. "Isabella, you know we can't. Your brother—"

"Yeah, yeah. I know," I cut him off with a roll of my eyes. "You look at me and see my brother, and it makes you feel guilty. I get it." The words taste bitter on my tongue, but they're the truth. Why did I think this time would be any different? "Forget I even said anything."

I turn, hoping I can escape, find Aurora, and pretend this conversation never happened. But before I can take a step, his hand wraps around my wrist, pulling me back. Ryan spins me around, and suddenly, I'm trapped against the wall, his body pressing into mine. The air between us thickens, my pulse quickens, and I can feel every inch of him against me.

A gasp escapes my lips when I feel his hard length brush against my stomach, and my body shivers involuntarily. His dark eyes lock onto mine. He's taller than me by a few good inches, and I have to tilt my head back to meet his gaze, my breath catching in my throat.

His hand reaches out, his fingers curling into one of my curls, tugging it gently. "Once again, you're fucking wrong, Isabella," he says, his voice low and damn near sinful. A shiver runs down my spine. "Your brother is the last thing I think about when I look at you," he grits out, and oh god, he smells so good. Has he always smelled like this? My brain goes foggy, my legs turning to jelly, and my heart is pounding in my chest. "That's the fucking problem."

I swallow hard, my eyes still locked on his. "Ryan…"

My eyes flutter closed as my body sways, and I stumble slightly. But before I can even react, his hands are there, gripping my waist, steadying me.

"Fuck. Alright, time for bed," he mutters.

I shake my head, a groan escaping me. I don't want to go to bed. I want to stay right here, with him, and figure out what just happened between us. "No."

"Yes," Ryan says, his voice turning serious. "You're drunk as hell and about to pass out. Christ, I should've cut you off earlier." His hands settle on my hips, as he tries to straighten me up. "C'mon, where's your roommate?"

I glance around the crowded room, my gaze landing on Aurora in the middle of the dance floor. She's moving like she's the only one here, arms flailing wildly, completely lost in the music. I envy her—how effortlessly she lets go, how she doesn't give a fuck about anyone here judging her.

"Shit," Ryan mutters, dragging a hand down his face. "I can't carry two drunk girls home." His eyes flick toward the back booth, spotting someone. "Cole," he calls out. "Help me out, man. Isabella and her roommate are both trashed, and there's no way in hell I'm putting them in a cab alone."

Cole, who's lounging in the booth with a girl draped over him, barely glances up before shaking his head. "Yeah, not fucking happening," he says with a bitter laugh, his lip curling a he steals a glance at Aurora on the dancefloor. "She's a snake. She'll bite me."

Ryan levels him with a flat look. "Come on, man. I'm not asking you to fucking marry the girl, just help me out. Please."

Cole clenches his jaw, nostrils flaring. He doesn't answer right away, and for a second, I think he's going to refuse again. Then he lets out a sharp exhale, muttering a low, "Fuck." With a heavy sigh, he pushes off the booth, not even sparing the girl beside him a glance before heading for the dance floor.

He reaches Aurora in two strides, wrapping a firm hand around her wrist and yanking her toward him.

"What the hell?" Her eyes go wide as she jerks back. "What the fuck are you doing? Get off me."

"Trust me, Viper, I don't want to touch you either," Cole snaps. "But you're drunk as shit. It's embarrassing."

Aurora glares at him, ripping her wrist from his grasp. "No one asked you to come save me."

Cole tilts his head, eyes darkening. "And what would your golden-boy boyfriend say if he saw you out here wearing a fucking belt as a skirt?"

Aurora arches a brow. "No one tells me what I can or can't wear. Not even him."

Cole scoffs, lips curling into a half-smirk. Then, without another word, he grabs her wrist again—firmer this time—and starts leading her toward the exit. "Let's go." He glances at Ryan as he walks past us, shooting him a glare. "You fucking owe me."

THIRTEEN

Isabella

I sink into the bleacher seat, the cold of the ice rink seeping through my jacket. I've always loved it here. It brings me back to those early mornings when my dad would wake Nathan and me up before the sun had even risen, pulling us out to his rink to skate.

Aurora drops into the seat beside me, immediately diving into her bag. A second later, she pulls out a crinkling bag of chips, a candy bar, and a small bag of popcorn.

I grin. "Came prepared, huh?"

She shrugs, already mid-chew. "Hockey games make me nervous. Food helps."

I nod, stealing a chip from her bag. "Because of your boyfriend?"

She nods, munching through her nerves. "Yeah. I always hated watching him get slammed into the boards."

I smirk, nudging her elbow. "I bet the part where you get to take care of him after was fun, though."

Aurora lets out a quick laugh, but it fades almost instantly. She sighs, staring down at the ice, fingers tightening around the candy bar. "God, I hate this long-distance crap. He's so far away, and we hardly ever talk. He's got games, practices, a whole life that doesn't include me, and I just…" She pauses. "He texts me to say whether they won or lost, but then…

nothing. Hours of radio silence." Aurora rips open her candy bar. "I know he's probably out with the guys, getting drunk… maybe with some girl hovering around, trying to get his attention."

Something tightens in my stomach, and the question slips out before I can stop it. "And you're okay with that?" I honestly couldn't imagine living with that kind of uncertainty, not knowing what my boyfriend is up to or who he's with.

Aurora snorts, shoving a handful of chips into her mouth. "Of course not. But I'm not gonna sit here and obsess over it," she says, tearing into the candy bar. "What am I supposed to do? He's out there, I'm here. I can't keep track of him every minute, right?" She shrugs. "If he wants someone else, then by all fucking means. I'm not gonna beg him to pick me."

She says it like it doesn't bother her, but I see the flicker of doubt in her expression.

"You guys have been together forever, right?" I say, nudging her lightly. "No way he's throwing that away."

Aurora exhales, glancing down at her snacks. "Yeah, I know." She rolls her eyes, a smirk pulling at the corners of her mouth. "Plus, there's no way he can find someone hotter than me."

I snort, bumping her shoulder. "Oh, how I love your humility."

She grins, grabbing another handful of chips.

I glance at my phone, check the time, then type out a quick message to Ryan. He gave me his number the night he drove me back to my dorm—just in case I needed anything, since I was pretty out of it. I haven't used it since, but this feels like as good a time as any.

Me:

Good luck on the game today.

I lean back in my seat, staring at the message for a second, suddenly way too aware of how nervous I feel. It's just a text—so why does it feel like my heart is trying to climb up my throat?

The dots appear. Then freeze.

Then they start moving again.

Ryan:

You rooting for me, Curls?

A smirk tugs at my lips. I sneak a glance at Aurora, but she doesn't even notice, too busy scarfing down her chips like they're her last meal.

Me:

Seeing as my dad's the coach of the team… yeah.

I hit send, and immediately, the three dots come back. My pulse quickens.

Ryan:

Wasn't my question.

I asked if you were rooting for me.

Feed my ego, Isabella. I need it right now.

I roll my eyes, but the stupid grin stays on my face. I'm about to type something back when Aurora shifts beside me, giving me a knowing look.

"Is that him?" she asks, a smirk creeping in.

She doesn't need to clarify who *him* is. We both know.

I roll my eyes, refusing to give her the satisfaction. "Eat your chips."

She chuckles, popping another handful into her mouth as I type out my reply.

Me:

I'm rooting for all the players on the team.

Ryan:

Isabella…

I bite my lip, fingers hovering over the keyboard before finally giving in.

Me:

I'm rooting for you, Ryan.

The second I hit send, my stomach twists with anticipation. The dots bubble on the screen, dancing for what feels like forever before his reply finally comes through.

Ryan:

I'll make sure to score a goal just for you.

I chuckle, feeling a buzz in my chest, something light and stupid and completely impossible to ignore.

We haven't really spoken since that night in the bar—since he pinned me against the wall and told me he doesn't see my brother when he looks at me.

And yet, at practice, he hardly looks at me. Just a quick nod, then back to the ice, like that night never happened.

Or maybe it didn't. Maybe I was just drunk out of my mind and imagined the whole thing.

I might have been drunk, but I made it clear—I wanted a rebound with him. And while I'd love to convince Ryan to fuck up his friendship with my brother, I can't keep waiting around for someone who's rejected me over and over.

I need to move on. Find someone else. Someone I can actually have fun with and forget about him.

The words slip out before I can stop them. "Have you ever had a one-night stand?"

Aurora pauses mid-chew, raising an eyebrow before shrugging. "Yeah, in high school. But I was absolutely wasted, can't even remember his name." She shakes her head with a small laugh. "But… yeah, it was kinda fun."

I cringe. "God, I don't think I could ever do that."

She shrugs again, biting her lip. "I get it. It's definitely not for everyone." Then her eyes widen slightly as she studies me. "Are you still thinking about the rebound?"

I shake my head. "I was. But now… I don't know. I think I need someone I actually know and trust."

Aurora grins, nudging me. "Like Ryan?"

"No." I laugh, nudging her back. "I've told you a million times, that's not happening."

She hums, rolling up the chip bag. "Mmm… I don't know. You two were definitely flirting at the bar the other night."

I narrow my eyes. "And what about you and Cole?"

Aurora scoffs. "You mean the literal Grim Reaper?" She rolls her eyes. "Yeah, we're not talking about him. Why are you dodging the question, though?" Her brows shoot up, eyes gleaming. "Did something happen between you two?"

"No." I shake my head. Nothing happened, *technically*. But then I pause, glancing at her from the corner of my eye. "Maybe?"

"Oh my god!" she squeals, practically jumping out of her seat. "I knew it! Tell me everything!"

I quickly glance around, noticing a few people looking our way. "Calm down," I mutter trying to keep my voice low. "Nothing happened. I just… offered him the position of being my rebound, he declined, and then pinned me to the wall and basically told me he wanted to fuck me, but couldn't because he's friends with my brother."

Aurora makes a face and blows a raspberry. "Lame. God, guys can be such *idiots*."

I chuckle, shaking my head just as the players start skating onto the ice, one by one. The sharp sound of skates slicing the ice cuts through the buzz, followed by the thump of sticks tapping and the crack of pucks slamming into the boards during warmups.

Then the lights shift and the starting lineup takes their positions.

I glance down, and there he is—Ryan. Number 27. His last name stretches across his jersey in bold letters, unmistakable even from up here. He leans forward, eyes locked in, every movement precise.

The ref drops the puck.

And just like that, the game explodes into motion and the crowd roars, rising to their feet.

Aurora leans into me, offering her chips. I take a couple, chewing them absently as I keep my eyes locked on the ice.

"You think the Wolves are gonna win tonight?" she asks.

I glance at her, blowing out a breath. "If the team can get their shit together. They're playing well, but they're getting outworked." I gesture toward the ice. "Look at that. They're too aggressive on the forecheck. They need to pull back and let the defense handle it, but they keep overcommitting."

Aurora laughs, clearly not grasping half of what I just said but nodding anyway. "Sure, *Coach*."

I focus back on the game, my mind racing through strategies. Something's off. The passes are a half-second too slow, the spacing's all wrong, and no one's stepping up to take control. They're playing like they're stuck in their own heads—and if they don't snap out of it soon, the other team's going to walk all over them.

A Thunderhawk player shoves one of our guys into the glass behind the goal, the impact echoing through the arena. The whole crowd winces in unison. Gloves fly off, shoving turns into fists, and suddenly, a full-on brawl breaks out right in front of us.

Aurora launches out of her seat, her voice somehow cutting through the noise. "Yeah! Take your top off!"

I lose it, laughing so hard I have to clutch my stomach. A few people throw us judgmental glares, which only makes it funnier. I glance at Aurora, raising an eyebrow.

"What?" She shrugs. "Hockey players are hot," she says with a wink.

I shake my head but turn back to the ice as the refs move in to break up the fight.

The Thunderhawk who shoved our guy skates off toward the penalty box.

Ryan skates over to Cole, patting him on the back, talking to him. But he doesn't see the Thunderhawk player coming up behind him. My eyes widen as the player closes in, his body shifting with brutal speed. Before I can even shout, the guy's shoulder drives into Ryan's with bone-crushing force, sending him hurtling into the boards.

The sickening crack echoes through the arena, and I feel my stomach drop as Ryan's body jerks violently, crumpling to the ice.

The noise of the crowd vanishes, when he doesn't move. My stomach knots so tight it hurts.

The trainer rushes onto the ice, dropping to his knees beside Ryan, checking him over.

Ryan is still on the ice.

Still not moving.

And I can't look away.

"Is he okay?" Aurora's voice barely reaches me, almost drowned out by the pounding in my ears.

I grip the seat in front of me, my fingers shaking uncontrollably. I don't have an answer. *I don't know*. "He has to be okay. He has to be," I whisper.

Aurora's hand suddenly clasps mine, her fingers firm, grounding me. I don't even realize how badly I'm trembling until I feel her warmth, steadying me.

And then, just as my chest feels like it might explode, I see it. Ryan shifts, a small movement at first, and then he's on one knee. Slowly. Wobbling. But he's moving.

My shoulders drop in relief as he stands up, shaky. The knot in my stomach loosens a little as the crowd clap.

Aurora releases a long, shaky breath beside me. "He's okay… he's okay," she whispers, squeezing my hand.

I nod, though I can hardly breathe, my eyes glued to Ryan as he makes his way off the ice. His steps are slow, every one of them showing how badly he's been hit. He lifts a hand, a weak thumbs-up for the crowd, but it does nothing to reassure me.

The buzzer blares, signaling the end of the game and the opposing team erupts in cheers.

The other team won.

FOURTEEN

Ryan

The final buzzer rings, and my stomach sinks.

Loss.

Again.

I rip my helmet off a little too fast, wincing as a sharp pain shoots through my shoulder. My ribs feel like they're on fire, each breath a reminder of the hits I've taken. My knee's throbbing, and there's this pounding pressure behind my eye, like I can still feel the boards slamming into my head. But none of that compares to the frustration eating at me.

We should've won this.

We had it. The plays, the setups… We were on the verge, and I blew it.

The locker room is dead silent. Not the quiet that comes after a hard-fought win, where everyone's too wiped to talk, but the kind that makes your shoulders sag, and your fists clench, and your mind race with all the shit you wish you could've done differently.

Skates scrape across the floor, too loud and too sharp. Sticks hit the walls, thrown down with way more force than they should be. Water bottles get crushed between clenched fists, the crinkling sound cutting through the silence. No one's saying a word. No one's even looking at each other. We're all too pissed, too embarrassed to make eye contact.

Nathan breaks the silence first, his voice attempting to sound reassuring. "Alright, I think we can all agree it was a tough game, but it was just one game," he says, yanking his jersey over his head. "We shake it off, come back stronger."

Easy for him to say.

I drop onto the bench, elbows on my knees, and roll my shoulder, testing the damage. I immediately regret it. Pain shoots down my arm, burning like fire. Every inch of me feels like it's protesting, but it's nothing compared to the mess inside my head. I rake a hand through my hair, exhaling sharply.

Fuck.

Austin shoots me a concerned look. "You good, man?"

"Yeah." The lie tastes bitter, sour.

"Could've fooled me," Austin mutters under his breath. "Yeah, you got slammed into the boards. You're not the reason we lost."

I shake my head, the words scratching their way out like gravel. "We were already losing before then." The hit was bad, but we were slipping before I slammed into those boards.

Cole rolls his eyes, his tone dry. "And that was on all of us. Stop whining about the loss."

Nathan shoots him a sharp look, his brow furrowing. "Ease off, will you?"

Cole shrugs. "What? He's acting like he cost us the whole game. We all played like shit."

I exhale through my nose, pressing my fingers into my temple. I don't have the energy to argue. Doesn't change the fact that I could've played better. That I *should* have.

Cole stretches his legs out, joints popping as he leans back, then glances over at me. "Alright, I need a fucking drink. You in?"

"Pass."

Austin raises an eyebrow, leaning against the doorframe. "Come on. One drink won't kill you."

"I said no." My voice comes out sharper than I meant. The guys exchange looks, but they don't push. One by one, they filter out of the locker room, their footsteps gradually fading until it's just me. Alone.

The silence is deafening, pressing down on every inch of this room. I stay rooted to the spot, staring at nothing, my bruised shoulder and battered pride throbbing in perfect sync.

I sit there for a few more minutes, trying to shake off the heaviness, but then my phone buzzes on the bench beside me. I glance at the screen, seeing a text from my dad. My jaw tenses as I swipe it open.

Dad:

Not your best game. Hope that shoulder isn't too messed up.

My fingers tighten around the phone. I know he means well, but it still stings. I feel a knot in my stomach, and the pressure in my chest grows.

I grab my phone, hesitating as my thumb hovers over Connor's number. We don't really talk much, and I don't know why I'm reaching out now. Maybe it's because I need someone to tell me this doesn't suck as much as it feels. Maybe it's just that I've got no one else.

I press the call button, and it rings twice before he picks up.

He's quiet at first. Then, after what feels like forever, he finally speaks. "Yeah?"

I close my eyes, rubbing my forehead. My shoulder's on fire, my ribs are a mess, and my brain's still buzzing from the hit. But none of that hits harder than the sting of knowing I let everyone down. "Saw the game?"

"I did," he says, a pause before adding, "You alright?"

I run my hand through my hair, trying to push the frustration down. "Not really."

Connor's quiet for a moment, like he's deciding if he should say something. "Talk to me."

I hesitate, unsure how to start. "I just—fuck, I don't know, man. I feel like I keep messing up. Like I'm never gonna be good enough."

He exhales. "Ryan, you are good enough."

I let out a humorless laugh, bitter and hollow. "Doesn't feel like it."

There's another pause, a slight shift in the background noise on his end before he speaks again. "Look, I know it's tough, but you're overthinking it. Bad games happen. Doesn't mean you're not a good player. You know how it goes. You just gotta keep working, keep pushing through it."

I drag a hand through my hair, frustration rising again. "It's not just this game," I admit, my voice coming out rougher than I want. "It's… all of it. Feels like every time I get close to getting my shit together, something knocks me back down."

Connor hums. "Okay. So, what are you gonna do about it?"

I frown. "What?"

"You can sit there and keep moping, telling yourself you suck… or you can get up, learn from it, and get better."

I grind my teeth, my jaw tightening. "That's not—"

"It is, Ry. It's all in your head. You play like you've already lost, guess what? You're gonna lose. Let this shit linger? Next game's gonna suck just as bad."

I rub my forehead, frustration bubbling up again. "Yeah, I know."

"Then do something about it," Connor says.

I let out a long breath. "You make it sound so simple."

"It *is* simple," he replies. "It's just not easy."

I lean back against the locker, staring up at the ceiling, my mind spinning. "You ever feel like you're running after something that's always just out of reach?"

Connor doesn't answer right away. The silence hangs between us, heavy. "Yeah. I have."

I glance at my phone, absently checking the time. It's late—way too late to be stuck in my own head, but here I am. "What'd you do about it?"

"I stopped chasing it," he answers. "Started focusing on what I could control. You can't change the last game, but you can decide how you show up for the next one."

I stay quiet, letting his words settle in. I can't change what happened tonight, but maybe there's something in that. Something I can work with.

Connor sighs on the other end. "Look, I'm not saying you shouldn't be pissed. Be pissed. Use it. But don't let it define you. You're a hell of a player, Ry, but if you let this shit mess with your head, it's just gonna screw with your game even more."

I swallow hard, feeling the sting of his words hit home. "Yeah, alright."

There's a pause, before he speaks up again. "You gonna be alright?"

Without even thinking, I lie. "Yeah."

I can almost feel him staring through the phone, like he knows I'm full of shit, but he doesn't push it. "Get some sleep, Ry."

"Yeah. Night." I hang up and toss the phone onto the bench, watching the screen fade to black. I lean back against the locker. My body aches—every muscle sore, every bruise reminding me of how much I've put into this game.

But it's my pride that hurts the most.

And the worst part?

I have no idea how to fix it.

FIFTEEN

Isabella

The arena's quiet.

It's always weird how fast it changes—one minute, the place is alive with the roar of the crowd, and the next, it's just empty seats and echoes. The silence is almost too loud.

I stroll down the hallway, my sneakers scraping on the floor with each step. My eyes flick toward the rink through the plexiglass. The ice is all scratched up from the blades, patches of melted water—remnants of a game that should've been different. A game that they should've won.

My fingers tighten around the notebook I've been clutching since the first period. I spent the entire night tracking plays, analyzing movements, noting down stats my dad had asked for.

I let out a slow breath, glancing toward my dad's office at the end of the hall. The door's closed. The lights are off.

That's weird.

He's always in there after a game. Win or lose, he's breaking down footage, running through plays, making notes, preparing for the next one.

My curiosity starts to itch, so I glance toward the locker rooms, and that's when I hear a low groan.

I stop in my tracks, my brows furrowing. There's no reason anyone should still be here. The guys all left a while ago, headed to grab drinks and forget about the loss. So why—?

I nudge the door open just a little, trying not to make a sound. The room is mostly dark, lit only by the soft glow of the hallway. But even in the low light, I catch a glimpse of movement.

I push the door open a little wider, stepping inside.

"Dad?"

A low, teasing chuckle cuts through the dark. "Not your daddy."

I roll my eyes, the tension in my shoulders easing slightly at the sound of his voice. I step further in, leaning against the lockers.

Ryan's slumped on the bench, elbows braced against his knees. He's peeled off all his gear, left with only his jersey and the tight compression shorts. Sweat clings to his skin, making the fabric stick. His hair's a mess, sticking up like he's run his hands through it a dozen times.

"You're still here?" I ask. "I thought you'd be out with the guys."

"Not really in the mood," he mutters, his eyes staring blankly ahead.

I study him for a second, the way he's hunched over, like he's carrying the entire team's defeat on his back. "You played well," I say with a small smile, hoping to lift his spirits.

His jaw tightens, and he finally looks up at me, his eyes full of frustration. "Did you watch the same game?"

I frown, pushing off the lockers. "Ryan, you were out there busting your ass."

He shakes his head. "Doesn't matter. We still lost. And that's on me."

I step closer to him, pulling out my notebook from my bag, scanning the notes I wrote down during the game. "You had three shots on goal, won most of your faceoffs, and were solid on defense. Plus, you set up Austin's goal."

I offer the notebook to him, but he just stares at the pages for a second before running a hand through his messy hair again, letting out a scoff, a short, bitter laugh following it. "And yet, we still lost."

"The team didn't lose because of you," I argue, narrowing my eyes at him.

He shakes his head, refusing to meet my gaze. "We were already down, and then I got fucking slammed into the boards. Spent a full minute trying to get my head straight. Feels like my fault."

"Ryan, one play doesn't decide the whole game."

"Maybe not," he mutters. "But I should've been better."

I watch him for a long moment, his eyes fixed on some point on the floor, his jaw tight. He drags a hand through his hair. "I let my dad down," he says, almost under his breath, like it hurts for him to admit it.

I pause, my brows pulling together. This isn't the Ryan I'm used to—the guy who's always cracking jokes, throwing out those smooth lines like nothing can touch him. Hearing him like this? It throws me off.

I step closer to him, watching the way he avoids my eyes, staring at the ground. "You don't need to prove anything to him or anyone else here, Ryan."

He looks up, his lips pulled into a frown. "I was supposed to do better. To make him proud." His voice falters for a second, and I see that flicker of doubt. "But I didn't. I never do. I still mess it all up. Every single time."

God, hearing that makes my stomach twist.

"You push yourself too hard," I say quietly, watching him.

Ryan exhales, tilting his head back against the locker with a thud. "Yeah, well. Somebody has to."

We sit in silence for a moment, his labored breaths the only sound between us. Then, I catch him shifting his shoulder, and a wince pulls at his face as he lets out a low groan.

"You're hurt," I say, my brows pulling together.

He brushes it off, but it's obvious that he's in pain. "It's nothing."

I arch an eyebrow and cross my arms, not buying it for a second. "Ryan."

He lets out a long, tired sigh. Slowly, he rolls his shoulder back, wincing as he does. "Took a bad hit. I'll be fine."

I frown, glancing down at him for a second before stepping closer, narrowing the gap between us. "Let me see."

He gives me a look like he's about to argue, but I'm not backing down. I've seen him take hits before, but there's something about this one that doesn't sit right with me.

Reluctantly, he shifts a bit, allowing me to get a better look at his shoulder. I step right between his legs, my heart skips at how close we are.

Ryan stays still as I press my fingers into his shoulder, feeling the stiff muscles beneath the fabric. He's warm, too warm, and when I dig into the sore spot, he exhales sharply, his body tensing.

"Jesus," I mutter, pressing a little harder. "You're completely locked up."

"It's not that bad," he mumbles, though his voice is tight.

I raise an eyebrow, pushing a little harder, ignoring his half-hearted protest. "Don't lie. This is pretty bad. You've got a rock for a shoulder."

He lets out a soft groan and the sound sends something hot curling through me, swirling in my stomach.

I don't acknowledge it. I *refuse* to acknowledge it.

I clear my throat, focusing hard on the muscle beneath my fingers. He shifts slightly, and I'm suddenly way too aware of how close we are. His eyes are on me, dark and heavy, and I can feel the heat radiating off of him.

"Feel better?" I ask, trying to keep my voice steady, but my pulse is thumping in my ears, drowning out everything else.

"Yeah," he says, his voice even rougher now, a little lower, and definitely not helping the weird energy zipping through the air. "Surprisingly."

I swallow hard, my fingers lingering on his skin a moment longer than necessary, my brain screaming at me to step back, but I can't move. His skin is warm beneath my fingertips, and I can feel the thrum of his heartbeat through his shirt.

The space between us feels like it's shrinking by the second. His face is so close, I can feel the faintest brush of his breath against my skin. His hands are light on my hips, just enough to keep me in place, like he's not ready for me to let go of me yet.

I don't know when he touched me, but it's like he's always had his hands there, pulling me closer without a single word.

His eyes are locked on mine—dark and intense—like he's trying to figure me out. Or maybe he is daring me to make the first move.

When I shift a little, his fingers tighten on my hips, and my breath hitches in my chest.

My pulse is pounding so loud in my ears that it drowns out everything else. My hands are still pressed against his chest, the muscles beneath my palms so solid, and the pull between us is magnetic—like neither of us can pull away, but neither of us knows how to make the first move either.

He moves his hand, just slightly, and my heart skips in my chest when his thumb brushes my hip. The heat shoots straight through me, and I bite my lip, trying to focus on anything except the way his eyes follow the movement.

Before I know it, his hands pull me forward, yanking me into his lap.

I gasp, my hands flying to his shoulders. "Ryan—"

He groans, the sound low and rough, like he's trying to keep control but doesn't have it in him anymore. "I know," he mutters, shaking his head like he's frustrated with himself. "Fuck, I know. I just... don't want you to stop."

I can feel him hard beneath me. His hands grip my hips, pulling me even closer, and the friction between us is so intense I can hardly think straight. It's too much, but it's also exactly what I want.

"What about what you said?" I breathe out. "The rules... and my brother?"

His lips twitch into a smirk as his fingers tighten on my hips. "I've always been a bit of a rulebreaker."

I want to believe him. God, I just want to let go, to lose myself in him—everything inside me is screaming for it. But the consequences hit me. All of the complications flood my thoughts of what will happen if we go ahead with this. I can't ignore them, no matter how badly I want to.

I bite down on my lip, trying to hold on to the last thread of control I have left.

"We shouldn't do this," I whisper, my voice shaking, torn between the desire to pull away and the temptation to give in.

Ryan nods, his breath ragged. "I know."

"This is a really bad idea," I say, fighting to hold onto the last shred of logic as my heart hammers harder with every second.

His jaw clenches. "The worst."

And yet, his hands don't move. Neither do mine. We're so close, and I can't look away from him, can't pull back. Something is happening, and I don't know how to stop it.

I'm not sure I want to.

His eyes flicker to my lips, and I can't breathe. My heart hammers in my chest so loudly I'm sure he can hear it.

"Fuck it," he murmurs, his fingers curling around my neck, pulling me closer before his mouth crashes against mine.

I gasp, trembling as he *finally* kisses me.

I've wanted this since that stupid welcome week party. Since the moment I first saw him, his cocky smirk and messy hair and stupidly perfect hands. And now it's finally happening.

He kisses me slow at first, like he's unsure if this is real or just a dream. I feel the hesitation in his hands—just for a moment—before they tighten, pulling me closer and tilting my head back to deepen the kiss. The world blurs, and I forget how to breathe.

He groans into my mouth, his fingers threading through my hair as he kisses me harder, deeper, like he's trying to make up for all the time we've wasted.

Heat coils low in my stomach, and I press closer, my hands fisting in his jersey, desperate to keep him close to me, to keep this moment from slipping away. His other hand skims down my back, gripping my waist, like he needs me just as much as I need him.

I don't even notice the sound I make against his lips—a quiet, needy whimper—until he responds with a rough curse, his grip tightening on my hips.

He tastes like mint, like warmth, like something I've been craving without even realizing it. *God*, he tastes so sweet.

Ryan groans, his lips trailing along my jaw, his breath hot against my skin. "Fuck," he mutters. "I don't want to stop. Please don't make me stop."

I shudder at the sound of his rough voice. A small part of me knows what we're doing is dangerous—the quiet voice at the back of my mind telling me we shouldn't.

But I can't pull away.

"Then don't," I murmur against his lips before I kiss him harder, my hands tangled in his hair, drowning out all the voices in my head. I don't know how to stop. I don't want to.

He pulls back slightly, his forehead resting against mine, and I can feel the heat of his breath mixing with mine.

"I'm so fucked," he whispers, his voice strained, before he kisses me again.

My hands slide up his chest, feeling the hard muscles beneath his shirt, his skin hot under my touch.

The kiss gets hotter, deeper. I can feel the heat of his body pressing against mine, the way his hands slide to my hips, gripping me, urging me closer. I move against him instinctively, my hips shifting, feeling his hard cock brushing against the seam of my jeans. He groans low in his throat, and it sends a shiver down my spine.

"God, Isabella," he groans again, his voice thick, dark and so sexy I'm losing my goddamn mind. "You have no fucking idea what you do to me."

His lips trail down to my neck, kissing, biting, and I let out a soft moan, my head falling back, giving him better access.

"You feel so good," he whispers against my skin, his voice low and dark. "I don't think I can stop." He sounds pained, like stopping would physically hurt him.

I moan softly, leaning into him, wanting more, *needing* more. All I care about is the way his lips taste, the way his body moves against mine.

"Do you want me to stop?" he asks.

I shake my head, the words trapped in my throat, but my body speaks for me. I grind against him again.

His hand slides down to my thigh, and he gently urges me to move against him, the friction building again, slow and deep. Every inch of me is on fire, my thoughts a jumble of everything I shouldn't want but desperately do.

"Ryan," I moan, my voice shaky as my fingers dig into his shoulders for leverage. God, I'm so close.

He groans, his chest rising and falling under my touch. "Ah, fuck. I don't know how much longer I can… shit."

I shudder, my fingers gripping his shirt, and then he—

"Hello? Who's in here?"

We freeze.

Panic slams into me as my dad's voice echoes through the locker room. "Shit. *Shit.*"

Ryan curses under his breath, his hands dropping from my hips as I scramble off his lap, my legs shaking like jelly.

My dad steps inside, his brows lifting when he sees us. "Oh. Didn't know you were still in here."

I clear my throat, fumbling for my notebook, trying to act normal even though my heart is still hammering in my chest. My hands feel shaky as I push myself off the bench, legs a little wobbly, and make my way toward my dad. "Yeah, I was… looking for you. I have the stats you wanted."

He nods, taking them from me with a smile. "Thanks, princess. You want a lift home?"

"Sure," I reply, attempting to keep my voice steady, even though I can feel the heat creeping up my neck, my mind still buzzing with the kiss.

He turns to Ryan, arching a brow. "What are you still doing here?" he asks. "You gonna sleep here or…?"

Ryan drags a hand down his face. "I'll head home in a bit. I just… need to take care of something first."

My stomach flips, warmth swirling in my core. I know exactly what he means. The innuendo is blaringly obvious, like a neon sign flashing 'we just dry humped,' but thankfully, my dad is oblivious to it all.

He shrugs and wraps an arm around my shoulder, steering me away. "Alright, make sure you clean up your shit when you leave," he tells Ryan, then pats my shoulder. "Let's go, kiddo. Your mom made me lasagna for dinner, and no way in hell am I missing out on that."

I let out a laugh, glancing back at Ryan once last time, feeling my stomach flutter at the reminder of everything that just happened.

As we walk out into the hallway, I let out a breath, doing my best to look normal, to act like nothing happened.

But I know, even if I try to bury it, things between Ryan and I have shifted. A line was crossed, and now, there's no going back.

SIXTEEN

Ryan

The second my skates hit the ice, I know it's gonna be a shit practice.

Everything's off.

My balance feels weird, like my legs suddenly forgot how to hockey. My strides are slow and heavy, like I'm skating through fucking quicksand. Even my stick feels wrong, like someone swapped it out for a shitty rental from the campus rec center.

I try to shake it off. Focus. The drills are simple, stuff I could do in my sleep. But still, nothing clicks. My passes are off, my shots are weak, and don't even get me started on my puck handling—I might as well be playing with a goddamn tennis ball.

And I know exactly why.

It's not the game. Yeah, we lost, and it fucked with me for sure—but I've had worse losses. It's not even the hit I took in the third period, even though my shoulder feels like someone took a sledgehammer to it.

No, it's *her*.

I haven't spoken to her since that night. The night she pressed into me, her hands clutching my jersey like she was desperate for me to pull her closer. The night I kissed her, like I couldn't stop myself, like I'd been starving for it. And the night she kissed me back like she'd been waiting for me to make that move since the day we fucking met.

And now? I don't know where we stand.

I haven't texted her. She hasn't texted me—except for that one message. The one I ignored.

The second I woke up the next day, I did what I always do. I grabbed my phone. Muscle memory. Habit. Call it whatever you want. I wasn't even fully awake when I saw the notification.

Isabella:

Hey.

I stared at it, my thumb hovering over the screen like an idiot. Didn't open it. Didn't answer. Just sat there, staring at that one word.

I told myself I'd answer later. That I was too tired. Too busy. But that was bullshit.

I didn't answer because I had no clue what to say.

How do I even talk to her now?

How do I look at her without thinking about how her breath hitched when I slid my hands down to her hips?

Without remembering the sounds she made when I kissed her?

Jesus.

I grit my teeth and squeeze my eyes shut, forcing myself to focus on something else, anything else. But it doesn't work.

I still hear her.

I still *feel* her.

My brain is fucking useless.

And apparently, so is my reaction time, because the puck zips right past me before I even see it coming.

"Jesus, Ryan," Logan mutters from across the rink, shooting me a look as he chases it down. "You playing in your sleep or what?"

I roll my shoulders, grip my stick tighter, and try to shake the distraction off. "I've got it."

"Doesn't look like it," Cole chimes in, skating up beside me. "What the hell's up with you today?"

"Nothing," I mutter, letting out a harsh breath.

Cole arches a brow. "You're acting like a damn zombie out here."

"Is your shoulder still acting up?" Logan asks.

The guys won't let up about last week's game, like I'm some fragile fucking rookie instead of the captain. They've been on me all week. I know it's their way of checking in, but I don't want to talk about it.

I shake my head, trying to focus, trying to make the next pass smooth, but I'm off—way off. The puck skids awkwardly across the ice instead of finding its mark.

Cole narrows his eyes at me. "What the hell was that?"

I scowl, frustration bubbling up. "Nothing. Just missed the angle."

Cole isn't buying it. He shoots me a look, his brow furrowing. "Missed the angle? Or still hung up on the game?"

I clench my jaw. "I'm fine," I repeat, more harshly than I intended. "I'm over it."

Nathan skates past and shoulders me lightly. "Clearly," he deadpans. "That's why you've been a miserable bastard all week."

I swallow hard, guilt coiling tight in my stomach. Jesus. Can't even look at the guy without feeling like I'm about to crack. Every time I do, it hits me just how much I fucked up.

Because he has no idea.

No idea that while he was out drinking with the team that night, I had his sister on my lap, her hands tangled in my jersey, and her body shuddering under my hands.

No idea that I kissed her.

No idea that I still fucking want her.

And now? I'm avoiding her like the plague, like somehow, I can erase that night and just pretend it didn't happen.

I shake off the thought and push harder, my legs burning as I tear down the ice, trying to outskate my own brain. Focus. Block it out.

But it's impossible.

Because I feel it. Clear as fucking day.

I don't even have to look up to know she's there, standing at the edge of the rink, clipboard in hand.

I can't look. I won't. Even though every instinct is screaming at me to turn my head, to acknowledge her.

Instead, I lock in on the puck. On the guys. On literally anything but her.

Doesn't matter. Her voice still cuts through the noise of the rink, sharp and clear.

"You're hesitating in transitions." Cool. Professional. Like nothing happened between us. "It's throwing off the plays. You're also pulling back on faceoffs instead of attacking."

My jaw ticks, grip tightening on my stick until my knuckles go white.

Coach's voice yanks me out of my own head. "Ryan, is your shoulder still bothering you?"

I don't flinch. Don't blink. Don't give him an inch. I'm so fucking tired of this conversation. "No."

Coach's stare is a full-body check. "Don't lie to me."

I exhale hard through my nose, my whole body coiled with frustration. "I'm fine."

There's a beat of silence, then Isabella's voice cuts through again.

"You're compensating," she says.

I feel her eyes on me, even though I refuse to meet them.

"You're holding back in contact drills," she says, voice calm but laced with something else. Concern, maybe? "Because it hurts."

My fingers flex around my stick.

I hate that she noticed. That she sees right through my bullshit. That she knows me well enough to know when I'm lying.

"I'll deal with it," I mutter, my voice rough, the words scraping their way out of my throat through clenched teeth.

"You don't have to," she says, softer.

And like an idiot, I look at her.

One split second. That's all it takes.

The noise of the rink fades. The sting in my shoulder? Gone. The shitstorm in my head? Silent. It's just her. Just us.

And I see it in her eyes.

She cares.

And I fucking *hate* that she does.

Because if I let myself go there—if I even *think* about her for more than a second—I'll crack. I'll say I'm sorry. I'll spill everything I've been choking down since that night.

That I haven't stopped thinking about her.

That I still feel her. Still hear those soft, breathy sounds she made when I—

Fuck.

And worst of all? I'll kiss her again.

I tear my eyes away, heat prickling at the back of my neck, and force myself to lock it down.

"Thanks for the notes," I mutter, the words stiff and dry in my mouth.

I don't wait for her to respond before I pivot, digging into the ice, and get the hell out of there—before I forget all the reasons I'm not allowed to want her and end up making the same mistake twice.

SEVENTEEN

Ryan

I try my best to avoid Greek row, given that they hate hockey players and think they run the school.

But the guys—or Austin, I should say—dragged me out of bed and threw a shirt at my face, telling me to get my ass up and stop wallowing in bed like a damn hermit.

I kinda wish I was Cole right now. Since that fight last month, he's been banned from frat parties altogether. He's probably at home, warm, comfortable, with no loud music and no girls shoving drinks in his face every two minutes. Lucky bastard.

Girls swarm towards us as soon as we walk in, their eyes glistening like we're some rare species on display. They size us up, checking out the team.

"Hey," Logan greets a blonde in the crowd, throwing her a flirty smirk that she returns right away. When I first met him, I thought he'd be a dead end with girls. He's the rookie, younger than all of us, and I figured he'd be the one sitting on the sidelines while the rest of us did our thing. But, nope. The guy gets more action than anyone, except maybe Cole. Who the hell knows what that guy does? He's a fucking enigma.

Logan flashes his signature grin and swings an arm around her shoulder. "I'm Logan. Single. Hot. Solid eight inches."

I roll my eyes, trying not to laugh.

Nathan scoffs and shakes his head. "Seriously? This is how you got two girls to go upstairs with you?"

Logan just winks at him. "Don't pretend you're not curious," he teases, turning to face the blonde. "So, what's your name?"

"Daniella," she says, practically melting into his side.

Logan chuckles, pulling her in closer. "You like what you see?"

She hums and stands on her tiptoes, leaning in like she's about to whisper something sweet in his ear. Instead, I hear it loud and clear. "I'd like it even more if there were no clothes in the way."

I snort, shake my head, and take a sip of my drink. If some girl said that to me, I'd probably burst out laughing. I'm not about cheesy pick-up lines. I like girls who tease me, who talk about something other than fucking hockey. I like—

"Izzy!"

My head snaps to the left so fast, I swear I hear my neck crack.

The noise of the party—laughter, the pulse of music, the clinking of glasses—fades into nothing. None of it matters. Not when she walks in.

My stomach tightens the second I spot her. Goddamn, she looks like she's been pulled straight out of my fucking fantasies. She's wearing a flowy, white top that hangs just right, and jeans that fit her like they were made for her body. Fuck, her curls are back, bouncing with every step, looking soft as hell, and all I can think about is how I had my hands buried in them, pulling her closer, kissing her, tasting her, feeling her grind against me.

Isabella doesn't even glance my way. Not a single look. It's like I'm invisible, standing here like a ghost. And honestly? I fucking deserve it.

I've been avoiding her ever since that kiss. Keeping my distance, trying to pretend it never happened. For her sake, for Nathan's, for my own damn sanity. I thought it'd be easier this way—acting like we didn't just tear down every line we had between us. But I can't forget it. It's all I fucking think about.

I keep my eyes on Isabella, watching her walk past me like I don't exist, and my stomach sinks.

"Didn't think you'd be here," Nathan says, lifting his chin toward her roommate. "Did you drag her out?"

Aurora scoffs. "Who else? If it wasn't for me, she'd have stayed at home all night crying over a documentary."

Isabella narrows her eyes. "The penguins were in love. It was sad, okay?"

I want to laugh, because it's so like her to cry over penguins she's never even met, but the tension in the air is thick, and I know better than to do that.

Austin swings his arm around my shoulder, shaking me slightly. "Same with this guy," he says. "He wanted to stay at home tonight but I dragged him out."

Isabella's eyes flick to mine. It's brief—probably just a second—but in my mind, it feels like fucking hours. I suck in a breath as I stare at her, those big brown eyes pulling me in, making everything else around me blur into nothing. Her face—that gorgeous face I can't stop thinking about—and those sweet, pink lips. God, I can still taste them.

I fucked up.

I messed around with my teammate's little sister. First mistake.

Then I ignored her. Pretended like nothing happened. Second, and the biggest mistake of all.

I shift away from Austin, letting his arm drop. "I need a drink," I mutter, turning toward the drink table. I don't actually want a drink. I want to apologize to Isabella. I want to kiss her again, to feel the rush of her lips against mine without any of the consequences hanging over us. But I can't.

So, drink it is.

"Hey, man."

I turn my head at the sound of a tap on my shoulder. It's Dylan, one of the football guys. Normally, hockey and football players don't tend to get along, but we've never given a shit about that.

"That was a hell of a hit last week. You good?"

I let out a sigh, my jaw tightening at the reminder. Not that anyone's let me forget it. "Yeah, I'm good," I mutter, nodding at him. "You know me. I'll get back up."

He chuckles, shaking his head. "Yeah, tell that to Jordan. The idiot gets hit once and sits out the whole season." He scoffs.

"Football guys are weak, man," I tease with a smirk as he laughs.

"Alright, alright, Reed's got claws."

I shrug, taking a sip of my beer. "I'm a wolf for a reason."

He laughs, and I take another sip, my eyes scanning the room. That's when I notice a group of girls staring at him, biting their lips and whispering. I can't blame them—the guy is tall as hell with broad shoulders, deep brown skin, and has the kind of face that belongs on a movie poster.

"Fuck," he groans, dragging a hand over his jaw, fingers brushing his goatee. "Who the hell is that?"

I follow his gaze, my stomach sinking when I see Isabella by the couch with Aurora. My heart stutters.

"The blonde?" I ask, hoping he says yes.

"The brunette." *Fuck.* "The one with curls and incredible rack."

Of fucking course he's interested in her.

"That's Isabella, Nathan's sister," I reply, gritting my teeth.

He lets out a low whistle, dragging a hand over his chin as a slow grin spreads across his face. "Damn. She's hot."

He's not wrong—she *is* hot. But she's more than that. She's beautiful in a way that knocks the air out of my lungs. Has a laugh that I can't get out of my head. Scrunches her nose when she's uncomfortable. She's smart, funny as hell, and one day, she's going to own every room she walks into, whether it's as a sports analyst, or running a team from behind the scenes.

But none of that matters to him. He doesn't see her like I do. Doesn't *know* her. And he sure as hell doesn't deserve to want her the way I fucking do.

You had her In your arms and you fucked it up.

Yeah, I fucking know.

Before I can react, Dylan's already making a beeline for her.

And I just stand here… watching.

My stomach twists with every step he takes until he's right in front of her. He's smooth, I'll give him that. Wears that cocky grin like armor, and somehow, she smiles back. *At him.*

The same smile that used to be mine.

My jaw tightens. My fingers clench around the red solo cup until the plastic creaks. Every word they trade, every laugh she lets slip, every time he leans in like he belongs there. It's like watching a car crash in slow motion, and I can't look away.

She's right there. Right fucking there. And I'm just standing here, watching her slip through my fingers while he makes it look easy. Like he doesn't even have to try.

And it's driving me insane.

I watch, like a glutton for punishment, as Dylan slides his hand around her waist and leans in to whisper something in her ear. She nods. Then lets him take her hand, following him toward the stairs like it's nothing.

Blood floods my head, a roar building in my ears. The world blurs at the edges. My fists clench, muscles coiled so tight they might snap.

No. *Fuck no.*

She's not going upstairs with him. I won't let that happen.

I move before I can think. Shoving through the crowd, shouldering past bodies and brushing off whatever noise or looks I get. I don't care. I don't give a shit about the consequences anymore.

I just know I can't lose her.

I take the stairs two at a time, and there she is—just reaching for the bathroom door.

Before she can disappear inside, I catch her wrist.

And without a word, I pull her into the nearest empty bedroom and shut the door behind us.

She whips around, eyes wide, breath catching in her throat when she finally looks at me.

"Ryan?" she breathes.

God, the way she says my name…

It's been too damn long since I heard her voice, since we laughed, since I had my fingers tangled in her curls, teasing her like it was second nature.

I miss it.

I miss *her*.

I swallow hard, my hand tightening around the doorknob. "What the fuck were you doing with Dylan?"

Her expression shifts, hardens like steel. "You have no right to ask me that," she snaps, narrowing her eyes at me. "*You* made it clear you regretted what happened." She glances away, shrugs like it doesn't cut deep. "And I told you I wanted a rebound."

The words hit like a gut punch.

She was really going to do it, wasn't she?

With *him?* In some stranger's disgusting bathroom?

No.

She deserves better than that.

Bitterness slips in before I can stop it. "I thought you said you couldn't sleep with someone you didn't know?"

Her head snaps back to me, her eyes locking onto mine, and my heart stumbles.

"Yeah, well," she says with a shrug, "I changed my mind."

"Changed your mind, huh?" I almost want to scoff, but I hold it in, taking a step closer.

She's so close now I can smell that sweet, familiar perfume—the one that's been stuck in my head for weeks, driving me fucking insane.

"Too bad," I murmur, my voice low as I lean in, closing the space between us until I can feel her breath on my skin. Her chest rises and falls quickly, and I feel the heat radiating off her. "Because I've changed mine."

She blinks, my words working through her. I watch, waiting for it to click, and when it does, she shakes her head and takes a step back—only there's nowhere to go.

"What are you doing?" she asks, her voice unsteady.

What am I doing?

Exactly what I *should've* done the first time I saw her.

What I wanted to do in the locker room, instead of walking away like a coward.

What I've wanted to do every damn time she's near me.

And this time?

I'm not fucking running.

I reach out, curling my hand around the back of her neck, my thumb brushing softly over her skin.

She gasps, breath catching, and her eyes flick to my mouth—lips parted, glossy, so damn kissable it hurts.

A low groan rumbles in my chest as memories crash over me—her taste, her sounds, her body pressed tight against mine.

I can't hold back anymore.

"Taking what I fucking want."

Before she can react, I yank her against me, crashing my lips to hers.

Every second I've spent denying myself, every night I've laid awake thinking about her—it all explodes the second our mouths meet. She doesn't stop me, doesn't pull away. She melts into me, her fingers curling into my shirt, gripping me like she needs this just as badly.

A low groan rumbles in my chest as I tilt her head back, deepening the kiss, sliding my tongue between her parted lips. Fuck, she tastes good. Addictive. Like something I've been dying for but never let myself have.

It's fire. It's reckless. It's *perfect*.

When I finally pull back, both of us gasping for breath, I take her in—the way her lips are swollen, the way her chest rises and falls too fast, the way she's still clinging to me like she's afraid I'll move away.

I drag my thumb over her bottom lip, smirking when her breath catches.

"You want your rebound?" I let my lips brush against hers again, feeling her shiver. "You fucking got it."

EIGHTEEN

Isabella

I don't even remember how the hell we got to my dorm, but honestly, I don't care. All I can focus on is the feel of Ryan's lips on mine, how his kisses make my entire body burn, how every touch of his hands seems to set fire to my skin.

The door clicks shut behind us, and as soon as it does, he's on me again. His groan is desperate, and I melt into it, losing myself as his hands slide down my back, pulling me closer. He deepens the kiss, his tongue tracing the curve of my lips, and I open for him. His tongue brushes against mine, with an intensity that makes me ache for more. I've never been kissed like this. Never felt so desired before.

"This fucking top," he grits out, his fingers gripping the hem of my shirt and tugging it up. His hand follows, trailing over my stomach, sending a shock of electricity through me.

"These fucking jeans," he mutters, his hand moving to grip my ass, squeezing hard, and I gasp. "Fuck, you're so hot," he breathes, his lips brushing over mine.

His words make a rush of heat flood my core, my body aching with need. Every second that passes, every touch, every kiss, makes the fire inside me burn hotter, deeper. I can't remember a time I've ever wanted someone this much.

"Take your shirt off," I whisper, my hands tugging at the fabric of his shirt, pulling him closer. "Please."

I can hear the amusement in his voice when he chuckles, the sound so damn sexy it makes my stomach tighten. "Begging already? Baby, I'm just getting started."

I want to roll my eyes, maybe push him away and tease him a little, but I can't. Not now. The need for him is so overwhelming, that I can't do anything but melt into him, and let myself feel every touch, every kiss.

He pulls back slightly, and I nearly whimper in protest, but before I can, his hands are already at his back, tugging his shirt off over his head. My eyes lock onto his chest, sculpted and toned, and I can't help the rush of desire that floods me. I let my gaze travel down, following the trail of dark hair that leads from his chest to his abs, disappearing into the waistband of his jeans.

I want to pull his jeans off, kiss my way down his body, and explore every inch of him.

Ryan's eyes darken, a low groan slipping from his throat as he takes a step forward, gripping my waist and pulling me against him. "Stop fucking me with your eyes or this will be over before you know it," he says, chest rising and falling with every harsh breath. "God, I swear, I could come from just your eyes on me."

"Quick on the draw?" I tease.

His laugh rumbles deep in his chest, and his tongue slides over his lips, making my pulse stutter. "More like you're hot as fuck, and I haven't slept with anyone in months." His hand runs through his hair as he groans. "Fuck, I'm gonna blow my load the second you touch me."

I raise an eyebrow, even though my core throbs at the idea. "You're setting yourself up for failure here. Should I have gone with Dylan instead?"

Ryan's eyes flare with heat, and a low, almost feral noise escapes him. Before I can blink, he's on me again, pulling me flush against him with a force that takes my breath away.

"You want someone to fuck you, you come to me," he snarls, his eyes boring into mine, hard and hungry. "No one else. Got it?"

I want to tell him that I don't want anyone else. That the thought of being with anyone else makes my stomach turn. But I keep it inside, not wanting to scare him off.

"I thought you didn't do relationships," I throw out, arching an eyebrow.

Ryan shakes his head, his grip tightening on my waist, his breath ragged against my skin. "I don't," he confirms. "That still stands." His lips find the soft spot below my jaw, kissing me with a tenderness that makes my heart skip. "I just want to make you feel good. Just this once." He pulls back, eyes searching mine. "Are you okay with that?"

The words make something in my stomach swirl. I know the deal. We both know the deal. But the thought of him walking away afterward, of watching him flirt with other girls, sounds like torture.

Despite everything, I nod, forcing the words out. "Duh, rebound, remember?" I tilt my head. "Do you think I'm going to beg you to fuck me again?"

Ryan's smile widens, his eyes sparkling with amusement. "I'd love to hear you beg."

I roll my eyes, pushing at his chest, but he doesn't budge. "Your ego is massive."

"As is my cock," he teases, a smirk playing on his lips before he pulls me in closer, kissing me again.

I pull back after a few seconds, catching my breath. His eyes are a little hazy and confused as he looks at me for an answer. I twist my fingers together nervously, and my lips part as I search for the words. "So, um… I kind of can't come with just penetration."

Ryan's brows furrow. "Oh?"

"It's not a guy thing," I explain, and his eyes stay focused on me. "I've tried plenty on my own… trust me."

His lips twitch, fighting a smirk, but he stays quiet, letting me go on.

"I just… can't get there from penetration alone. So don't take it personally if I don't come." I let my fingers trail lightly over his chest, a teasing smile playing at my lips. "I promise I'll still enjoy every second of this. Thoroughly."

Ryan's eyes flicker with heat, and his smirk widens as his hands tighten on my waist. "Oh, you'll come," he says, his tone radiating with confidence as his lips brush against mine. "If not from my cock, then from my fingers and mouth."

His hands glide down to my ass, squeezing, his fingertips digging into my skin as he pulls me closer, and I moan against his lips, my body reacting to him instinctively. He groans back, the sound sending a shiver down my spine. "God, you make the hottest noises. Fuck, I need to see you."

Before I can respond, Ryan pulls away, his hands moving to the hem of my top, tugging it over my head. The fabric hits the floor, and his gaze drops to my chest, eyes locking on the purple lacy bra.

A noise crawls from his throat. "Purple just might be my favorite color, too."

I let out a chuckle, but Ryan groans, his breath hitching as he tilts his head back slightly. "Fuck, why are you so beautiful?

Why do you drive me out of my mind? Why did it have to be you I bumped into that day?"

His question hangs in the air, a flutter of emotions rushing through me. I can't stop myself from asking him the question running through my mind. "Do you regret it?"

His fingers dig into his hair, tugging it as he exhales sharply. "It ranges from so-fucking-much and my stomach cramping from guilt, to not a single fucking ounce of regret." He lets out a soft, almost sheepish chuckle, his smirk returning. "The latter usually wins," he adds with a sigh. "My mind is confused." His eyes flicker down to his crotch, thick and bulging through his jeans. "My dick is too."

I can't help but laugh. Reaching behind my back, I undo the clasp of my bra, letting it fall to the floor. "Does this help?"

Ryan's eyes darken, and he exhales shakily, his eyes locked on my tits, which makes my nipples harden with every second his eyes are on me. God, I want him to touch them, to lick them, to just do… something.

"Yeah," he says licking his lips. "Yeah, that helps a lot." He moves closer, cupping my tits, and my head lulls back, letting out a moan when his thumbs brush over my nipples. "Fuck, you have the prettiest tits." He lifts his gaze to mine. "Want me to play with them a little?"

I nod rapidly which he chuckles at, and clutches my waist, bringing his lips to mine as he walks us toward my bed, lying me flat on the bed. He cups my breast, playing with my nipple, twisting, pulling, rubbing and *god*, I'm so wet I can feel my thighs slipping against each other.

"You're wet, baby, aren't you?" he whispers against my lips. "Fuck, I want to feel you." Unbuttoning my pants, he doesn't even bother pulling them down, instead he slides his hand down my jeans and into my panties, parting me with his fingers.

I moan into his mouth when he rubs my clit with the pad of his middle finger, dragging it between my folds.

"Oh *fuck*, you're drenched," he moans and my pussy clenches around nothing. There's nothing hotter than a guy moaning. I want him in my ear groaning and moaning and making it known how fucking good he feels. And even though I'm not touching him in any way, he's getting pleasure from feeling me. And that is the hottest thing I have ever experienced.

His finger slips inside me, just to his knuckle before pulling it out and thrusting it back in. My back arches off the bed when his mouth closes around my nipple and his tongue swirls around it, tugging and sucking and making me lose my mind.

"That's it, baby, let me know how good I'm making you feel."

He doesn't stop, his mouth dragging lower, wet kisses trailing heat along my skin until he pauses just above the swell of my other breast, lips parted, breath warm. His teeth graze my skin, sucking slow and deep until it aches.

My hips twitch up into his hand, helpless. He groans, his tongue flicking over the bruise blooming beneath his mouth before turning his attention to the other one.

I close my eyes, letting the pleasure surround me when suddenly it stops. I snap my eyes open and Ryan pulls his hands out of my panties and his mouth away from my breast and before I can tell him to get back to work, he shuffles until he's lower on the bed and tugs my jeans and panties off.

He doesn't take them off all the way, though, he stops halfway, until just my ass is exposed, bends my legs up into my chest and dives in with a flick of his tongue.

"Oh god," I moan when his hot mouth sucks on my pussy.

His hands cup my ass as he spreads me open and his tongue licks the length of me, sucking up my arousal. He focuses his tongue on my clit, kissing my pussy like he would my mouth, hot and *torturous*.

"Ryan," I moan, gripping the sheets in agony. "Fuck, just make me come."

He chuckles against my skin, his tongue drifting down to lick my entrance, cleaning me up. "Patience. If I only get to have one night with you, I'm doing it right and taking my sweet ass time."

I open my mouth to tell him this doesn't have to be a one-time thing, but I don't. My eyes squeeze closed when his finger fills me up. It's so long and thick and *god*. Tipping my head back, I let out a loud, filthy moan I'm sure other people can hear, but I don't give a fuck right now.

"Fuck, your moans are sexy as hell," Ryan says, his words breathy and choppy. "You like my fingers inside you?" he asks, sliding another one in, curling them inside me.

"I need…"

"This?" he guesses, pressing a soft kiss to my clit, which makes me jump from the contact. "You want me to kiss your pretty, little pussy while I fuck you with my fingers?"

I moan in response, and he continues licking me while his fingers work me open.

"Fuck," he groans as he lifts from between my legs. "Goddamn, I need you bare." Tugging off my jeans and panties, he pulls them down my legs and onto the floor before spreading my legs wide open and settling between them, his mouth returning to my clit.

I tip my head back, sliding my fingers through his hair, while he drives me insane. God, I can't remember the last time I came, never mind the last time someone else made me come, but I can feel it building and building, cresting to the top until…

Ryan groans, spreading me wider, eating me harder, deeper, faster, leaving no part of me untouched, and the orgasm hits me hard and blinding, my legs shaking in Ryan's grip.

"That's it, baby. Come on my tongue. Fill my mouth with your cum."

A moan rips from my throat as I grip his hair in my fist, bucking my hips as the orgasm crashes through me, his dirty words making the pleasure last infinitely long. When I come down from the high, Ryan groans, giving me one last lick, which makes me flinch.

He presses a soft kiss to my clit before he crawls up my body and leans down to kiss me.

"So." *Kiss.* "Fucking." *Kiss.* "Hot." He groans into my mouth, our tongues tangling together as he grinds against me, still wearing too many damn clothes for my liking.

"Off," I moan, making work of his buttons. "Need. Inside me."

He chuckles against my lips. "Damn, I made you come so hard, you're speaking with broken words."

I roll my eyes, shoving at his chest, and he climbs off the bed, tugs his jeans off, and pulls them down along with his boxers. My eyes zone in on his long, hard, thick cock, and my breath catches in my throat. *Holy shit.*

My eyes snap to his at the sound of his chuckle. "Gotta say, watching you go speechless over my cock is one hell of an ego boost."

"I just—" I shake my head. No words. I have absolutely no words. The only cock I've seen—other than porn—was Jacob's. And Ryan is *much* bigger than him.

His hand flies to his cock and he starts stroking it leisurely. "You've got to stop looking at me like that. I'll blow my load before you even fucking touch me."

I let out a scoff. "How promising."

He chuckles, shaking his head as he climbs back on the bed, crawling over my body to tug my nipple. "Stop being a little tease and open those pretty legs."

I bite my lip in anticipation and run my hand through his hair, letting my legs fall apart. He shifts between them, kissing me as one hand cups my breast, his thumb rubbing my hard nipples. "You got a condom?" he murmurs against my lips.

I nod, keeping my hand lodged in his soft hair. "Night stand."

He attempts to move, but I don't let him, my legs tightening around him, keeping him right where I want him. I kiss him deeper, desperate for him, and he chuckles against my mouth.

"Baby, I need to grab a condom."

I whimper in protest, but Ryan lifts his head, glancing down at me. His grin is downright sinful as he drags his thumb over my bottom lip.

"I wanna keep kissing you too," he murmurs, voice thick with hunger. "But I'm also dying to be inside you."

I sigh. "Alright. Hurry."

He reaches over and opens my nightstand, pulling out a box of condoms I bought on a whim after deciding I needed a rebound. Never thought it'd be him using them, but I'm so glad it is.

He rips one open and rolls it onto his cock, giving it a couple of strokes before settling between my legs, his eyes flying to mine. "You ready?"

I nod, widening my legs for him, and he leans on one hand while the other grips his cock and slides it inside me. I'm drenched, so fucking wet, but he's still thick and bigger than anything I've ever had, so it takes a few times for him to finally slide inside me.

"Ah fuck," he groans, squeezing his eyes closed when he finally fills me. "Fuck. Fuck. *Fuck*. You feel so good. Oh shit." He pulls out and thrusts back inside me. "Goddamn, Isabella. Fuck, I forgot how good sex is."

I moan in response because… I've never had sex that felt like this.

He leans forward, capturing my lips with his. "Please tell me it feels good for you too."

"So good," I reply with a moan, feeling so full, pleasure curling up my spine.

And god, I can feel every vein, every inch, thick and stretching me open. My fingers claw down his back without thinking, my nails dragging hard enough to leave lines, sharp little scrapes that make him hiss above me.

"Fuck," he groans. "Do that again."

I dig in deeper as he thrusts harder, my thighs bracketing his hips, heels pressing into his ass, pulling him closer, deeper, wanting him to never leave my body.

I tilt my head and bury my face in the curve of his neck. God, he smells so good—spicy, a little sweaty, musky and masculine and utterly intoxicating—and I breathe him in, let myself drown in the scent of him as my lips part. I press kisses up the side of his throat, my tongue flicking out to taste the salt of his skin, and then I suck, slow and dirty, hollowing my cheeks and leaving my own mark on him.

"Ah fuck," he rasps. "You're gonna make me lose it."

He lifts onto his knees, dragging his cock almost all the way out before driving back in, slow and thick and *deep*. His eyes never leave where we're joined, watching the slick stretch of my pussy around him like it's the only thing in the world worth looking at.

"Holy fuck," he groans, voice hoarse, raw, wrecked. One hand grips my thigh, holding me open, while the other slides down to my lower belly and pressed down firmly. I feel it— feel *him*—right under his palm, the way he moves inside me making something feral coil low in my stomach.

"Shit… I can see it," he growls, pupils blown, sweat beading on his brow. "I can see my cock inside you, baby. Look at how full I've got you."

I glance down and the sight makes my pussy clench around him. His thick cock disappears into me again and again, and where his hand presses into my stomach, I can *see* the bulge, the outline of him making my body to take every inch.

My moan breaks out, my hips jerking up to meet every thrust. "Ryan," I gasp as my fingers find my clit, rubbing frantically.

"Fuck yeah," he pants, the rhythm of his thrusts turning punishing, relentless, his fingers tightening where they press down, like he wants to feel every time he pushes into my body. "Rub that clit. Make yourself come."

My voice hitches as my head tips back, a cry breaking free when he cups my breast, rough fingers rolling my nipple until it's tight and aching. His other hand slides between my thighs, spreading me wider, holding me open for him as he sinks deeper, so deep I swear I can feel him in my fucking throat.

His pace picks up, hips snapping forward with more hunger, each movement a little more desperate, a little less controlled. I moan and my hand slips away from my clit. Ryan doesn't miss a beat. He catches my wrist, presses a kiss to my palm, then takes over, his thumb sliding right where I need it, circling my clit in perfect time with every stroke of his cock.

"Fuck, I can feel you squeezing me so tight," he groans, his voice shredded with lust, eyes locked on mine. "You close, baby? You gonna come all over my cock?"

I nod, my thighs trembling, heat crashing through my body in hot waves. His breath fans across my face, ragged and matching mine, and he doesn't let up—not his thrusts, not the way his thumb keeps working me over, relentless and so good it burns.

My head falls back against the pillows, my lips parted, moans spilling out as the orgasm crashes through me. "Oh my god. Ryan," I cry, my body clenching around him, as I come hard, my legs shaking and my back arching off the bed.

He grits his teeth, groaning. "Oh fuck, I'm gonna come," he pants, desperate, chasing his own release. He grips my hips so tight it's gonna bruise, yanking me down into each thrust until I feel him twitch inside me.

With a ragged moan, he pulls out of me, fumbling the condom off, tossing it blindly aside as he fists his cock, jaw tight, his breath coming in sharp bursts.

"Fuck," he groans, and then he's spilling across my stomach in hot, thick ropes, cum striping my skin while his whole body shudders.

I watch him through hooded eyes, wrecked and panting, his chest heaving. My fingers trail lazily down my belly, and I gather his release, sticky and warm on my fingertips. I lift my hand to my lips and suck one finger into my mouth, my eyes locked on his as I taste him.

Ryan's breath catches, and his gaze darkens as he watches my mouth wrap around my own fingers.

A crooked grin pulls at the corner of his lips. "Fuck, you're hot as hell." His lips find mine again, his hand gently cupping my face, thumb brushing softly over my cheek. Every time he touches me like that, my stomach flutters, like it's the first time.

I melt under it, pressing closer, kissing him again, swallowing down the groan that rumbles in his throat. He breaks the kiss first, resting his forehead against mine, his nose brushing mine as he glances down, smirking at the mess he's made of me.

"You got a towel or something?" he asks. "To clean you up?"

"Yeah," I breathe, my lips still tingling from his kisses. "Nightstand." I motion weakly with a flick of my fingers, too boneless to move.

He chuckles, shifting just enough to lean over me, opening the drawer with one hand while the other stays on me—like he doesn't want to lose contact even for a second. His fingers graze my thigh as he grabs a hand towel, and brings it to my skin.

"Hold still," he murmurs, his thumb brushing idle circles on my hip as he cleans me up gently. "Fuck… you make it look so goddamn pretty."

I let out a chuckle as he tosses the towel, and for a moment, neither of us speaks. We just look at each other, the silence hanging between us, trying to figure out what happens next.

A few seconds pass, and Ryan finally runs a hand through his hair, letting out a heavy sigh. "I have to go."

"I know," I say, my voice not matching the knot in my stomach. I don't *want* him to leave, but we both know what this was. Just once. No strings.

A pained look crosses his face, and he steps back slowly, his body tense. "I don't want to," he admits.

I can't help but let out a small laugh, despite the lump in my throat. "Me neither," I confess, my heart hammering. I want him to stay. I want to wrap my arms around him and pull him down beside me. I want to pretend this is something more. I want to believe that look in his eyes means what I *wish* it meant.

But we both know it doesn't.

With a resigned sigh, Ryan starts pulling his clothes back on.

I grab the sheet, pulling it over myself, but even that feels ridiculous. He's seen every part of me, been inside me, moaned my name into my neck. But now… It's over.

Once he's dressed, he looks back at me. His gaze is heavy, his eyes tracing the curve of my face, studying every detail like he's trying to hold onto it. He sighs again, a low curse slipping out, and then, before I can say anything, he crosses the space between us with long strides, and kisses me one last time.

It's different this time. This kiss is soft, slow—nothing like the urgent, hungry kisses from earlier. This one feels like a goodbye.

When he pulls back, his thumb brushes over my cheek, just like before. His gaze locks onto mine. "Are we good?"

I nod, offering him a shaky smile, trying to push past the ache in my chest. "That was a hell of a rebound," I tease, trying to lighten the mood, but the knot in my stomach tightens all over again.

Ryan scoffs, shaking his head with a smirk. "And an amazing way to end my dry spell."

I laugh, but the sound feels hollow as his smile slips, and he leans closer, pressing his forehead to mine. His breath is warm against my skin, and it sends a jolt straight to my heart.

"I'm glad it was me," he whispers, pulling back just enough for his lips to brush against my forehead.

And then he pulls away.

He gives me one last smile, then he turns toward the door. My chest tightens as he opens it, and without another word, he walks out and shuts the door behind him.

NINETEEN

Ryan

The rink is freezing, but I'm sweating my fucking balls off like it's mid-July.

Practice is always brutal, but today? Feels like Coach is actively trying to kill us. My legs burn, my lungs are on fire, and my jersey sticks to my back as I push off, carving deep into the ice just as the whistle shrieks through the arena.

"Again!" Coach shouts from the bench.

I grit my teeth and dig in, lungs screaming as we run yet another breakout drill. I set up at the blue line, stick on the ice, tracking the play as Logan carries the puck through the neutral zone. He's quick on his edges, shifty as hell, but I match him stride for stride, forcing him wide toward the boards.

The second he shifts, I drop my right knee and extend my stick—poke check, clean, puck gone. I sweep it off his blade and transition instantly, snapping a pass up to Austin, who's streaking up the weak side.

"Nice fucking try." I smirk, gliding backward as Logan groans.

"Yeah, yeah," he mutters, coasting past me. "Still faster than your slow ass."

I snort, pivoting to shield the puck before threading a crisp pass back to Austin, who's cutting toward the slot.

"Back door!" I call, reading the play before it happens.

Austin one-times it, but Nathan is already there, tracking the puck like a goddamn hawk. He drops into a perfect butterfly, glove snapping up like lightning, and robs him blind.

"Fucking hell," Austin groans, throwing his head back as Nathan smirks behind his mask. "Take a goddamn break, man."

"Maybe shoot better," Nathan taunts, casually tossing the puck aside like it wasn't the filthiest save of the day.

Logan skates by, patting Austin on the helmet. "He's got a point, buddy."

Austin shoves him. "Eat shit."

Coach blows the whistle. "Switch it up! Power play unit, get on the ice!"

I skate to the center, glancing toward the boards—and freeze.

She's here.

Of course she is. She's at every practice, standing on the sidelines with her clipboard in hand, taking notes like it's just another day at work. Which it is. She's just doing her job, and I should respect that. Should stop fucking staring.

But knowing that doesn't stop my body from reacting like a goddamn idiot every time she's in the rink.

Because now all I can think about is her under me. Her back against the mattress, fingers curling in my hair. Her breathy little moans in my ear as I kissed my way down her—

Something hard smacks against my shin guard.

"Fuck!"

I whip around, and Cole is staring at me, brow arched. "You're staring," he says flatly.

Shit.

"Staring at what?" I feign ignorance, even as my face burns hot.

Cole scoffs, shaking his head before skating off, leaving me standing there like an idiot.

I know I'm being obvious, but I can't help it. Can't stop looking at her—thinking about her—since that night. Since I met her, actually.

The thought of her going home with some other guy at the party the other night had my jaw clenched so fucking hard I thought it might snap.

I knew I wanted her. I just didn't know how bad.

And now that I've had her—now that I know what she sounds like, tastes like, feels like—I can't stop wanting her.

The whistle blows, snapping me out of it.

"Reed!" Coach's voice cuts through the rink. "The fuck are you doing standing there like a statue? Get moving!"

I shake off the distraction, grip my stick, and push forward, skating hard through the drill. The ice is smooth beneath my skates, the air cold on my face, sweat dripping from my brow.

Logan passes me the puck, and I take it, pushing forward before sending a hard pass to Austin. His stick wobbles, and the shot flies wide.

"Fuck," he mutters, shaking his head in frustration.

"Try opening your stance more," a voice calls from the boards. Isabella's.

Austin turns, his eyebrows furrowed, looking between her and Coach. "You sure?"

Coach doesn't even glance up. "Listen to my daughter and do what she says."

Austin stands taller, hand to his forehead in a salute. "Sir, yes sir."

He straightens up, gets in position, and waits for the puck again. When it comes, he opens up, adjusts his angle, and fires. The puck slams into the top corner of the net.

"Well, what do you know," Austin grins, tapping his stick on the ice. "Baby Hayes knows her stuff after all."

I chuckle as Austin skates past me, my chest lighting up with pride.

Yeah, she fucking does.

I shake off my thoughts and drop into position as we start the power play drill. The puck drops, and I immediately battle Logan for possession, tying up his stick and kicking the puck to my blade.

I pivot, my eyes scanning for an opening, and fire a quick saucer pass to Austin.

"Back to me," I call.

Austin sends it right back, and I drop low, loading my stick for a slap shot. The second the puck touches my blade, I rip it, feeling the force of the shot as it screams toward the net.

It pings off the crossbar with a crack.

"Fuck," I mutter under my breath.

Nathan's chuckle is audible even through his mask. "So close, buddy."

I don't waste a second, regrouping and shifting into position as Logan takes possession and starts a rush the other way. I backcheck hard, pushing my legs to the limit as I close the gap between us.

"Little slow today, Reed," Logan taunts, a playful grin on his face.

"Little ugly today, Gray," I shoot back, matching his pace.

His shoulders shake with a laugh, but I'm already focused, getting my stick in his lane. In one smooth motion, I poke-check the puck loose before he can get a shot off, sending it sliding toward our zone.

Coach nods from the bench. "Good stick, Reed."

I catch his praise as my eyes flick to the boards. Isabella's still there, clipboard in hand, watching. She's biting her lip, brow furrowed in concentration, and damn, she looks so fucking cute.

I quickly look away, snapping back to the drill before I get distracted.

The rest of practice feels like it drags on forever. My legs burn like fire, but I power through, and every time I glance at the boards, her eyes are there, following me, studying every move I make.

I know I shouldn't, but as I skate past her during a water break.

"Careful," I tease. "Staring like that might get you in trouble."

I take a slow sip from my bottle, watching her every movement, how her throat works as she swallows.

"Shut up," she mutters, but the flush creeping up her neck tells me everything I need to know.

I chuckle, shoot her a wink, and skate back into the drill.

By the time Coach finally calls it, my jersey's soaked, my arms feel like dead weight, and I'm one more drill away from collapsing on the ice.

"Hit the showers," he barks. "Film in an hour!"

A collective groan echoes through the rink, but I don't have the energy to join in.

"Fuck, I'm starving," Austin grumbles, rubbing his stomach. "I need, like, five cheeseburgers."

"That's cute," Logan shoots back. "I need six."

"Jesus," Nathan mutters. "You guys are actual garbage disposals."

As they argue over which fast food joint has the best post-practice meal, I hang back, my eyes flicking over to the boards.

Isabella's still there. Still watching me. Like I'm the only thing in the rink.

And damn if that doesn't do something to me.

I skate toward her, feeling a smile slide onto my face. "Good watching out there."

She raises an eyebrow, her lips curling into a small smile. "Good playing out there."

I smirk, leaning in just enough to drop my voice. "Thanks. You did good with Austin. Any pointers for me?"

She watches me for a long moment, her gaze lingering before her tongue darts out to wet her lips, just the tiniest hint of a challenge in her eyes. "You could've hit that one-timer."

"Yeah?" I step closer, feeling the heat between us. "What else?"

She tilts her head slightly, lips twitching into a small grin. "You were a little distracted on the ice."

"Hmm," I nod slowly. "I think we both know the reason why."

Her eyes flicker. She licks her lips again, and I barely resist the urge to grab her right here, and press her against the boards. Fuck, I want to taste those pretty lips again.

"Reed!"

Coach's voice cuts through the air, pulling me back to reality.

I step back, my heart pounding, like a guilty fucking teenager caught in the act.

"Stop distracting my daughter and get the fuck in the locker room."

"Right. Sorry." I throw Isabella a grin. "Was just telling your daughter she did a great job. Really amazing. Best practice ever."

We both know I'm not talking about hockey.

Her lips curve into a knowing smile, and she rolls her eyes, shaking her head. I chuckle, finally turning toward the locker room, but not without one last glance at her—just to see if she's watching me walk away.

The second I step in, music blasts through the room, vibrating the walls, like always.

"Shotgun on the showers!" Aiden yells, yanking his jersey off.

"There's like five showers, man, calm down," Logan retorts, rolling his eyes.

I shake my head, peeling off my own jersey. The undershirt sticks to my chest, soaked from sweat, and I rip it off, wincing as the cold air hits my skin.

"Well, well, well. Reed finally got some."

I frown, glancing up to see Logan smirking at me, his eyes locked onto my neck.

Nathan strolls by, takes one look at me, and snorts. "Holy shit."

I turn to the mirror, my eyes widening when I see what they're talking about.

Shit.

A massive, dark, impossible-to-miss hickey.

Logan whistles. "Damn. Someone had fun."

Nathan just smirks. "Hope she was hot."

She was. She also happened to be your sister.

Austin bursts into laughter, taking a few steps closer. "Holy shit, Reed, did you get attacked by a vampire?" And of course, he's completely fucking naked.

"Jesus," I mutter, stepping back and holding my hand up as if that will protect me. "Put your dick away if you're gonna stand that close to me."

He just laughs, slipping his boxers on with zero fucks given. "Congrats on ending the dry spell. Who was the lucky girl?"

"Or guy," Logan adds, wiggling his brows.

Nathan nearly chokes on his water.

I arch a brow. "Not a guy."

"So, it *was* a girl?" Austin grins, eyes glowing with curiosity. "Who?"

Shit.

"Yeah, I'm not fucking talking about this with you guys."

"Aww, come on," Austin groans. "I've been rooting for you to get laid for months."

"Was it Brenna?" Logan asks. "She was all over you at the party last week."

I have no fucking clue who Brenna is. But I can't exactly admit that, can I?

I glance at Cole. He's leaning against the locker, chewing his gum slowly, eyes flicking between me and the rest of the room.

"Yeah," I lie, swallowing hard. "It was… Brenda."

"Brenna," Austin corrects, a grin tugging at the corner of his mouth.

"Right. Sure. Her."

Nathan chuckles from across the room, his voice dripping with amusement. "Damn, she really marked you up. Shouldn't you remember her name?"

I let out a laugh that's way too forced, feeling it scrape at my chest. Jesus.

My face burns, and I force my hand through my hair, pretending like I'm unaffected. But deep down, I'm spiraling.

If only they knew who actually gave me that hickey. If only they knew I'd left my marks all over her perfect tits, leaving my fucking scent on her skin.

My best friend. My teammate. A guy I consider like a brother. And I betrayed him.

I fucked his little sister.

And goddamn it, I want to do it again. Because deep down, no matter how many times we agreed it was a one-time thing.

Once will never be enough.

TWENTY

Isabella

"I'm not going," I announce, flopping back onto the bed.

Aurora, standing in front of my closet, doesn't even look at me. She pulls out a tiny black dress, holds it up between two fingers, and stares at me, waiting.

"You're wearing this," she says, the dress hanging in the air like it's the obvious answer.

I groan and let my head fall back onto the pillow. "I'm staying in."

Without missing a beat, she tosses the dress onto me. "You're going out."

I roll my eyes and flop back down onto the bed. "I'm not in the mood. I've had a long week, and a good movie and junk food are all I need right now."

She pulls out a pair of shoes, keeps rummaging through my closet, and doesn't seem affected by my protests. "You've been cooped up in here long enough."

I sigh, looking up at the ceiling. "I just don't feel like seeing Ryan tonight. Not after everything."

Aurora turns her head so fast, I almost get whiplash. "Everything?" she asks, eyes narrowing. "What does everything entail? What are you not telling me?"

I haven't told her about me and Ryan yet. I don't know why. Well, scratch that—I do know why. Because I was stupid enough to think I could sleep with him one time and forget it ever happened. And now, Aurora wants me to go to this party and see him there with other girls, and the thought alone makes my stomach churn.

"We slept together."

Aurora freezes in place. "You what?"

I chew on my lip, feeling my face turn bright red. "Saturday night."

Aurora's eyes widen. "And you didn't tell me?"

"I'm telling you now," I reply with a shrug

"Isabella!" She grabs her makeup brush and throws it at me. I dodge it just in time, bursting into laughter.

"I… forgot?"

"You forgot?" Aurora halts in her tracks, her jaw practically touching the floor.

"Well, I didn't forget, obviously," I mutter, running a hand through my hair. "It just… happened. And I didn't know how to tell you."

Aurora shakes her head, narrowing her eyes. "You're lucky I love you. If you ever do that again without a heads-up, I will murder you."

I roll my eyes, but a grin sneaks on my face anyway. "What? Should I send a play-by-play mid action?"

"I'm not asking for a play-by-play," she adds with a smirk. "but a few juicy details wouldn't hurt."

I breathe out a laugh and shake my head. "I regret telling you this already."

Aurora turns to me, eyebrow raised, the lipstick still in her hand. "So, was it good?"

I blink, memories of the other night flashing in my head. "Yeah," I admit, my lips curling into a smirk. So fucking good.

I've never had sex like that before. Granted, I've only been with one guy before, but still.

She narrows her eyes. "But?"

I hesitate, the words sitting in the back of my throat. "But it's not happening again," I tell her, lifting my shoulder in a shrug.

She pauses, the lipstick hovering just above her lips, her gaze locked on me. "Wait, what?" She narrows her eyes. "Why not?"

I chew on my lip, wishing I could just bury myself in my bed. "We agreed it would only be a one-time thing."

Aurora's eyebrows lift, and she blows out a breath, turning her attention fully to me. "Oof. You've made a big mistake."

I furrow my brows, confused. "How so?"

She shrugs and sits beside me on the bed. "You desperately needed a rebound, don't get me wrong, and Ryan's hot and I could tell you liked him… But there's no way you can hang out with him every day, flirting and teasing, and not catch feelings for him."

I frown, pulling the sheets up to my chin. "Which is exactly why I need to stay in," I mutter. "He's going to be at the party, and I—"

"Hell no. You're not cowering away," she interrupts, giving me a pointed look as she tugs at the sheets. "You made your choice, and now you have to live with it."

I sigh, frustrated. "I don't know if I can handle it."

Aurora leans in, locking eyes with me. "You can. You see him every day at practice. This is no different."

I beg to differ. At practice there are people noting my every move at all times. My dad by my side, my brother on the ice, and the other guys surrounding him. But at parties, there are so many quiet places, dark corners where I can lose my inhibitions and melt into a puddle with a simple glance from him.

"Plus. Showing him how hot you look won't hurt," Aurora adds with a grin.

I chuckle despite my nerves. "Okay, fine. I'll go. But you can't leave me alone. I have no willpower when it comes to him."

Aurora chuckles and turns to face me, her hands on her hips. "I won't leave your side. Now, get dressed. I need to sext Chase while my makeup still looks good."

I scrunch my nose. "Ew. I did not need that visual."

She scoffs, leaning in front of her mirror to touch up her makeup. "Please. Like you've never done it."

"Absolutely not," I reply, raising an eyebrow.

Aurora winks at me, her tone smug. "Well, the night's still young."

I shake my head, but I laugh as I strip out of my sweatshirt and slip into the black dress she picked out for me. "I don't even know why I'm friends with you."

She winks again. "Because I'm irreplaceable."

By the time Aurora and I get to the party, it's already packed. The bass from the speakers is so loud it vibrates through my bones. The kitchen's a mess of half-empty beer bottles, plastic cups, and the stale smell of spilled alcohol. The air is thick with heat and full of the mix of too many bodies crammed into one space.

Aurora hands me a cup without a word. "Drink. Mingle. Have fun. In that order."

I look at the neon pink liquid in the cup. "What is this?"

She takes a sip of hers. "Does it matter?"

Yeah, that's not reassuring, but I take a sip anyway. The sweetness hits me first, followed by something citrusy, and then the burn of cheap alcohol. I cough. "Jesus. This tastes like soda and nail polish remover had a baby."

Aurora chuckles. "Yeah, but it does the job."

I roll my eyes but follow her as she leads the way through the crowd. People are everywhere—guys trying to dance like they're in a movie, a couple making out like they've never seen each other before, and some guy who looks way too proud of himself for being able to drink from a beer funnel without dying.

Aurora moves through it all with ease like it's second nature. I can't help but glance around the room, my eyes drifting, scanning the crowd for any sign of Ryan.

We see each other every day at practice; aside from a few stolen glances, nothing's changed. And yet, I can't stop thinking about it. About him. About how it felt.

The way his hands gripped my waist, the heat of his breath against my skin, the way he kissed me like he couldn't get enough.

But none of that matters. Because here I am, obsessing over every detail of that night, while he…

Well, I don't know what he's thinking.

But I have a feeling it's not *this*.

Aurora must notice me zoning out because she raises an eyebrow. "What's up with you?"

I snap my gaze away, shrugging it off. "Nothing."

She tilts her head. "Uh-huh, sure. Just checking out the room for no reason at all, right?"

I roll my eyes. "I'm not looking for Ryan," I lie. Not convincingly either, because Aurora lets out a scoff as she leans back against the wall.

"Yeah, okay And I definitely don't stalk my boyfriend's Spotify activity."

A laugh bubbles out of me, but before I can argue, a guy stumbles into our space, his chest puffed out. His breath reeks of cheap alcohol, and his confidence is a little too loud for someone who can barely stand straight.

"Hey," he slurs, zeroing in on Aurora. "Haven't seen you around before."

Aurora barely spares him a glance. "That's because I wasn't around."

He laughs, clearly drunk enough to think he's hilarious. "You're funny. I like that."

"How tragic," she sighs.

His grin widens, too far gone to catch the insult. "What?"

Aurora takes a sip, and gives him a deadpan look. "That you think I'm even remotely interested."

The guy's grin drops, irritation flickering across his face. "Being a bitch isn't attractive, you know."

Aurora arches her brow at him. "And what makes you think I'm trying to attract you?"

I bite back a laugh, watching the exchange. The guy scoffs before turning his attention to me. "What about you, sweetheart?"

I scrunch my nose, the stench of alcohol hitting me even from this distance. "No thanks."

He mutters something under his breath, his face flushed with embarrassment, before he stumbles off into the crowd.

Aurora raises her cup, her lips twitching into a smirk. "To being unapproachable."

I clink my cup against hers, a small laugh escaping me. "Cheers."

We're still laughing when a groan cuts through the noise.

"Great. Viper's here to ruin the party."

I turn, my gaze falling on Cole. He's standing nearby, arms crossed, and his eyes are locked on Aurora with a look that could melt steel. He drags his gaze down her body, pausing at the low neckline of her top, and then flicks his eyes back up to her face with a tight expression.

Aurora doesn't seem fazed. She takes another sip of her drink, her lips curling into a half-smirk. "Wow, you're already in my business? That was fast."

Cole scoffs, his eyes running over Aurora's outfit once again. "Do you ever wear clothes that actually cover you?"

Aurora's gaze sharpens. "Stop looking at me and it won't be a problem."

Cole's smirk fades, his jaw tightening. "Trust me, I'm not fucking looking."

The tension between them thickens, heavy and suffocating. I glance back and forth, my curiosity bubbling up, but before I can say anything, Cole saunters off without another word.

"Okay, what's with you two?" I ask, raising an eyebrow at Aurora. "You look like you're ready to kill each other."

Her face screws up in disgust. "That would involve me getting close enough to touch him. Not happening."

I arch a brow, but she offers nothing more.

I take a long sip of my drink, the coolness of it running down my throat as I scan the room, letting my gaze bounce from one face to the next. The noise of the party hums around me, a blur of voices and laughter blending with the pulse of the music. It's all just background noise—until I freeze.

There he is.

Ryan.

Leaning against the far wall, looking effortlessly perfect. His dark hair's a little tousled, and his sleeves are rolled up just enough to show off the muscles in his forearms. And because the universe has a cruel sense of humor, he's surrounded by a group of girls—each of them with their attention locked on him.

My stomach drops.

He got what he wanted, and I was stupid enough to give it to him. And now, I'm just another girl in his past.

Aurora's eyes flick back down to her phone when it buzzes and she chuckles, a grin tugging at her lips.

"Chase?" I ask, already knowing the answer.

She looks up, her grin widening. "He got my picture," she says, shooting me a wink. "He's asking for another one," she adds, tilting her head at me. "You'll be okay for a minute, right?"

"Yeah, I'll be fine," I reply with a chuckle.

She blows me a kiss and she spins on her heels and heads upstairs.

I take another sip of my drink, letting out a long breath. It's not like anything will happen with Ryan, anyway. A part of me thought he'd see me and feel like he made a mistake setting that one-time rule. But I was just being delusional. He doesn't need me. He never did. He's got his pick of girls—girls who don't come with complications, who he can hook up with without consequences.

It doesn't matter how much I want to be the one to catch his attention. It doesn't matter what I thought we had. I'm just another girl, fading into the background like every other one before me.

I take a deep breath, trying to force my mind onto something—anything—other than Ryan and the damn knot forming in my stomach. I focus on the ice in my cup, the way it clinks together as I stir it absently. Anything but the sick feeling in my chest.

But then I glance around, and my gaze drifts back to the spot where he was just standing.

He's gone.

And so are the girls.

The empty space gnaws at me for a second before my stomach twists even tighter. Did he leave with them? Of course, he did. Why wouldn't he? I'm not what he's looking for. I was just a momentary distraction.

Swallowing hard, I try to push the lump in my throat away, but it doesn't work. The ache doesn't stop.

But just as I'm about to give in to the bitter wave of self-pity crashing over me, someone tugs at my wrist.

TWENTY-ONE

Ryan

Isabella gasps as I grab her wrist, pulling her through the crowded hallway. The music pounds around us, people laughing, shouting, but it all blurs into the background, drowned out by the pounding in my chest. All I can focus on is her. The way her dress hugs her body, teasing me with every step, the way her dark curls bounce against her shoulders like they were made to be wrapped around my fingers.

Fuck, she looks perfect.

Gorgeous, with a trim waist and hips that make it impossible to think straight. My fingers tighten around her wrist as I push forward.

We reach the bathroom, and I shove the door open with my foot, pulling her inside. Her chest rises and falls, her eyes flicking up to mine—unsure, excited, nervous.

"Ryan?" she breathes.

I run a hand through my hair, exhaling hard. My pulse is a wreck. My hands shake. I lock the door because I need to, because if I don't, I'll second-guess it, and I can't second-guess this.

"I tried to stay away from you." My voice comes out rough, low. I swallow hard. "I fucking *tried*, Isabella. But I can't. I can't do it anymore."

Her lips part slightly, and I watch as her breath catches. I know what she tastes like, and every inch of me aches to kiss her, to feel her lips on mine again.

"I thought you said it was just a one-time thing," she whispers.

I let out a short laugh. "Yeah, well. That was a dumb fucking idea."

My gaze drags down her body, and my restraint starts slipping. The dress—fuck, the dress. It's too short, too tight, riding up her thighs like it's trying to kill me.

"One time isn't enough." I grit out, reaching for her, because I can't spend another second without my hands on her. "Not even fucking close."

Before she can respond, I grab her hips and lift her onto the counter. Her legs part instinctively, and I step between them, my body pressing into hers. Our breaths mingle, her pupils dilate, her lips part slightly and before I fucking know it, my mouth is on hers.

Oh fuck, I missed this. Missed her. Christ, kissing this woman is unlike anything I've ever experienced. Her mouth tastes like vodka, and I want to drown in it. My hands are everywhere. Her waist, her ass, her thighs.

She moans into my mouth, when my fingers push up under her dress and trace over her cotton panties.

"Fuck. You're already dripping," I murmur against her lips. "This all for me?"

She shudders, nails digging into my shoulders. "Yes."

"Yeah?" My lips brush against her jaw, down to the sensitive spot on her neck. "Tell me how bad you want it."

A groan leaves her lips. "Shut up and fuck me."

I chuckle as I crash my mouth against hers again, my hands trailing over her body. But then I blink. Look around at the bathroom in some stranger's house. And her, gorgeous and flushed and desperate, looking at me like I'm the only person in the universe that matters.

I freeze, my breath catching in my throat. "Fuck. No. Not here."

She blinks, brows drawing together. "What?"

"You deserve better than this," I mutter, running a hand through my hair. "Not some bathroom at a par—"

Her hand covers my mouth, cutting me off.

"I don't care where," she says, shaking her head, her chocolate brown eyes locked on mine. "I need you."

My brain short-circuits.

"Please," she breathes. "Please, Ryan. I need you so bad."

Her words wreck me, the desperate plea, filled with need, and fuck, I'm gone.

I drop to my knees, sliding her dress up to her hips and tugging down her blue cotton panties. I look up at her, a slow grin spreading across my face. "I think I changed my mind. Blue's my favorite color after all."

I don't give her a chance to reply before leaning forward and licking up her soaked slit, groaning at how wet she is. She cries out, one hand in my hair as her back arches.

"Tastes so fucking good," I groan as I suck her sweet clit, sliding a finger inside her, curling deep.

"Oh god." She shakes, her thighs trembling around my head, then fists my hair hard and pulls me up. "Later," she gasps. "Fuck me now."

I don't even answer. My cock strains against my jeans, throbbing with need, and I can't take another second without being inside her. My fingers fumble at my zipper as I yank my jeans down just enough to free my cock, thick and already leaking. I grab her hips, dragging her to the edge of the sink. She watches me, biting her lip.

I position myself at her entrance, the tip just barely pressing into her. "Is this what you want?" I taunt, dragging my cock against her, teasing her, making her squirm.

Her breath stutters, her body arching into me. "Stop messing around."

I grin against her neck. "Where's the fun in that?"

She groans, and I let out a chuckle, done with teasing her. I reach into my pocket, quickly pulling out a condom. Fucking thank God Austin always carries these damn things on him.

I roll it on, making sure it's snug and I don't waste another second.

I line up and push in, in one deep stroke, swallowing her gasp as she clenches around me. Oh fuck. She's so soft. Perfect. Hot, tight, and so wet I almost black out.

"Fuck," I groan, my fingers tightening on her hips. "Look at you, so fucking desperate for me. You want me so bad, don't you, baby?"

Her body moves with mine, matching my pace, her breath coming in soft, desperate moans. She clings to me, her nails scraping down my back, her legs tightening around my waist.

"Harder," she whispers.

I chuckle darkly, snapping my hips forward. "You think you can handle that?"

She nods frantically, her breath coming in sharp, uneven gasps. "Yes. Fuck me harder, Ryan. Please."

My head drops to her shoulder, my lips brushing against her skin as I thrust harder, deeper, until she's gasping, her body arching against mine.

"I'm going to make sure you feel me for days, baby. Every inch of you will remember this."

Her nails bite into my skin, and she moans, her head falling back. I groan, watching the way her lips part, her eyes fluttering shut.

"You love this, don't you?" I murmur. "Knowing someone could walk in? Knowing we shouldn't be doing this?"

Her breath hitches, and she nods, cheeks flushed, eyes dark with lust. "Yes."

Something tightens in my chest, and I grip her jaw, tilting her face toward mine, needing her to see me. "No one else gets to see you like this." My thumb brushes over her parted lips. "No one else gets to hear these sounds from you."

She doesn't answer. Can't. Her breath catches, a moan breaking free, and I don't let her think. I kiss her deep, claiming her lips. She clings to me, pulling me closer, matching my rhythm.

My mouth lowers, my lips leaving soft kisses along her jaw, down to her collarbone, smelling her sweet perfume mixed with a light layer of swear. A groan rumbles in the back of my throat and I sink my teeth in, drawing a gasp from her lips, followed by a moan when I seal my mouth over the spot and suck. Hard.

Her body bucks under me, thighs clenching around my waist.

"God, I wanna mark you." I shift lower, and my teeth find another patch of skin, just beneath her collarbone. I flick my tongue over it before I close my mouth and suck. "Here."

She whimpers and I can feel the noise travel through her chest into my mouth.

"And here." I drag my tongue up across the line of her shoulder, tasting salt and sex and *her*. "I want every inch of you marked by me."

Her body tightens around me, pure fucking heaven, and just as I tip my head back with a groan, there's a knock on the damn door.

Isabella tenses, her eyes widening, but I'm not stopping. Not now. Not when we're this close. I stay buried inside her, my pulse hammering.

"Get the fuck out of here," I yell to whoever is at the door, thrusting deeper inside her.

She gasps, her head falling back, a moan slipping from her lips.

"Ryan?"

Fuck.

Cole's voice makes my stomach drop. Isabella's eyes snap open, her breath hitching.

I freeze, my jaw tight, but she doesn't. No, the little tease squeezes around me. My whole body jerks in response, a strangled groan escaping before I can stop it. *Jesus Christ.*

She bites her lip, her expression entirely too smug, and I shoot her a warning look.

"It's… occupied," I manage, my voice wavering by the pleasure curling up my spine. My hands grip her thighs harder as I slowly thrust into her, unable to stop moving from how fucking good she feels.

Isabella clenches around me again. I snap my head up, pinning her with a dark look.

"Problem?" she asks with a teasing smirk.

I growl under my breath. "Yeah, I got a fucking problem." I slam into her harder, grinding my hips against hers, making her whimper.

She gasps. "Oh god. Ryan—"

I cut her off with another thrust. "Not so cocky now, huh?" Christ. I can't stop. "Your pussy feels so fucking good," I whisper, thrusting into her. "So tight, so fucking perfect around me."

I hear Cole snicker from the other side of the door. "Yeah, I can tell. Tell *Brenda* I said hi."

Isabella's smirk vanishes. Her brows knit together, suspicion flashing across her face. "Brenda?" she repeats.

For fuck's sake.

"Ignore him. He's just a dumbass." My fingers dig into her hips, making sure she feels every inch of my cock still buried inside her. "Stop thinking about Cole and kiss me."

I brush my lips against hers, swallowing any lingering doubts. My thumb finds her clit, rubbing slow, teasing circles. Her breath stutters against my lips, her body jerking in response. I can feel her getting closer, can feel the way she's gripping me, pulling me deeper.

"Fuck," I groan against her lips. "You're squeezing me so tight. Can you feel how deep I am inside you?"

She moans, her hands clutching at my shoulders as she moves with me, desperate, frantic.

"That's it, baby," I rasp, dragging my teeth along her jaw, my hips snapping into hers. "Come on. Take what you need."

Her breath comes in short, desperate gasps, her thighs trembling around my waist. I can feel how close she is. How badly she wants to let go. And fuck, I need it just as much.

I keep my thumb on her clit, circling slowly, watching her squirm, and shift my hips, hitting that spot that makes her entire body tense.

Her hands slip under my shirt as she rolls her hips, chasing the friction she needs.

I thrust into her harder, groaning at how perfect she feels.

"I don't want to pull out, baby." I mutter against her lips, fisting a hand through her curls. "I want to stay inside you forever, feel you squeeze me like that."

Her breath catches as she bucks against me. I can feel the tension building, her body shivering.

"You close?" I ask, grinding into her, pushing deeper, harder, watching her face twist with pleasure as she gasps for air.

She whimpers, barely able to nod.

I grunt, my hips snapping against hers as my thumb rubs her swollen clit. "Then come for me, baby," I whisper, watching her fall apart.

She breaks, her back arches, a loud cry slipping out, and I slap a hand over her mouth to muffle it. Her body jerks as she comes, her pussy pulsing around me like a fucking vice.

"Fuck, you feel so good," I groan, my hands gripping her tighter, pulling her into me. "So tight—so wet—*fuuuck*."

Her orgasm is like a tidal wave, and it sends me spiraling. My own release follows fast, my body jerking as I slam into her one last time, my groan mixing with hers.

I stay inside her, letting the waves of pleasure roll through me as I catch my breath, resting my forehead on hers. *Fuck.*

Isabella's warm breath hits my cheek, her body still shaking from the orgasm.

When I pull out, I can't help myself. I cup her face, my thumb running over her cheek, just taking a second to get lost in those big brown eyes. My chest is still pounding, and I swallow, trying to steady myself. I lean in, kissing her slowly, holding onto this moment for a little longer.

I reach up, tucking a strand of hair behind her ear, my fingers brushing against her skin, unable to stop myself from savoring how soft she feels.

I know this is a mess. And I know if we're not careful, this will end in disaster. But as I look at her, I know I can't walk away from her.

There is not a fucking chance in hell this thing between us ends now.

TWENTY-TWO

Ryan

The first thing I feel when I wake up is sore.

The second thing? Smug as hell.

I stretch, then wince when a dull ache flares in my shoulder. It's been a few weeks since that hit, but it still sneaks up on me sometimes. Probably should've iced it last night.

Ah, well. I was doing something way more fun.

A grin tugs at my lips at the reminder as I sink deeper into my pillow, my muscles still heavy with sleep.

My mind plays a loop of the memories from last night. Her hands on me. The way her breath hitched when I kissed down her neck. The way her fingers curled against my back, pulling me closer. The way she tightened around me even when we were interrupted.

Heat creeps up my neck, my skin tingling with the ghost of her touch. I should probably feel guilty. Maybe a tiny part of me does. But mostly? It just felt too fucking good. Too right. Nothing has felt as right as being with Isabella has.

I run a hand over my face, groaning as I force myself to sit up, and glance around my room, my eyes adjusting to the morning light spilling in through the blinds. My clothes from last night are crumpled in the corner along with my shoes.

I scrub a hand through my hair, debating whether I have the energy to shower or if I can get away with just throwing on clean clothes and calling it a day.

Food first. Shower later.

I glance down, realizing I'm in nothing but my boxers. Not exactly an uncommon sight in this house. Logan walks around like this all the damn time, not a single ounce of shame in his body.

I push off the bed and head to my dresser, grabbing a pair of sweatpants and stepping into them, then pull a hoodie over my head. My stomach growls as the scent of bacon drifts under my door, and I take that as my cue to move.

The guy's voices get louder as I open my bedroom door and climb down the stairs.

When I walk into the kitchen, Nathan's at the stove, flipping bacon. Austin is leaning against the counter, scrolling through his phone, probably texting his latest situationship. And Logan's at the island, popping grapes into his mouth one by one, feet kicked up on the chair across from him.

Logan looks up first, a sly grin tugging at his lips. "Well, well, well. Look who finally decided to wake up."

I grunt in response, rubbing my shoulder as I step into the kitchen.

Austin smirks from his spot at the counter, glancing over his shoulder with a playful gleam in his eyes. "Yeah, what the hell, man? You never sleep in."

I reach for a mug from the cabinet, trying to keep my cool. Trying to act like nothing's out of the ordinary. Chill. Definitely not like a guy who spent last night with a girl he shouldn't have. "Needed the rest."

Nathan looks up as he plates up the bacon strips, his eyebrows arched. "Rest from what?"

I shrug and pour myself some coffee. "Just tired." I lift the mug to my lips. "Practice has been killing me."

Austin side-eyes me from across the room. "I thought you said your shoulder wasn't hurting anymore."

Shit. "It's not," I lie. "Just… you know coach. He's a beast."

Austin chuckles, grabbing a bacon strip from the plate and munching on it. "Oh, I fucking know. He made me skate fifty laps because I called his wife hot."

Nathan groans. "Are you fucking kidding me?"

"What?" Austin lifts a shoulder in a lazy shrug, a shit-eating grin plastered across his face. "Your mom's a MILF, Nathan. Embrace it." He winks.

Nathan groans, chucking a piece of toast at him.

I breathe out a laugh, shaking my head. Austin's got no filter, and he knows exactly how to press someone's buttons.

I let out a laugh, shaking my head, when Logan nudges my shoulder. "Where the hell did you go last night?" he asks. "We looked for you, but you just vanished."

Austin raises an eyebrow. "With Brenda again?"

I force a sip of my coffee, stalling as I try to come up with something that won't make me sound like a total idiot. "Nah, that's… over. I went home."

Austin snorts, his eyes flicking over to me with suspicion. "Alone?"

I meet his gaze squarely, my expression blank. "Yep."

Austin doesn't look convinced, his gaze narrowing. "Hmm. Okay."

I'm not really in the mood for an interrogation, I steal a piece of bacon off his plate, stuffing it into my mouth, hoping they'll drop it.

But Logan's still staring at me, his brows tugged together as he studies me. "You're acting different," he says, which makes me raise a brow.

"Different how?"

Logan gestures vaguely, his hand floating in the air like he's trying to find the right words. "I don't know. You're… smiling. A lot."

I wipe the grin off my face way too fast. "I'm not." *Am I?*

Logan squints, then his eyes widen, almost popping out of his head. "You got laid last night."

My hand jerks, nearly spilling my coffee as I choke on it. I cough hard, trying not to make a complete fool of myself. The hot liquid burns a line down my throat as I struggle to keep my face neutral. "What?"

Austin leans in, his usual smirk spreading wider. "Went home *alone*, did you?"

"The rook is spewing bullshit," I lie, rolling my eyes to try and mask the lie. "I didn't get laid last night."

God, I'm a terrible liar. My heart's pounding in my chest like it's trying to escape. I swear it's gonna blurt out the truth for me. But I can't let that happen.

"Bullshit," Austin says, crossing his arms over his chest, his brow arched. "Who was she?"

I grumble, grabbing a piece of bacon and stuffing it in my mouth like it'll somehow make them back off. But deep down, I know better than to think they will ever shut up.

Austin grins, shaking his head with a chuckle. "Look at him. She must be special if you're hiding her from us."

I roll my eyes, trying my best to act unaffected, though I can already feel the heat creeping up my neck. Before I can respond, my phone buzzes in my pocket, and I freeze the second I see the name on the screen.

Isabella:

You gave me a hickey!

I almost drop the phone trying to lock the screen, hoping the guys don't catch a glimpse.

"Was that her?" Logan asks, leaning in too close.

I shoot him a look and turn around, swiping her text open before typing a reply.

Me:

You gave me one last time.
Thought I'd return the favor.

Isabella:

Aurora noticed.

Me:

Yeah? What'd you tell her?

Isabella:

What do you think? I can't lie to her.

I have to wear a high neck top now.
There's no way I can cover up this bruise.

I feel the smirk tug at my lips before I can even stop it. I like knowing she has my mark on her.

A throat clears behind me, and I glance up to see Logan, his eyes gleaming with amusement. "Bro, you're smiling again."

I try to force the smile away, but it's no use. "Don't you guys have anything better to do?" I ask with an eye roll.

Austin scoffs, dropping his half-eaten bacon on his plate and giving me a once-over. "Nah, this is more interesting."

Nathan leans against the counter, his arms folded and a grin spreading across his face. "We'll find out who she is eventually," he says, which makes my gut churn.

Trust me. You don't want to know who she is.

I force my lips into a thin line and push the tension down as I brush past them. "I'm heading back upstairs. Need a shower."

Their laughter follows me as I climb the stairs.

Once I'm in my room, I slam the door shut behind me, throw myself on the bed, and grab my phone, knowing damn well I can't resist texting her back.

Me:

> It's not a bruise. It's proof.

I hit send, already leaning back against the headboard, kicking my feet up. I let out a breath, watching the text bubble pop up on the screen almost immediately.

Isabella:

> Proof of what?

I let out a chuckle, running my hand through my hair, thinking for a second before replying.

Me:

> That I was there.

I type another response, a playful grin sneaking onto my face.

Me:

Don't hide it. Let them see who's leaving their mark on you.

Isabella:

You're impossible.

Me:

But you like me anyway.

Isabella:

Yeah. I do.

I grin and I can't fight off. I've never had this much fun with a girl before, never wanted to be around someone like I do her. Never missed a girl like I do her.

Before I can second-guess myself, I call her.

When she picks up, her voice is breathy, clearly caught off guard. "Hey."

My stomach does this flip, and a grin I can't fight pulls at my lips. "Hi." I run a hand through my hair, nerves kicking in. "Sorry. I didn't mean to call, I just—" I hesitate, then huff out a laugh. "Actually, that's bullshit. I did. I wanted to hear your voice."

She laughs softly, and I can hear that smile in her voice. "I'm glad you did."

I lean back against the headboard, the phone pressed to my ear. "Yeah?" A smile spreads across my face. "I'm glad too."

For a second, neither of us says anything, and I exhale, rubbing a hand down my face. "Fuck, I wanna see you."

She lets out this amused little huff, and I can practically see her raising an eyebrow. "You saw me last night. Have you already forgotten?"

A low groan rumbles in my throat. "Oh, I haven't forgotten. I can't *stop* thinking about it."

There's some shuffling on her end, and then the call cuts.

I pull the phone away, staring at the black screen. "What the hell?"

Did she seriously hang up on me?

I'm still processing when a new notification pops up.

Incoming video call.

My pulse jumps, and I hit accept without thinking.

And then she's there.

Lying on her side, one arm tucked under her head, the other steadying her laptop. Her hair's messy, falling over her shoulder in soft waves. Her tank top's slipping just enough to make it hard to focus on anything else. There's a flash of toned stomach between the hem and a pair of sleep shorts that look more like underwear than actual clothing.

"Fuck, Isabella." My voice comes out rough as I rake a hand through my hair, already feeling way too hot for how far away she is.

She smirks. "Thought you wanted to see me."

"I did. I do. I just—fuck." I blow out a breath, dragging a hand down my face. "I just didn't expect you to show up looking like that."

Her eyes flicker with amusement as she glances down at her own chest, like she's just now noticing how the thin straps of her tank top barely hold her in. "What?" she asks innocently, batting her lashes. "Am I distracting you?"

I groan, letting my head fall back against the pillow. "You know exactly what you're doing to me." My fingers curl around my phone, grip tightening. "Fuck, I wish you were here. In my bed. With me."

Her laugh softens, and her lips pull into a smile that makes everything in my chest tighten.

"So," she says, tracing her fingers over her blanket, her teeth sinking into her bottom lip, "you wanna see me again?"

I sit up straighter, arching a brow. "Thought that was obvious."

She shrugs, like she's trying to play it cool, but there's a flicker of something in her eyes. "Last time you said it was a one-time thing and—"

"That was *before*." I cut her off. "Before I got to fucking taste you and then had to see you every day knowing I couldn't touch you again. Before last night."

Her breath catches, but she doesn't say anything. Just watches me.

I lean closer to the screen. "We're not done, Curls."

Her breath hitches. "No?"

I shake my head. "Not even close."

Her smile grows, slower this time.

I smirk, my eyes scanning her gorgeous face through the screen. "I can't stop thinking about you. It's a problem."

Something shifts in her expression. A flicker of heat in her gorgeous eyes. "What are you thinking about?" she asks, voice low, teasing… curious.

I let out a short laugh, shaking my head. "Thinking about how the hell you managed to turn my entire world upside down in one night."

She lets out a breath, arching a brow at me. "Not sure if I should be flattered… or worried you're about to ghost me."

I shake my head, firm. "I'm not going anywhere." Then I pause, because I owe her honesty. "But I meant what I said last night. I'm not looking for anything serious. Hockey's kind of my whole life right now, and I suck at juggling shit. I don't want to mess this up by pretending I've got it figured out."

She nods, not looking the least bit surprised. "I get it. You don't owe me anything. I'm not looking for anything crazy serious. I just want to… spend time with you. That's all."

I smile before I can stop myself. "Spending time with you sounds pretty damn good."

She smiles, tilting her head. "How's your body feeling?"

My lips twitch. "You mean after last night or after the game?"

She rolls her eyes, but her smile slips through anyway. "The game, idiot. You got rocked into the boards, Ryan. That kind of hit doesn't just disappear."

I shrug, leaning back into the headboard. "I'm fine."

She gives me a look. "Liar."

I sigh. "Alright, maybe I'm a little sore. But I'll survive." I shift, adjusting against the headboard. "Talked to my brother about it."

Her brows lift slightly. "Yeah?"

I nod. "I was just… so fucked up about what happened and—" I blow out a breath, fingers tightening around my phone. "I feel like I'm always trying to catch up with him, and the more I do, the more life throws me a fucking curveball and puts me ten places behind."

She's quiet for a second, then lets out a soft sigh. "Yeah. I know exactly what that feels like."

Her gaze drops to her hands, her thumbs brushing over the hem of her sleeve.

"I love Nathan," she says, lifting her eyes. "But sometimes… being his sister makes it harder to be taken seriously." She swallows, fingers still tugging at the fabric. "I've worked my ass off to get here, but it doesn't matter how hard I work. People look at my last name and assume I only made the cut because I have the right connections."

I frown. "Has anyone *said* that to you?"

She shakes her head, but there's a tension in the way she chews on her bottom lip. "No, I just… feel it. The stares. The looks of confusion. It's like I'm constantly trying to prove that I belong."

I lean forward a little, my brows tugging together. "You *do* belong."

She blinks, looking at me.

"I've seen you at practice, Bels. You've helped out the team a lot more than any of us have ever managed to do." I shrug, my voice rougher than I expected. "Fuck what they think. They're just pissed because you're better than them and they can't use their last name to justify being average."

Her lips tug into a small smile. "You're kind of hot when you go all motivational speech on me."

I chuckle. "Baby, I'm *always* hot," I tease, watching her roll her eyes. But her smile fades a little, her gaze shifting.

She sighs, looking down at her hands. "I just wish people saw me. Not just Nathan's little sister."

Her words hit harder than I expect. I want to tell her that I see her. I see her all the fucking time, even when I close my eyes, she's the only one I see. Whenever she's around me, it's like the whole damn world fades away, including her brother. I don't think about Nathan when I see her. I don't think about any of the noise. I only see her.

But the words get stuck in my throat. Instead, I sigh, the truth spilling out before I can stop it.

"Yeah. Same here." I rake a hand through my hair, trying to shake off the tightness in my chest. "People already compare me to my brother every chance they get, and I just know it's gonna get ten times worse when I join the NFL." I scoff. "If I even make it, that is."

Her eyes snap to mine, narrowing in disbelief. "Are you serious right now?" She shakes her head like I'm crazy. "Ryan, you're amazing. I have zero doubt you'll make it into the NFL. And no one's gonna compare you to your brother."

I let out a bitter scoff. "You dream big."

Her face softens, and for a second, I'm frozen. Her eyes—those dark, beautiful eyes—are locking onto mine with an intensity that has me second-guessing every thought in my head. All I want is to reach through the screen and kiss her.

"I'm serious," she says, her voice steady. It's that certainty that hits me hardest. "You're not just Connor Reed's little brother. You're *you*. You'll make your own name. You just have to believe that."

"You really think that?" I ask her.

"Yeah, I do," she replies with a nod. No hesitation. Just confidence. Like it's the easiest thing in the world.

I can't help the laugh that escapes me. "I could listen to you talk about me all day."

She rolls her eyes, but the smirk that's tugging at her lips tells a different story. "You're such an idiot."

I hum, stretching my arms over my head, grinning. "You weren't calling me an idiot last night," I tease, feeling way too smug about it.

Her cheeks go pink, and I can't help but grin even wider. "I love talking to you," I tell her, feeling my chest crack open at the sight of her.

She exhales softly, her smile lighting up the screen. It's so goddamn pretty, I almost forget how to breathe. "Me too."

God, I miss her. Is it possible to miss someone this much? Because I do. I don't care what we do—I just want her here. Beside me. Kissing me. Touching me. Talking to me. Just here.

She stretches her arms above her head, her tank top riding up slightly, revealing a sliver of smooth skin. And fuck, it doesn't help. I'm already craving her, and now all I can do is stare like an idiot and imagine what it'd be like if she were in my bed instead of on my screen.

"I swear, if I have to write one more paper on sports analytics, my brain is going to shut down."

I chuckle, leaning back against my pillows, trying to act casual while every part of me wants to reach through the screen and pull her into me. "Didn't you choose to be a sports major?"

She groans, rolling onto her stomach and burying her face in the pillow. "Don't remind me. I have a paper due tomorrow, and I should be working on it instead of talking to you."

I hate how much I don't like that answer. I'm not the kind of guy who sits on calls. I don't do long convos or late-night talking—never have. Usually, I'm counting down the seconds until I can hang up.

But with her? I don't want this to end. I don't want the screen to go dark.

I shouldn't feel this way. I don't get attached. I don't get needy.

But then again, no one's ever been Isabella.

"Lay it on me," I say, nodding toward the screen. "Tell me what you need help with, baby."

Her lips curve into the prettiest, softest smile. "Won't you get bored?"

I let out a scoff. "You could read the dictionary out loud and I'd still be hanging onto every word."

She chuckles, cheeks pink, and I don't even think she realizes she's blushing. "You're such a sap."

I shoot her a lazy grin. "And you'd rather talk to me."

"Not even close."

I laugh, scrubbing a hand through my hair. "Don't lie to me. Just admit it. I'm way more interesting than your assignment."

She sighs, fighting a smirk as she swings an arm over her face. "Fine. Maybe."

"There it is." I lean back, hands laced behind my head. "That's all I needed to hear, gorgeous."

She peeks at me from under her arm, a small smile tugging at her lips. Then something shifts in her expression. Her smile drops and she lets out a low sigh, shaking her head.

"I just… I want to walk into a room and have people know I earned my place there."

"You will," I say, with no hesitation. "I don't have an ounce of doubt in you."

Her gaze flicks to mine, a little uncertain. "You really think so?"

Of course you can, Bels. You're basically a pro already. Smart, confident, and you handle cocky athletes like it's nothing, even the giant pain-in-the-ass kind."

She lets out a chuckle. "Like you?"

I smirk, shooting her a wink. "Exactly like me."

She goes quiet for a beat, then says, soft and a little shy, "Thank you."

I exhale, head tipping back against the wall, a grin tugging at my lips. "Anytime, baby."

Her cheeks flush, and she tries to hide it with a sigh. "Okay, seriously. I need to go."

"Tragic," I say, dramatically clutching my chest. "Abandoning me in my time of need."

She rolls her eyes, but her smile stays. "Later, Reed."

"Later, Curls," I say, just before the screen goes dark.

I drop my phone onto the mattress and stare up at the ceiling for a second, trying to remember what the hell I was supposed to be doing before she called.

Food. Shower. Pretend to be productive.

But all I can think about is how I already want to see her again.

I don't even realize I'm grinning like an idiot until my cheeks start to ache. I rub a hand down my face, then roll out of bed and head for the shower.

I was so damn hesitant about starting something with her when I knew she was a relationship girl through and through.

But we're on the same page.

We're having fun.

A friends-with-benefits arrangement with the hottest girl I know?

Yeah. I'd be an idiot not to enjoy every second of it.

TWENTY-THREE

Isabella

Sports management has always been a boys' club.

Not officially, of course. If you look at the course catalog, the brochures, the university website, they'll all tell you that it's an open field, a career path for anyone passionate about athletics, business, and strategy. But sit in a classroom like this, surrounded by guys who don't think twice before dismissing you, and it becomes painfully clear that isn't the case.

I try not to let it get to me as I take my seat in the small, cramped group of desks shoved together at the back of the classroom. The professor just finished explaining our first major project of the semester—developing a team strategy for a hypothetical sports franchise. The goal is to take everything we've learned so far—roster management, player statistics, financial planning—and create a game plan that makes sense for our assigned team.

I should be excited. This is the kind of thing I love, the kind of work I actually want to do in the future. But as I glance around at the four guys I've been grouped with, I already know I'm going to have to work twice as hard just to be heard.

None of them look at me as I sit down. Two are on their phones. One is doodling in the margins of his notebook. The last one, a guy with a buzz cut and a smug expression, leans back in his chair like he's already decided this whole project is beneath him.

Great.

I clear my throat. "So, should we start by assigning roles?"

That gets their attention. Kind of. The guy closest to me—blue eyes, athletic build—raises an eyebrow. "We don't even know what sport we're working with yet."

"Right, but the professor said we should think about the key elements of team strategy first. What makes a team successful, what their biggest challenges are—"

Buzz Cut smirks. "Damn, you're really into this, huh?"

I resist the urge to roll my eyes. "Well, yeah. That's kind of the point of taking the class."

The blond guy finally looks up. "Aren't you the girl that works with the hockey team?"

"Yeah, I—"

He scoffs, cutting me off. "So, you, what, hand out water bottles?"

I freeze for a second, my brows dipping. "What?"

His lips twitch like he's fighting a smile. "Or, like, pick out the jersey colors? That's cute."

Buzz Cut chuckles, shaking his head. The other guy snickers under his breath. The only one who doesn't laugh is the dark-haired guy across from me, but he doesn't bother to correct them, either.

I grip my pen tighter, my nails pressing into my palm. I shouldn't be surprised. This isn't the first time someone's dismissed my job like it's nothing more than a hobby. But that doesn't make it any less frustrating.

"Actually," I say, keeping my tone even, "I track game stats, help with scheduling, and sit in on meetings. But yeah, let's go with 'picking jersey colors.'"

There's a beat of silence. Then the blond guy lets out a low whistle. "Damn, alright," he says, before going back to his phone, like that's the end of the conversation.

Buzzcut chuckles, his eyes flicking over me. "That's nice and all," he says, leaning forward, "but come on. No offense, but this isn't really your place."

I blink, thrown off by how casually he says it, like it's just a fact. "Excuse me?"

"I mean, you're obviously smart, but you really think a pro-team is gonna listen to a girl when it comes to strategy?" he asks. "Name one female GM in the NHL."

I stare at him for a long second, debating whether or not I should even waste my breath. Then I inhale slowly, setting my pen down.

"Ava Caldwell," I say, meeting his gaze without flinching. "Assistant GM of the Seattle Storm. Maya Kincaid, the league's first female scout. Riley St. Clair, senior director of player development for the Chicago Phantoms. Want me to keep going?"

The corner of his mouth twitches like he's about to argue, but I don't give him the chance.

"Just because there aren't many doesn't mean there won't be," I say, leaning back in my chair. "You're acting like sports is a 'boys-only' club. Hate to break it to you, but it's not. Are any of you actually working with a sports team right now?" I glance at them, waiting for an answer. Of course, there's none.

The blond guy looks up from his phone, arching an eyebrow. "Let's be real. You only got that job because of your dad."

The air in my lungs turns razor-sharp, but I don't flinch. I've seen the looks. Felt the judgment every time I walk into a room. I knew they were thinking it.

But hearing it out loud? It makes my stomach churn, knowing all of my suspicions were true.

"It's not like they're actually listening to you," he continues. *You do belong.*

Ryan's voice cuts through the noise in my head, steady and sure. I breathe it in. Let it anchor me.

Because I know how this works. I know what they see when I walk in—my last name, my brother, my dad. Not the hours I've put in. Not the late nights or the early mornings or the fact that I've had to be twice as prepared, twice as sharp, just to get a seat at the damn table.

But I'm not here to make them comfortable. I didn't work my ass off to be quiet and grateful and small.

They can underestimate me.

They can doubt me.

But I'm not going anywhere. I didn't work my ass off to sit here and shrink and let them take over.

I lean forward, resting my elbows on the desk, eyes locked on his, daring him to keep talking. "You ever sat in on a game strategy meeting?"

Silence.

"Ever gone through a player's stat sheet, helped make a call on whether they should be in the starting lineup?"

Nothing.

I nod slowly, watching his face redden. "That's what I thought. See, while you were busy acting like this industry belongs to you, I was actually working. Learning. Earning my spot. So, tell me. If I don't belong here, why am I already doing the job you're sitting in this class hoping to get?"

His face flushes deeper.

I let the silence stretch before leaning back, crossing my arms. "Now, are we actually gonna work on this project, or are you gonna keep proving me right?"

The professor, who's been circling the room, must have overheard the conversation, because suddenly, he's standing next to our group. "Something I need to step in for?"

Buzz Cut clears his throat, shaking his head. "Nope."

The professor glances around the table before settling his gaze on the guys. "Sports management is about skill, not gender. If you think otherwise, you're in the wrong field."

I glance at the guys before adding, "And for the record, I don't need any of you to believe in me. I know what I'm worth."

The room goes quiet. And for the first time since I stepped into this class, I'm looking forward to proving them wrong.

TWENTY-FOUR

Ryan

The steam from the shower still clings to the air as I step out, towel wrapped around my waist. I wipe my face, rubbing my hands through my wet hair, and toss the towel onto my bed. The bathroom mirror fogs up as I grab my phone from the counter, checking the time—just after eight.

My brain's still a little mush from my psychology class earlier. Some days, balancing hockey and school feels like a lot, but I'm still glad I took this path instead of following my brother.

Downstairs, the guys are probably already hyped up for the game. Austin's probably bouncing around, yelling at the TV, since it's his favorite team playing tonight. Normally, I'd be right there with them, ready for a night of noise, snacks, and shit-talking. But honestly? I'm way more interested in something—or rather, someone—else right now.

I swipe open my phone and text Isabella.

Me:

You up?

I lean against the bathroom sink, waiting for the little bubbles to pop up. A few seconds later, my phone buzzes.

Isabella:

> It's eight. Of course I'm up.

I chuckle, that familiar smart-ass tone of hers making me grin.

Me:

> I miss you. And that smart mouth of yours.

Isabella:

> You're trouble…

Me:

> If by trouble you mean the best time ever, then yeah, I am trouble.

I can't help it. A stupid, goofy grin spreads across my face. My phone buzzes again. I grin even wider. I can practically hear her rolling her eyes at me. I feel my phone vibrate again and quickly glance at it.

Isabella:

> You're ridiculous. But I'll admit, I kind of miss you too.

My chest does this stupid flutter and my smile widens. Yeah, I like hearing that from her. A lot. I've never been a guy who craves attention or affection, but from her? It's different. I want it. All the time.

Me:

> So… what are you doing? Besides missing me, obviously.

I could be down there with the guys, but honestly, nothing sounds better than just talking to her. I know they'll be fine without me. Hell, I'm usually the one who bails on them.

Isabella:

> Trying to finish some stupid assignment for tomorrow. But it's not happening.

Me:

> So what you're saying is, I should come over and help you procrastinate?

I smirk, imagining her sitting at her desk, probably with a cup of coffee or something. She's so driven, but I know she doesn't mind putting things off for the right distraction. I could be that distraction.

Isabella:

> Did you forget I have a roommate?

I groan out loud, dragging a hand down my face as I head into my bedroom, and throw on a t-shirt and some shorts.

Fuck, I knew it was a long shot, but… I just want to see her. But since she lives with a roommate, that isn't an option. Not to mention I'm surrounded by guys—Logan, Austin… and her brother. It's like the universe conspired to keep me and Isabella in a constant state of sexual frustration.

Less time alone. Less touching. Less of her.

More of me slowly losing my damn mind.

Me:

> You're killing me, Curls.

Isabella:

You'll survive.

Will I, though? Because I swear, if I don't see her soon, I might actually lose it. Every time she texts me, I want more. Every time I hear her voice, I miss her harder. It's becoming a serious problem I don't know how to deal with.

Me:

I don't think I will. Need you.

There's a pause. Long enough to make me question if I came on too strong. But then—

Isabella:

Yeah?

My mouth curves into a slow, crooked grin as I type out a reply, my fingers moving fast.

Me:

So fucking bad.

Isabella:

Me too.

Fuck. My heart kicks like I just hit the winning shot in overtime. I stare at those words, that little admission, and my pulse takes off.

She needs me too.

Me:

Come over then. My place.

I don't expect her to actually say yes—but I send it anyway, hoping.

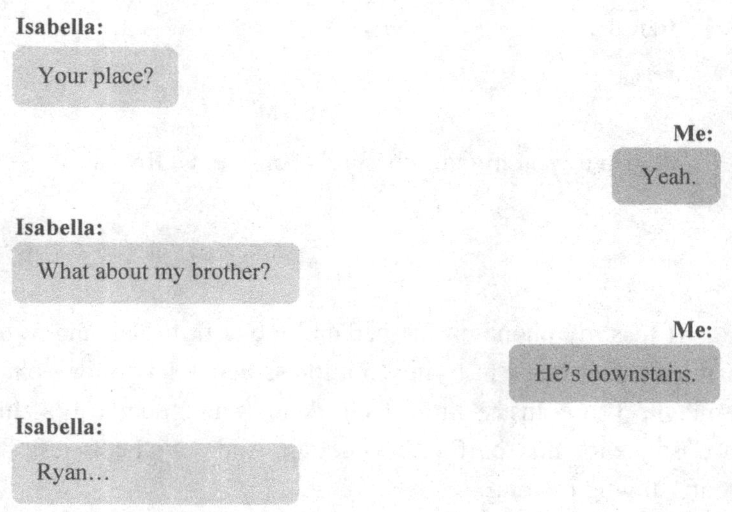

I can hear the warning in her voice, the hesitation. It only makes me want her more. I can't stand the thought of waiting any longer.

Me:

I'll sneak you in.

Because I'm not spending another night without her when I could be holding her in my arms instead.

I know I'm taking risks. Big risks that could come and bite me in the ass if we get caught. But damn, I'm enjoying the reward.

Another pause. Long enough to make me shift in place, my fingers drumming against my thigh, trying to tap the nerves away. She's hesitating. I can feel it through the silence. Drawing it out just to torture me—has to be.

Then finally, my phone lights up.

Isabella:

> Fine.

A grin tugs at my mouth. She's coming. Hell yeah.

Me:

> Meet me at the back entrance.

I toss my phone on the bed and move fast, glancing at the mirror. Not that I'm trying to impress her or anything—okay, maybe I am. Just a little. I check my shirt, decide it's fine. Casual enough. Comfortable enough. And, let's be honest, it's not staying on long.

My phone buzzes ten minutes later, pulling me out of my thoughts as I try to clean my room up a little.

Isabella:

> I'm here.

I don't even try to fight the grin spreading across my face.

I slip out of my room, heading down the stairs as quiet as I can. The guys are all in the living room, yelling at the screen. Austin's fully invested, so the volume's basically maxed out. They're too locked in to notice me slip past.

Perfect.

I head for the back door and crack it open.

There she is.

Hood up. Arms crossed. Looking like the best and worst decision I'll ever make.

"Took you long enough," she says, one brow raised.

I lean against the doorframe, shooting her a smile. "Had to make myself look good for you."

She rolls her eyes, but there's the ghost of a smile playing on her lips. "Didn't work."

I clutch my chest, mock wounded. "Ouch. Really? After all that effort?"

She steps into the doorway, brushing past me with a smirk. "You should've tried harder."

God, I love how she teases me.

I attempt to close the door quietly. Naturally, I do the exact opposite—clearing my throat louder than I mean to as I ease it shut.

The sound echoes way too much down the hall.

Shit.

I wince, and sure enough, she whirls on me with a look that could scorch drywall.

"Really?" she hisses. "That was the *loudest* way to close a door."

I can't help the grin spreading across my face as I shake my head. "Sorry. My brain isn't working right now. Not when you're here, wearing that."

I glance down at the oversized hoodie barely covering those denim shorts clinging to her legs. It doesn't make any sense. It shouldn't be so fucking hot. But somehow she makes it look illegal.

She rolls her eyes, like she's immune to my flirting, but the pink creeping into her cheeks says otherwise.

I nudge her forward, my hand sliding into hers. "Come on," I murmur, keeping my voice low. "Before someone actually notices."

We slip past the living room, and Isabella tiptoes up the stairs ahead of me, hoodie riding up just slightly, and yeah, I'm definitely not looking away.

I stifle a groan as my eyes land on her ass in those denim shorts, dying to get my hands on her.

We reach my room, and I swing the door open, letting her in first. She walks past me, and I step in behind her, easing the door shut until it clicks.

Quiet this time. Lesson learned.

"That was a little too easy," she says, arching a brow at me.

I lean back against the door, letting my eyes drag over her slowly—the way the hoodie lifts a little when she crosses her arms, how those shorts sit on her hips. Want her so bad. Goddamn.

"Almost like I know what I'm doing," I reply with a smirk.

She shoots me a look. "So… I'm not the first girl you've snuck in?"

I push off the door and close the space between us, watching the way her gaze flickers from my face to my chest like she can't decide where to land. "Would it make you feel better if I said no?" I tease.

She doesn't like the idea. I can tell. And honestly? I don't blame her. If some other guy was sneaking into her room, I'd lose my damn mind.

Her eyes narrow, her arms still pressed against her chest. "It'd make you an asshole."

I laugh under my breath. "Well, lucky for you," I murmur, "I haven't snuck anyone in before."

I mean it. I don't bring girls back here. This is my space. My room. My bed. But with her? All that went straight out the window. I want her here more than I want anything.

She doesn't say anything right away, just studies me. Then her expression softens, and she lets out a short breath. "Good," she finally says.

Before I can move in again, her eyes drift to the shelf beside my bed, and she tilts her head. "Are those old video games?"

I glance over. "Yeah."

She steps closer, crouching slightly as she reads the spines of the DVD cases. "Oh my god. Is that the original Mario Kart?"

A grin pulls at my lips as I walk over to stand behind her. "Yep. Mario Kart 64. Still works, too," I tell her. "The Graphics are shit, but I grew up playing this with my brother."

She looks up at me, arching a brow. "You like the old ones better, huh?"

"Hell yeah," I say with a chuckle. "Nothing beats the classics."

"I love this game," she murmurs, running her fingers over the cartridge. "I used to wreck my brother," she replies, her lips turning up into a smile. "He'd storm off every time I hit him with a red shell."

I shake my head, a laugh bubbling out of me. "You're telling me you're a sore winner?"

She smirks, turning those gorgeous eyes on me. "I'm telling you I'm undefeated."

I raise a brow, stepping closer again. "Dangerous words."

"Prove me wrong."

"I might have to," I murmur, stepping in closer, backing her toward the bed, my smirk tugging at the corners of my mouth.

My fingers slide under the hem of her sweatshirt, brushing warm skin. Fuck, I've missed this.

"Did you miss me?" I ask.

Her eyes find mine, that playful spark lighting them up. "No."

I lean in closer, letting my breath fan across her cheek, my grin widening. "Liar."

She rolls her eyes but doesn't move away. "I saw you two days ago," she says.

I scoff, letting my fingers skim along her waist. "Exactly. That's way too long." I tighten my hold on her hips, pulling her closer. "Come on, Bels, just admit it. You missed this."

She lifts her chin, mouth tugging into a smirk. "If I say yes, will you stop being so smug?"

I laugh, shaking my head slightly. "Probably not." I lean in closer, lips hovering just above hers, teasing her. "Say it, baby. Tell me you missed me. We both know you did."

She doesn't reply for a second, just keeps those eyes on me, before grabbing my shirt, hard, and yanking me into a kiss that shuts me up instantly.

I groan into her mouth, my hands gripping her waist as she melts into me. She's warm and soft and so fucking addictive, and I'm already forgetting how to think straight. I want to savor this and take my time. But all I can think is that I need her closer. I deepen the kiss, my body running on instinct, chasing more of her.

God, I'm never going to get tired of this. Kissing Isabella is like nothing I have ever felt. It messes with my head in the best way and makes my heart slam against my ribs, like she's rewriting every damn part of me to erase every other person out of my mind and shaping me to fit perfectly with her.

Her fingers slide into my hair, her nails slightly grazing my scalp in that slow, dangerous way she knows drives me crazy.

It's not just a kiss—it's her staking a claim, and shit, I might just let her.

My hands trail under her sweatshirt, feeling her soft, warm skin, groaning as I continue to lift it higher and higher. She raises her arms, letting me pull it over her head in one smooth motion. The second it's gone, my hands are on her, fingers tracing the curve of her waist, up to the soft swell of her chest.

A knock hits the door.

We freeze.

Isabella's eyes fly wide, her breath catching against my mouth. "You said they wouldn't notice," she whispers.

I press a finger to her lips, listening.

"Ryan?" It's Logan. "Game's started, man. Are you coming down?"

I clear my throat, trying to get rid of the raspiness in my voice. "No, I'm… a little tired. I'm gonna crash."

"Alright, goodnight," he replies before heading back downstairs.

The second we're in the clear, Isabella arches a brow. "You suck at sneaking me in. Next time, I'm picking the place."

I smirk, cocking a brow. "So, there's gonna be a next time?"

She rolls her eyes, but the corner of her mouth twitches, and I know I've got her.

I chuckle against her lips as I push her down onto my bed, capturing her mouth with mine. She melts into me instantly, her fingers slipping under my shirt. My entire body tightens at the sensation, the warmth of her touch, the way she moves beneath me.

I shift, pressing into her just enough for her to feel what she's doing to me, and she exhales a soft sound that sends a sharp bolt of heat through my veins.

Her hands curl into my shirt, fisting the fabric. I reach for her denim shorts and pop the button. She kicks them off, along with her shoes.

"Don't stop," she breathes, her fingers tugging at my belt.

I groan when her knuckles brush over the bulge straining my sweatpants. I help her out, kicking them off fast, my boxers going with them, and my cock springs free—thick, already leaking, aching for her.

She stares for a second, her lips parted, and I swear her breath stutters.

"You sure you're ready for all this?" I murmur, voice low as I stroke myself, watching her throat moving as she swallows.

Her hand flattens against my chest, pushing me back onto the bed, and a second later she's on me, straddling my thighs.

I can't help but grin, my hands sliding up her smooth legs, dragging her even closer. "You look good up there, Bels."

My chuckle dies in my throat when she moves above me, rolling her hips in a slow, torturous grind that has me instantly hard.

Fuck.

My fingers dig into her waist, pulling her down against me, making sure she feels every inch of my hard cock against the seam of her panties. "Ah fuck," I moan, tipping my head back.

She moves again. Grinding slowly against my hardening cock, which sends a sharp jolt of heat straight through me.

I groan, already impatient. I want to take my time, to tease her, to pull those breathless little gasps from her lips—but then she moves against me again, her body pressing flush to mine, and I can't fucking take it anymore.

I need her out of these clothes. Now.

Her hands slide up under my shirt. I sit up, let her yank it off, toss it wherever, and I reach behind her, fingers finding the clasp of that tiny black bra. One flick—gone, and I groan out loud the second I see her bare. Prettiest tits I've ever seen. Perfect handfuls, nipples hard and flushed, begging for mouth.

I capture her mouth in another kiss, my tongue sliding against hers, while I rub her taut, perky nipples with my thumb.

She pulls back just slightly, breathless, but arches her brow. "That's the best you've got?"

A smirk breaks out onto my face. She wants to play? Let's fucking play.

I lean in to brush my lips against hers. "Trust me," I murmur. "You'll be begging for more in a minute."

She doesn't have time to react before I grip her waist, flipping us so she's underneath me once again. She gasps, but it quickly melts into a laugh as her fingers curl in my shirt.

"Competitive, are we?" she teases.

I smirk, dipping my head until my lips graze the sharp line of her jaw. "Only when there's something worth winning."

I let my eyes drop down her body, taking in the black panties she's wearing. I pause for a beat, looking down at her with a grin.

"I've always been a fan of black."

She chuckles, shaking her head. "Are you going to change your favorite color every time?"

I shrug, sliding a hand over the curve of her hip, fingertips brushing the fabric of her panties. "Guess I'm just a sucker for whatever you're wearing."

I let my fingers drift lower, tracing the heat beneath the thin fabric, and a soft moan slips past her lips.

"Fuck, look at you. You're soaked." I hook the lace of her soaked panties to the side, baring her soft, swollen pussy to the air. She's spread open under me, legs bent, pussy bare, glistening in the dim light.

My cock throbs hard at the sight.

I slide my fingers through her, dragging through all that slick heat until they shine with her mess, then push them inside her.

Her body shudders, her nails digging into my shoulders. And the little, choked whimper she lets out might be the hottest thing I've ever heard.

"You like that?" I whisper against her ear, my teeth nipping at her earlobe. I curl my fingers inside, rubbing slowly along that spot that makes her thighs try to close around my wrist. "Tell me how bad you need me."

She shudders. Her breath falters.

"S-so bad…"

I press my thumb to her clit and rub harder, faster, until she's gasping, her hands gripping my wrist like she can't decide if she wants to stop me or make me keep going.

I tug her drenched panties off with a smooth drag down those perfect legs, toss them, and spread her open with both hands. My mouth actually waters.

Fuck me.

Her pussy's glistening, flushed, lips soft and swollen, glinting in the low light like she's already been edged for hours. I groan under my breath, dragging my thumb slow through the slick mess coating her slit.

So fucking pretty.

I lean in, plant a kiss low on her stomach and she sucks in a sharp breath, and I can't help the smirk that creeps across my face.

"Fuck, look at this pussy," I groan, spreading her open wider with both hands. "Dripping all over my sheets." I lick my lips, dying for a taste. "You want my mouth, baby? Want me to tongue-fuck this tight little cunt until you're begging me to stop?"

She gasps, her breath hitching in her throat.

I smirk, dragging my mouth just close enough that she twitches. "Say it. Tell me you want me to eat you like the filthy little slut you are. Say you want my tongue buried in this sweet, soaking pussy."

Her whole body trembles.

"Be a good girl," I murmur. "Open those legs and tell me how bad you want me to make you come with just my mouth."

Her hips roll, needy, that soaked, glistening pussy throbbing under my breath. "I want your mouth," she whispers, a soft whimper leaving her lips. "I want your tongue on my pussy. Right now. Please, Ryan."

I groan, the sound vibrating against her thighs. "Yeah? you want me to suck that pretty clit until you're shaking?"

"Yes," she breathes. "I want it. I need it. Please, Ryan. Fuck. Just give me your tongue."

I trail soft kisses down her body. On her belly, the crease of her thigh, down the inside, right where her skin gets hot and sensitive. She shivers, a soft whimper caught in her throat when I blow a warm breath over her soaked pussy. My hands slide under her thighs and spread her wider.

Then I finally give her what she wants.

My tongue flicks up her slit, and her entire body jerks. I groan into her heat, flicking my tongue over her clit, hearing her choke on a moan.

Fuck, she tastes sweet.

She fists the sheets, her legs twitching, back arching up off the mattress as I suck her clit into my mouth and circle my tongue over it.

"F-fuck, Ryan—oh god—"

I dip my tongue down, fuck into her with it while my nose nudges her clit, and she cries out, trying to close her thighs around my head. I don't let her. I grip her hips tight, pin her to the bed, and keep going. Fast, wet licks, open-mouthed kisses, sucking that swollen little bud until she's practically vibrating in my hands.

"You gonna come, baby?" I murmur against her, every word vibrating through her core. "Come on my tongue. Let me taste it."

She jerks, her whole body seizing. She cries out, her nails clawing into the sheets and hips grinding against my mouth.

"You taste so good," I groan, licking up every drop of slick leaking out of her ruined, twitching pussy. "Could stay down here all night."

My hands spread her open wider, holding her still while I feast, groaning into her pussy until she twitches.

I pull back just enough to look up at her—panting, glassy-eyed, a total wreck already.

"Too much?" I ask, voice thick, lips shining with her.

She shakes her head fast, biting her lip. Her thighs are shaking, but she doesn't want me to stop.

Good.

Because I'm just getting started.

I grin against her skin and flip her onto her stomach in one move.

She gasps when she lands on her stomach, panting, her hair a mess across her back.

"On your knees, baby," I tell her, smacking her ass, watching it ripple and turn the cutest shade of pink. "Face the headboard."

She hesitates, for half a second. Then she shifts up, her elbows digging into the mattress, back arched, ass in the air, looking like every one of my dirty dreams.

I grab her hips, my thumbs pressing into those dimples at the base of her spine, and just watch her for a second. I smack her ass again, the sharp sound filling the room as she moans, pushing back into my hand.

"You know what this pussy needs?" I murmur, dragging the tip of my cock through her. "It needs to be fucked. Needs to be filled, doesn't it?"

She whines, nodding frantically, arching her back even more, pushing her hips back into me.

"Patience, baby," I mutter, reaching into the drawer beside my bed. I rip open the foil with my teeth, roll the condom on quick, and stroke my length once, twice. Then I'm crawling back over her, lining up at her entrance, the head of my dick pressing just barely against her tight, dripping hole.

I push in slowly, and holy shit, she's tight. So warm, so wet, squeezing around me like her body's trying to memorize mine. She gasps, her fingers gripping the sheets, and I grip her hips harder to keep myself grounded.

"Fuuuck," I groan, buried halfway. Her pussy is gripping me so good, I have to stop, breathe, hold myself from pounding into her like I want to. I lean over her back and kiss her shoulder. "You feel so fucking good, baby," I whisper against her skin. "So goddamn tight."

She moans, rocking her hips back, taking me deeper. Her lips part on a soft, broken sound when I bottom out.

I grip her hips and pull every inch out before slamming back in. Her body jolts, her tits bouncing under her. She whimpers, fisting the sheets, hard. Her ass hits my hips with a wet slap with every thrust.

I'm fucking lost in her. Drowning in the way she takes me so deep I forget my own name. The way her body wraps around my cock like it belongs to her, like she's the one fucking me with every needy roll of her hips.

"Ryan," she moans, breathless. It makes my heart pound in my chest. Fucking love hearing her moan my name. Like I'm the only man that's ever touched her. Like I'm the only one who ever will.

And fuck me, I want to hear her scream it.

I slam into her with one smooth, brutal stroke, hilting deep, her gasp swallowed by the echo of skin on skin. She clenches around me, tight as a goddamn fist, and my control's hanging by a fucking thread.

"Fuck, you feel so good," I groan, my eyes rolling to the back of my head.

She lets out a loud, needy moan—too loud—and my hand is on her mouth instantly.

"Shh, baby," I murmur low into her ear, breath hot against her skin. "You need to be quiet."

As much as I want her to scream my name, we both know if the guys heard her, we'd be in deep shit.

She whimpers against my palm, her hips still trying to move even though I've got her pinned. I drive into her again, slow but hard, and she moans into my hand, muffled and filthy and desperate.

"That's it," I groan, my voice rough. "Be good for me. Be quiet, and I'll give you my cock. I'll fuck you so hard you forget your own name. But you gotta earn it. Can you do that, huh? Can you keep those pretty sounds inside?"

She nods. But she can't stay silent. Not with the way I'm fucking her. Her thighs start shaking again, and her muffled cries only get louder, her body straining against my grip. My hand presses tighter over her mouth, her moans breaking into these wrecked little sounds that I feel all the way through me.

"Such a good girl for me," I murmur, my voice breaking as I thrust harder, grinding deep on every stroke. "Take it. You can take it."

She's so close. I can feel it. I let go of her mouth, and the noises she makes sends shivers down my spine.

"I need more," she gasps, her voice trembling as she glances at me over her shoulder, her hair stuck to her cheek. "Please—"

I freeze, my breath ragged as I look down at her. A slow, wicked grin spreads across my face when it finally clicks.

"Oh, baby." I pull out slowly, savoring the slick glide as she tries to hold onto me, and ignore the needy noise she makes as I reach for the nightstand. "You just had to ask."

My fingers wrap around exactly what I need. The second I turn on my massage gun, the low hum vibrates through the air.

Her eyes widen. "Ryan—"

I press it to her clit and she jerks, her body lifting off the bed.

"Fuck—fuck—oh god—"

Her legs shake, knees slipping on the sheets, fingers clawing at the mattress. I keep one hand on her hip, the other holding the makeshift vibrator right where she needs it.

She's sobbing, moaning uncontrollably, her voice breaking. "I need—"

I slide back inside her.

"Ahh—oh fuck, fuck, fuck—" Her gasps turn to sobbing moans.

Her whole body seizes, trembles, shakes against me, and I can feel the flood of her release gush around my cock—soaking me, soaking the sheets, leaking down her thighs.

She lets out broken whimpers, her face buried in the sheets. "R-Ryan—oh god—"

"Fuck, Isabella—" I groan, grabbing her hips and pounding into her once, twice, and then I'm gone. The orgasm slams into me, and I come deep inside her, my entire body shuddering as I spill into her.

I keep rocking into her through it, slowly, groaning every time a rush of pleasure curls up my spine.

I kiss her neck. Her shoulder. Trail my lips up to her mouth and kiss her slow, messy, breathless.

"You still alive?" I ask against her lips.

She lets out a broken laugh. "Barely."

I chuckle, kissing her again. Fuck, I can't get enough of this girl.

I finally pull out of her, both of us groaning as I do and roll to my side, holding her against me. She's dazed, her eyes half-lidded, lips red and swollen, and her thighs slick, pussy stretched and full.

She looks wrecked.

And so fucking beautiful it hurts.

For a moment, neither of us moves. We just lie there, tangled up in each other, our hearts still racing.

I chuckle, tossing the massage gun aside. "That good, huh?"

She lets out a weak, breathy laugh. "You're… a genius."

I smirk, pulling her in closer. "Told you I'd have you begging for more."

A satisfied hum slips from her lips, her fingers tracing lazy shapes along my skin.

Yeah. I'm completely fucking ruined for her.

My eyes drift shut, the tension in my body starting to ease, but then she shifts, lifting off the bed. My brows pull together as she reaches for her clothes.

I shoot out a hand, my fingers curling around her wrist, stopping her. "Where are you going?"

She glances back at me, brows drawn. "I have to go, Ryan."

"No, you don't." I tug her toward me. No way in hell I'm letting her leave.

She laughs, breathless. "Oh yeah?" Her smile wavers slightly, tension slipping back into her face. "What about the guys?"

I lean over her, bracing myself on either side of her head, caging her in. "They don't come in here," I murmur, dropping my lips to her ear. "Which means I get to keep you all to myself."

Her eyes meet mine, lighting up. Fuck, they're so pretty. "You want me to stay?"

"Hell yeah, I do." I brush my mouth against hers. "You're mine for the night."

She pretends to consider it, but I already know she's not leaving. "Fine," she says, rolling her eyes. "But if you snore, I'm kicking you."

I let out a scoff. "I don't snore. I'm a fucking gentleman."

"We'll see about that," she mutters, scrunching her nose in that way that makes me want to kiss her stupid.

"Shut up and let me hold you," I whisper, pulling her against me. She fits perfectly, like her body was made for mine. Warm, soft… perfect.

My arm drapes over her waist, my fingers drawing lazy circles on her hip. She shifts, her leg hooking over mine, and it settles me in a way I didn't know I needed, or even wanted.

"I like this," I mumble feeling more comfortable than I have in a while.

She shifts, her lips curling into a smirk. "Me being naked in your bed?" she teases.

I laugh quietly, squeezing her a little tighter. "Well, yeah, but it's not just that. I like having you here. These quiet moments, when it's just us… with no one around."

She tilts her head, catching my gaze. "You're getting soft on me, Reed."

I grin, brushing my nose against hers. "Maybe I am, but I've never had a girl as a friend before. Someone I can just hang out with."

She raises an eyebrow. "Did I just get friend-zoned?"

I laugh, leaning in to kiss her quickly before pulling back to meet her eyes. "Not even close, Curls. I want you in ways no friend should want another friend."

She tries to hide her smile but it beams out of her anyway. "Yeah?"

I nod, brushing a strand of hair behind her ear. "Yeah."

I kiss her again, deeper this time, feeling the way she melts into it, her fingers tracing the side of my neck. When I pull away, she's still grinning, a little out of breath.

"I like these moments too," she says, her voice soft, sending a flutter through my chest.

I press a kiss to the crown of her head, and close my eyes. I could stay like this forever.

But of course, I can't help myself.

I crack one eye open, glancing down at her curled against me, a smile tugging at my lips.

"Psst…" I whisper.

She stirs, her sleepy gaze meeting mine.

"Can I be the little spoon?"

She lets out a soft laugh, shaking her head. "You're ridiculous," she mutters, swatting my chest before nestling back in.

I wrap my arms around her tighter, the grin refusing to leave my face. Her warmth seeps into me, her breath soft on my neck, and for the first time in a long damn time… I fall asleep with a smile on my face.

TWENTY-FIVE

Ryan

I love sleep.

The silence. The stillness. The way my body sinks into the mattress, a half-dreamy buzz in my brain, and absolutely no responsibilities waiting for me.

What I don't love?

The loud-ass banging that rips me right out of it.

I groan as another knock rattles through the room, echoing like a goddamn drumline in my skull. "Shut up," I mutter into the void, dragging the pillow over my head and squeeze my eyes shut, silently begging whoever it is to go away.

No such luck.

"Ryan, you up?"

Nathan.

Shit.

My entire body goes rigid, but my brain's still fuzzy, still catching up. I blink at the ceiling, trying to piece together why my sheets feel warmer than usual—and then freeze.

There's someone beside me.

Someone warm. Someone soft.

My heart launches into a sprint, slamming against my ribs as I glance down and take in the absolute chaos of limbs tangled in my sheets and curly brown hair spilling across my arm.

Fuck.

Fuck.

Fuuuuuck.

Nathan is banging on my door.

And his sister—his *very naked* sister—is in my bed.

I swallow hard, every nerve lighting up like a damn fire alarm.

"Ryan?" Nathan calls again, knocking louder this time.

Panic stirs in my chest and I slide a hand over Isabella's bare back, giving her a gentle shake. "Isabella," I murmur.

She makes a sleepy little sound, her body curling into mine like she's chasing the warmth. My lips twitch despite the full-body panic setting in.

Fuck, she's cute.

Focus, dumbass.

"Bels, you need to wake up," I whisper, a little firmer.

She shifts, groggy, her fingers dragging across my stomach as her lashes flutter open. "Ryan?"

"Yeah, baby," I say, my voice still rough with sleep. My hand settles on her hip without thinking. "You spent the night in my bed, remember?"

Her lips curve into a lazy smile, eyes still hazy. And for a second, I completely forget I'm supposed to be panicking. All I can think about is last night. How she sounded, how she felt, how perfect she was underneath me.

And how badly I want her again.

Bang. Bang. Bang.

"Ryan, you up?"

Nathan's voice slices through the moment like a goddamn buzzsaw. Isabella's eyes snap open, and her whole body stiffens. Before I can say a word, she's bolts upright and scrambles out of bed.

My eyes follow her, taking in every inch of glowing skin, every curve, every second I'm not supposed to be enjoying right now.

She's fucking stunning.

I blink hard, trying to reboot my brain. "Yeah—uh—just give me a sec!" I shout.

Fuck, I just want to enjoy this. I've never slept beside a girl before—especially in my own bed—and instead of having a lazy morning, soft kisses, and morning sex, I'm picking up her clothes off the floor and tossing them toward her.

She catches them and tugs her sweatshirt over her head, sliding into her shorts a second later. She bends to grab her sneakers, and I catch myself staring again, wanting to pull her back to me, to kiss her, to do everything I'm not supposed to.

"Are you naked or something?" Nathan calls through the door. "You know I've seen your junk more than I'd like to, right?"

I groan. "Just—fuck. Hang on."

I dive for my sweats, yanking them on.

Then Isabella drops to her hands and knees and crawls under the bed.

"What are you doing?" I whisper.

"What do you think?" she hisses back, halfway under already.

Jesus. This is so fucked.

I don't want her to hide. I want her right here, preferably back in my arms, definitely not on the ground and under my bed.

But if Nathan walks in and sees her in my room?

Yeah. Goodbye balls.

"What the hell are you doing in there?" Nathan grunts from outside the door.

I let out a breath when Isabella finally gets fully under my bed, squaring my shoulders. "I'm good. You can come in," I say, forcing my voice to sound normal.

The door swings open, and Nathan steps in. I cross my arms and lean back against the dresser, trying to look like I'm not sweating bullets.

Does this look weird? It looks weird, right?

Nathan narrows his eyes at me. "Why are you acting weird?"

"I'm not," I say, though I know I look as guilty as a kid caught with his hand in the cookie jar. I sit on my bed, leaning back on the mattress. "What's up?"

"Did you forget we have practice this morning?" Nathan raises an eyebrow. "You're late, and still half-dressed."

Trust me. I'm more dressed than I was a few minutes ago.

"Yeah, I know. Thanks."

I want to glance at Isabella—just a quick look, to make sure she's still hidden—but if I do, I'm dead. Nathan will catch me, and that's not how I plan on dying today.

Nathan groans, rubbing the back of his neck. "My shoulder is killing me."

My eyes flick to him in desperation. Fuck, I need him to just get out.

"Can I use your massage gun real quick?"

I blink. "Yeah, sure," I say, waving him off. My brain is still stuck on how the hell I'm gonna get Isabella out of here without Nathan noticing.

But then my eyes widen as I watch him reach for the massage gun and something clicks in my mind.

Oh, fuck no.

"NO. You cannot!" I shout, jumping on top of the massage gun, panic flooding my chest.

Nathan freezes, his eyes widening. He raises his hands, confused. "Jesus. What's the big deal?"

"I just… don't want to share it," I say, shrugging, praying to whatever gods might be listening that this works.

Nathan stares at me, his eyes narrowing. "What? Why not?"

Shit. What do I say? I can't tell him the truth—that would traumatize him and seal my fate in one shot.

"I… I…" I let out a long sigh, pinching the bridge of my nose in frustration. "I came on it."

Fuck my life.

Nathan's face drops. "*What*?"

Fuck, am I really doing this? There's no turning back now. "I was jerking off, and—"

"No," Nathan cuts me off, shaking his head, holding his hand up to stop me. "Jesus fucking Christ. I did not need to hear that."

"You asked," I point out.

"And I fucking regret it." He glares at me, muttering under his breath. "Fucking hell, I'll buy my own massage gun."

Without another word, he storms out of my room, slamming the door behind him.

I stand there for a second, breathing out a deep sigh of relief.

"You can come out now," I tell Isabella, watching her slowly crawl from under the bed, her lips pressed together in amusement.

"Really?" she asks, arching a brow. "That was the best you could come up with?"

I roll my eyes, trying to push down the embarrassment. "I didn't know what else to say. I didn't want to traumatize him, baby," I tell her, my hands instinctively reaching out to smooth her messy curls away from her face.

Her sleepy eyes meet mine, and a small smile tugs at her lips. She looks so damn cute without an ounce of makeup, just glowing in the soft morning light. All I want to do is pull her back into bed, wrap her in my arms, and just hold her. Kiss her more. Touch her more. Fuck her again.

But we both know we can't.

"Any ideas how to sneak me out of here?" Isabella asks.

I chuckle, already formulating a plan in my head. "We need a diversion." I grab my phone, quickly typing out a message to Austin.

Me:

I need a diversion. No questions asked.

I hit send, tapping my fingers nervously against the screen as I wait. I'm not sure if he'll come through, but I can only hope.

Before I have time to second-guess myself, a loud crash echoes from downstairs, followed by some yelling.

Isabella raises a brow, a grin tugging at the corners of her lips. "Was that the diversion?"

I shrug. "Why don't we find out?"

I walk toward the door, peeking out through the crack. The hallway is empty.

"C'mon," I mutter, holding out my hand to her.

She follows me down the hall, her soft footsteps echoing behind me.

"Are you five years old?" Nathan's voice floats up from downstairs. "How the hell did you break all of our plates?"

I stifle a laugh as we slowly descend the stairs. That was one hell of a diversion.

"It just slipped, alright?" Austin replies.

The yelling gets louder as we move down, and I round the staircase, heading toward the back exit. We turn the corner, and I slip through the hallway to the door. I hold it open for Isabella, letting her go first.

She squeezes past me, heading outside, but before she can fully step out, I tug on her wrist, pulling her back toward me.

Her eyes widen in confusion. "Wha—"

I cut her off, leaning down and crashing my lips to hers. My hands cup her face, feeling the softness of her skin beneath my fingertips.

When I pull back, I can't help but smile, smoothing a few stray strands of her hair from her face. "Couldn't let you leave without doing that."

Her smile widens, a playful glint in her eyes as she shakes her head. "Just say you're obsessed with me already," she teases, leaning in to press another kiss to my lips before stepping back.

I chuckle quietly, watching her slip through the door. I close it behind her, leaning my forehead against it.

She's not wrong. I'm fucking obsessed with that girl, and it scares the hell out of me.

I pull my phone out, the screen buzzing with a message. Austin's name flashes across the screen.

Austin:

You're welcome.

Also, we need new plates.

I can't help but laugh, shaking my head.
Fuck, that was way too close.
And yet, I regret nothing.

TWENTY-SIX

Isabella

I push open the door to the coach's office, the familiar smell of stale coffee hitting me immediately.

Dad's sitting at his desk, flipping through some papers. He looks up when I step in, a grin spreading across his face.

"Well, well, if it isn't my favorite daughter," he teases.

I roll my eyes, stepping inside and closing the door behind me. "I'm your only daughter."

He waves me off. "Same difference. Bringing me lunch again, or just stopping by to see if I'm still alive?"

I chuckle, swinging the brown paper bag onto his desk. "You're lucky I am. If Mom had her way, you'd be eating steamed vegetables and quinoa every day."

Dad groans loudly as he grabs the sandwich I bought for him. "Love your mom, but I need some fucking meat." He takes a bite, chewing with a look of pure relief on his face.

I sit down across from him, and he devours his sandwich, gulping it down.

"How's school going?" he asks, before taking another bite. "Keeping up with everything?"

I shrug, leaning back in the chair. "Yeah, it's fine. Boring. You know how it is." I make a face, because I know he knows exactly what I mean.

"You having a good time working with me at the rink?" he asks, arching an eyebrow.

I smile, my lips curving without even thinking about it. "You know I love it."

Dad's face softens a little, his eyes lighting up. "Love to hear it," he says, then leans back in his chair, studying me carefully. "I thought for sure one of the guys would try something with you, but it looks like they're keeping their heads straight, huh?"

My pulse kicks up, but I plaster on a smile. "They know better than to mess with Coach's daughter."

Dad laughs. "Good. I've got enough on my plate without worrying about that." He takes another bite of his sandwich, then shoots me a look. "But if anyone even thinks about it…" He raises a brow.

I snort. "You gonna bench the entire team?"

He grins. "Don't tempt me."

I keep smiling, but inside, I'm spiraling. Because someone already *has* thought about it. Touched. Kissed. Definitely done more than that.

I push the thought down, burying it under about a hundred layers of denial. Because if he finds out about Ryan? Game over. I don't even know for who—me, Ryan, both of us, the team?

"You know I've gotta protect my little girl," Dad says, still smiling.

Before I can respond, a knock interrupts. I turn my head seeing Nathan at the door, Ryan close behind. My pulse skips when my eyes meet Ryan's, and that familiar smirk on his face is enough to make my stomach flip.

I force myself to look away, pinning my bottom lip between my teeth.

It's been days since the whole sneaking-out mess, and God, I didn't realize how much I'd missed him until now. Every time I think about it, I feel this strange tug in my chest, this longing I didn't sign up for. We haven't had the chance to see each other since then, and it's driving me crazy.

"Hey, Dad, you got your car keys? I left my hoodie in the backseat last night, and it's freezing in the rink," Nathan says.

Dad sighs, already digging into his pocket. "You're worse than me at losing shit." He tosses the keys over, shaking his head. "First, though, I want to get your guys' opinion on something."

Nathan catches the keys. "Alright, shoot."

Dad leans back in his chair, glancing between us. "What would you guys say if I gave Isabella a little more responsibility and let her work on the next set of plays for the game against Westbrook?"

I blink, caught completely off guard. "Wait, you want me to—what? Seriously?"

He gives a little shrug. "You've been showing me more than enough in practice. I think you're ready for it."

A rush of excitement floods my chest, quickly followed by a wave of nerves that makes my stomach tighten. "I—uh, I don't know. That's a lot of pressure."

Nathan scoffs, rolling his eyes. "You think too much. Dad's right, Izz. You'll nail it."

Ryan nods, lips curling into a smile. "I know you'll kill it," he adds.

I glance between the two of them. Their confidence is almost overwhelming. It feels nice to hear, but…

I bite my lip, the nerves gnawing at me. I'm not sure I'm as ready as they think. A part of me wants to rise to the challenge. Another part is terrified of failing and disappointing them.

"What if I mess it up?" I ask, the doubt creeping through.

Dad shrugs. "Hey, that's part of the game. But I have a feeling you won't. And if something goes wrong, it's not just on you. We work together and try again."

I let his words sink in, but my stomach churns.

"What do you say?" Dad asks again, raising his eyebrows. "Do you want to make us proud?"

I take a deep breath, trying to shake off the nerves. Maybe I can do this. I think I can. It's a good chance to prove everyone wrong—especially the ones who still think women don't belong in sports.

"I'm in," I say, blowing out a breath.

Dad flashes me a proud smile. "You're gonna do great, princess." He pushes off the desk, standing. "C'mon, I need to grab the tablet anyway."

He and Nathan leave, the door clicking shut behind them, leaving Ryan and me alone. The silence stretches between us, and for a few seconds, neither of us moves.

I'm not sure who makes the first move—maybe it's me, stepping closer to him, or maybe it's him, reaching for me— but before I know it, our lips meet.

It's fast, a little messy, and exactly what we both need. When we finally pull apart, Ryan's forehead rests against mine, his breath coming in short, ragged bursts. His eyes are half-lidded, and the sight makes my stomach flutter.

"Fuck, I missed you," he murmurs, and I can't stop the smile that tugs at my lips.

"You're gonna get us caught," I tease, though I'm not exactly complaining.

Ryan shrugs, a smirk playing at the corners of his mouth. "Don't even know if I care anymore."

I laugh softly, letting my hands move up around his neck, pulling him in closer. "You say that now, but you won't when you're getting your ass kicked by my dad."

Ryan groans, his hands sliding down to my hips, pulling me even closer. "Being with you is fucking dangerous." His voice turns low, dark. "And so fucking hot."

I don't even bother trying to fight it. His lips find mine again, and I get lost in him. My fingers tangle in his hair, urging him closer, making sure he knows I'm not going anywhere.

When we finally pull apart, my heart's still racing, and I'm still buzzing from the kiss. But there's still that nagging doubt lingering in the back of my mind.

"You really think I can do it?" The words come out a little shakier than I'd like. "The Westbrook game?"

Ryan meets my eyes, and his expression softens. "I wouldn't have said it if I didn't believe in you, Bels." His grip tightens on my hips. "I've seen you at practice. Austin's been playing a lot better than before. I am too, and that's all because of you."

I feel a little spark of pride, but it doesn't totally quiet the voice in my head. The one that says this might all blow up in my face. "You guys are the only ones who think so," I mutter, exhaling hard.

Ryan's expression shifts. His jaw tightens, brows pulling together. "Did someone say something to you? Give me names. I'll handle it."

A scoff escapes me as I shake my head. "That isn't necessary. I can handle them myself. I don't need my fuck buddy fighting my battles for me."

Ryan's eyebrow quirks, and a smirk tugs at his lips. "Is that what I am?"

I hum, leaning in until our lips are inches away. "Would you prefer 'booty call'?"

"Call me whatever you want," he murmurs, his hand drifting down to my waist, pulling me a little closer. "Call me your fuck buddy. Call me your booty call. Call me in the middle of the night. Call me yours—"

His mouth crashes into mine before he can finish, the word swallowed by the kiss. A moan slips from my lips, and he swallows it greedily, groaning as his tongue traces the seam of my mouth. I open for him, fingers digging into his shoulders.

The kiss steals the breath from my lungs. It makes my pulse hammer, my blood burn, my—

Footsteps.

We freeze.

The footsteps get closer. Louder. Too loud.

Shit.

I stumble back, nearly tripping over my own feet as Ryan jerks away, his hands already halfway in his pockets, face flushed. My pulse is a wild, erratic mess. The heat of his mouth is still on mine when—

The door swings open.

Dad steps in. Nathan follows right behind him. Both of them stop, their eyes flicking between us. "You're still here?" he asks Ryan.

Ryan freezes for a split second. He clears his throat. "Uh, well, she wanted to go over some things with me before I head out. Practice stuff. For next week's game."

Dad gives Ryan a brief nod, buying the excuse without a second thought. "Alright, we'll go over that now," he says, walking into the office and settling into his chair. "We've got a lot to do before next week's game."

"Let's go, man," Nathan says, standing by the door. "Austin's probably hoarding the showers by now."

Ryan nods and looks at me one last time before following Nathan out of the room. The door clicks shut behind them, and I'm left standing there, my heart still racing from the close call.

We can't keep doing this—sneaking around, dodging close calls, pretending like this thing between us doesn't have disaster written all over it.

But when he looks at me like that, when he kisses me like I'm the only thing he wants in the world?

Stopping doesn't feel like an option.

It feels impossible.

TWENTY-SEVEN

Ryan

The bus ride to an away game always smells like sweat and way too much Axe. Same cramped seats. Same idiots yelling over each other the entire ride.

Honestly? I kinda like it. It means game day. It means I get to hit the ice and stop thinking about everything else for a few hours. Westbrook plays fast and loose, which means we just have to hit harder and outskate them. Simple plan. Just gotta stick to it.

But there's something different about the team bus this time.

Because she's here.

Isabella climbs onto the bus, her hair pulled into a ponytail that I want to tug and—*Jesus*. Focus. She doesn't even glance my way at first, scanning for a seat near the front.

Still, my eyes are on her.

Can't help it.

She finally looks up, and for half a second, our eyes meet. That's it. That's all I get. But it's enough to make my chest tighten and a dumb smile tug at the corners of my mouth.

I look away before it becomes obvious. Before someone— anyone—picks up on something they shouldn't.

Fuck, she looks good. Always does. But today? She's wearing that fitted jacket that hugs her waist just right, and those leggings—Jesus. Tight enough to short-circuit my brain.

Nope. Not going there. Last thing I need is to sit through a four-hour bus ride with a boner surrounded by sweaty hockey guys.

She's always at practice, but this is the first time she's traveling with us. First time she's taking the lead on anything big. Coach handed her the plays for Westbrook, which is kinda huge. And I know she's nervous, but she's ready.

I'm so fucking proud of her. I have no doubt that she'll do great.

Her eyes find mine for half a second before she glances away. She doesn't smile. Doesn't give anything away, and yeah I get it. We can't afford to slip, not with a bus full of guys who live to talk shit.

Still, part of me wishes she'd smile at me and walk straight to the back and sit beside me.

But that would definitely raise a few eyebrows.

The rest of the guys, a mix of rookies and bench players, pile in behind her and take their usual spots up front.

Logan hops on next, taking a deep, dramatic inhale and sighs. "Ah, you smell that? That's the scent of victory, boys."

Austin snorts as he steps on. "No. That's the scent of your rank-ass gear. Jesus."

Logan just grins like an idiot. "Still smells like winning to me." Then he turns and throws me a look. "You ready for tonight?"

"Always," I reply with a shrug. "Westbrook's fast, but their D is a mess. We hit hard, push early, they'll fall apart."

Logan nods, and just like that, his game face clicks in. He jokes a lot, but when the puck drops, he flips the switch. "Think they'll come for you early?"

"They can try," I say, smirking. "I'll be ready."

"Good." He leans back in his seat. "I got twenty bucks on you throwing the first hit."

I chuckle, but my head's already in the game. First shift. First hit. First goal.

And maybe, if I don't totally screw up, a glance from the girl standing on the sidelines—who I'm not supposed to want.

Yeah. That too.

Cole gets on next. Doesn't say a word. Just beelines it to the back, drops into his seat. Pops a piece of gum in his mouth and stares out the window.

Austin—who has never been quiet a day in his life—flops onto the seat in front of me. Stretches like he's been doing hard labor, cracks his neck, and glances around.

"All right, boys. Who's getting lucky tonight?"

I groan. "Jesus, Austin."

Logan grins. "It's a legit question."

Cole doesn't even bother looking up. Just raises a brow and mutters, "Not you."

Austin, used to Cole's charming personality, blows out a breath. "Sounds like jealousy to me."

Nathan's got his headphones on, like always. Zoned out, probably blasting music. We all know better than to mess with him pre-game.

I shake my head, leaning back in my seat. "Let's focus on winning first."

Austin smirks. "Winning on the ice or winning in bed?"

I level him with a deadpan stare.

He chuckles. "C'mon. You guys know away games mean girls are dying to—"

A throat clears. Loudly.

The entire bus goes silent.

Isabella stands in the aisle, arms crossed, one brow raised. "Excuse me?" she says.

Austin looks like he's about to shit himself. "Uh—team bonding. We were talking about team bonding."

Her eyes move slowly from Logan to Cole to Austin, unimpressed. "You do realize I'm right here, don't you?"

No one says a word.

I bite the inside of my cheek to keep from laughing. She's got all of them terrified, and honestly? It's kinda hot.

Austin's brows lift, and he shrugs. "Well, shit, we're not about to leave you out. You looking for a date too?"

Before she can fire something back, Coach's voice slices through the bus.

"Rhodes!"

Austin throws his hands up. "Right, right. Sorry, Coach." Then he swivels to Isabella again, that dumbass grin stretching wider. "But if you *are* looking for a date—"

Coach sighs like his soul is slowly dying. "Christ. Isabella, come sit up front with me and get away from those idiots."

Her eyes slide to me, and something tightens in my chest. *Fuck*. I wanted her next to me. Four hours with her beside me? Would've been the best part of the damn trip.

I slip my phone out from under the seat and type fast.

Me:

I need another no-questions-asked.

Austin's phone buzzes and he glances down. I catch the way his lips twitch into that cocky-ass smirk, and a second later, my phone vibrates with a text.

Austin:

> You're gonna owe me big time. What is it?

Me:

> Sit next to Coach.

He reads the message, brows pulling together. I don't even care if he knows at this point. He stands, stretches, and slides into the seat beside Coach.

"Hey, Coach. Mind if I join?"

Coach turns his head slowly, eyes narrowing. "I mind *very much*—"

"Sweet," Austin cuts in, draping an arm across the headrest. "So, I was thinking about coaching strategies—"

Coach exhales the deepest, most soul-weary sigh I've ever heard and pinches the bridge of his nose.

I tune the rest out. Don't care. Because Isabella's already walking toward me.

She doesn't look at anyone else. Just slips into the seat beside me like it's the only available seat, given the full bus.

I glance over at her, my heart hammering in my chest. There's nothing suspicious about this… right? She just prefers sitting at the back.

Who the fuck am I kidding?

It's suspicious as hell, and if Coach glances back and sees his daughter sitting with me, I'm so completely busted.

But it's worth it—just to be close to her.

Her eyes narrow, lips curving into the start of a smirk. "That was your doing, wasn't it?"

I shrug, letting out a quiet laugh. "A 'no questions asked' gets me a long way."

She shakes her head, but I catch the smile she's fighting. "You're ridiculous."

I smirk, leaning back slightly. "And yet, here you are. Sitting beside me."

The bus hums beneath us as the engine starts, all I can focus on is her.

The warmth of her leg pressed against mine. The faint scent of her perfume that smells so sweet. I shift slightly, pressing my thigh into hers.

She glances around the bus, scanning for anyone watching. Austin's still up front, talking Coach's ear off like I told him to. The rest of the guys are mid-convo about god knows what, and Cole's still got his eyes out the window.

No one's looking.

So, I take the chance.

I reach over and find her hand. She tenses for a second when my fingers brush hers, but she doesn't pull away. When I lace our fingers together, her grip tightens like she's been waiting for me to do it.

I bring our joined hands into my lap, letting my thumb trace slow, lazy circles over the back of hers. Her skin's soft and so warm. I drag my thumb over the curve of her wrist, feel her pulse thrumming beneath it.

My brows tug. "You're shaking."

She lifts her head slightly, eyes flicking to mine before looking away. "Yeah. I'm a little nervous," she says, blowing out a breath. "This is a big game for you guys, and if I screw up, it's all on me."

I shake my head. "We're the ones out there on the ice. If one of us screws up, it won't be on you."

Her gaze drops to our hands, her thumb brushing lightly over mine, like she's trying to believe me. "I don't want to let anyone down."

I squeeze her hand a little tighter. "You won't."

She swallows. The silence stretches.

"You nervous for the game?" she asks softly.

I almost laugh, giving a small shrug. "Yeah. Always."

She tilts her head, her eyes narrowing. "You don't seem like the type to get nervous about anything."

I smirk. "That's because I don't let it show. But of course I get nervous, Bels. I'm the captain. I'm supposed to lead the team, and Westbrook plays dirty."

She watches me for a second. "You worried you'll get hit again?"

My lips twist. "I dunno. I've been hit plenty. I just…" I shift in my seat, dragging my thumb over her hand again. "Losing. Fucking up. Letting people down. That's what gets to me."

She goes quiet, her gaze on mine. "I've seen how the team looks at you. You won't let them down."

Something in my chest pulls tight. I glance at her, searching her face, looking for any sign she's just saying it to make me feel better—but there's nothing. Just honesty. Conviction.

Her brow lifts slightly, like she knows exactly what I'm thinking. "And if your family can't see that, then they're wrong. You're not the failure they make you out to be."

Fuck. Her words hit hard. Like she peeled back the part of me I don't show anyone and touched it without flinching.

I drag in a breath, trying to cover the ache with a grin. "That confident in me?"

She hums, her eyes still on mine. "I know you better than you think."

And maybe she does.

Maybe that's what's so fucking terrifying.

Because the more she sees, the less I want to hide.

And I've never felt that with anyone.

She shifts slightly. "So… are you going out with the guys later?"

I let out a chuckle. "You don't even know if we're gonna win," I point out.

"Yeah, but the guys will want to go out whether you win or lose."

I press my lips together. She's got a point.

"Either way, I think I'd rather stay in with a certain girl," I tease, my eyes glinting.

Her eyes light up and a smile curls onto her lips, but it falters a little as she tilts her head, something flickering behind her gaze. "Are you sure you don't want to go out with them? Get laid? Find some easy pussy?"

I scoff, shaking my head. "Austin's an idiot."

She raises a brow. "You didn't answer the question."

I pause, my stomach sinking. Is that what she really thinks? That I'd ditch her to go hook up with some random girl?

Without thinking, I lean in a little closer, my grip on her hand tightening. "You know damn well the only girl I want is sitting right here."

She exhales, shaky and soft, and fuck, it sends a jolt straight through me. Her gaze doesn't waver. Her lips curve into a smirk that could ruin me.

"Yeah?" she says.

I nod, thumb gliding over her skin. "Yeah."

I want to kiss her.

But we both know we can't.

Holding her hand under the radar is one thing. Kissing her? That's a whole different level of reckless.

Still. That doesn't stop me from wanting her.

I glance around the bus again. The guys are still distracted, talking over each other, and Coach is too busy with Austin to notice anything else.

I shift slightly, angling my body toward her. "Spread your legs."

Her breath catches, and she turns toward me, eyes wide and startled. "Ryan—"

I squeeze her thigh, my fingers pressing into the soft fabric of her leggings. "Quiet, baby," I whisper, and she swallows hard, glancing around to make sure no one is watching. Despite her hesitation, she slowly spreads her legs for me.

A smirk tugs at my lips. "Such a good girl for me."

I feel her exhale sharply, low, but just enough for me to hear how I'm affecting her.

I drag my hand up her thigh, slowly, my fingers brushing over the waistband of her leggings, then slip beneath the fabric to trace the delicate lace of her panties. She flinches slightly, and I tighten my grip on her leg. "Shh, baby," I whisper against her ear. "You need to be quiet."

Her fingers dig into my arm. "You're insane," she whispers.

I chuckle. "And yet, you're not stopping me." Her breathing becomes shallow as I slide my fingers lower, pressing against the heat beneath the lace.

"You're soaked," I say with a cocky grin.

She squeezes her eyes shut, her breathing uneven. "You're the worst," she whispers, half-teasing, half-surrendering.

I dip a finger inside her, my cock twitching in my pants when a low moan leaves her lips. "Am I?"

She doesn't answer, her body does all the talking, shifting toward my touch as if she can't help herself.

I smirk. "You like getting fingered on the team bus, don't you?"

A tiny, muffled sound escapes her—a mix of a whimper and a soft curse. I curl my finger further, teasing just enough to make her squirm. "That's it," I whisper. "Be good for me. Stay quiet and I'll give you what you want."

Her entire body shudders under my touch as I press my thumb against her clit, drawing slow, lazy circles. Her breath stutters, and I know she's fighting to hold back a sound.

I slide another finger inside her, curling it just right to make her thighs tremble. "Fuck," I breathe out. "You're gripping me so tight."

I move my fingers faster, my other hand steadying her by gripping her thigh, keeping her perfectly open for me. I can feel how close she is. Every part of her is trembling, her fingers clutching my arm like she's holding on for dear life.

A smirk tugs at my lips as I murmur, "Come for me, baby."

Her eyes squeeze shut. She bites her lip hard, and falls apart, silently—or as quietly as she can. Slow, soft moans leave her lips and she presses her hand over her mouth, to stifle her moans.

Her body goes limp beside mine, breathing heavy, her skin flushed.

I can't help but grin as I lift my fingers to my mouth and suck them clean, which earns a wide-eyed look from her.

I groan as her sweet taste covers my tongue. "Fuck, I can't wait for tonight."

She narrows her eyes slightly, her lips curling into a sly smile. "What's happening tonight, exactly?"

I chuckle, raising an eyebrow. "You're going to let me fuck you properly after we win," I tease.

"Am I?" she asks.

My leg's still pressed against hers. My dick's half-hard and throbbing in my jeans, aching with everything we didn't get to do. I can still taste her on my tongue.

I lean in, my gaze flicking to her lips, but before I can reply, Coach's voice roars from the front of the bus.

"Jesus Christ, Rhodes."

We freeze.

Isabella's eyes go wide, her smile vanishing as she whips her head toward the front, my heart pounding as Coach stomps down the aisle.

When he reaches us, he drops into the empty seat beside us. "That kid is fucking killing me," he grumbles.

I swallow hard, my jaw tight as I try to look anywhere but at Coach. The tension's thick enough to choke on. I glance at Isabella. Her lips are pressed into a firm line, her posture a little too stiff, like she's trying not to twitch. The nervous energy is radiating off her, and I feel it in my bones.

Fucking hell. That was way too close.

TWENTY-EIGHT

Isabella

The bus rolls to a stop, the sudden jerk making everyone shift in their seats. I grab my bag, sling it over my shoulder, and wait for the doors to open. The second the bus comes to a full stop, the guys practically scramble out, eager to stretch their legs.

"Aw, sick," Austin says, practically bouncing as he steps down the first step. His eyes are already scanning the house. "Dibs on the master bedroom!"

"That's not happening," my dad says, stepping off the bus.

Austin turns, his brows drawn together. "What do you mean? I'm paying for the pizza tonight. I deserve the best room."

"I paid for the house," he replies with a dry look. "I decide who sleeps where."

I step off the bus, taking in the house. It's tucked away in a quiet corner, surrounded by trees and wild grass that could probably use a trim, but it's light, modern, and way bigger than anywhere I've stayed before.

The guys all rush past me, but Ryan falls in step beside me, glancing over the house. "Not bad," he says.

"Not bad?" I ask, my eyes widening. "It's gorgeous. There's a hot tub, a pool, and it's huge."

"Fair point," Ryan says with a grin, his eyes flicking toward me. Then, without warning, he gently tugs me aside, pulling me behind some bushes near the side of the house, out of sight from the rest of the guys.

Before I can ask what he's doing, his lips are on mine. He groans against my mouth, like he's been waiting for this moment, and honestly, so have I. His hand finds its way to my waist, pulling me closer, and I can feel the rapid thump of his heartbeat against mine.

"Missed you," he mutters, his forehead resting against mine. "Fuck, I *really* missed you."

I can't help the soft laugh that escapes me, still a little breathless. "I've been sitting right next to you on the bus all day."

He grins, brushing his thumb over my cheek. "Yeah, but I couldn't kiss you," he says, his gaze dropping to my lips. "Couldn't touch you."

A warmth blooms in my chest. I roll my eyes but can't fight the smile pulling at my lips. "Let's go inside before the guys start wondering what we're up to," I say, stepping back reluctantly before I end up kissing him again and we get caught.

Ryan just grins, reaching down to grab my bag before I can. "Lead the way, baby."

We walk into the house together, my eyes widening when we step inside. The living room is massive, with plush leather couches scattered around a grand fireplace. A flat-screen TV stretches across one wall, and the place smells like fresh wood and clean linens. To the right is an open kitchen with a marble countertop, and snacks are already set out on the island.

Austin's lounging across the enormous sectional in the living room, his arms behind his head. "Holy shit, this couch is so soft. I'm never leaving."

Coach doesn't even glance at him as he drops his duffel near the door. "If you wanna pay four hundred a night, be my guest. One less headache for me on the bus ride back."

Austin's eyes go wide. "Four hundred? Jesus." He lets out a low whistle, shaking his head. "Okay. I see why your wife sticks around, now."

Coach just grumbles in response, and I bite back a laugh. Austin is always chirping my dad about my mom, and it never gets old. My mom's stunning and totally head-over-heels for my dad, in a way that makes Nathan and I groan whenever they start making out in front of us. But Austin thinks it's his personal mission to remind my dad that he's got a thing for her, every chance he gets.

The rest of the guys trickle in, tossing their bags wherever they please. Logan heads straight for the kitchen, yanking open the fridge. "Is there any beer?"

Coach shoots him a look. "We got water."

Logan groans, slamming the fridge shut. Meanwhile, Nathan's already scoping out the place, mentally calculating where everyone's sleeping, figuring out where to stash the gear, and making sure Austin doesn't burn the place down.

I start walking toward the stairs, and Ryan's footsteps follow behind me.

"I call dibs on whatever room's closest to yours," he murmurs low enough for only me to hear.

A laugh slips from my lips. "Should we just share a bed and make it obvious we're fucking?"

His lips quirk up in that mischievous way I love. "Don't really feel like getting my ass kicked, but if you need help testing yours out, I'm happy to volunteer."

I roll my eyes, though a smile tugs at the corners of my mouth as we reach the top of the stairs. Ryan chuckles, his hand reaches out, toying with my ponytail. "You look cute when you blush."

My skin flushes at his flirting as we walk down the hallway. Most of the rooms have already been claimed, but I spot a smaller one at the very end. Cozy. Private. Perfect.

Ryan leans against the doorframe, crossing his arms, his eyes scanning the room with a grin. "Cute."

"Are you gonna help me unpack or just stand there looking pretty?" I drop my bag on the bed and shoot him a playful look.

His grin widens, and I feel my knees go a little weak. God, he's so hot. "I do both equally well."

Before I can respond, Logan calls out from down the hall. "Reed. There's a room over here."

Ryan sighs dramatically. "Guess that's my cue."

We glance down the hallway, where Logan is standing, and the room he's talking about is at least four doors away, a little too far for my liking.

A chuckle leaves my lips when Ryan groans. "Guess you're not getting lucky tonight after all."

Ryan's eyes meet mine and he steps closer, his scent messing with my head in the best way. He lifts his hand, his fingers brushing against my jaw, slowly.

A grin breaks out onto his face, enjoying the effect he has on me. "Baby, *you're* here. I'm already lucky enough."

I smile before I can stop myself. He's being ridiculously, annoyingly cute, and my heart hammers against my chest so hard it feels like it might actually explode.

For a second, I let myself enjoy the way his words make my chest flutter, the warmth bubbling up in my throat.

But then my brain catches up.

The smile falters, just enough for the truth to sneak back in. This is supposed to be fun. Casual. No strings. No feelings.

So why does my stomach twist like I'm seventeen and falling for the first time?

I shake my head, trying to clear the fog and snap myself out of it.

But Ryan catches the movement.

His eyes narrow, sharp and curious, like he can read every thought I'm trying to bury. "What was that look?" he asks.

"Nothing," I say too quickly, stepping distance might help the churning in my stomach. "Let's just… focus on the game first."

Ryan's grin widens, that cocky tilt to his mouth making it almost impossible not to smile back. "You gonna wear my jersey, Curls?"

I lift a brow. "That would be a little obvious, don't you think?"

Something flickers in his eyes—disappointment maybe— but it vanishes as quickly as it came, masked by a hand dragging through his hair.

"Yeah, yeah. I know," he sighs, glancing away for a beat. "I just… wanted to see you wear my name, I guess."

The flicker of vulnerability in his eyes punches straight through my chest.

I hate it.

Because the truth is, I want that too. I want to wear his jersey, to cheer him on.

But I can't.

So instead, I step in close. My lips brush his ear as I rise on my toes, hands splayed against his chest.

"I'll moan your name instead," I whisper.

I don't wait for his reaction.

Just turn on my heel and head into my room, heat crawling up the back of my neck, fully aware of his eyes locked on me.

But the low groan I hear as the door clicks shut behind me?

Yeah… this weekend is going to be fun.

TWENTY-NINE

Ryan

The sweat's already starting to bead on my forehead, but it feels good. The game's moving fast, like every pass and every turn are charged with energy. The rink's cold, but I'm burning up, muscles working overtime, eyes locked on the puck.

I drop back into position, eyes on their left winger trying to sneak in behind me. He's quick, but I've seen this move before. He wants to slip inside, catch me off-guard.

Not tonight.

The puck hits my stick, and I flick it up the boards.

"Wheel!" Isabella's voice cuts through the noise from the bench.

I curl around the net, see Austin open up. I pass it toward him.

Austin catches it in stride, weaving around two Westbrook guys with that easy confidence he always has when he plays.

"Right side!" Logan calls out.

I shift left to cover, just as one of their forwards barrels in hard. I plant, shoulder him off, and he stumbles. Shoots me a look like he wants a rematch.

Bring it.

Westbrook's scrambling, and I can feel the shift in the game. Their defense is slow to react, and Austin's already moving, cutting through their guys like it's second nature. He takes the pass clean, shifts left, and in one smooth motion, he's got the perfect shot lined up.

The puck flies, and before their goalie even knows what hit him, it's in the back of the net.

The buzzer sounds off, and the crowd erupts.

Austin skates back, a grin on his face, fists pumping in the air. "Let's go, baby," he yells.

He's grinning like he's just won the damn lottery, high-fiving everyone within reach. Nathan shoots us a quick thumbs up from the crease, his eyes locked on the puck, focused as ever, despite the score. We're up by two, and Westbrook's starting to get desperate.

The whistle blows, and one of their forwards ignores it—charges in and hammers Cole from behind.

He slams into the ice hard, his stick flying, his feet slipping out from under him.

"Fuck," I grit under my breath. Instinct kicks in before thought does. I lunge forward.

Westbrook's guy doesn't let up, not even with Cole down on the ice.

I slam into him, hard enough that I'm pretty sure I hear his teeth rattle, but the asshole doesn't fall, just stumbles slightly.

Cole's up fast. He throws a punch that lands with a crack. Gloves are flying, refs are yelling, and bodies are tangled. It's a fucking mess.

The ref's whistle cuts through, but neither of them back down. Their elbows are flying, sticks tangled, bodies crashing on the ice.

As soon as Cole and the Westbrook guy hit the ice again, the whistle blows, and the refs pull them off each other. One of them points straight at Cole and the Westbrook player, signaling for the penalty box.

"Both of you. Box. Now."

Cole skates off the ice, breathing hard, his eyes still locked on the guy who hit him like he's about to rip through the glass and take another shot. I watch him as he skates past me, jaw tight, his face a mask of pure focus, blood still dripping from where he took the hit.

I follow him to the penalty box, slowing down to fall in step beside him. "You good?" I ask, as I roll my shoulders.

Cole flexes his hand, his fingers curling and uncurling like he's still itching for a fight. He doesn't look at me, just mutters, "Guy's a dick."

"You took that hit like it was personal."

"Felt personal." He heads into the penalty box, ripping off his helmet and throwing it to the floor. His chest heaves, eyes locked on the ice like he's already planning round two.

"I need you on the ice, not in the box," Coach snaps. "Stop taking the bait."

Isabella's already scribbling on her clipboard, her eyes meeting mine when she lifts her head. "Run play five next shift. They're leaving the left side wide open."

I nod and push off the boards, refocused as the game continues. The clock is ticking down and I skate back in my zone, keeping my eyes locked on the puck. Westbrook's throwing everything they've got at us, but Nathan's been a fucking wall in net. I can feel the win in my bones.

Logan meets my eyes, and he sends the puck zipping my way.

"One hard!" Isabella calls, warning me there's pressure coming fast.

I spin on my skates and take the shot, quick and clean, just as the goalie shifts to the other side.

For a split second, everything slows down. It's just me, the puck, and that goalie reaching out with everything he's got, but it's too late.

It hits the back of the net. Buzzer goes off. Game over.

We win 3–1.

The bench clears. Helmets off, sticks thrown in the air.

Everyone's on me; hands slapping my back, yelling, high-fives flying.

They drift to the boards, waving at the crowd, pointing up at whoever showed up for them.

I pull my helmet off and swipe the sweat from my forehead. The crowd's roar is still ringing in my ears, but I can't help but look around, letting my eyes drift to the stands.

Yeah, I played for the team. But if I'm being honest?

A part of me was playing for her too.

And then, I find her.

She's perched on the edge of the stands, her eyes locked on me, waiting for me to notice her. And I do. Instantly.

She's standing with her arms in the air, and her mouth wide in a cheer I can't hear. Her curls are pulled back in a loose ponytail, her cheeks are pink from the cold, and her smile is so damn wide it knocks the air out of my chest.

A smile tugs at my lips before I can stop it, a rush of warmth spreading through my chest. My heart skips a beat as I picture myself walking toward her, grabbing her by the waist, pulling her close, kissing her right there in front of everyone.

But then, my gaze flickers to her jersey.

And even though I can't see the back of her jersey, I know *Hayes* is sprawled across it in bold letters.

For a second, my stomach drops, a tight feeling creeping into my chest. I get it. She's here for her brother, celebrating his win like any sibling would. But there's a gnawing feeling at the back of my mind that won't go away. A small part of me wants it to be my name she's wearing. My jersey. Just once. Just to see what it feels like.

It's stupid, I know. I've never cared about who wore my jersey before. Hell, a lot of girls have had my name across their backs, but I never gave two shits. But with Isabella? I want it. I don't even know why.

The crowd shifts all of a sudden, and I feel the attention move away from me. Reporters start huddling around someone, and I squint, trying to figure out what's going on.

Then, through the crack of people, I spot him.

Connor.

The hell? What's he doing here?

Confusion hits me first, but then it quickly morphs into a sharp, uncomfortable twist in my chest. I watch as a swarm of reporters, teammates, and fans crowd around him, jealousy curling in my gut.

Everyone's scrambling to get close, trying to get his attention. It stings more than I care to admit. I just scored, just won the game, but it feels like I'm an afterthought now. Like everything I worked for in that moment is already forgotten.

Connor catches my eye from across the rink, and a smile spreads across his face as he waves the reporters off, and in a few quick steps, he's making his way toward me.

When he reaches me, he lifts his chin, his cap shifting a little. "Nice goal."

I shake my head, half-smiling. "Yeah, thanks."

He claps a hand on my shoulder. "You looked good out there."

I shrug, not sure what to say to that. "What are you doing here?" I ask. No one ever comes to my games. It's been that way since—hell, I don't even know—probably since I was eleven or so. So, seeing him here? Yeah, it's throwing me off.

His hand drops from my shoulder and he shrugs. "Had some time off. Wanted to see my little brother do his thing."

I laugh, dryly, cocking my head. "You flew in to watch a college game?"

"No," he says. "Flew in to watch *your* game."

I freeze.

His lips twitch. "I'm glad I did. You played like a beast out there."

I let out a breath, rubbing the back of my neck. "Took your advice. I put all that aggression on the ice."

Connor gives me a once-over, his eyes lingering on my face for a beat longer than usual. "Glad to hear it. Your shoulder feeling better?"

I roll it, the ache gone now. "Yeah. It's good."

He nods, but then before he can say anything else, I hear the sound of my girl's laugh, and turn to see her running toward me.

"I told you you'd do amazing," she says, grinning so brightly that it almost knocks the air from my lungs. She throws her arms around my neck before I even have the chance to react, she pulls me in close.

I close my eyes as I feel the warmth of her body pressed against mine, her familiar scent filling my senses. I can't help but sink into the feeling, one hand instinctively reaching to her head, my fingers getting tangled in those gorgeous curls of hers.

I breathe her in, the familiar scent of her shampoo making the stupid flip in my chest happen all over again. The world could burn down around us, and I wouldn't care.

I just want to hold her.

"It was all you, Curls," I murmur as I pull back to look at her. "Your strategy kicked ass."

She chuckles, and my gaze drops to her lips, lingering for a second too long, the urge to kiss her overwhelming.

Fuck.

But then, I hear a throat clear, and I glance at my brother, and realizing we're in the middle of a room full of people. Coaches, players, and of course—her dad and brother.

I swallow as I shift away from her.

I clear my throat and force a smile. "This is Isabella. My… friend," I say, though the word feels awkward on my tongue.

That word doesn't belong beside her name.

Because Isabella is so much more than a friend.

But I can't say that right now. Not with everyone surrounding us.

Connor looks between us, his expression unreadable for a beat, before he finally shifts his focus to her. "Nice to meet you."

She grins at him. "Yeah, you too. You're amazing, by the way. I grew up watching your games."

My brother chuckles, but a groan leaves my lips. "Bels. Can you not fawn over my brother? Please?"

She laughs, shrugging innocently. "Hockey legend, Ryan. What do you expect?"

I roll my eyes. "He gets enough of that." Part of me doesn't like how easy it is for her to gush over Connor. Another part of me knows it's just how it goes—he's been a pro for years, and I'm just… me.

"Izzy!"

At the sound of Nathan's voice, Isabella's face lights up, and she grins before waving goodbye to me. Then she rushes toward him, and he pulls her into a quick hug.

A grin pulls at my lips as I watch them. They have the kind of sibling relationship I've always envied.

"Friend?" Connor's voice slices through my thoughts, a smirk tugging at his lips as he raises an eyebrow.

I roll my eyes, but there's no hiding it. He's right. I'm lying to myself

"She's Nathan's sister," I clarify.

Connor's brows shoot up, but he doesn't say anything. He just waits for me to say more.

"And Coach's daughter," I add, and I can feel my jaw tighten when his eyes go wide.

"Fuck."

I let out a breath, running a hand through my hair. "Yeah."

Connor chuckles, crossing his arms. "That's… brave."

"Stupid, probably," I admit, shaking my head. Because, yeah, that's what it is. Stupid. Reckless. Dangerous. And so fucking worth it.

He doesn't argue, and I'm kind of grateful for that. It's not like I need anyone to tell me what a mess this is.

I press my lips together, the urge to get out of here hitting me. "I should go," I say, trying to keep my voice steady.

Connor nods. "Yeah, go celebrate. You earned it."

A smile tugs at my lips, and I turn to leave. But then I stop, glancing back at him. "Thanks. For… you know, coming out here to see me."

"Anytime," he says with a smile.

I head toward the guys, still thinking about the one girl I can't have. I glance back at her. She's laughing with Nathan and her dad, her smile lighting up the whole space.

"Alright, alright!" Austin calls out, cutting through the noise. "Who's getting some tonight?" He winks, and the guys all laugh.

But I look at her again, and I can't focus on anything but her.

She's the one I want to see tonight.

And maybe every night after that.

THIRTY

Ryan

We pull into the driveway of the Airbnb, the buzz from the game still buzzing in the air. The ride back was nothing but shit-talking and post-win adrenaline, and the energy hasn't dropped a bit.

"Man, we fucking destroyed them," Austin says, bumping his shoulder into mine as we head up the steps. "Easily your best game of the season, Ry."

Nathan claps me on the back, a grin pulling at his lips. "He's right—for once—you were on fire out there."

Coach gives me a nod as the rest of the team trickles inside. "Good work, Reed. That's how you lead a team."

I nod, a rare warmth settling in my chest. Praise like that doesn't come often—not from my family, anyway. Connor's the one who gets all the attention, the golden boy tearing it up in the NFL, while I… skate in his shadow. If I called my parents right now to tell them I had the best game of my season, they'd probably say "Good job" before flipping the conversation to his latest highlight reel.

But tonight? Tonight's mine. We won.

The house is already a mess when I walk in. Austin's raiding the fridge, Logan and Nathan are ribbing on each other, and the rest of the guys are piled up on the couch, joking around.

But I'm not paying attention to any of that. My eyes are already looking for her.

She's leaning against the kitchen counter, watching me with that look like she's been waiting, like she knew I'd be looking for her. And honestly, it's all I fucking do these days.

"You killed it tonight," she says with a smile.

I should say something back, but instead, I move. Because the second I hear her voice, and see her smile at me, I know I need to kiss her.

But not here.

Not in the middle of the kitchen, with half the team just a few feet away. Not where anyone could walk in and see Coach's daughter pressed up against me.

So instead, I grab her wrist and tug her down the hallway, pushing open the nearest door—a dimly lit laundry room. The second the door clicks shut behind us, I press her back against it, my mouth already on hers.

My hands are in her hair, my lips on hers, full of desperation and urgency, knowing we shouldn't be doing this—but not giving an ounce of a fuck anyway. She fists the front of my hoodie, pulling me closer, and *fuck*, it's not enough. It never is.

We pull apart when my phone buzzes, and I reach for it, glancing at the screen, chest jumping before I can stop it.

But when I swipe it open, that flicker of hope crashes fast.

It's not them.

No missed calls.

No texts.

Not even a fucking thumbs up.

I stare at the screen for a second too long, the buzz from earlier fading.

"Everything okay?" Isabella asks.

I shrug, lock the screen, and shove the phone into my pocket. "Yeah, just…" I pause. Her brows are pulled together. No point lying, not when she's already reading me. "Thought it might be my dad congratulating me about the game or something."

Her expression softens, and she steps in closer, her frown deepening. "He didn't watch?"

"Oh, he probably watched," I say, shaking my head. "He just doesn't care enough to say anything unless it's to critique," I tell her with a bitter laugh. "If Connor so much as sneezes on the field, they're calling to talk about how 'driven' he is. I play my best game of the season and get nothing."

And yeah, I'm used to it by now. But it still pisses me off. Still gets under my skin like it's the first time. Doesn't matter how old I am or how far from home—I'm still checking my phone like an idiot, hoping this time will be different.

She doesn't say anything for a second. Doesn't try to give me some motivational quote or tell me my dad loves me in his own way or whatever bullshit people usually say.

She just rests her hand on my arm. "I'm sorry."

"I know I should be over it, but I'm not," I admit, the words coming out in a rush. "Every time I think I don't care anymore, I still check. I hate that I do, but I can't stop."

She reaches for my hand, laces her fingers with mine. "Maybe he'll never say what you want to hear, but what you did tonight was still incredible, Ryan. Your brother was proud of you. I could see it in his eyes." I press my lips together, keeping my eyes on her—the only solid thing in my life right now. "Your teammates. My dad… Me," she finishes, giving me a sweet smile. "We're all so proud of you."

My hand flexes around hers. Somehow, without even trying, she's become the one person I actually want to share shit with. The highs, the losses, the parts I usually keep buried.

I glance down at her, my fingers brushing the side of her waist. "*Fuck*, I really wish you were wearing my jersey right now." Would have turned around this shit mood seeing my name on her back.

She tilts her head, lips twitching in amusement. And then— without a word—she grabs the hem of her *Midnight Wolves* Jersey, with her brother's name stitched across the back.

Slowly, she pulls it over her head and lets it drop to the floor, revealing another jersey underneath.

For a second, all I see is her—flushed cheeks, bright eyes, a smirk playing at her lips. But then she moves, turning just enough for me to catch the name across her back.

The deep blue fabric, the white sleeves, the sharp silver detailing along the edges. And across her back, stitched in bold block letters. *Reed.*

My breath catches. My pulse stutters.

Because *fuck*, there's something about seeing her in it, about knowing she put it on under her brother's jersey, knowing she wanted me to see.

A rough sound escapes me, low in my throat. My hands are on her before I even think about it, my fingers gripping her waist, feeling the heat of her skin through *my* jersey.

"You're actually trying to kill me, aren't you?" I mutter, voice rough.

She bites her lip, fingers toying with the fabric. "You like it?"

My gaze drags over my name stretching across her back, and something tightens in my chest.

"You have no idea what this is doing to me," I mutter, my hands sliding over her waist.

"I think I do," she murmurs, biting her lip.

I step in, closing the space between us, pressing against her. She shifts just slightly—just enough for her ass to brush against me.

"Reed? Where are you, man?"

Austin's voice makes us both freeze. Isabella's eyes widen in panic, and she steps back, her fingers scrambling to pull her brother's Westbrook jersey over mine, covering up my name.

Fuck. This is stupid. Too risky. Sneaking around in a house full of people who'd kill us if they knew what was going on.

I can't help but glance at her—her hair's a mess, her cheeks flushed. She looks so beautiful.

"Uh, just a second!" I shout, my voice coming out way too high.

She mutters a quiet, "Shit" under her breath as she adjusts her hair.

I just wanna pull her back in my arms and kiss the shit out of her, mess her hair up all over again.

My forehead lightly presses against hers for a second, and I close my eyes. "I just wanna be alone with you," I whisper against her skin.

She nods against me, her fingers curling around the nape of my neck.

I take a deep breath, trying to steady myself, and pull away from her, pushing open the door, making sure the coast is clear.

I step into the empty hallway and head toward the living room.

Austin's lounging on the couch, and as soon as he spots me, he throws his head. "Fucking finally. Where the hell were you?

Never mind, forget it. Get dressed. We're hitting the bar to celebrate."

Coach looks over at me a hint of a smile crossing his broody face. "You guys did good tonight. You deserve a little fun. I'll even turn a blind eye to the drinking."

Nathan lifts his brows. "You in?"

A grin pulls at my lips, the guys' excitement about celebrating our win hits me. But the idea of being at a bar, girls hitting on me left and right when the only girl I want is one I can't have? Yeah, that doesn't sound like celebrating. I just want to be with her. But obviously, I can't tell them that.

"Uh, nah. I think I'll stay in tonight," I say, running a hand through my hair.

Coach gives me a hard look. "You good, kid?"

I feel the heat rise in my skin under his stare, and I scramble for something that sounds halfway believable. "Yeah, yeah. Just… feel like staying inside." I clear my throat and fake a cough, hoping that sells it.

His frown deepens. "Are you sick? You gonna be good for the next game?"

Shit. "No. I'm fine. Just a… uh, day cough."

He raises an eyebrow. "Day cough?"

"Yeah." Christ. This sounds fucking dumb. "Must be the dust or something. It'll be gone by tomorrow."

Coach doesn't look entirely convinced, but he doesn't push it. He studies me for a second longer. "You want me to stay?"

Since I want to fuck your daughter in every position imaginable, I'd say that's a big fat fucking no.

I clear my throat. "Nah, I'm good."

Austin lifts his shoulder in a shrug. "Well, your loss, man. The bar's gonna be a blast."

"Have fun," I mutter as the guys head toward the door, my mind already back on Isabella. I can't wait until I can get back to her.

Coach looks over at Isabella, his lips twitching into a proud smile. "You coming, princess? You should be celebrating too. Your plays helped us win this one."

Isabella shakes her head, a small smile playing on her lips. "It's been a long night. I think I'll just stay in and watch a movie or something."

"Yeah, I might join you for that," I lie through my teeth. We both know we won't be watching a damn movie once they leave. Hopefully Coach doesn't catch on.

To my surprise, Coach just nods, wrapping his arm around Isabella's shoulders. "Alright. Get some rest. You killed it tonight. Proud of you."

She smiles back, that usual warmth in her eyes. "Thanks, Dad."

He walks out and the second we hear the door close, I'm on her, pulling her into another kiss.

My hands move instinctively, sliding down her back, pulling her even closer. Her body is so warm against mine; her lips are so soft, and I can't get enough of the way she fits against me. It's all I can focus on—all I want to focus on.

I pull back just enough to breathe, my chest rising and falling fast. I look at her—at the way her lips are swollen from our kiss, how her cheeks are flushed.

"You're gorgeous," I murmur, my voice rough and raspy before I kiss her again, sliding my hands down her sides, feeling the curve of her body as I pull both of the jerseys up. She lifts her arms, letting me strip them off her.

"Fuck," I murmur, feeling my pulse speed up at the sight of her.

My hands are everywhere, sliding up her sides, down her back, tracing every inch. She presses into me, chest to chest, and I let out a low groan before I even realize I'm doing it. I'm hooked. Can't get enough. Every time she moves, I want more.

She leans in and kisses my neck, slow and wet, and it short circuits my brain. I tilt my head without thinking, giving her more, chasing that feeling like a goddamn addict. My fingers tighten on her waist. She's not even trying hard and I'm already losing it.

"You make me crazy," I mutter, my lips brushing her throat as I work my way down. I can feel her heartbeat against my mouth. She sucks in a breath when I hit the right spot, and that sound? It goes straight to my dick.

Her hands are sliding under my shirt, nails grazing up my spine, and I'm burning up. I drop my head, kiss along her collarbone, and start tugging at the waistband of her jeans, pulling her closer, grinding up against her. I want her. Right here, right now, in every way.

I pull back, just for a second, breathing hard. "Wanna hit the hot tub?"

She shoots me a smirk. Kills me in the best way. "Yeah."

We step outside, the cold air hitting me as I strip out of my clothes and lower myself into the water. I let the heat crawl up my spine, and lean back, eyes closed, just for a breath, until I hear her behind me. I turn.

And Jesus.

She's standing at the edge of the tub, her skin glowing in the soft light, wearing this white cotton bra with these tiny little blue flowers, and matching panties. The fabric barely covers her, and I can't help but check out her legs—*fuck me.*

She grins at me, biting her lip again, and then steps in slowly. The tips of her curls float in the water, her skin glistening, her nipples hard under the wet cotton. She's fucking beautiful.

"You're staring," she says, voice teasing.

I grin, dragging a hand through my hair. "You look like you want me to stare, baby."

She raises an eyebrow and swims closer, the water rippling around her as her body presses into mine. I feel the heat coming off her even through the steam and the water and she leans in, her lips brushing the edge of my jaw.

"Remember what you asked me?" she says, blinking up at me with those wide, dark eyes that somehow manage to look innocent and absolutely filthy at the same time.

I squint, a little thrown, my brain still half-stuck on the way her chest is pressed against mine, on how her skin's slick and hot and goddamn perfect. "What did I—"

Before I can finish, she's straddling my lap. Her arms slide around my neck, her thighs locking around my hips, and holy fuck, she fits against me like she was made to be on my lap. I slide my hands down her back automatically, settling on her hips, and feel every inch of her soaked, warm skin under my palms.

She leans in again, lips grazing my jaw, her breath warm against my skin. "You asked if I'd let you fuck me properly…"

My cock's already hard as steel under the water, pressing up against her through my boxers. I groan, deep in my chest, my fingers curling around her hips like I'm holding on for dear life.

"Yeah," I breathe, trying to stay in control. "I remember."

She shifts her hips again, slow, dragging her soaked panties over the length of my cock and I gasp through my teeth. It's too much and nowhere near enough.

Her smirk curls up again as she grinds down a little harder. "Does this answer your question?" she asks, her eyes locked on mine, with a sexy as fuck smirk on her pretty lips.

I let my hands slide down, my thumbs brushing the dip of her waist, as I grab her ass. I pull her down harder against me, feeling the pressure of her pussy right up against the curve of my cock through the thin barrier of cloth between us. She's wet, and not just from the tub—she's soaked, warm, soft and perfect against me.

"Not quite," I mutter against her throat, my mouth brushing against her wet, smooth skin. I kiss along her neck, tasting her, feeling her shiver in my arms. "I think I need to hear you say it."

She lets out a breathless laugh and moves her hips again, slower, dragging her clit right over the thick length of me.

"You need me to spell it out for you?" she whispers, her fingers sinking into my hair, tugging just enough to make my hips jerk up into her. she drops her head, her voice low and hot and heavy in my ear. "I want you to fuck me, Ryan," she whispers, grinding against me. "Right here. Right now."

That's all I need to hear.

My hands grip her ass I pull her harder against me, making her gasp out loud, her back arching just a little. "Then we need to take these off," I grit out, my fingers sliding under the waistband of her panties, feeling how the fabric clings to her— tight, soaked, practically melting against her skin.

I hook my thumbs and drag them down her thighs, peeling them off, inch by inch, until she's bare above me, sitting in my lap, skin flushed and wet, eyes dark and wide and so fucking gorgeous. I toss the panties up onto the deck and look back at her.

She reaches down, tugs at the waistband of my boxers under the water, and slides them off. Her fingers wrap around my cock, teasing me, stroking me, making my head fall back at the feel of her soft, warm hand.

"Fuck, Bels," I mutter, my eyes locked on hers as she shifts, lifts herself up just enough for the head of my cock to press against her slick entrance.

She rolls her hips again, letting my tip drag against her entrance, not letting me in yet, just teasing. She bites her lip, looking down between us, and it's the hottest fucking thing I've ever seen.

I grip her hips, lift her just enough, and then pull her down onto my cock in one slow, agonizing thrust. She gasps, her nails sinking into my shoulders as I fill her, stretching her inch by inch, the water rippling around us.

Her mouth falls open in a silent moan, her body trembling as she takes me.

I groan, my head tipping back. "Oh fuck, you feel so fucking good. Jesus. It's so good. Too good," I grind out, barely keeping control as she clenches around me, impossibly tight, impossibly wet.

She moans, rolling her hips, her eyes fluttering. "God, you're so deep."

I groan, gripping her ass and pulling her even closer. "You can take it."

She whimpers, adjusting, rocking against me, dragging herself up before sinking down again, her slick heat gripping me inside her.

My hands roam over her body, until I find the clasp of her bra. It falls away, revealing her perfect tits, her nipples hard and the prettiest pink shade I've ever seen as water beads over her skin.

"Much better," I murmur, cupping her breasts, rolling her nipples between my fingers just to hear the breathy little gasp she makes.

I chuckle, leaning down to flick my tongue against the peak of one breast before sucking it into my mouth. "You love having these tits played with, don't you, baby?"

She groans, grabbing my face, forcing my gaze up to hers. "Fuck me, please."

A hot as fuck girl is naked on my lap begging me to fuck her? Yeah, no way in hell am I denying her. I grip her hips and thrust up, hard, burying myself to the hilt. She cries out, and I do it again, and again, setting a brutal rhythm that makes the water slosh over the sides, that makes her breath stutter, her moans spilling out in broken gasps.

"This what you wanted?" I groan, thrusting deep, grinding against her sweet spot. "You wanted me to fuck you properly?"

She nods frantically, panting. "Yes—fuck, yes—"

I slide a hand between us, rubbing tight circles over her clit, making her whole body shudder.

"Ryan—fuck, I'm close," she gasps, hips jerking, thighs trembling around mine.

She rides me harder, her tits bouncing with every movement, and I lean forward, my tongue lapping over her nipples, sucking her into my mouth.

"Shit. Just like that," I mutter, hands sliding up her back, gripping her ass, guiding her movements. "You feel fucking incredible, Bels."

She gasps, her walls fluttering around me, and fuck, my cock throbs inside her, feeling how fucking tight she is around me.

"Ryan," she moans, clinging to me. "Harder—"

I snap my hips up, slamming into her, making her gasp, making her pussy squeeze around me.

"You gonna come on my cock, baby?" I murmur, sucking a mark into her neck. "Gonna soak me right here where anyone could walk out and see you bouncing on my dick?"

She moans, loud and wild, biting down on her lip to muffle it but not managing to hold it in. She's shaking, clenching tight around me, and I can feel her start to fall apart, her body locking up.

"Ryan—oh fuck, fuck—"

I thrust up again, my thumb pressed against her clit, and she shatters. She cries out, body tensing, her walls pulsing around me, gripping me so fucking tight I nearly lose it right then and there.

I hold out—barely—fucking her through it, grinding up into her while her orgasm wracks through her.

She's wrecked, her head tipped back, lips parted, still gasping out little whimpers.

I grip her hips tighter as I snap my hips up, grinding as deep as I can. I know she's spent, but I don't stop. I slide a hand up to her throat, forcing her to look at me as I thrust into her again.

"I'm not wearing a condom," I warn her, watching her pupils blow even wider, watching the way her lips tremble. I didn't even fucking think about it. I just wanted her so bad.

Her breath catches, her lips parting as her eyes widen. There's a flicker of something in them—shock, heat, *want*.

"I'm on the pill," she whispers, and my cock twitches so hard inside her I nearly lose it on the spot.

"Jesus fuck," I groan, my grip tightening on her hips. "You want me to fill you up? Want me to fuck my cum so deep in you you'll still feel it tomorrow, next week, and every time you sit down?"

She whimpers, her thighs trembling as she clenches around me. She likes it. Loves it. I feel it in the way she bucks her hips into me, the way her hands slide up my back like she can't get close enough.

"Tell me," I growl, slamming into her again. "Tell me how bad you want it."

"I want it," she gasps. "I want you to come inside me, Ryan. Fill me up. Make me yours—"

My control snaps and I thrust up hard, one last time, burying myself as deep as I can inside her as I come with a groan, her name breaking on my lips. My cock throbs, spilling hot, thick streams of cum into her, and she cries out at the feeling, her pussy still fluttering around me, squeezing every drop of cum out of me.

I hold her against me, nothing but the sound of our breaths and the water lapping around us. Her forehead presses to mine, eyes still hazy, lips parted, just barely brushing against my own.

"Fuck," I whisper.

She laughs, and shifts her hips into mine one more time, like she wants to push my cum deeper, hold it inside her. And fuck me, my dick twitches, already hungry for another round.

"I fucking knew it!"

The sound slices through the air, and we freeze at the sound of Austin's voice.

My grip tightens around her, pulling her in close, tucking her into my chest on instinct, shielding her with my body, though it's too late and we both know it. My heart's thudding so loud it drowns out everything else.

Fuck. Fuck. Fuck.

We're still in the hot tub. I'm still buried inside her. There's no hiding it. No playing it off. No making this look innocent.

And Austin sees everything.

"Get the fuck out," I bark, shooting him a glare.

He scoffs, shaking his head as he steps fully into view. "You sneaky motherfuckers. How long has this been going on, then?"

I don't answer. My arms are tight around Isabella, her bare skin warm against me, her face still pressed to my neck like she's trying to disappear.

"None of your fucking business."

He scoffs, crossing his arms. "I *told* you not to go there, Ryan. From day one."

"Yeah, I fucking got that. Thanks for your concern." I force myself to swallow, meeting his gaze. Fuck. This is so not how I wanted to get caught. "Please don't tell anyone."

Austin smirks, tilting his head. "Hmm," he hums, dragging the sound out, his gaze flicking between us. "I dunno. What's in it for me?"

I can't help the frustration that flares in me. "Austin—"

His grin widens, and he takes a step closer. "Can I join?"

Isabella makes a choked sound against my neck.

I shoot him a glare. "Get the fuck out of here."

The asshole lets out a laugh as he lifts his shoulder in a shrug. "Eh, doesn't hurt to try." He bends down, scooping his wallet off the poolside table and shoots us a wink. "You two have fun," he adds as he walks off, before the door clicks shut behind him.

Isabella exhales, a long, shaky sound, then groans and buries her face in her hands. "Holy shit."

I run both hands down my face, jaw aching from how tight I'm clenching it. "Yeah. Holy shit."

We sit there, the water around us sloshing quietly as we both try to figure out what the fuck just happened.

My eyes flick to Isabella, and I can see the panic in her eyes.

I don't know what the hell to do. We've been sneaking around for months, knowing it was dangerous as fuck. And now, here we are—caught.

It could've been anyone walking through that door, but it was Austin. As much of a pain in the ass as he is, he's not the one I'm worried about.

Because if Coach or Nathan ever find out, then it's over for us.

And I'm not ready to let go of her yet.

THIRTY-ONE

Isabella

"**I** don't even know why I bother anymore," Aurora mutters, tugging the cropped denim jacket tighter around her chest, a shiver running through her despite the biting cold. She doesn't seem to care, still rocking that short denim skirt and crop top. "I swear, if my professor makes me critique one more 'avant-garde' painting that's literally just a blank canvas, I might drop out."

I raise an eyebrow, glancing over at her as we keep walking toward the party. "Aren't you supposed to appreciate all forms of art?"

Aurora scoffs, throwing her hands up dramatically. "Not when it's complete bullshit." She keeps walking, her boots clicking on the pavement with every step. "I spend hours on my stuff. My hands cramp, I get paint in my hair, and then some guy turns in a white canvas with a single red dot in the corner, and suddenly, he's a genius."

I can't help the snort that escapes me. "You're kidding."

She shakes her head. "He didn't even use paint. It was ketchup."

My brows knit. "Ketchup?"

"From his fast food order," she replies with a wave of her hand. "He said it 'represents consumerism.'"

I blink a few times, trying to picture it. "And what did the professor say?"

Aurora groans, throwing her head back. "That it was thought-provoking and great social commentary."

I lose it. Laughter bubbles up uncontrollably. Aurora shoves me lightly, though she's clearly trying not to laugh too.

"It's not funny," she mutters, but the grin she's fighting to hide tells me otherwise. "You'd be pissed too if you spent three days on a piece just to get the same grade as the Ketchup King."

I wrap my arm around her shoulders, pulling her into a side hug. "I'm sorry. If it's any consolation, I think you're an amazing artist."

Aurora lets out a long dramatic sigh, slouching against me. "God, why do I even try? The only thing that's keeping me sane is knowing I'm heading to Westbrook this weekend."

I glance over at Aurora, catching the hint of a smile tugging at the corners of her mouth. "You're seeing Chase?"

She nods, her gaze flicking ahead. "Feels like forever," she murmurs with a sigh. "I wish I could've gone to his game last week."

My fingers curl slightly around the strap of my bag, and a quiet kind of pride settles in my chest. I'm still riding the high from that game. The guys actually listened to my advice, my dad stayed out of the way, and for once, I wasn't just the coach's daughter on the sidelines. I was the one calling the plays. Tweaking strategies. Watching them execute what I'd drawn up.

And it worked. We won.

"Anyway. Enough about me," she says waving a hand. "Let's talk about you and Ryan."

"Oh god," I groan, already bracing for her questions.

"Still hooking up with him?"

I exhale. "Yes."

She gives me a skeptical look. "And?"

I glance at her, lifting a shoulder. "We're just having fun."

Aurora narrows her eyes. "Really?"

"Mhmm."

She lets out a slow, knowing hum. Ugh, I hate when she does that. She's always been way too good at reading me before I even have a chance to lie.

She shoots me a sideways look, eyebrow raised. "So, if he, I don't know, hooked up with someone else tonight… that wouldn't bother you?"

My head jerks toward her before I can stop it.

"Oh my god," she stops dead in her tracks, a grin splitting her face wide open. "You like him."

"Shut up."

"You didn't even try to deny it."

"It was a stupid question."

"Isa." She halts and pulls me to a stop with her. "Just be honest. Do you like him?"

I could lie. Say no and move on. Keep pretending I don't have feelings for him. That Ryan's just a distraction.

But I let out a long sigh, knowing there's no point in lying to her. "Maybe."

Aurora's eyes widen in disbelief. "Holy shit."

I roll my eyes. "It doesn't matter. He doesn't do relationships."

She raises a brow. "And you don't do casual."

"Exactly." My voice comes out tighter than I mean it to. "I thought I could handle it, but…"

My throat tightens. I don't finish the sentence.

She bumps her shoulder into mine. "Then be real about it. If you can't do casual, you need to tell him before you get hurt."

I let out a harsh breath.

Yeah. I hate that she's right.

After Austin caught us. Ryan snuck over to my room later that night, and we talked. About everything. His family, mine, school, what we wanted for our futures We only fell asleep at five in the morning. It didn't feel like just casual fun, it felt real, like we were actually connecting. And for a second, I convinced myself that maybe he felt the same, that he'd changed his mind about relationships and was willing to give one a try… with me.

But when I woke up, he wasn't in my bed. He'd slipped away before I even opened my eyes, back to his room.

He told me from the beginning what this was—nothing more than fun. And I'm just fooling myself in thinking it's anything else.

We turn the corner, and the bar finally comes into view. There's a line already, people packed along the sidewalk, their breath fogging in the cold.

Aurora glances at me. "Have you decided what you're going to do?"

I exhale slowly. "I don't know."

"Well, you better figure it out," she replies, flashing a flirty smile at the bouncer. He glances at our fake IDs before waving us through.

The heat hits us as soon as we walk inside. Sweat, cheap drinks, cheap cologne.

My eyes scan the crowd, and I pause when I see him.

Ryan's over by the pool table, with a drink in his hand, and that stupid easy grin on his face. He's surrounded by a group of girls hanging onto every word he says. One has her hand on his arm. Another's leaning in way too close. They all look perfect. And the worst part?

He doesn't seem to care.

My stomach twists.

And I hate that it does.

It's stupid. I *knew* this wasn't serious. Told myself a hundred times. It's just fun. No strings. But still…

An ache creeps up my chest and I can feel Aurora watching me, but I can't drag my eyes away from him.

The idea of seeing him with someone else?

It was hypothetical. A question. A test.

But this is real. This is happening right in front of me.

I have no right to be upset. None. But that doesn't stop the sharp, sour feeling clawing its way up my throat.

Aurora follows my gaze and lets out a low whistle. "Yikes."

I don't answer. I don't need to.

"You okay?" she asks, her voice softening.

I nod, even though the answer is definitely no. Not even a little bit.

She studies me for a second like she's trying to decide if I'm lying. I am. "Do you want to leave?" she asks, placing her hand on my arm.

Yes.

I want to leave. I want to pretend I didn't see any of it, that it doesn't matter, that I'm not currently doing everything in my power not to launch a pool cue across the room.

But instead, I shake my head. "No. Let's get a drink."

She doesn't push. Just leads the way, slipping through the crowd. I follow close behind, my eyes fixed on anything but him.

We make it to the bar, and Aurora slides right into a stool, ordering us a drink. I wrap my fingers around the glass, when the bartender places it in front of us, and take a long sip.

The burn helps. Sort of.

I steal a glance, even though everything in my body tells me not to, and the moment I turn my head, I see Ryan watching me.

His smirk widens a little, and my stomach dips like an idiot.

I should look away. Pretend I wasn't watching him with five girls all over him. Pretend I don't care.

But I don't. I keep looking at him.

He says something to the girl in front of him. She says something back, flashing a smile at him, but his attention isn't on her anymore. It's on me.

My heart kicks into overdrive as he walks toward me, pushing past people before he stops in front of me.

His eyes scan my face, his expression faltering when I don't say anything. "You're quiet."

I lift a shoulder, shifting my weight. "Not much to say."

It's a lie. I have *too* much to say. All of it stuck in my throat.

Ryan doesn't respond right away. He just watches me, his head tilting slightly.

I spin around, but before I can, his fingers slide into mine. "Ryan—"

"Come with me." His hand tightens slightly around mine, but he doesn't tug, just waits—giving me the choice.

I pause, my heart hammering in my chest with every second his eyes are on me. I should say no. But my feet are already moving.

He weaves us through the crowd. The music fades as we move toward the back, neon lights flickering overhead, casting him in blue and red and gold.

And then he pulls us into a bathroom and shuts the door behind us.

It's quiet. Too quiet. The only sound is the dull bass bleeding through the walls and the buzzing in my ears.

Ryan drops my hand and turns to lean back against the sink.

I cross my arms over my chest. I don't look at the way his sleeves are pushed up, revealing the kind of forearms that should be illegal. I don't look at the way his jeans sit just right on his hips.

I don't.

Except I do.

And when I meet his eyes again, I know he noticed.

"What's wrong?" he asks, keeping his eyes on me.

"Nothing," I reply, avoiding my gaze. Because if I keep looking at him—at those stupid eyes, and that even stupider jawline—I'll forget that I'm mad.

I'm supposed to be walking away, not letting him back me into a dimly lit room like I'm his. Like we're something.

Ryan lets out a slow breath, and rakes a hand through his hair. "C'mon, Bels. Tell me why you're not looking at me."

"I can't do this," I blurt out.

Ryan's brows furrow, confusion flashing across his face. "What?"

My chest tightens, the words sitting heavy in my throat, but I manage to force them out. "I… I want to end this."

There's a beat of silence. It feels like the room is shrinking around me, and every second that passes only makes the air thicker. He doesn't say anything right away, just stares at me, his eyes searching my face like he's trying to figure out if I'm serious.

His jaw clenches, a muscle ticking in his cheek. My heart races, but it's not because I'm nervous. It's because I already know what comes next. I've been fooling myself for too long, convincing myself this could be something more.

"You were right," I say, my voice dropping. I swallow hard, trying to keep my composure. "I can't do the casual thing. I thought I could, but…" My words trail off, and I can't finish the sentence.

I should've never let this get this far.

Ryan's face hardens, the teasing glint in his eyes fading as he starts to pace. His footsteps are the only sound in the small room, shoes scuffing against the floor, each step loud in the silence between us.

I watch him, biting my lip. My stomach twists, a familiar ache creeping up, but I can't take the words back now. I shouldn't have said them, but part of me knew from the start it was inevitable. The second I let myself get too close, I knew it was all going to unravel. I just didn't think it would happen this fast.

"You can't do the casual thing?" he asks, shaking his head. "You're the one who wanted a rebound."

"I know," I say with a nod, exhaling sharply. "I thought I could handle it," I murmur, shaking my head. "But I was wrong. I—" I swallow, my throat dry. "I tried not to catch feelings. I really did." I feel a lump in my throat, the words sticking there. "But I did. And I can't keep pretending I don't."

Ryan stops pacing and stands still for a beat, his eyes on me. The tension in the room is thick, suffocating. It feels like the air is too heavy to breathe, and I wonder if I should've just kept my mouth shut. But now it's out, and there's no taking it back.

His gaze flickers over my face, studying me like he's looking for something. What, I don't know, but I don't think he finds it. "You want to date me."

I swallow, shaking my head. "I never said that."

Ryan's eyebrows pull together, and he runs a hand through his hair, messing it up even more. "You're ending things because you can't do casual. What else would that mean?"

I swallow the lump in my throat. "It means I don't want to feel like this when I see you with other girls, like I'm just one of many."

"One of many," he repeats with a bitter laugh, his voice cold. "You seriously believe that?"

I meet his gaze, my heart pounding in my chest. "C'mon, Ryan. You're not my boyfriend. You don't owe me any explanations, but don't lie to me. You were surrounded by girls out there."

There's a flicker in his eyes, before he steps closer, his posture stiffening. "And I know none of their fucking names," he snaps, cutting me off. "You want to know who the only person I was thinking of tonight was? You. You're the only person I think of every damn night since you spilled your drink on me at the welcome week party."

My breath catches in my throat, and I forget how to breathe. I don't know if it's the way his words hit me or the intensity in his eyes, but I can't look away. I don't want to.

"You're the *only* person in my head, Isabella," he says, his voice softening as his hand reaches up to brush a curl behind my ear. "I dream of your curls, your sweet perfume, the shape of your lips, of you with your clipboard in hand, standing on the side of the rink."

I want to step back, to put some space between us, but my body betrays me. I stay rooted, frozen, every word he says wrapping around me like a whisper I can't escape. I can't breathe. My mind is spinning, and I don't know how to stop it.

"Ryan," I whisper, but he doesn't stop.

He takes another step closer, and it feels like he's everywhere, his warmth enveloping me, his presence overpowering. "Tell me you don't want this. Tell me you don't want me, and I'll walk away."

I bite my lip, every nerve in my body screaming at me to fight, but I can't lie. I don't want to walk away from him, but I also don't want to keep falling for a guy who will never be mine.

"Damn it, Bels," he mutters with a frustrated groan as he steps closer again. "You want me to be your boyfriend? Fine. I'll be your boyfriend."

I blink, caught off guard. "What? I—That's not—"

He closes the gap between us, his hand landing on my hips and pulling me closer until we're almost flush against each other. His chest presses into mine, and I can feel his heart pounding as fast as mine. "I'm not losing you," he says, his eyes locked on mine. "Which means I'm your fucking boyfriend."

I shake my head, trying to clear the fog clouding my thoughts. "You can't just... It's not as simple as—"

"It is," he finishes as he cups my face, forcing my gaze to meet his. "I want this, Isabella. I want to be with you."

My heart stumbles in my chest. "Ryan," I whisper, shaking my head. "You said you don't date."

"I didn't," he corrects, his eyes softening just a little, like he's letting me see the side of him that's usually hidden. He exhales slowly, a grin tugging at the corners of his lips. "But you also said you don't date hockey players. Guess we're both making exceptions."

I stare at him, trying to process everything he's saying. The words don't come. My brain is in overdrive, and my heart's already falling for him, whether I'm ready to admit it or not.

Ryan's thumb brushes against my cheek, his touch sending a shiver down my spine. "I want to do this," he murmurs. "I want to be with you."

My brows furrow, despite the way my heart is screaming at me to just say yes and jump into his arms. "You really think you can just walk in here and claim me like that?"

Ryan leans in closer, his smirk growing as he presses his lips to my ear. "I don't think, Isabella. I know."

I roll my eyes, fighting a smile. "You're impossible."

Ryan chuckles, a rich, warm sound that makes my chest tighten. "And you're mine," he says, his lips finding mine before I can say another word.

In a swift move, he lifts me up into his arms and my legs swing around his waist. His hand slides down, grabbing a handful of my ass.

He pulls back, a wicked grin spreading across his face. "This is going to be so much fun. Get ready, baby, because I'm going to be a great boyfriend."

God help me, I think I believe him.

THIRTY-TWO

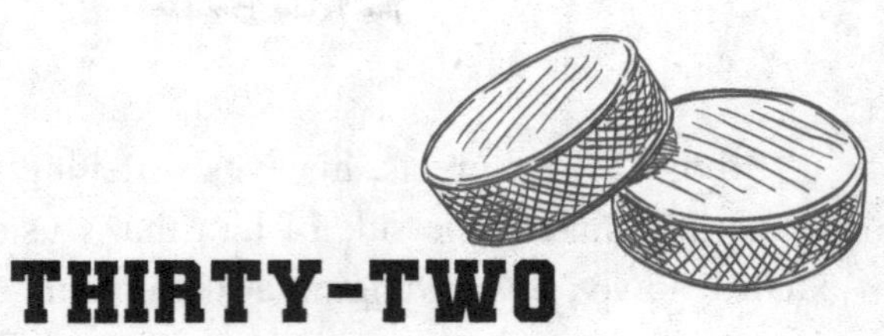

Ryan

I never thought I'd be taking a bath with a girl, but here we are.

I snuck her in while the guys were out, and we fucked the minute she walked into my bedroom. I made her come three times after she kicked my ass at Mario Kart, and then we finally got in the tub to clean up.

Washing her hair took way longer than I expected—guess I had the wrong shampoo for her curls—but I didn't mind being there. I love taking care of my girl. There's something about making her feel good that makes everything else seem unimportant. And I did just that, with a special toy I bought to use on her whenever she stays over.

I made her come again in the bathtub until she pushed my hand and the toy away, telling me she was too sensitive to have another orgasm.

I press a kiss to her shoulder, water beading off her skin as she sits between her legs, with her bare back pressed against my chest.

It should feel awkward. Uncomfortable. But it doesn't. It just feels… right.

And the craziest part?

I'm her *boyfriend*.

That word still feels foreign. I've never been someone's boyfriend before. Never wanted to be. Never thought I could be. But the night Isabella looked at me, and told me she wanted to end things, all I could think was…

Losing her is scarier than staying.

So I stayed.

Her fingers trace idle shapes on my knee beneath the water. Lazy little loops and lines that vanish before I can figure out what they're supposed to be. She's quiet. Comfortable. Happy.

Which makes the guilt hit harder.

Because sneaking around with Nathan's sister—my best friend's little sister—was one thing when this was just casual. When it was late nights and locked doors and pretending it didn't mean anything. Though it *always* meant something. I was just too stubborn, too stupid, to admit it.

But she's not some secret hook-up anymore.

She's mine.

My girlfriend.

And I don't want to hide her. I don't want to keep ducking glances and sneaking kisses behind closed doors. I want to kiss her in the middle of campus. I want to show her off. Let the whole damn world know she's taken, and that I'm off the market. Fully, completely, and absolutely hers.

"You're quiet," she says, breaking me out of my thoughts.

I lower my chin to the crown of her head. Her hair smells like my shampoo and I inhale it, my chest lighting up. "Thinking."

She tilts her head up just enough that her cheek brushes my collarbone. "About what?"

About how I have no fucking clue what I'm doing. About how this—*us*—should feel like a trap, like a countdown to when I mess it all up. But instead, it feels like the safest place I've ever been. Like maybe I haven't wrecked everything I've touched.

I don't say any of that.

"Dunno."

She chuckles, shaking her head. "You know, for someone who's really good with his mouth, you're terrible at using it sometimes."

My lips twitch. "Is that a compliment or an insult?"

"Both."

I smirk, dragging my hands up her arms, my thumbs brushing across her shoulders. Her skin's slick and warm, like silk under water.

I've never been so happy in my life.

Her fingers keep tracing shapes on my knee as we sit in silence. "Do you think I could still work in sports if it wasn't for my dad?"

I frown, twisting my head to look down at her. "Where is this coming from?"

She shrugs, like it's no big deal, but I can tell by the look on her face that something is eating at her. "One of the guys in my class said the only reason Westbrook lost was because they got distracted by my boobs."

I tense behind her, arms tightening just slightly. "What the fuck?"

She shrugs. "It's fine. I'm used to it."

"You shouldn't be," I cut in, my brows drawing together. "What the fuck, Bels? Who the hell said that?"

She glances back at me, shaking her head. "I just want to know if you really think I could have a future in sports… or if I'm just kidding myself."

"Yes," I say, no hesitation. "Of course you can."

"Really?" she asks, eyebrows lifting.

"You're amazing as hell, Curls. You don't need my opinion, but you already know where I stand." My jaw tightens. "Don't let those idiots make you question your skills. You shouldn't have to prove yourself to a bunch of insecure assholes who couldn't run a fantasy league if their lives depended on it."

That makes her laugh, and I feel some of the tension in her shoulders ease.

"You're smarter than all of them," I continue. "Never met the idiots, but I have no doubt that you work harder than any of them. You belong in that room just as much, hell, more than they do."

She leans her head back against my shoulder, eyes flicking to mine. "You think so?"

I nod. "I know so. You're amazing, Isabella. Don't let them make you forget that." A smirk curls on my lips. "And for the record, your boobs weren't the distraction. I mean… they are for me, but—"

She rolls her eyes, and I chuckle.

"We beat them because of your plays," I tell her honestly. "Because you stepped in and showed us where we were screwing up. We beat them because they suck. Nothing to do with you being a woman, baby."

She laughs, the sound soft and so beautiful, and leans fully into me again. Her head rests on my shoulder, and I press a kiss to her damp curls.

This feels so right. Fuck. Why did it have to be with the one person I can't have?

"We should probably tell your brother about us soon," I say, though neither of wants to think of her brother when she's in my arms, naked.

She lets out a groan and flops her head back against my chest. "Do we have to?"

"I feel like it'd be worse if he walked in on us and got the shock of his life."

She sighs, knowing I'm right. "Fine," she says. "I guess we'll have to tell him eventually… but not tonight."

My hands slide down from her arms to her waist, my fingers drifting over soft, bare skin beneath the water. "So, what I'm hearing is… we've got the whole night to do whatever we want?"

She tilts her head to the side, her eyes gleaming. "That depends."

"On?"

Her fingers skate along my thigh beneath the water, featherlight and maddening. "What exactly do you want?"

A deep hum rumbles in my chest as I lean in a little closer. "Where do I start?"

I push her hair aside, my fingers trailing down the curve of her shoulder, and press my lips to her damp skin. I kiss a line up her neck, stopping just below her ear.

Her breath catches. "Ryan…"

I grin against her skin. "Hmm?"

She lets out a little huff. "You're annoying."

"You know I love teasing you, baby." I bite down, gently, enough to make her gasp, enough to make her hips shift against mine.

Fuck.

My hands slide down beneath the water, gripping her hips, anchoring her in place. Or maybe anchoring me. Because she moves again—slow, on purpose—and it's like she wants me to lose control.

"You need to stop if you don't want my cock inside you again."

Her next movement is even slower. Torture. Absolute torture. I groan and grip her tighter, fingers digging into her skin. My hand slips up, wrapping around her throat to tilt her chin back.

I kiss her because I need it. I need her.

She moans into my mouth and I pull away just long enough to kiss down her throat, across her collarbone, down to her perfect tits.

"You really like torturing me, huh?"

She hums. "Oh, absolutely."

I laugh, rough and low. "You're gonna be the death of me." And I'll die a happy man if it means I get to be with her.

Her gorgeous face breaks out into a grin as she threads her fingers through my hair, tugging just enough to make me groan. I nip at her shoulder, my hand sliding down to her—

Knock, knock.

We both freeze.

Her eyes widen, and mine imitate hers.

What the fuck? The guys were supposed to be out all day, so I didn't even think to lock the door.

I open my mouth, no idea what I'm about to say—but before a single word can come out, she vanishes beneath the water with barely a splash.

The door creaks open.

"Oh—shit." Nathan stands there, his eyes wide. "Sorry, I didn't know anyone was—wait… are you taking a bath?"

I blink. "Yes."

He looks around. "…Alone?"

My brain short-circuits. Fuck, if he glances down at the bathtub, there's no doubt he'd see another figure in there under the bubbles. "I've had a really long, hard day."

Nathan frowns. His gaze drifts to the edge of the tub… and stops.

Sitting there—clear as day—is the purple silicone suction toy I bought for Isabella.

His brows lift slowly. "What the hell is that?"

I stare at it.

Then at him.

Back at it.

Back at him.

I consider death as a viable option.

"I uh, use it… for sore muscles."

His face scrunches. "*Where*?"

I open my mouth.

Nothing comes out.

Nathan takes a slow step backward, holding his hands up. "You know what? I didn't see anything. Not a damn thing."

And just like that, he's gone, the door shutting behind him.

Isabella bursts up from under the water a few seconds later, coughing from holding in her breath.

"Oh my God," she gasps, clutching her stomach. "Who was it?"

I drop my head back against the tub, already imagining my inevitable death. "Your brother. He saw the toy I bought for you. Thought it was mine."

Her eyes widen, and then she bursts into laughter.

I sigh, bracing for the worst, rubbing a hand down my face. "He's gonna kill me."

She chuckles. "I'll miss you," she says with a teasing smirk.

I look down at her, my eyes narrowing. Before she can react, I pull her toward me, lifting her so she's straddling me—completely naked, water dripping down her chest, her breath hitching in surprise.

"Yeah, fuck that. If he kills me, I'm haunting the fuck out of you. I'll be with you forever."

Her smirk widens and she leans closer, her hair falling over her bare shoulder. "You'll haunt me?"

My hands slide to her waist, gripping her damp skin and nod. "If you think you can get away from me, think again, baby. You're stuck with me."

Her eyes darken just a little, her hands resting on my chest. "Yeah?"

"Yeah." I pull her closer, my lips brushing against hers.

I brush her hair back from her face, and when we pull apart, her smile falters for a split second, like she's nervous. "We need to tell him."

I let out a long breath, nodding. "Yeah, I know."

She's quiet for a moment, her eyes flicking to mine. "You know he's gonna lose his shit over this, right?"

I nod, pressing my lips together. I know I'm about to get my ass handed to me—by Nathan and Coach—and honestly, I probably deserve it. I knew the risks, and I still jumped in, headfirst.

"I don't wanna hide you anymore," I say, brushing a wet strand of her hair off her shoulder. "I don't want this to be a secret, not from him, not from anyone." Her eyes soften, that glint in them making my heart skip a beat. "Let me take you out on a date."

She raises an eyebrow, smirking. "What?"

"That's what boyfriends do, right?"

She shrugs, shaking her head. "I don't know. My ex didn't take me on dates. Just quickies in his car."

I groan, grip tightening on her hips as I pull her closer. "Don't talk about another man when your tits are in my face."

She chuckles. "Jealous?"

"Yes," I say with no hesitation. Her eyes widen at my admission and I clear my throat, shaking my head. "I've never done this before. I've never gone on a real date. But I want to go on one with you. What do you say?"

She goes quiet for a second, her brows lifting. "You really wanna go on a date?"

A soft lazy smile pulls at my lips at how shocked she is to hear that. "Of course I do, baby. I love spending time with you."

She rolls her eyes. "That's just because I blow you."

I let out a laugh. "That's definitely a perk. But no. I like hanging out with you, clothes or no clothes. I wanna do it somewhere other than a bedroom."

My eyes drift to her, unable to look away. Her wet, curly hair clings to her skin, droplets of water trickling down the slope of her nose, catching the light before they fall onto her lips—those lips, red and full, like she's just eaten cherries. They look so sweet. And I know they taste just as sweet. I swallow hard, trying to focus. But I don't want to focus. I just want to look at her for the rest of my days.

"You're my best friend, Bels," I admit, feeling something fluttering in my stomach.

Never thought I'd say that about a girl. Never thought a girl would be my best friend. But this girl right in front of me is just that. We may do some… very non-friendly things, but when it comes down to it? She's my person. I tell her shit I've never told anyone. She's the first one I want to talk to when anything happens—good, bad, or in between.

She smiles at me, soft and sweet. But then her eyes glint, that little smirk creeping back onto her face. "You're so obsessed with me," she teases.

I roll my eyes, but my stomach flips a little because, honestly? She has no idea how much. "Just say yes, Curls. You know you want to."

She sighs like she's debating it, but then she wraps her arms around my neck, pulling herself closer. "Fine. Yes."

I break out into a grin, because she just said yes. To me. To this. And I don't think I've ever wanted anything more.

I pull her in and kiss her, trying to tell her everything I don't know how to say. That I'm all in. That I'm hers. That this is real. And I'm so fucking lucky she chose me.

When I finally pull back, my forehead rests against hers, and I breathe her in and I think—how was I ever scared to be someone's boyfriend?

Because this?

This doesn't feel like pressure.

This feels like home.

THIRTY-THREE

Isabella

I stare at my reflection in the tiny dorm mirror, tugging at the hem of my dress for the fifth—no, sixth—time.

"This works, right?" I twist left. Then right. Then back again, trying to see myself from every possible angle. "I don't look like I tried too hard? But also, not like I just threw something on? Like, I want to be hot, but effortlessly hot. Cool, but put together. Like, I—"

"Okay, *woah*. You need to calm down," Aurora cuts me off, flopping down onto her bed. "It's just a date."

I shoot her a glare. "First of all, rude. Second, I haven't been on a date in… ever," I admit, blowing out a breath. "I have no idea how this works." I press my lips together. "I just don't wanna embarrass myself. I like him, and—"

"And you're spiraling." She smirks. "Deep breaths, babe. If you didn't like him, you wouldn't be having a breakdown over an outfit."

I shoot her a glare, grab a pillow and chuck it at her head.

She dodges it, letting out a laugh. "So violent. I'm just saying, this is a good thing. It means you actually care about him. Unlike your ex."

I press my lips together. "Jacob wasn't that bad."

Aurora snorts. "Since coming here all you've talked about was Ryan. Be honest. Did Jacob ever make you nervous?"

I open my mouth, but nothing comes out.

"Did you ever overthink a text? Get butterflies when he called? Debate for six hours over what to wear?"

I groan. "Okay, okay, point made."

The relationship I had with Jacob was purely physical. I grew to be accustomed to it, to expect that to be what a relationship is. But from the moment I met Ryan, everything between us has been completely different.

We might have had a physical relationship, and snuck around at first, but it was worlds apart from what I had with Jacob. We actually talked, and spent time together.

"You look hot," she assures me, flashing me a smile. "He's not gonna know what hit him when he sees you."

I sigh, glancing at the mirror again. "But what if—"

"Nope." Aurora sits up, stabbing a finger in my direction. "We're not doing this. No self-sabotage. You like Ryan. Ryan likes you. End of story."

"My brother won't like it," I say with a harsh breath.

I still don't know how we went from *only once* to *okay, let's hook up in secret* to now... *in a relationship*. All while my brother and my dad have no idea.

Aurora gives me a look. "You're both adults. If Nathan has a problem with it, that's a him issue. Besides, what he doesn't know won't hurt him."

I blow out a breath. "I guess."

"Good. Now, stop touching your hair before I physically restrain you." She hops off the bed and grabs her curling iron. "Sit."

I take a seat, and Aurora helps me curl my hair, fixing the pieces I couldn't reach.

By the time she's done, I've mostly stopped freaking out.

But then there's a knock at the door.

My stomach flips.

I take a deep breath, smooth out my dress, and open it.

The door swings open and Ryan stands there with his hands in his pockets, dark jeans sitting low on his hips and a black tee stretched across his chest. His hair's a little messy, like he ran a hand through it on his way here, and his eyes sweep over me in a way that makes my skin warm.

"Wow," he says, dragging a hand across his mouth. "Fuck, Bels. You look—"

Aurora steps directly in front of me, blocking his view before he can finish that sentence. "Alright, Romeo. Listen up."

Ryan freezes.

She crosses her arms. "I've been rooting for you two since the welcome week party. But if you hurt her… I *will* make sure you never reproduce."

Ryan blinks, thrown by her threat. "Uh—"

"And I mean that literally," she says, completely serious. "Screw with my best friend, and you'll find out."

"What the hell are you doing?" I ask, my lips curving into an amused smile.

She shrugs. "Just making sure we're clear."

Ryan recovers quickly, chuckling under his breath. "Duly noted."

Aurora stares him down for another second before stepping aside. "Alright. You may proceed."

Ryan shoots me a grin like none of that just happened. "Ready?"

"Please," I mutter, brushing past her before she starts listing methods of castration.

Ryan's hand finds mine, our fingers intertwining as he leans down to press a kiss to my cheek. "I like her."

"She's a menace," I say with a dry look.

"She just loves you," he says, his grin softening as he glances at me.

When we reach his car, he opens the passenger door, and I stop, raising an eyebrow.

"What?" he asks, looking confused.

"You're being all… polite. It's suspicious."

He shuts the door with a grin, and when he slides into the driver's seat, a chuckle leaves his lips.

"It physically pains me that you think it's suspicious I'm doing something nice for you," he says, reaching across the console to cup my face. His thumb brushes the corner of my mouth. "I'll only ever make you feel like a princess, baby. Nothing suspicious about that."

My heart stutters in my chest.

He leans in, kisses me, then pulls back and shifts the car into drive.

"So," I say, turning toward him, "where are we going?"

Ryan glances over, a grin spreading across his lips "It's a surprise. Sit back, relax, and let your boyfriend handle it."

I raise a brow. "Boyfriend, huh?"

His smirk deepens. "Hell yeah. The best boyfriend you've ever had."

I roll my eyes, but I can't help but smile.

The drive is quiet, with the radio playing music on low, one hand on the wheel, the other occasionally resting on my thigh. And by the time we pull up outside a small studio, I'm too curious to be nervous anymore.

I squint out the window. "Wait… this is my pottery studio."

Ryan lifts a brow. "Look at you. Knew you were smart."

I narrow my eyes at him as he kills the engine and unbuckles. "Why are we here?"

He jogs around the car and opens my door, holding a hand out. "Figured I'd impress you with my total lack of artistic talent."

I laugh, sliding my hand into his and letting him tug me out. His hands settle on my hips automatically.

"Lucky for you, I actually know what I'm doing," I say, bracing my palms against his chest.

"Perfect." He grins. "You can teach me."

He slides his hand into mine as we walk inside, and my brows tug together when I look around the place.

It's quiet. Empty. No instructor, no staff. Just soft music playing overhead and dim lighting casting shadows across the studio floor. In the center of the room, only two pottery wheels sit waiting.

I stop short and turn to him, brows raised. "You rented out the whole place?"

Ryan shrugs, hands stuffed in his pockets. "Wanted our first date to be special."

I shake my head, already smiling. "You're ridiculous."

"But charming," he adds, flashing me a wink.

"Jury's still out."

His chest shakes with a chuckle as he closes the door and we walk into the empty studio.

I break the eye contact, and walk over to the wheel and sit down on the stool, preparing the clay and glance over my shoulder.

A slow smile curls onto his lips as he shifts closer. His eyes never leave mine—or the way my hands move as he takes a seat on his stool beside me.

"What made you want to do pottery?" he asks.

I shrug, focusing on centering the clay. "It became my hobby over the summer. I needed something that could keep my mind busy." I chuckle as the wheel spins a little too fast and I have to steady it. "Clearly I'm not amazing at it, but—"

"Don't do that." He nudges my shoulder gently. "I've seen your pieces in your room, baby. You are amazing."

I pause, warmth blooming across my cheeks. "Thank you."

He arches a brow as he watches me. "I think I got the hang of it. Lemme try."

I move aside as he settles in front of the other wheel, rolls up his sleeves, and dives in like he's done this before.

He has very clearly not.

Within minutes, his hands are covered in clay, his concentration so serious it makes me laugh. But the thing he's creating is… well, unidentifiable.

I bite my lip, trying so hard not to laugh. "Wow. That's… really something."

He glances at his sad, lumpy mess and then flicks a bit of clay at me. The tiny blob lands on my cheek.

My mouth falls open. "You did *not* just do that."

Ryan flashes an unapologetic grin. "What? It was an accident."

I scoop up a chunk of clay and smear it across his forearm. "Oops."

His brows shoot up. "Oh, so that's how it's gonna be?"

"Maybe," I reply, my lips twitching into a smirk.

Before I can react, Ryan's hands are on my waist and I'm suddenly lifted off the stool, a squeal ripping from my throat as he hoists me into the air.

"Ryan!" I laugh, kicking my feet. "Put me down!"

He chuckles. "Say I'm the greatest artist of our generation," he demands.

"Never!"

His fingers dig into my sides and I squirm, caught between gasping and giggling.

"Okay—okay! You're a genius!"

He grins as he lowers me back down, hands still warm on my waist. "That's what I thought."

I swat at his chest, but I'm grinning too hard to mean it. Clay is smeared across his arm, there's a smudge on his jaw, and I'm sure I look just as messy, but I can't remember the last time I had this much fun doing something so stupid.

The kind of fun that makes your cheeks hurt from smiling and your stomach do flips.

Ryan keeps his eyes on mine, the laughter dying between us. The air shifts. Or maybe I imagine it. Either way, I feel it.

Something flutters in my chest and I know without a doubt…

I could really, *really* fall for him.

I think I already am.

We're quiet for a second, before he leans in and kisses me. His lips are warm. His clay-slicked fingers brush my jaw like I'm something delicate, and I swear the ground wobbles under my feet.

When we finally break apart, I'm breathless and one hundred percent blushing like an idiot.

"What was that for?" I whisper.

Ryan doesn't answer. Just gives me that crooked smile that messes with all my internal systems and nods toward the pottery wheel.

"Come on, Picasso. Show me how it's done."

I arch a brow. "You want to try again? After that mess?"

Ryan moves behind me and plops down on the stool. "Yup. I'm a fast learner. Teach me."

I roll my eyes, but I'm already moving to sit between his legs, my back pressed to his chest. His hands find mine, guiding my fingers to the spinning clay.

We start shaping the clay, but it's impossible to focus with him this close, and his breath ghosting against my neck.

"You know," he murmurs, "this is kind of hot."

I snort. "We're elbow-deep in wet clay."

He hums. "Still hot."

I roll my eyes, but I can't keep the smile off my face.

We start slow, our palms slick with clay as we guide the shape together.

"We're basically recreating Ghost."

I laugh under my breath, tilting my head toward him just slightly. "You wish you were Patrick Swayze."

He smirks, the curve of his lips grazing the skin beneath my ear. "I dunno, I think I'm doing a pretty good job."

His eyes flick to my lips. Mine do the same. And before I can process it, his mouth is on mine.

His hands slide from mine to my waist, and just like that, the rest of the world disappears.

The clay spins, forgotten on the wheel. The mess, the studio, every reason why we shouldn't be together—it all fades.

It's just him. Just us.

His fingers slip under the hem of my dress, his palms skating over my skin. "You have no idea how long I've been thinking of this," he murmurs, his voice rough, lips still pressed against mine.

I smirk, nipping at his bottom lip. "Oh? And what exactly have you been thinking about?"

His hands tighten on my hips, pulling me closer. "You. Just like this. A little messy. A lot turned on," he says with a rough grunt. "Been thinking of it ever since I saw those clay covered overalls in your dorm."

My heart stutters at the admission. That was months ago, before he had ever even kissed me, before we even knew each other that well.

I hum, letting my fingers trail up his chest, feeling the way his muscles tense beneath my touch. "And what else?"

Ryan exhales sharply, his grip flexing. "You really wanna know?"

I nod, biting my lip.

He leans in, his voice breathy and sinful against my ear. "I've thought about having you like this. Covered in clay, with my hands all over you." His fingers slip beneath the hem of my dress, skimming my bare thighs. "Making you whimper while I touch you. Getting you so worked up you forget how to breathe."

Heat pools low in my stomach, spreading with every word. "You talk a big game," I tease.

Ryan chuckles, slow and cocky, his tongue flicking against my bottom lip. "I back it up, too."

His lips find my throat, kissing, nipping, sucking until I gasp. His hands roam, exploring, learning the curves of my body. Just when I think I might lose it, he pulls back, leaving me breathless.

"You're playing dirty," I whisper, my voice shaking with need.

Ryan grins against my skin, his teeth grazing my collarbone. "I can make it so much dirtier, baby."

I let out a shaky breath as he pushes my dress up inch by inch, until my thighs are bare. His fingers dig in, thumbs stroking the sensitive skin, coaxing my legs apart as he presses closer. I can feel him, hard, hot, thick underneath me.

His hands slide back to my hips. "Hold that thought," he murmurs.

I blink back at him, dazed, lips swollen from his kisses. "What—?"

He grins, kissing the corner of my mouth before pulling back. I make a soft sound of protest, my thighs instinctively squeezing together, but Ryan just chuckles as he takes a step back. "Don't worry, baby," he drawls, heading toward the utility sink at the corner of the studio, turning on the water. "I'm not stopping. Just not about to fuck my girl with mud all over my hands."

When he comes back, he grips my hips and lifts me up, placing me on the worktable.

"What's my favorite color today, Isabella?" he asks, his eyes flickering down between my legs.

I bite my lip, shaking my head. "I'm not wearing any."

A groan crawls out of his throat as he pushes my legs apart, and stares down at the evidence. "Fuck," he grunts, dragging his thumb over my wet, swollen clit, gathering the proof of how much I need him. "You've been dying for me, baby. Haven't you?"

I don't answer, can't. Not when his fingers are moving, circling, teasing, making me arch into him.

"Say it," he demands. "Tell me how bad you want it."

I exhale shakily. "Ryan…"

He clicks his tongue. "Try again."

I whimper when he slides a finger inside me, stretching, filling me. My thighs quiver and my hands grip the edge of the worktable so tight my knuckles turn white. "I want you… So bad," I whisper, desperate for him.

His breath catches, and then his other hand is on my chin, tilting my head back so he can kiss me, his tongue sliding against mine as his fingers keep working me open. He swallows every moan, every gasp, his body pressing harder against mine.

"That's better," he murmurs against my lips. "Gotta hear you beg for it."

I can't think anymore. I don't want to. All I want is him— more of him, all of him.

"Lay back," he orders.

I do just that, my back hitting the cool surface, with my dress bunched around my waist, and my breath coming in shallow pants.

Ryan steps between my legs, his hands running up my thighs, as he spreads me wider, as he takes in the sight of me laid out for him. "Fucking perfect," he murmurs, almost to himself.

Then he's undoing his jeans, shoving them down, freeing his cock, thick and flushed, leaking at the tip. The sight of him—so hard, so ready—makes my stomach tighten, heat coiling low in my belly. I bite my lip, my hips lifting slightly.

Ryan groans. "Look at you. You're fucking dripping." He fists himself, stroking once, twice, aligning himself.

He pushes inside me slowly, making me feel every thick, pulsing inch of him. I cry out, legs wrapping around his waist.

Ryan curses, his hands gripping my waist so tight I'll have bruises tomorrow. "Fuck, you're tight. I love sinking into you, feeling you take me inside your body, having you clenched around me." He pulls back, almost all the way, before slamming back in, making me moan so loud it echoes through the studio.

He thrusts into me deep, slow at first, dragging it out, making me feel every inch, every thrust. His hands roam, squeezing my breasts through my dress, his thumbs circling my nipples, making me whimper. His lips find my throat, my collarbone, kissing, biting, marking.

"You like this, baby?" he grunts, his pace picking up, hips snapping into mine, making the table creak beneath us. "Like me fucking you here, where you work, where you make your pottery pieces?" His hand slides between us, his fingers finding my clit, rubbing in time with his thrusts. "Gonna think about this every time you sit at that wheel, aren't you? Gonna remember how I stretched you open, how I made you come all over me?"

I'm gone—completely undone, my body burning, shaking, pleasure coiling tighter and tighter. "Yes," I gasp, nails dragging down his back, my hips lifting to meet every thrust. "Ryan, I—"

He groans, his thrusts growing erratic, harder, deeper. "That's it. Say my name when you come."

I whimper, my thighs tightening around him, my body arching as he drives deeper, hits the spot that makes me see white. He groans, gripping my chin, tilting my face up so I have to meet his eyes, have to see the hunger there, the possession burning through him.

"You're mine," he breathes, his forehead pressing against mine, his pace slow but brutal, every thrust sinking deep, stealing my breath. "*I'm* your boyfriend. No one else gets to have you like this. No one else gets to see you like this—spread out, messy, dripping, fucking begging for me."

My cry is swallowed by his mouth as he kisses me, his hips rolling into mine, making sure I know who's inside me.

His voice is ragged, his breath hot against my ear as he thrusts deeper, harder. "You're mine," he rasps. "*My* fucking girl."

His words send a wave of heat crashing through me, make my walls clench tight around him. Ryan groans, his body shuddering against mine.

"Say it," he demands, his breath ragged across my face, his hand finding my clit, rubbing in slow, devastating circles. "Tell me who you belong to."

I'm breaking apart, pleasure tightening in my core. I can't fight it, don't want to.

"You," I gasp, my back arching off the worktable. "Yours, Ryan—fuck, I'm yours."

His fingers press harder against my clit, his cock hitting the perfect spot, and then I'm shattering—my body tightening, my vision going white as pleasure crashes over me, my cries breaking into gasps. Ryan follows, burying himself deep, his body tensing, a low, wrecked moan spilling from his lips as he pulses inside me, filling me with his cum.

"Damn right you are," he groans, kissing me, swallowing my cries as we both shatter together.

The world goes quiet. Just the sound of our breathing, and the faint hum of the wheel still spinning behind us.

My head drops back, landing on the worktable with a thud, my heart still racing out of my chest.

Neither of us moves right away, but then Ryan shifts, his hands slipping beneath my thighs. I barely have time to react before he's tugging me down the length of the worktable and lifting me into his arms.

I gasp, legs instinctively wrapping around his waist. "Ryan—"

He kisses me before I can finish. Slow this time.

His fingers find my hair, brushing it back gently. His eyes lock on mine—still dark, still burning, but softer now.

"You," he murmurs, voice low and warm, "are going to kill me."

I smile, still breathless, still clinging to him. "You'll survive."

He chuckles, presses one last kiss to my lips, then lets his forehead rest against mine.

"So, uh…" he says, glancing behind his shoulder. "You think we can still save that vase?"

A snort escapes me, tired and giddy. I glance back at the ruined lump of clay spinning awkwardly on the wheel. "I'm afraid not."

He chuckles, arms tightening around me like he's not ready to let go. "Guess we'll just have to make a new one."

THIRTY-FOUR

Ryan

My legs are burning.

Practice ran long, but I don't even care. Nothing beats the rush of being on the ice.

Near the entrance, Isabella stands off to the side, beside her dad. Her curls fall over her shoulder, but it's the dress that kills me. White, and way too tight for sanity. I can already picture what's under it.

Her brown eyes lock on mine, sending a jolt through my chest. Instant. Total. Fucking hunger.

I'm a fucking idiot for ever thinking I could only have one night with her. Months of this, of sneaking around—stealing kisses, tangled limbs in the backseat of my Jeep, her breathy moans bitten into my neck when we shouldn't even be in the same room. And it's still not enough.

Never will be.

I don't think there will ever be a time when I'm not completely obsessed with her

I smirk, walking past her slowly, then throw in a wink for good measure. Her lips twitch, fighting back a grin.

God, I want to kiss her.

I want to pin her against a wall. Want her thighs around my waist. I want to make her whimper, make her moan my name in that breathy voice of hers. Fuck.

The guys are filing into the locker room ahead of me. I should keep walking. Should hit the showers.

But instead, I move toward her.

I grab her wrist, and pull her with me. She gasps, but I don't look back. Don't check if anyone sees. I shove open the storage room door and pull her inside.

It slams shut behind us, and the dim fluorescents flicker overhead.

"Ryan!" she gasps. "Are you insane? We could get—"

I press her against the wall and kiss her, cutting her off, groaning into her mouth, my chest lighting up with the need I have for her. She pulls back slightly, shaking her head.

"You're gonna get us caught," she whispers against my lips, but her arms are already around my neck, her body already arching into mine.

"I don't care," I murmur, kissing down her neck, pushing her cardigan off her shoulders. My hand finds her hip, slides up under that dress—warm skin, soft and smooth. "What's my favorite color today, Curls?"

I hook a finger into the thin band of her panties, and pull them down—tiny pink lace that slides down her legs and puddles at her ankles.

"Pink," I murmur as she steps out of them. I scoop them up and shove them into my pocket without hesitation.

"Keeping these."

"You're insane," she whispers, biting her lip.

Yeah, insane for you.

I reach for her again, my hand between her thighs, fingers parting her slick folds—fuck, she's wet. *Dripping.*

"I want to make you feel good," I say, rough, breath shallow. "Let me get on my knees. Let me taste you."

She gasps, her back hitting the shelf behind her as I sink to one knee. But she grips my shoulders, before I can do anything. "No," she says shaking her head. "No time."

I look up, desperate for a taste of her. "Are you gonna make me beg you for a taste? Because I gladly will."

Her eyes twinkle, and I can tell she loves the idea, but she shakes her head. "Someone could come in here. There's no way I could relax enough to come."

I lift onto my feet with a groan, pressing my forehead against hers. "Fuck," I grunt, my cock heavy and thick in my pants. "I need you, baby."

"Me too," she replies, her breathy heavy against me cheek. "But I can still do this."

Before I can even process it, she's already switching places with me, dropping onto her knees, her hands already at my waistband, tugging my boxers down along with my pants. My cock springs free, hard and aching and already leaking precum, and she just licks her lips and looks up at me with those big brown eyes like she's about to ruin my entire fucking life.

My spine snaps straight.

"Jesus, Isabella. Look at me like that again, and I'll come right down that pretty throat."

"Good." Then she wraps her lips around the head of my cock and sucks.

"Oh fuck," I groan, my hand hitting the wall behind me.

Her tongue swirls, slow at first, just enough to tease the ever-loving crap out of me, then she sinks deeper, wet heat sliding down my shaft, her hand curling around the base to stroke in time with her mouth. Her pace picks up, messy and fucking perfect, spit pooling at the corners of her lips, dripping down her chin, glistening on my cock every time she pulls back.

She moans around me, a low, needy sound that vibrates up my spine, and I damn near fall apart right then.

"God, yes—like that—fuck, don't stop—"

Her eyes never leave mine, even when she starts bobbing harder, her throat stretching to take more.

And I'm so close, so fucking close—

Knock. Knock. Knock.

I freeze. My whole body seizes up. Panic claws up my throat.

But Isabella doesn't stop.

She pulls me deeper instead.

"Jesus fuck—" I hiss through clenched teeth, my legs trembling as I lean back against the wall.

She moans around my cock, slurping noisily, determined, fucking relentless. I'm right there, white heat rushing through me, balls tightening, hips jerking.

"Gonna—fuck—gonna come—"

And I do.

Hard.

My knees damn near buckle as I shoot down her throat, my teeth grinding to keep from groaning loud enough for the whole damn rink to hear. She swallows every drop, her eyes fluttering, like she fucking *lives* for it.

When she pulls back, she wipes her mouth with two fingers, licking them clean while staring up at me with that smug, wicked glint in her eye.

"You're evil," I pant, dragging her up and kissing her. She tastes like me and I fucking love how messy it is.

She grins against my lips. "You're welcome."

I press another kiss to her lips, before pulling on my pants and fixing my hair.

I creak open the door, and we sneak out slow, quiet, creeping down the hall.

But as soon as we round the corner, Austin's there, raising an eyebrow so high it could scrape the ceiling.

"Seriously?" he says, smirking. "Storage closet?"

I exhale hard, running a hand through my hair. "Thanks for knocking," I reply dryly. "Really helped speed things along."

Austin chuckles, shakes his head. "What if Coach had gone in there?"

"Then I would've died of embarrassment," Isabella mutters, glancing up at me with a smirk I can't help but return.

And then, like the fucking timing gods are laughing, Coach steps out of the office, frowning as he looks between the three of us.

"What are you guys still doing here?"

"Uh… I got lost." Jesus, I fucking suck under pressure.

Coach narrows his eyes at me. "Get to the lockers and out of here."

Isabella takes a step back and our eyes meet for a second before she vanishes around the corner.

I let out a sigh and head for the locker room. My cock's still sensitive. My pocket's still holding her panties.

And I'm still fucking obsessed.

"You suck at lying," Austin says with a chuckle.

I roll my eyes. "Yeah, I fucking know."

A group of figure skaters passes as I reach the tunnel. Austin accidentally bumps into one of them—a curvy brunette in a perfectly neat bun.

She stumbles, but Austin flashes that lazy, cocky grin that works way more than it should. "My bad, sweetheart."

She narrows her blue eyes onto Austin, unimpressed. "Watch where you're going."

It's always kind of funny how hockey players and figure skaters don't exactly mix. I don't know if it's because they think we're all brain-dead meatheads or because we spend half the time dodging each other on the ice, but there's definitely an unspoken rivalry. Not that I care. They do their thing, we do ours.

Austin jogs beside me, pressing play on his playlist.

I shove open the door to the locker room and step inside.

"Turn that shit down," Nathan mutters, dropping onto the bench.

Austin grins, cranking the volume up instead. "What was that? You love it? Thanks, man."

Nathan glares, but Austin just shoots him a wink.

I shake my head, tossing my gloves onto the bench and yank my jersey over my head.

"Please tell me someone is down to grab food after this," Austin groans, ripping his skates off. "I'm a growing boy. I need food before I pass out and die."

Logan shakes his head, an amused smirk curling his lips. "Don't you have class after this?"

Austin shoots him a glare. "Why would you say that?"

"Because I know you haven't been to a lecture in, what… two weeks?"

Austin scowls. "That is wildly inaccurate."

Logan raises a brow. "Oh yeah? When's the last time you went?"

Austin opens his mouth, then shuts it, thinking way too hard. "It's not about when I went. It's about the fact that I am enrolled, and that, my friend, is already a win."

Logan snorts. "You're actually insane."

"I prefer gifted," he replies with a wink.

Nathan sighs. "You know, it wouldn't kill you to show up once in a while."

Austin waves a lazy hand. "That's what finals are for. Show up once, pass, disappear again. It's a system."

Logan snorts. "A bad system."

"It works."

Nathan sighs heavily, rubbing his temples like dealing with us is his full-time job. "You know, one day, your bullshit is gonna catch up with you."

Austin shrugs. "Yeah, but not today."

I breathe out a laugh and start to strip out of my gear, desperate to get in the shower and wash off, especially after what just happened in the storage room.

But as I do, something falls out of my pocket. My lips drop into a frown, and I glance down just in time to see a flash of pink.

Oh, shit.

Isabella's lacy pink panties slip out of my pocket and land right in the middle of the locker room floor.

For a second, there's silence. Then Nathan's gaze flicks to them, his brow arching. Logan tilts his head, and Austin—of course—immediately sits up, his eyes widening and that shit-eating grin of his spreading across his face.

My brain short-circuits, and my mouth moves before I can think.

"Uh... those are... mine."

Nathan blinks. "Um... Okay?" His brows tug together. "I thought you were gonna say they were from some girl you hooked up with."

I clear my throat. "Yeah… that would've been better," I admit, rubbing the back of my neck.

Austin bursts out laughing, sputtering water all over the floor as he laughs harder.

Nathan tilts his head in his direction. "You good, Austin?"

Austin clears his throat, wiping his chin, still grinning. "Peachy," he mutters, slapping his chest, trying to stop the coughing fit. Then, he smirks at me. "Pink lace, man? Didn't take you for a soft and sweet kinda guy."

I shoot him a glare. He knows damn well who they belong to, and he's enjoying every second of my misfortune.

The tension in my jaw tightens, and I feel like the guilt swirling in my stomach.

Nathan's still watching me, as I grab the panties, shoving them into my bag as fast as I can.

Cole glances up from his spot across the room, just raising an eyebrow as he watches Austin, clearly piecing it together. His lips curl slightly, but he stays quiet, chewing gum like nothing's going on.

Shit.

Two of my teammates already know.

And it's only a matter of time before Nathan finds out. And when he realizes whose underwear just made a surprise appearance in the locker room?

Yeah. I'm fucked.

THIRTY-FIVE

Isabella

I've gotten way too used to the smell of grease and beer. I guess that's what coming to the bar almost every week does to you. I slip inside alone, the blast of warmth hitting my skin as I scan the room.

Aurora's over at Westbrook visiting her boyfriend for the weekend, and the second I walked into my empty dorm, the quiet started creeping under my skin.

I needed noise. Something that felt alive.

I weave my way through the crowd, stopping when I see him, but he doesn't see me.

Ryan's posted up at the bar, leaning back on his stool with one foot hooked around the leg, nursing a beer. His hair's a little messy, and his white T-shirt stretches over the shoulders I know too well. The rest of the team is here too, spread across a long table littered with half-finished drinks and empty baskets of fries.

My phone buzzes before I even make it to the bar, and I read the texts Ryan sent before I left.

Ryan:

What are you wearing?

Me:

Wouldn't you like to know.

Ryan:

> I would actually. Send me a pic
> and maybe I'll behave tonight.

Me:

> You never behave.

Ryan:

> Exactly. So pic, baby. I'm
> hard already thinking about it.

I roll my eyes, biting back a grin as I step up beside him. He glances over, his eyes widening at the sight of me before they drag down the length of me.

"Fuck, this is so much better than a picture," he murmurs, his voice rough.

I breathe out a laugh as I slip onto the stool beside him.

"I didn't know you were coming tonight," he says as he turns his body to face me.

I shrug. "I didn't want to stay in my room all alone," I admit, meeting his eyes. "Besides, I wanted to see you."

It's dangerous, I know. We're surrounded by the team—including my brother—but sneaking around is hard.

Ryan should glance away, put some distance between us. But his thigh bumps mine as he turns slightly, and the way his fingers brush against my wrist makes my pulse jump. We don't touch in public. Not really. Not when Nathan's in the room.

"I always want to see you," Ryan whispers, his lips curling into a smile, those brown eyes of his that I love twinkling.

We break apart at the sound of a throat clearing and I glance to my side, seeing Cole slap a hand on the bar, to garner the bartender's attention.

His eyes flick to me the second he feels my stare.

"You came alone tonight?" he asks, his brow arched.

I've never really spoken to Cole before, don't really know much about him, other than that he fights a lot and Aurora hates him… and that—based on his timely throat clearing—he knows about me and Ryan.

I nod. "Yeah, Aurora's visiting her boyfriend this weekend."

A bitter laugh rattles out of him. He takes a sip of his beer and mutters a low, "Good," before heading back to the table.

Ryan snorts quietly beside me. "What's the deal with them? Has Aurora told you anything?"

"Not a thing," I reply with a shake of my head.

Ryan tips his beer toward his lips, and I flag the bartender for a drink, but before it even hits the bar, I hear the familiar echo of a few voices that make my stomach twist.

I turn around, spotting the guys from my Sports Management class entering together.

They stroll in, laughing loudly as they sit at a table. They don't see me, and I thank the lord for that, because I know what happens when they do. The backhanded comments. The smug looks. The not-so-subtle reminders that I don't belong in their little boys' club.

Ryan's hand tightens on mine, breaking me out of my thoughts, and I glance at him.

"You good?" he asks, his brows tugging together.

"Yeah," I lie, swallowing harshly.

His brow lifts, noting something's off, and shakes his head. "Try again."

I exhale through my nose, squeezing my eyes closed. "The guys from class are here," I tell him, seeing his jaw tighten. He knows exactly who I'm talking about.

He doesn't say anything—just sets his beer down and moves.

I grab his wrist. "Ryan—"

He turns back to me, and the muscle in his jaw ticks. "Stay here."

He walks straight to their table and flips a chair around, straddling it backwards, his forearms resting on the top.

I hop off my stool and head closer, trying to listen.

"Oh shit," one of them laughs nervously. "Reed, what's up, man?"

Ryan doesn't smile. Doesn't blink. "I don't give a fuck what you're about to say."

They blink, taken aback, but before any of them can reply, Ryan cuts them off.

"I just want to know which one of you disrespected my girlfriend."

They exchange confused glances.

Ryan leans in, narrowing the distance between them. "The girl in your class?" he continues. "The one you clearly think isn't worthy of being there, just because she's a woman?" He pauses. "Ring a fucking bell?"

No one answers. No one *dares*. But they know exactly what he's talking about. I see it in their wide eyes, and short glances at each other.

Ryan's lips curl into a cold, dangerous smile. "Here's the deal, assholes. You don't get to disrespect her. Not now, not ever. I don't give a fuck what you think your fragile masculinity is entitled to. If I catch any of you treating her like she's anything less than the incredible smart as fuck woman she is, I'll make sure the only thing you're managing is a hospital bill. Got it?"

One of them swallows hard. Another nods.

Ryan smiles, tapping the table. "Glad we got that sorted."

He pushes the chair back and walks off, like he didn't just threaten them into silence. My heart's pounding. Half from the adrenaline, half from the way he's looking at me when he comes back.

Like I'm his.

And he's not sorry about it.

"I thought I told you to stay there," he says with an arched brow.

I just smile, completely and utterly, without a doubt, in love with him. "Thank you."

"You don't need to thank me, baby." His hand brushes my hair behind my ear, giving me a sweet smile I feel tingling all over my body. "I will always protect my girl."

His eyes flick to my lips, and I know he wants to kiss me—hell, I want to kiss him—but we both know he can't, so he sighs, grabs his beer and we head to the table where the rest of the team are.

I sit beside my brother, and Ryan slides on the other side, his eyes locked on mine.

Austin slings an arm around the back of the chair and grins at me. "Hey, baby Hayes. Glad you could make it. You're practically one of us now."

I raise my glass, letting out a chuckle. "I'll take that as a compliment."

"It is one," he replies. "Best thing Coach did was hire you."

A smile curls on my face, and I meet Ryan's eyes, seeing a similar smile on his. It always surprises me how proud he is of me and my achievements.

The guys are talking about… something. I'm not exactly sure what, because all I can focus on is the boy across from me, his thumb brushing casually over the mouth of his bottle and his eyes on me.

My tongue runs over my bottom lip as I watch him, and he watches me. He shifts, adjusting slightly and I track his movements as he brings his bottle to his lips and takes a sip. He grins, chuckling to himself at my blatant ogling, and glances down at his lap.

A second later, I feel my phone buzzing and I take it out of my pocket, my eyes widening when I see a message from Ryan lighting up the screen. My heart skips a beat, and I quickly glance around the table to make sure no one's paying attention before I swipe it open.

Ryan:

> Stop undressing me with your eyes. We're in public.

I grab my drink to keep from making a noise. My hand slips instinctively over the phone, shielding the screen.

I shift in my seat, crossing my legs, but all it does is make the ache worse.

Ryan notices, and his mouth curves wickedly, and within a few seconds, another text comes through.

Ryan:

> You wet for me, baby?

I don't respond. Can't. Not with Nathan right here. But Ryan doesn't need a reply. He knows.

Another message lights up.

Ryan:

> You're lucky this table's between us, or I'd have you bent over it and take you right here.

> (Respectfully)

I bite my lip, my body flushing, and not from the booze. I quickly type back, and hit send.

Me:

> You're all talk, Reed.

His phone buzzes a second later. He picks it up and reads the message, then looks at me like he's two seconds from climbing across the table.

He shoots me a look and the next thing I know, my phone lights up again.

Ryan:

> If I had you alone right now, I'd have your legs over my shoulders and your voice hoarse from begging me to give you more of my cock.

I set my phone down and grab my glass. I need a drink. *Desperately.* Just a few sips to cool the fire licking down my spine before I lose the last of my self-control and text Ryan to meet me in the bathroom.

The vodka-lime mix hits my tongue, but it does nothing to settle the ache building low in my stomach. Nothing to stop the heat crawling across my skin.

Another vibration rips through the table, the soft glow of the screen lighting up.

And suddenly, everything tilts.

My body freezes. My blood goes ice-cold.

From the corner of my eye, I see Nathan glance down—just a casual flick of his eyes. But then he pauses, his brow furrowing.

No. *No, no, no.*

Time slows to a crawl as his gaze narrows. He tilts his head, his focus locking on the screen, and his jaw goes tight.

My heart drops as Nathan's eyes hover over the screen. The message on my phone is *not* something I want him to see.

"Nathan—" My voice comes out strangled, too late.

His hand moves and he grabs the phone and reads the message.

His body tenses, his shoulders squared, jaw clenched. His nostrils flare once, and his eyes lift. Dark and sharp and *furious.*

Right to Ryan.

"Are you fucking serious?" he growls.

The room goes silent.

Ryan's posture stiffens immediately. Nathan's eyes never leave him, and I feel my heart race out of my chest. Everything is happening way too quickly.

"Woah, man." Ryan's hands go up in defense as he stands up. "Listen, it's not what it looks like, alright?"

Nathan doesn't back down. He takes a step toward Ryan, his eyes narrowing. "So, you weren't sexting my fucking sister just now?"

Logan's brows shoot to his hairline, glancing between them. "Ryan and Hayes?" he asks, shock coating his tone.

Austin scoffs. "You're a little late, buddy."

Ryan shakes his head. "It's not like that, alright?"

But Nathan doesn't listen to him. He shoves Ryan, hard.

He stumbles back, his eyes locked on my brother. "Hit me if you need to," Ryan says, his voice tight, but his eyes are locked onto Nathan's, unwavering. "I know I fucked up and betrayed you, but just listen to me."

But Nathan doesn't listen. He shoves Ryan again, and this time, it's harder. His face is twisted with anger. "My little sister, man."

"Nathan, stop!" I push my chair back, standing up to try and put myself between them. "Just let me explain."

I can feel my heart pounding in my ears as I take a step forward, my eyes darting from Ryan to Nathan. The words I want to say won't come out. I can't believe this is happening. This is everything I didn't want to happen.

Ryan's hands find Nathan's chest again, his voice desperate now. "Will you just fucking listen to me when I tell you it's not like that! I fucking love her, okay? *I love her*. It's not just fucking around for me."

The words hit me like a tidal wave. I freeze, my breath catching in my throat.

He loves me.

Nathan's movements stop too, his body going rigid as he processes what Ryan just said. His eyes flicker from Ryan to me, confusion clouding his anger.

I slowly turn to Ryan, my chest rising and falling with every heavy breath I take. "You… You love me?"

He steps closer, his hand reaching for my face. His fingers are warm, comforting against my skin as he gently cups my cheek. "I love you," he repeats, and I feel something shift in my chest—like a key turning inside me, unlocking a part of me I didn't even know was locked. "I fucking love every single part of you, Curls."

My lips part and I shake my head, unable to believe he's telling me this. I've never had a guy tell me he loves me before. I told Jacob I loved him when he wanted to break up, hoping he'd say it back and realize it was a mistake. But he just told me this would be for the best, and he was right.

Because what I felt for Jacob was a mere fraction of what I feel for Ryan.

"I love you too," I say, the words trembling as they leave my mouth. I step closer, my hands sliding up his chest, wrapping around his neck as I press my forehead against his.

"Fuck this," I hear Nathan say behind me, his voice bitter and cutting. He shakes his head in disbelief and turns, heading for the door.

Ryan looks at me, a pained expression crossing his face. "I'm so sorry, Bels," he murmurs, heavy with regret. "I didn't want it to happen like this. I didn't want him to find out like this."

Me neither.

We stand there for a long moment, my hand in his, neither of us speaking.

"We'll fix this," Ryan replies, pressing his lips to my forehead. "I swear we will."

I really hope he's right.

THIRTY-SIX

Ryan

I can't focus.

Not with Nathan glaring at me from the net, and the sounds of skates scraping up the ice.

The whole team's off today, and it's all my fault.

I should've stayed away from Isabella. I shouldn't have kissed her. I shouldn't have fallen for her, but I did. And now Nathan's treating me like I'm the fucking enemy. Hell, the whole team feels the tension.

They all notice the way Nathan won't talk to me, won't even look at me. I knew he'd be pissed, but I didn't expect him to shut me out this way.

I push the puck forward and take the shot, but instead of moving to block it, he just lets it hit the net. Doesn't even acknowledge it.

My teammates shoot me confused looks, but I don't even know what the fuck just happened.

I skate up to the net, frustration starting to boil over. "Come on, Nathan, don't be like this."

He doesn't move. Doesn't look at me. Nothing. Just keeps staring in front as if I'm not even on the ice.

Jesus. I can't fucking stand the silence from him. "Are you that pissed at me that you can't even look me in the eye? You're seriously gonna pretend I'm not even here?"

He freezes, his back straight, and without a word, he pushes himself up and skates toward me.

He jabs his finger into my chest, hard. "You gonna pretend like you didn't lie to me for who knows how long?" I open my mouth, but the words get stuck in my throat. "You think you can sneak around with my sister behind my back, and everything's just gonna go back to normal?"

"You think I wanted this to happen?" I spit out, my jaw clenched so tight it aches. "I tried to stay away from her."

Nathan scoffs, shaking his head, his lip curling into a snarl. "Well, you did a fucking great job, huh?"

Fuck, this is everything I didn't want to happen. And it blew up in my face anyway. "I tried, Nathan. I really fucking tried. But I just couldn't stay away."

Nathan rips off his mask, then his gloves, his fingers shaking with anger.

I heave out a breath, ripping off my helmet, and throwing it down onto the ice. "Alright, you wanna do this? You wanna hit me?" I don't back down. "Go ahead. Hit me for kissing her. Hit me for thinking about her. Hit me for wanting her when I know I shouldn't have."

He steps closer, his hands balling into fists, his jaw tight with rage. He grabs the front of my jersey and yanks me toward him.

"I told you not to go near her," he spits.

"I know, man," I reply, shaking my head. "I know. It wasn't about the sex for me, alright? I fell in love with her."

Nathan's face twists, and he shoves me back. "Oh yeah? You loved her from the start, did you?" he sneers. "You just knew? You knew the second you met her that you'd be in love with her?"

I wince, trying not to let it show, knowing at the beginning it was just pure attraction and only sex between us. But even back then, I knew that what we were doing was more than sex. I just wanted to see her. To kiss her. To talk to her. Sex was a perk. A really good, fun perk.

"I… I don't know when it happened, alright?" I bite back. "But this thing between us is real. And I can't walk away from it. I didn't mean for any of this to happen, but now that it has, I'm not going anywhere."

Nathan's glare turns sharper, colder. "Bullshit, Ryan. You can't even keep your attention on a girl for longer than a week. What makes my sister so different?"

"I don't know, Nathan," I tell him honestly. "I don't. But what I do know is that I've never felt this way before. I love her, man. And I'm not going to hurt her. Ever."

His eyes narrow, and I can see the doubt still clouding his judgment. But at least for a moment, the silence hangs heavy between us, and something in his eyes softens, like he believes what I'm telling him.

But Coach's booming voice cuts through, making both of us snap to attention.

"What the hell is going on here?" he asks, stepping onto the ice. "You two are supposed to be practicing, not about to tear each other's throats out!"

The previous look in Nathan's eyes is erased, replaced by a glare as his jaw ticks. "You want to tell him, or should I?" he asks.

My stomach sinks, dread twisting inside me like a knot. I know what's coming. And I can't do shit to stop it.

He turns toward Coach before I can say anything. "Ryan's been messing around with Izzy. They've been sneaking around behind our backs."

Coach's face hardens, his eyes narrowing as he processes what Nathan just said. For a long moment, he just stares at me, like he's trying to figure out if we're just messing with him. But then his jaw tightens and his face turns red. "My *daughter*, Ryan? Are you fucking kidding me right now?"

I can't even look at him. Coach is waiting for an answer, but I don't have one. Not a good one, anyway. There's nothing I can say that will make him not want to wring my neck.

Austin picks this moment to chime in. "Coach, come on. You can't be pissed he fell in love with her. He wouldn't have kept it this quiet for so long if it wasn't important."

Coach whips his head toward Austin like he's ready to strangle him. "You knew about this?" His eyes narrow, pinning him in place.

Austin blinks, looking like a deer caught in headlights. "Uh… knowledge is a tricky thing."

Nathan groans, his hands clenched into fists at his sides. "Austin…"

Austin sighs, defeated. "Yeah, I knew. I walked in on them in the hot tub fuck—I mean… kissing," he finishes, his eyes widening, and I kiss my good looks goodbye.

Will Isabella even want to be with me after they're finished pummeling me into the ground?

Coach spins his attention to me, his brows tugged in anger. "You had sex with my daughter in the hot tub?"

Nice going, Austin.

I wonder what's beneath this ice. Can I crack it and drown, please?

"The hot tub I then went into for a relaxing midnight dip?" Coach groans, his hand going to his forehead like he's about to pass out. "Oh Jesus. I need to wash my body with fucking bleach. I'm gonna have a fucking rash."

I want to tell him I actually came inside her—not in the water—but I doubt it'd bode well so I keep my fucking mouth shut, pressing my lips together to keep from laughing.

Coach is still grimacing, looking like he's seconds away from having a breakdown. "Christ, this is gonna give me a heart attack."

Nathan's eyes are still burning with rage. "Do I have permission?" he asks his dad, his fists still clenched.

Coach rubs his temples. "Fine. Just get it over with."

Nathan's already stepping up and before I realize what he's doing, he lands a punch straight to my jaw. My head snaps back, and for a second, I forget where I am, everything goes blurry.

"Fuck," I choke out, swallowing the sting. "I deserve that."

Because if this is the price for being with her?

Then I'll take every hit he's got.

Nathan's still standing there, breathing heavy. "Yeah, you fucking do. Messing around with my fucking sister?"

I force myself to meet his stare. "I told you, I'm not just messing around, here," I tell him. "Have you seen me with anyone else this year?"

He lets out a sharp, bitter laugh. "Brandy."

I shake my head, wiping the blood from my lip. "That was your sister."

His brows pinch, confusion flickering behind the anger. "The toy in the bath?"

I drag a hand down my face, sighing. "You really don't wanna know."

His eyes narrow. "The panties in the locker room?"

I groan, looking up at the ceiling. "Just punch me again."

Nathan steps forward, and for a split second, I brace myself, thinking maybe he'll hit me like before. Instead, his knee slams hard into my balls.

The air gets knocked out of me, and my knees buckle.

"Fuck," I wheeze, doubled over as my vision blurs.

"Alright, that's enough," Coach barks. "Both of you. Showers now."

Nathan finally steps back and drops his stick onto the ice before he skates off.

I take a deep breath, trying not to pass out.

Because I want nothing more than to be with Isabella.

Even if I lose everything else in the process.

THIRTY-SEVEN

Isabella

Meeting the family usually comes with a handshake. Ryan got a busted lip.

I shouldn't be here. Ryan told me not to come.

But when your boyfriend texts you 'Don't freak out, but your dad kinda found out. And your brother punched me', staying at home isn't an option.

I shove open the office door without knocking, my eyes immediately finding my boyfriend.

Ryan's slouched in a chair, one ice pack pressed to his eye, another resting on his groin. His jersey halfway off, shoulder pads tossed beside him, blood dried at the corner of his mouth. He's bruised and beaten—and still, somehow, manages to look hot. But my stomach twists at the sight.

Because this isn't supposed to be happening.

I knew they'd be mad when they found out. I just didn't think they'd take it this far.

Nathan's in the corner, his arms crossed over his chest. Dad is standing behind the desk, jaw tight, arms folded like he's trying very hard not to lose his temper.

Too bad. I already lost mine.

I step fully into the room, letting the door swing shut behind me. "What the *hell* is wrong with you two?"

My voice slices through and their eyes snap toward me.

Nathan turns to Ryan, his eyes narrowing. "You snitched?"

Ryan shrugs, wincing as a smirk tugs at his lip. "I wanted her to kiss it better."

Nathan groans and steps forward, rolling his neck. "My fist will kiss it better."

I move toward him, eyes scanning the damage to his face. "God, Ryan…"

Nathan exhales sharply through his nose. "Izzy—"

"No." I whip back toward him and Dad. "You found out I'm dating someone and your reaction was to punch him in the face? You don't get to play protective big brother and stoic dad after this. I knew you'd be mad, but you had no right to punch him."

Nathan shrugs. "He deserved it."

Ryan sighs behind me. "Can't say I disagree."

I whirl around, shooting him a glare. "You're not helping." I take a deep breath, turning back to my dad and brother. "You don't get to dictate my life. You don't get to decide who I date. You don't own me."

Dad exhales through his nose. "We're trying to protect you, princess."

"From what?" I throw my hands up. "From being happy?"

Nathan shakes his head. "From getting hurt."

I let out a dry laugh, disbelief washing over me. "Getting hurt? Newsflash, Nate—you're the one who just punched my boyfriend in the face, so forgive me if I don't take your concern all that seriously."

Nathan shifts, like he's holding back whatever angry older brother speech he's been rehearsing since birth.

"I didn't ask for your permission," I continue, my eyes locked on theirs. "And I don't need it. If this is how you treat someone I love, then don't expect me to ever bring anyone else home again."

They both open their mouths at once, but I lift a hand and cut them off.

"No. You've said enough." My tone sharpens. "You don't get to act like this is about protecting me when all you're doing is trying to control me."

There's a beat of silence, and then a throat clears behind me. Ryan.

I turn slowly to find his eyes narrowed. "Anyone else?"

My heart stutters.

I step closer, cupping his face without a second thought, brushing my thumb over the bruise on his cheek.

"No one else," I assure him. "Just you."

He exhales, long and shaky, and I lean in, pressing my lips against his. He hums against my mouth, his fingers curling around my waist.

Nathan groans behind us. "Jesus. Do you have to do that here?"

I turn just enough to raise an eyebrow. "Would you prefer if we texted you a time and location first?"

Ryan chokes on a laugh, and Dad mutters something that sounds like a prayer.

Nathan glares. "This is not funny."

"It's a little funny," I say, shrugging. "Especially the vein popping out of your forehead right now."

Nathan glares at Ryan. "You can't blame me for being skeptical. You've never had a relationship in your life."

Ryan shrugs, his eyes finding mine. "Guess I was just waiting for your sister."

Nathan makes a gagging noise.

Dad starts to say something else, but I hold up a hand. "Nope. We're done here. You've both officially lost your talking privileges. You don't get to decide who I'm with. You don't have to like it, but you will respect it." I grab Ryan's wrist, tugging him up from the chair. "Come on, Ryan. Let's go have sex."

Ryan blinks. "Uh—"

Nathan throws his hands in the air. "For the love of God, at least use protection!" he yells. "I am way too young to be an uncle."

"Don't worry," I shoot back. "He'll pull out."

The silence that follows is immediate and *painful*. Dad looks like he's just had a stroke. Nathan opens his mouth, then closes it again like his brain short-circuited.

I grab Ryan's wrist and drag him toward the door.

As soon as we're away from the office, Ryan comes to a halt, scratching the back of his neck. "Not that I'm against the idea, babe, but… I did just get my nuts kicked."

I sigh, turning toward him and reaching up to gently touch his jaw. His skin is warm beneath my fingers. My thumb brushes his busted lip, careful not to hurt him.

"God," I murmur. "What did they do to you?"

Ryan just smiles, that stupid crooked grin that got me into this mess in the first place. "Worth it."

I shake my head, laughing despite everything that just happened. "You're ridiculous."

He slides his hands around my hips, pulling me closer. "I'd take a hundred more beatings if it meant being with you."

My heart squeezes in my chest.

"I really hope it doesn't come to that," I say softly.

He grins, leaning in until his forehead rests against mine. "Me too. But hey, there is a silver lining to all this."

"Yeah?" I reply, raising an eyebrow. "What's that?"

His hand curls around the back of my neck, his thumb brushing against my skin—the way he knows I love. He stares into my eyes, a smile tugging at his lips. "We don't have to hide anymore. Your brother knows. Your dad knows. The team knows."

My smile widens at the realization, and then he leans in, capturing my lips with his.

Ryan pulls away from the kiss, still grinning. "Guess there's no turning back now, huh?"

I laugh, shaking my head. "Nope. You're stuck with me now."

He tugs me closer, his hands sliding down to my hips, his grin widening. "Good. Cause I wouldn't want to turn back even if I could."

THIRTY-EIGHT

Ryan

The house is suffocating.

It's been a week since Nathan found out about me and Isabella and he still hasn't spoken to me. He's barely acknowledged I exist, except for that one time when he punched me. But hey, at least he hasn't punched me again, right? Progress, I guess. I dunno.

I drag myself downstairs, the soreness in my face reminding me of the last conversation I had with Nathan. The bruises are still there, but I've gotten used to it. It's the silence that's harder to handle.

Logan and Austin are sprawled out on the couch when I walk into the living room. Logan's flicking through the TV channels, barely paying attention to whatever's on. Austin's tossing a hockey puck in the air, catching it like it's second nature. As soon as they hear me, both of them glance up at me, their eyes taking in the state I'm in.

Logan raises an eyebrow. "Jesus, you look like shit."

I grunt, dropping down onto the couch. "Thanks. Feel like it too."

Austin shifts, clutching the puck in his hand. "You talked to Nathan yet?"

I shake my head, running a hand through my wet hair. "Nah. Won't even talk to me." I glance between them. "Has he said anything to you guys?"

They both exchange a glance, and Logan shrugs. "Nothing. Every time we bring up the subject, he either checks out or walks away. He's pissed, man."

I exhale sharply, leaning back against the couch. "Yeah, I know."

There's a knock at the door and I push myself up from the couch and make my way to the door. When I open it, the last person I expect to see right now is Isabella, but there she is standing in the doorway with that soft smile of hers that always makes everything feel better.

"What are you doing here?" I ask, surprised.

She shrugs. "Wanted to see you." She hesitates, eyes flicking past me toward the stairs. "Can I come in?"

I step back, nodding fast. "Yeah, yeah, of course." Once she steps inside, I shut the door behind her and glance down at her, my brows pulling together. "Your brother's upstairs, though."

Isabella nods. "I know, but..." She gives me a knowing look. "We don't have to hide anymore, right?"

A real smile breaks through, the first one I've had in days, and I pull her into me, kissing her softly, savoring the feeling of finally being close to her again. We haven't seen much of each other—given the situation—and I missed her like crazy.

It's like she's the missing piece of me I didn't know I was searching for. When she's in my arms, everything else fades away, and for the first time in a long while, I feel like I'm exactly where I'm supposed to be.

I try to show her everything I feel in that kiss, cupping her face, my fingers threading through her soft curls as I deepen it, letting her know just how much she means to me.

Before I can pull away, a pillow smacks me square in the head. I break the kiss, glaring up, my expression darkening, but Austin's grinning like a jackass.

"I'm happy for you guys, and everything. But my room's right next to yours," he calls out. "Don't be too loud. I need my beauty sleep."

Logan snorts and shoves Austin, his grin teasing. "Cut them some slack, man. They've been in hiding long enough."

I roll my eyes, grabbing Isabella's hand and pulling her toward the stairs. "Come on," I say, flashing them a smirk. "Let's go before they start launching more stuff."

We don't stop until we're in my room, the door clicking shut behind us. Isabella leans against it, watching me carefully for a moment before sighing.

"You okay?" she asks, her voice low and soft.

"Yeah," I murmur, giving her a lopsided smile. "Just tired. It's been a long week."

She steps closer, her hands finding their way to my chest. "I don't want this to keep being an issue. I hate that Nathan's mad at you."

I shake my head, pulling her closer. "Hey, this is my issue, not yours, baby. We'll figure it out. We've been best friends since freshman year."

She doesn't look convinced, her eyebrows tugging together and I brush a curl behind her ear, staring into her eyes. "I don't regret this, Bels. I don't regret a single second of being with you."

She smiles, her arms swinging around my neck. "I don't either."

For a few long moments, we stand in silence, just breathing each other in, but then her eyes flick over my shoulder, and her brows bunch. "What's that?"

I follow her gaze, noticing the basket of stuff I've been collecting. "Oh," I murmur, turning back to glance at her. "That's just some stuff for you," I say with a shrug.

She blinks, taken aback. "You bought my shampoo, too?" she asks.

I shrug again. "It's the good kind, right? At least Aurora told me that's the one you like to use."

"You asked Aurora?"

"Yeah," I say, scratching the back of my neck. "I guess I wanted you to feel like you could stay… if you wanted to, and you'd have all the essentials here."

Her eyes search mine. "Ryan," she breathes, and she steps closer, sliding her hands up to my neck.

I lean in and press my lips to hers again, wanting to show her how much I want her, how much I need her.

My hands move to her waist, pulling her closer, and her hands slip beneath my shirt, her fingers trailing along my skin.

"Ryan," she breathes against my lips, her voice trembling slightly.

I lift her shirt over her head slowly, my fingers brushing the smooth skin of her stomach. She shivers under my touch, her breath catching. She's perfect in every way, and the way she looks at me right now… it makes me forget about everything else.

"We don't need to rush anymore," I murmur, my lips trailing down her neck, my hands moving to unbutton her jeans.

"You're so fucking beautiful," I whisper, the words catching in my throat. My thumbs trace the subtle dip at her waist. "Kinda makes it worth having a busted lip."

She lets out a breathy laugh, and her fingers curl behind my neck, playing with the ends of my hair. I watch her smile bloom slow, and it melts something inside me.

I slide one hand up, fingers brushing the underside of her bra, and unhook it with a snap. Her breasts spill free, full and soft, her nipples already tight, and I let out a quiet groan and cup her, my thumb grazing over her nipple as I lower my mouth to her shoulder, dragging kisses up the curve of her neck.

Her hands are already under my shirt, tugging, insistent, and I pull it over my head and toss it aside. Her fingers trail over my skin like she's memorizing me by touch, and I swear I feel every inch of it all the way down.

"You don't even know what you do to me," I murmur, kissing down her chest, between her breasts, tasting her skin, lingering just to feel her tremble. "Every time you tuck your hair behind your ear when you're concentrating. Every time your brow furrows when you're working on new plays. Every time you look at me like this—like I'm the only thing you want."

I take my time pulling her jeans down, inch by inch, my fingers dragging along her thighs, leaving her in nothing but simple, soft panties, molded to the shape of her pretty pussy.

She moans when I kiss the inside of her thigh, her fingers tightening in my hair, and her hips rise just barely off the bed.

I ease her panties down slowly, and I feel her breath hitch when the cool air touches her. I toss it to the side and slide up her body until we're pressed together again, chest to chest, skin to skin, the heat of her slick against my stomach, begging, pleading.

Her legs curl around my waist, pulling me down into her, and I grind against her. She gasps into my mouth, clutching at my back, her body already starting to shake.

She touches my face, holds it like she's afraid I'll disappear if she lets go and I lean down to kiss her. I line up with her, letting the tip of my cock nudge against her soaked pussy. She's so wet already it makes me groan.

I push in slow, careful, watching her eyes roll back just a little, her hands scrambling up my arms to anchor herself. She's tight, warm, slick—perfect. Her mouth drops open, and she lets out the prettiest moan as I sink deeper.

"Fuck, Isabella," I breathe, forehead against hers, buried all the way inside her. "You feel so fucking good. You were made for me, baby. Every inch of you."

Her legs tighten around me, pulling me deeper, her heels pressing into my ass, and I start to move. Slow strokes, grinding into her, feeling her body stretch and take me with that perfect squeeze.

"You know what I love about you?" I pant, my hips rolling into hers. She shivers under me, whimpering, her nails digging into my back.

She shakes her head, her lips parting on a gasp when I bottom out again, staying there a second just to feel her pulse around me.

"I love the way your eyes light up when you laugh," I say, kissing the corner of her mouth, then her jaw, then down her neck. "The way you tease me. God, it drives me crazy."

She lets out a tiny breathless, which turns into a gasp when I angle my hips just right and hit that spot inside her that makes her thighs shake.

"You always know what I need," I keep going, my voice rough, getting lost in the feel of her. "It's like you can read my mind."

I push inside her again, keeping the pace slow. Her moans get louder, her head falling back, her neck falling back, and I take that as my opportunity to kiss down the line of her throat."

"And you're so damn smart, Isabella," I groan into her skin. "You're so ambitious… I know you'll get everything you want, and I'll be right here, cheering you on every step of the way."

She moans and grabs my face to kiss me again, tongues tangling, teeth clashing a little. It's messy and so fucking good.

"I'm so obsessed with you," I mumble into her mouth between thrusts. "God, you make me wanna follow you anywhere. You could drag me to the pits of hell and I'd follow with a smile on my face."

She whimpers again, her body tightening. I feel her getting close, biting her lip, eyes fluttering, breath catching with each stroke. I grab her hand, lace our fingers together above her head, pinning her like she's mine. Because she is. Every inch of her.

"You gonna come for me, baby?" I grunt, kissing her temple, her cheek, her lips again. "Come all over my cock while I'm telling you how in love with you I am?"

"Y-yeah," she moans, grinding up into me, meeting every thrust. "Don't stop, please don't—"

"I won't," I say, and I don't. I fuck her while whispering every single thing I love about her. Her hair. Her eyes. Her lips.

Every part of her, inside and out. I'm so in love with this woman.

Her body tightens around me, and then she throws her head back, her mouth open in a silent cry, her thighs locked around me. I don't stop. I let her ride it, let her fall apart, whispering into her skin.

"I love you," I say again and again. "I love you, Isabella."

I kiss her neck, and she whimpers when I roll my hips again, her body twitching around me. She's soaked, completely wrecked, but I want more. We don't have to rush anymore. I want my time with her.

"Baby…" I groan against her throat, and she shifts under me, her eyes fluttering open. I brush the hair from her face, and she leans into my touch. I lean in, kiss her cheek, her jaw, then her lips, sucking lightly on her bottom lip until she lets out that little whimper that drives me fucking insane.

"You think you can get on top for me?" I murmur against her mouth, my cock still buried inside her, twitching at the thought. "I wanna watch you ride me."

"Yeah?" she says, her voice all breathy, sending a zing of pleasure up my spine.

"Fuck yeah," I breathe, shifting us, careful as I pull out of her. She lets out a needy, wrecked moan at the loss, and it almost makes me say screw it and fuck her back into the bed. But I want this. Want to see her.

I roll onto my back, my hands flying to her hips, watching her as she straddles me, her thighs sliding over mine, hair falling around her face. She looks down, body flushed and glistening, tits bouncing slightly as she adjusts herself. Her hand wraps around my cock, and fuck, the sight of her stroking me, lining me up again, nearly undoes me.

She sinks down slow, her eyes locked on mine the whole time, her mouth falling open when I stretch her out again.

"Jesus—fuck, you feel so good," I groan, hands gripping her hips, holding her there.

She starts to move, grinding on my cock, her hips rolling in this hypnotic rhythm that has me biting back curses. Her hands land on my chest, and I watch her ride me slowly, her lips parting as pleasure builds inside her again.

Her tits bounce with every grind, every rock of her hips, and I can't stop my eyes from devouring her, drinking her in.

"I love watching you work that tight little pussy on my cock," I hiss, my lips grazing hers. "So, fucking greedy for it, baby. You can't get enough, can you?"

She moans, and grinds down harder, her clit rubbing against my pelvis with every movement.

"I swear I could come just from the way you look. You're so fucking hot like this, Bels. So tight around me, fuck—you're squeezing me so hard."

She leans down, presses her forehead to mine, our lips brushing together and she moans my name again as she tightens around me.

I grab her hips, thrusting up to meet her halfway, and she lets out a choked cry, her whole body trembling.

"Keep going, baby," I pant, thrusting up harder, my hips snapping into hers, making her gasp. "Ride me."

She lets go, a loud, desperate moan spilling out of her as her body spasms, pussy pulsing around me, soaking me as she comes hard.

I grip her tighter, keep fucking her through it, chasing my own release.

I don't last long. Her pussy's too good, too tight, and with a loud groan, I come hard, deep inside her.

We're both shaking, gasping, her body draped over mine, skin slick, her thighs still trembling from the aftershocks. She collapses against me, her tits flush against my chest. I wrap my arms around her back, holding her close, our bodies still locked together in every way.

"Goddamn," I whisper into her hair, lips brushing her ear as I breathe her in. "I love you so fucking much, Isabella."

She breathes it back into my throat, her mouth barely moving, just the ghost of a kiss pressed to my skin.

She shifts just slightly, her hips tilting to adjust the angle, my cock still thick inside her, twitching with the aftershocks. She lets out this tiny sound, a satisfied little hum, and presses a kiss to my collarbone.

"Don't pull out," she whispers, her voice quieter, a little shy. "I want to sleep with you still in me."

My cock twitches, still nestled deep where I came. And fuck if that doesn't make me harden a little. My hand slides up her back, my fingertips tracing the dip of her spine, and I kiss the side of her face.

"You sure?" I murmur into her skin. She nods and she cuddles tighter, her legs curling around mine, our bodies molding together.

"Feels good," she breathes. "Feels… right."

She's right. It does. My cock is still inside her, still wrapped in her warmth, soft and soaked, every throb of her body echoing in mine. I feel the mix of us leaking out around the base, wet and warm between her thighs, but she doesn't care, doesn't move—just sighs again, content, melted over me like we're one breath, one heartbeat.

I close my eyes, my arms wrapped around her, our bodies fused. The world shrinks to her weight on my chest, her pussy snug and wet around me, our breaths syncing as we start to drift.

"I've never slept like this," I whisper.

She smiles into my neck, half-asleep. "Get used to it."

I think I definitely could.

THIRTY-NINE

Isabella

Dinner smells amazing.

Mom made her famous roasted chicken with garlic mashed potatoes and buttery green beans. It always reminds me of home, the times when we'd all sit at the table together, talking and laughing over stories from practice or whatever else was going on in our lives.

Except tonight, the mood is tense.

Nathan's barely looked at me since we sat down. Dad hasn't said much, either, which is honestly worse because the man *never* shuts up. If he's quiet, something's definitely off.

Mom, on the other hand, keeps shooting me knowing glances, like she's waiting for me to bring up the obvious elephant in the room.

I set my fork down and exhale slowly. "Alright, let's get this over with."

Dad lifts a brow. "Get what over with?"

I give him a flat look. "The part where you and Nathan act like I've committed a federal crime."

Nathan snorts. "Pretty sure dating Ryan *is* a crime."

"Yeah?" I shoot back. "Then what does that make punching him in the face during practice? Community service?"

Nathan rolls his eyes, dropping his fork. "I barely touched him."

"His lip split."

"Should've ducked faster."

Mom gasps. "Nathan!"

He shrugs. "What? He disrespected Dad."

"Oh my god." I push my plate away, my appetite gone. "This is exactly what I mean. You two are acting like I betrayed the family or something."

"You did," Nathan replies, dryly.

Dad finally speaks up, cutting into his chicken. "Nathan's right. He stepped out of line."

Mom kicks Dad under the table.

He flinches. "Ow—What was that for?"

"Don't encourage this," she says.

Dad raises both hands in surrender. "Yes, dear."

"Napkin," she adds.

He obediently wipes his mouth. "Anything else while I'm at it? Want me to recite the national anthem?"

Mom smiles sweetly. "I've got a better use for your mouth."

"Christ, mom," Nathan groans.

I try not to gag at the flirtatious sparkle in her eye, but Dad's already glancing at me again, his expression serious as he sets his knife down on the table.

"Listen, princess. You've got to understand… this isn't just some random guy you started dating. He's my player. Nathan's teammate."

Nathan crosses his arms. "Locker room's a fucking mess."

Dad nods. "And now I've got half the team thinking I play favorites."

"Oh, please," I scoff. "If anything, Ryan's getting less playing time now."

Nathan picks up his fork, mumbling, "Good."

Mom sighs, pressing her hand to her forehead. "Can we all just eat before the chicken goes cold?"

I stare at them, frustration bubbling to the surface. "Why do you hate this so much? Do you really think I'm stupid and can't make my own choices?"

Nathan doesn't answer. He just clenches his jaw and shovels mashed potatoes into his mouth.

Dad shakes his head. "It's not that we don't think you can make your own choices."

"Could've fooled me."

"It's about making sure you're taken care of. I've seen the way guys in hockey act. I don't want that for you."

Mom snorts. "If I remember correctly, you'd dated half of campus before you met me."

Dad's whole demeanor shifts. "That was different."

She raises an eyebrow. "How?"

He pauses, then smiles. "Because I didn't know what I was missing until I met you."

I blink. "Did you guys just… flirt in the middle of this?"

Nathan groans, burying his head in his hands. "They do this all the time. I'm begging you. Make it stop."

Mom shrugs, a smile curling on her lips. "Sorry, love. Marriage perk."

I turn back to Dad. "If *you* could change when you met Mom, why is it so hard to believe Ryan changed when he met me?"

He watches me for a beat, then sighs. "He really makes you happy?"

"Yes." I don't even hesitate. "He treats me with respect. He listens. Which is more than I can say for the two of you right now." I close my eyes for a second. "Look. I get that you're protective. But I'm not twelve anymore."

There's a long pause, the kind where it feels like the whole table is holding its breath.

Then Dad leans back in his chair and lets out a heavy sigh. "You love him?"

I nod. "Yeah. I do."

He exhales slowly, lips pressing into a line. "Then I guess we'll deal with it."

Across the table, Nathan gapes. "*Seriously?*"

Dad shrugs. "She's an adult. What else can I do?"

Nathan glares at him. "You could bench him."

Dad's eyes gleam. "Or kick his shin."

Mom sips her wine. "Or—here's a thought—you could just invite him over for dinner."

Nathan makes a wounded noise. "Please no."

Dad eyes her. "You sure that's a good idea?"

She lifts her brows. "Did I stutter?"

He sighs. "No, ma'am."

Nathan drags a hand down his face. "I'm skipping Sunday."

"No, you're not," Mom chirps. "Family dinner. Attendance is mandatory."

Dad stabs a green bean. Mom sips her wine with a smirk. And Nathan looks like he's plotting Ryan's murder.

I sit there for a second, the tension still hanging in the air, just not as sharp as before. No one's exactly thrilled. There's no big speech or heartfelt moment. Just a quiet, grudging acceptance.

Not exactly what I hoped for.

But no one stormed off. No one flipped the table.

Honestly? I'll count it as a win.

FORTY

Ryan

I roll my shoulders back and stare at the front door for a second longer than necessary, my hand hovering just over the handle. The porch light flickers slightly above me, and I swear I can hear my own heartbeat in the quiet suburban street.

I shouldn't be this nervous.

It's just dinner.

It's just her family.

I've sat across from Coach Hayes before. I've been in the locker room when he's ripped into us after a bad game. I've seen him in the stands with his wife, watching our team play. But this—*this*—is different.

Because tonight, I'm not Ryan Reed, defenseman.

I'm Ryan Reed, the guy sleeping with his daughter.

And I have no idea if that means he's going to shake my hand or break it.

Less than a week ago, Nathan barely wanted to look at me. Now, suddenly, I've been *invited* over for dinner? Something must have changed. I just don't know what. And I can't shake the feeling that I'm walking into a test.

I drag in a breath, mutter a quiet *fuck it*, and knock.

The door swings open instantly.

Coach Hayes's arms are crossed, like he was standing there, waiting. He's wearing the look that usually comes right before he makes us run suicides until someone pukes—and I've got a bad feeling that someone is about to be me.

"Ryan," he says, stepping back just enough to let me in.

"Hi, sir," I manage, my voice an octave higher than usual.

He blinks. Not a big reaction, but enough to make me second-guess myself. I've never called him *sir* before, but I don't exactly think *Coach* fits the situation either.

Christ, this is awkward as hell.

I step into the house, trying not to visibly sweat. The place feels… weirdly homey. Framed hockey jerseys line the hallway, something garlicky and delicious floats from the kitchen, and pots clink softly in the background.

Then I hear *her*.

Isabella's voice, light with laughter, carries from the next room. The sound eases something in my chest, at least for a second. And when she steps into view, her dark curls pulled back, cheeks flushed from whatever she was just doing, the nerves settle a little more.

"Hey," she says, smiling as she moves toward me, looping her arm through mine. "Come on, we're just setting up."

I let her lead me toward the dining room, where Nathan is already at the table, scrolling through his phone. He barely acknowledges me at first, but when he finally does, he nods once. "What's up?"

It's not exactly a warm welcome, but it's better than the silent treatment. I'll take it.

"Not much," I say, which is a fucking stupid answer, but whatever.

Mrs. Hayes glances up from the kitchen, smiling warmly at me. "Ryan. It's so nice to have you here. Isabella, can you help me with the plates?"

Isabella squeezes my arm before slipping away, leaving me alone with Coach and Nathan.

I take a seat across from Nathan, who finally puts his phone down and raises an eyebrow at me.

"So," I start, tapping my fingers against my knee. "How's the season?" I ask, mostly to fill the silence.

Nathan gives me a look. "You're *on* the team."

"Right," I say, blowing out a breath. "Just trying to make conversation."

Coach takes the seat at the head of the table, resting his forearms on the wood. "How's school going?"

I sit up straighter. "Good. I mean, I hate gen eds, but I've only got one left next semester, so that's something."

Nathan smirks. "Which one?"

I groan. "History."

Nathan winces. "Oof. Sucks for you."

Coach shakes his head. "History's important, Ryan. It teaches you not to repeat past mistakes."

The way he says it makes me pause. Is that a general statement, or a direct fucking warning?

Before I can figure it out, Isabella and her mom return with the plates, and the air shifts as they sit down and we begin to eat.

The food is *good*—garlic chicken, mashed potatoes, roasted vegetables. My stomach growls the second I take a bite, which earns me an amused look from Coach.

Conversation flows easier after that. Mrs. Hayes asks about hockey, Isabella talks about a project she's excited about, and Nathan tells a story about one of our teammates getting nailed in the face with a full water bottle.

It's… surprisingly normal. Like, suspiciously normal. For the first time all evening, I'm starting to believe I might survive this.

Then Mrs. Hayes turns to me. "So, Ryan, your brother is Connor Reed, right?"

I blink, caught off guard. "Uh, yeah. That's him."

Coach leans back in his chair. "He's doing well?"

"Yeah," I say, setting down my fork. "He's having a hell of a run right now. One of the best seasons of his career."

Mrs. Hayes smiles. "That must be exciting. You two are close?"

I shrug, because I never know what to say when people bring him up. "I guess. My parents are really proud of him. They've kind of… always been focused on his career. Which, like, fair. He's the one living the dream. I mean, I'm just playing college hockey. It's not the same."

Coach sets his fork down and leans back in his chair. "College hockey is still a damn impressive achievement. You're playing at a top level, balancing classes, staying in shape, performing under pressure. That's not 'just' anything."

I blink, a little surprised that he's complimenting me. "Thanks."

He grumbles something under his breath and reaches for his glass. "Don't let it go to your head. I'm not letting you off the hook."

And there it is.

"If you hurt my princess," he says, dead serious, "I *will* kick your shin."

I blink. "Kick my shin?"

Nathan doubles over, wheezing.

Isabella groans. "Dad."

Coach shrugs, like this is a totally reasonable threat. "You ever had your shin kicked?" he asks me. "Hurts like hell."

Isabella grabs my arm and mutters, "Ignore him. He's lost his mind."

Coach just lifts an eyebrow, and I decide maybe I shouldn't push my luck.

Mrs. Hayes sighs from across the table. "Hunter, we talked about threats at dinner."

"I'm not threatening," Coach says, his eyes slicing through me. "I'm warning."

I glance at Isabella, who mouths, *Sorry,* with a wince.

But honestly? This is the most terrifying, hilarious, oddly heart-warming dinner I've ever had.

And, weirdly, I don't want it to end.

Later, after the table's cleared and Coach is helping his wife with the dishes, Isabella walks me to the door.

"Thanks for coming," she says, slipping her arms around my waist.

"Thanks for not letting your dad kick me."

"He still might."

We both laugh, and she leans in to kiss me. I slide my hand to cup her face, holding her as I pull back and stare into those big brown eyes that sucked me in from day one. "I love you," I say earnestly, my heart feeling so full.

Her smile is immediate. "I love you too."

And just like that, all the tension, all the stress, all the weird shin-related threats… gone.

Well. Mostly.

Isabella pulls back, out of my reach. "I'll be right back. Let me grab my purse."

She gives my arm a quick squeeze and slips out of the room.

Coach comes out of the kitchen a few seconds later, his sleeves rolled up to his elbows, looking every bit the gruff, intimidating guy I've always known.

He doesn't say anything at first. Just stands there, wiping his hands on a towel, his gaze fixed on me.

I shift uncomfortably, but it's not like I have any choice but to face him.

Then Coach breaks the quiet with a grunt. "You seem to make her happy."

I raise an eyebrow, unsure if it's a compliment or just a grumble. "Yeah?"

He shrugs, one corner of his mouth twitching like he's holding back a smile. "Could be worse, I guess."

I chuckle, running a hand through my hair and step forward. This is it. Time to rip the band-aid off.

"Coach… I'm in love with your daughter. I didn't plan for any of this shit, and I know I'm probably not the guy you had in mind for her, but she makes me happier than anyone has before, and honestly, I can't picture my life without her. I know this is a total mess, and hell, you can bench me, kick me off the team, whatever you want. But I won't—I can't—walk away from her."

He looks up at me, his expression unreadable for a beat. Then he sighs.

"That was a good speech," he says. "Of course, that doesn't change the fact that you were sleeping with my daughter behind my back."

His wife's voice rings out from the kitchen. "Hunter!"

Coach winces. "Sorry. That was—sorry."

I fight the urge to laugh. "It's okay."

He clears his throat, leaning forward slightly. "Just… treat her right."

"I will," I say without an ounce of hesitation. "Always."

He nods once. "Alright then."

And that's it. No hugs. No handshake.

And for now, that's enough.

I give him a hesitant nod, not sure if I should say something else. But before I can come up with anything, Isabella reappears, her purse in hand and flashes me a quick smile that melts my braincells.

"Okay, let's go," she says, sliding her hand in mine before turning to face her dad. "Bye. Love you."

They say a quick *love you* back and I open the front door, and step outside.

Coach is still watching me from his front door, his arms crossed over his chest, and I can't tell if he's done hating me or if he's just waiting for me to screw up.

I won't screw up, though. I have the best thing in my life right beside me, and I will do everything to keep her.

I open the car door for her, and she slides into the seat, flashing me a smile before thanking me. I lean down, kiss her and close the door before heading to the other side.

My mind is still spinning from everything as I get into my seat and start the engine.

I might have just survived dinner, but whatever comes next with her? I'm all in.

FORTY-ONE

Ryan

The final buzzer echoes across the rink and the crowd goes wild. The game's over. We won—6-4. My teammates rush to each other in celebration.

Logan slaps me on the back as he skates by. "Hell yeah! That last pass was a fucking masterpiece."

Austin's already looking for the postgame snacks, clearly more concerned about his stomach than the victory, but I can't blame him. We all earned a good meal after that game.

"You killed it," Nathan says, slapping me on my back. It's been less tense between us since the family dinner, and honestly… I missed my friend.

"Thanks, man, you too," I reply.

He turns and skates over to his family. His mom's cheering from the stands, his dad pulling him into a hug, and his sister's there too. I feel a weird kind of twist in my stomach.

I look up at the crowd, searching… for what? I don't know, but I'm not expecting to see anyone since I—

I blink, my heart stopping for a split second. No way. What the hell?

But there she is. My mom is in the stands, smiling down at me like she hasn't in… fuck, years. And it's not just her—my dad's there too. Right beside her.

What the hell is going on?

I feel my legs freeze for a moment, my mind scrambling to process it all. I've been busting my ass to get their attention for years, and I can't remember the last time they were at one of my hockey games. And now… now they're here? For me?

I push through the confusion and start heading toward them.

When I finally reach them, I'm not sure what to expect. A polite nod? An awkward pat on the back? But my mom surprises me. She's smiling. Like… she's actually proud.

There's something else in her eyes, too. A mix of guilt and something close to regret, maybe. Or maybe I'm imagining that part.

"Great game, Ryan," she says. "You played really well."

I nod, smiling, my chest fluttering at the words. "Thanks, Mom." I try to keep my voice even, steady. "I appreciate that."

My dad stands beside her, hands jammed deep into his coat pockets, his expression unreadable. His eyes meet mine for a brief second before they flick away.

"You looked good out there," he says. "Smart passes. Solid game."

I blink, thrown off. It's the kind of thing he's said to Connor a million times. But to me? It's rare. Foreign even.

"Thanks," I say, though it comes out more like a question than anything else. I don't know what to do with this version of him.

For a second, none of us says anything. We just stand there in this weird bubble of silence, the noise of the crowd and my teammates' laughter muffled around us.

Then my mom speaks again. "Connor called us," she explains and suddenly it makes sense. Because they never once have attended any of my games at Colton. She swallows before continuing. "He had a talk with us and said he thought we should come watch you. That maybe we hadn't been… as present as we should've been."

I exhale slowly, blowing out a laugh. "Better late than never, I guess."

"We didn't mean to make you feel like you didn't matter," she says. "That was never the intention."

I nod, swallowing the lump in my throat. "That's how it felt, though," I admit, wincing the hurt flicker in my mom's eyes. "Every game, every practice, every win… I kept looking for you. Expecting a call or even a text, but the only thing I got were my failures."

My dad finally looks at me, his lips pressed into a thin line. "You've always been driven," he says, almost like he's thinking aloud. "I thought… maybe you didn't want us involved. That you wanted space. You never asked."

"I didn't think I needed to," I say with a shrug. "You didn't need to be asked for Connor."

He doesn't defend himself. Just nods once, solemn. "I'm sorry, son. I got it wrong. I thought pushing you meant I was supporting you. I didn't realize I was making you feel like you were always second best."

I swallow hard, because that's the first time I've ever heard my dad admit he might've screwed up. The first time he's actually said sorry.

"I'm not trying to be Connor," I tell him. "I respect everything he's done, but I want to build something that's mine. Not a copy of his career. My own path."

My dad clenches his jaw, but he gives a short nod. "I get that. And I'll try to be better at seeing it."

I turn at the sound of footsteps, and there she is.

Isabella.

Her cheeks are pink from the cold, her curls wild around her face, and her smile—God, that smile—hits me harder than any goal ever has. It's the kind of smile that makes everything else fade into the background.

She makes her way toward me, weaving past the guys and parents and chaos of postgame noise, like she's moving through her own little tunnel straight to me. When she reaches me, she doesn't say anything at first. Just wraps her arms around my neck and presses her face against my chest.

"You were incredible," she murmurs.

I rest my chin on the top of her head, breathing her in. She smells like vanilla and candy and something I can never quite name but always know is her.

"Thanks, baby," I say, my voice low, a little rough. "I needed that."

When she pulls back, she tucks one of her curls behind her ear—something she does when she's nervous—and glances over my shoulder.

I already know who she's looking at.

My parents.

"Want to meet them?" I ask her.

She nods, a smile lifting her lips. "Yeah. If you want me to."

"I do." I've never introduced a girl to them before, never had a girlfriend before Isabella and I'm excited about showing her off to them.

I take her hand and turn toward my parents. My mom straightens slightly, and my dad's eyes flick down to our joined hands.

"This is Isabella," I tell them with a smile. "My girlfriend."

Isabella offers them a warm smile. "It's really nice to meet you both."

My mom nods, glancing between the both of us. "You too."

"You've got a pretty amazing son," she says, glancing up at me with those big brown eyes that sucked me in from day one. "On and off the ice."

My mom smiles, her gaze flicking to me. "Yeah. We know."

"Reed!" I turn my head, spotting Nathan standing beside Austin and Logan and he arches his brow. "We're heading to Morley's to celebrate. You coming?"

"Go on," my dad replies. "We'll leave you to it. Go celebrate."

I nod, giving them a smile. "Thank you for coming. Seriously. You have no idea how much it means to me."

I tighten my hand in Isabella's and turn, walking toward the exit. I steal one last glance at my parents. They're standing there like strangers beside each other.

They've barely spoken in years. Their marriage was a silent unraveling, one I witnessed in slow motion growing up.

And for a long time, I figured that's what love always turned into. Something temporary. Conditional. Disappointing.

I didn't let myself believe in forever, not really. Didn't let anyone get close enough to want it.

Until her.

With Isabella, it's never felt like something that might fade or fall apart. It's the opposite. Every day with her, it just gets deeper. Stronger. Like she's not just part of my life—she *is* my life.

And there's not a chance in hell I'll ever end up like them. She's it for me. No doubt in my mind.

She looks up at me as we step out into the cold night air, her curls dancing in the wind. "You okay?" she asks.

I nod. "More than okay."

"I'm so proud of you," she says, her eyes sparkling in the night sky.

I grin, the adrenaline still buzzing through my veins, but it's nothing compared to the way she makes me feel. "You have no idea how much I needed to hear that." I slide my arm around her waist, tugging her in until there's barely any space between us. My voice drops as I look down at her. "And I can't wait to show you how much I love you tonight."

Her breath hitches and I lean in, about to kiss her when a loud groan cuts through the moment.

"Jesus Christ," Coach mutters. "I'm standing *right here*. Gonna need to bleach my ears after that."

He unlocks his car and opens the passenger door.

Mrs. Hayes slides in with a smile, catching our eyes just before the door closes. She gives us a warm, knowing look, like she remembers exactly what it's like to be young and crazy in love.

Isabella hides her grin, and I wrap my arm around Isabella again, pulling her close as we watch them drive off.

"Maybe next time, we wait until we're out of earshot," she says, still smirking.

I kiss her temple. "Nah. Let him suffer."

And in that moment, with her by my side, warm under my arm, I know nothing could ruin this moment.

Not a damn thing.

FORTY-TWO

Isabella

The bar is loud, packed with people, but all I can focus on is the warmth of Ryan beside me. His arm rests along the back of my seat, fingers playing absentmindedly with the ends of my hair like he doesn't even realize he's doing it.

I've never had this before.

My last relationship had been secrets and whispers. But this? Sitting beside Ryan, with his hand in my hair, and his thigh pressed against mine, it's the kind of thing I never thought I'd get.

And I'm so damn glad that he's the first person I get to have it with.

Ryan leans closer, his breath warm against my cheek. "You keep staring at me," he murmurs, a smirk tugging at his lips. "If I didn't know any better, I'd say you're obsessed."

I snort, elbowing him lightly. "And if I didn't know any better, I'd think you like it."

His grin is slow, easy, as he shifts, his lips brushing against my ear. "I do."

A little shiver runs down my spine. We've been together for months now, but I still feel flutters around him, like it's the first time he kissed me in that locker room.

"I like this," I admit softly. "Being with you. Out in the open."

His fingers tighten ever so slightly in my hair, and he shifts closer, his thumb brushing the back of my neck in a way that makes my brain short-circuit.

"Yeah?" he murmurs.

I nod.

For a second, neither of us moves. We just sit there, the noise of the bar buzzing around us while we're in our own little bubble. Then Ryan leans in and kisses me. The kind of kiss that makes me forget everything except the feel of his lips and the way my fingers curl in the fabric of his shirt like I don't ever want to let go.

We don't get far before Nathan groans beside us.

"Come on," Nathan says. "If you're gonna date my sister, can you not make out with her like five inches from my face?"

Ryan grins against my lips before pulling back. "You'd rather we move to the other side of the table?"

Nathan raises his eyebrows. "I'd rather you both develop a sudden and incurable fear of PDA."

I just roll my eyes. "You've known for weeks. Get over it already."

"I will never get over it," Nathan deadpans, chugging his beer.

"Better get used to it, man," Ryan says with a shrug, reaching for his drink. "I'm not going anywhere."

Aurora slides into the seat beside me, flipping her blonde hair over her shoulder. "You two are disgustingly in love. I love it."

I snicker, but the moment is immediately ruined when Cole walks past, his dark eyes flicking toward her with pure, unfiltered disdain. "Jesus. You're here."

Aurora glares. "Trust me, I'm just as disappointed to see you."

Cole takes a seat and leans against the table like he owns it, gum snapping between his teeth, the sleeves of his cut-off tee doing absolutely nothing to hide the tattoos running down his arms. He looks like a warning label, especially with the way he scowls at Aurora.

"Do you *have* to hover?" she mutters, taking a long sip from her cocktail.

"No one asked you to be here," he says flatly.

"No one asked you to breathe, but here we are."

Austin slides in across from us, smirking as his eyes flick between them. "God, you guys are better than cable."

Logan strolls up to the table, tapping Austin on his shoulder. "I'm heading home."

Austin blinks up at him. "What Already?"

Logan just shrugs, a smirk tugging at the corner of his mouth. His eyes flick over his shoulder—toward a guy leaning against the bar, watching him with a smirk. Tall. Dark hair. Broad shoulders.

Then Logan turns back, shooting Austin a wink. "Don't come home for a good hour."

Nathan chokes on his drink and his eyes bounce between Logan and the guy. His throat bobs as he swallows. "I—" He clears his throat. "I thought you were straight?"

Logan shakes his head. "Nah, man. I'm bi." He pauses, his gaze sharpening. "That a problem?"

Nathan's eyes widen slightly. "What? No. Of—Of course not."

Logan studies him for a beat, then claps him on the shoulder. "Good." He grabs his jacket. "See you guys later."

He disappears into the crowd, and a moment later, Nathan takes another long sip of his beer.

Austin raises a brow at my brother, amusement in his eyes. "You okay there, champ?"

Nathan nods a little too fast. "Yeah. Fine."

The night stretches on, and when I glance over at Ryan, I feel a familiar warmth spread through my chest.

He catches me looking, brows lifting. "What?"

I shake my head, smiling. "Nothing. Just happy."

"Yeah. Me too." Ryan's lips curl into that signature smirk of his, his lips grazing mine just before he kisses me again. "I'm really glad you spilled your drink on me that night."

I laugh softly, teasing, "I'm glad you gave me my rebound."

Ryan chuckles. "And now you're stuck with me for the rest of your life." He leans in, pressing his forehead against mine, before our lips meet in a soft kiss.

I can't help but feel it in my bones that no matter what comes next, I'll be exactly where I'm supposed to be. Right here, with him.

"Yeah," I whisper, my fingers intertwining with his, "I think I'm okay with that."

EPILOGUE

Isabella

I pull open another drawer, sorting through clothes and mentally checking off the list of things I need to do before we leave. Ryan got traded to a new team, which means another move. Moving isn't anything new for us, and honestly, I've gotten pretty good at making it work.

As I sort through the piles of jeans, shirts, and jackets, I take a quick glance at my phone, my thumb swiping across the screen to check emails. Data analysis reports. Game footage I need to review. Player performance stats.

I can't help the smile that tugs at my lips. I love what I do. The flexibility of working remotely is my perfect fit, and it's one of the perks that lets me follow Ryan wherever he goes.

I can practically see the next few months unfolding in my mind. We'll settle in a new city, I'll find a quiet corner to work, and I'll be there for Ryan, supporting him as his career continues to evolve. The beauty of my job is that as long as I have Wi-Fi, I can do it anywhere. And the best part? I get to be with my husband through it all.

I grab a T-shirt from the pile, my brows tugging together when I feel the sticky fabric between my fingers. My eyes widen when I realize it's the one I spilled my drink on the night I met Ryan.

That night feels like a lifetime ago, and yet, every time I look at this shirt, I'm reminded of how far we've come.

Ryan walks into the room, his eyes scanning the space before landing on me. "Baby, have you seen my—"

I hold up the T-shirt, rolling my eyes. "Seriously? You're still holding onto this shirt?"

He grins, leaning against the doorframe, that playful glint in his eyes that still makes my knees weak. "It's a classic."

I shake my head, the smile never leaving my face. "More like a relic."

Ryan steps closer, his hand drifting over my stomach where our son is growing, his fingers brushing gently over my belly. His touch is soft, tender, and it makes me smile.

"Well," he murmurs, his voice low, "I'm keeping it. It's a piece of our history. I want to show our son one day and tell him how I met you."

I glance up at him, my heart swelling as I look into his eyes. He's still the same Ryan in so many ways—messy hair, that signature grin, and the way his eyes light up when he's happy.

I rest my hand on his, feeling the matching wedding band on his finger.

"Are you okay with the trade?" he asks, his expression turning serious as he searches for something in my eyes.

I nod, offering him a smile. "Yeah. It'll be a change, but it's exciting, and besides, you'll get to play on the same team as Austin again. I know how much that means to you."

Ryan's grin widens, and his hand moves to cup my face, his thumb brushing gently over my cheek. "Yeah, I'm looking forward to that. Getting to play with the guys again, especially Austin. It's gonna be like old times. But no matter what, you and our son come first. Always. I'll take care of you two, you can count on that."

My heart flutters at his words. I've always felt safe with him, and now, with our little one on the way, that feeling only grows stronger.

I rest my hand on his chest, feeling his steady heartbeat beneath my palm. "You make it sound so easy."

Ryan leans down, pressing a soft kiss to my forehead. "Because it is. Moving, being a part of this life—yeah, it's not always easy. But being with you? That's the part that's always been easy." He grins, squeezing my hand. "I couldn't do any of this without you by my side."

I chuckle softly. "Good thing you don't have to."

Ryan gently rubs my belly again, and he pulls me in for a kiss. When he pulls away, he looks at me with that soft, loving smile that makes my heart race. "You're my favorite person, Curls. You know that?"

I nod, my voice soft. "You're mine, too."

We've grown so much over the years—Graduating, the NHL, the constant travels and trades—but it's all worth it. Because we've always been through everything together.

"So, what do you think?" Ryan asks, holding my face in his hands as a smile curls onto his lips. "You up for another five years of this?"

A laugh bubbles up from me. "Let's make it ten."

Ryan's grin widens, and before I can say anything else, his thumb brushes over my cheek as he leans down until his breath fans over my lips. "How about forever?"

My heart skips, the thought of forever with him settling deep into my chest. "Forever sounds perfect."

The End

Acknowledgements

First of all, I want to thank you all so much for picking up this book. Whether it's your first time reading one of my books or you've been here since the start, I'm seriously so grateful for giving me a chance. I really hope you enjoyed your time with Isabella and Ryan, and the rest of the gang at Colton U.

To all of my amazing followers and supporters, your undeniable excitement over my books has kept me going when I wanted to throw my keyboard out of the window.

To my Patreon members: Thank you for being my hype team when I share every early teaser. Thank you for being in it with me and for reminding me that people actually care about these fictional characters I love so much. I adore every single one of you and I am so grateful to have a little community of people who want to know more about my work.

Sophie—thank you for editing this book, and for all of your patience and kind words. I'm so glad I get to work with you.

And finally, if this book made you laugh, swoon, laugh, or fall in love with a fictional hockey player, I've done my job. I hope you stick around for the rest of the series. It only gets even more fun from here.

About the Author

Stephanie Alves is an avid reader and writer of smutty, contemporary romance books. She was born in England, but was raised by her loud Portuguese parents. She can speak both languages fluently, though she tends to mix both languages when speaking. She loves to write romantic comedies with happy endings, witty banter and sizzling chemistry that will make you blush. When she's not writing, she can be found either reading, or watching rom coms with her two adorable dogs cuddled up beside her.

You can find her here:
Instagram.com/Stephanie.alves_author
Stephaniealvesauthor.com